LOWDOWN

LOWDOWN

ANTHONY SCHNEIDER

THE PERMANENT PRESS
Sag Harbor, NY 11963

For information, address:
  The Permanent Press
  4170 Noyac Road
  Sag Harbor, NY 11963
  www.thepermanentpress.com

Library of Congress Cataloging-in-Publication Data

  Schneider, Anthony (Novelist), author.
    Lowdown / Anthony Schneider.
    Sag Harbor, NY: The Permanent Press, [2018]
    ISBN: 978-1-57962-523-8
        1. Romantic suspense fiction.

  PR9369.4.S37 L69 2018
  823'.92—dc23   2018030321

Printed in the United States of America

For Max

Even this late it happens:
The coming of love, the coming of light.

—MARK STRAND
"The Coming of Light"

You gonna come back around
To the sad, sad truth, the dirty lowdown.

—BOZ SCAGGS
"Lowdown"

Do You Have Anything to Say

Jimmy

The first seven years you're in the can, all you can think about is revenge. Kill the cocksucker who put you there. The next seven years you crave freedom and things you remember from before— a walk on a beach, Russian hooker, steak dinner, queen-size bed, sunlight. You want to get laid more than you want to get even. After that you're not so sure. You know you want to be on the other side, but you don't trust your memories. People have died, gone to prison, disappeared. Places you remember have closed down. Freedom is just a dream, something you imagine often but incompletely. Part of you is scared of it. Prison has become your life. You may hate it, but it's home. You're not even sure if you hate it anymore. That's what twenty-five years in the calendar shop does to you.

Do you have anything to say? That was the last question the state asked of him, after extracting nearly half of his life. You didn't fuck with the state. He said no sir, and the man in the yellow shirt nodded and the woman beside him nodded, and the senior parole commissioner nodded and closed his manila folder, and then the guard rose and took him back to the small waiting room. Where they waited. The guard's face was blank; he didn't know shit. Jimmy looked down at his shoes. He'd answered questions, expressed remorse and responsibility, just as his lawyer had coached him. His prisoner's statement contained a list of the skills he'd learned and courses he'd taken in prison. There was a commendable behavior report and a letter from a Brooklyn assistant district attorney ("considerations do not warrant a retrial but do shed favorable light"), which had magically appeared not long before Jimmy became eligible for parole. There was a letter from Father Steven, and one from a potential employer, Jimmy's cousin Richie, who sold mattresses on Long Island and promised there would be a job waiting for Jimmy. There wouldn't be, but someone in the Ruggiero family had paid Richie to put the job offer in writing, and they would pay him to say Jimmy continued to work there, if it ever came to that. Richie wasn't doing this out of the goodness of his heart. The lawyer who had coached Jimmy for his parole hearing said there was a good chance, given that his application contained a letter signed by an assistant district attorney and he had good-time credit. But everyone knew none of it meant a goddamn until you were outside those prison gates.

They sat there five minutes, ten, more than enough time for Jimmy to wonder if he would sit in this room again, in another year or two, and to think about crimes he had committed and crimes he had not. That's what he always came back to. He did feel remorse. And he'd made his peace with serving time. After all, he had done illegal things. Lots of illegal things. But the punishment didn't fit the crime, not the way he saw it. Still, his struggle with injustice, fate, and cocksuck luck was a thing of the past. You do your time. He had done his time. Like a man. Like a prisoner. And he would submit. To more time or to freedom. The choice wasn't his; it never had been. The state was stupid, but the state was strong. He was an insignificant cog in the mighty criminal industrial complex. He wondered if they still sold Ding Dongs and Ho Hos and if the cigar shop on Eighth Avenue was still there, and then he stopped himself wondering. It wouldn't really matter if he wasn't released. Didn't pay to speculate. Cross that bridge when you're out of the can.

There was a knock on the door. The guard rose and escorted Jimmy back into the hearing room and they took their seats.

The tables were clean. Papers had been stacked or put away, briefcases and bags on the floor.

The board members all looked at Jimmy, then the senior commissioner—gray suit, gray skin—spoke about responsibility. Early release was a privilege, an act of grace, not a right. Yellow shirt nodded.

Two weeks later Jimmy emerged, squinting in the midday sun, carrying a suitcase and a Bankers Box, twitchy and thirsty in his scratchy suit.

You are outside the prison gates. You're fifty-eight years old and a newborn. On a bright summer day that feels like a song, a guard hands you your belongings and you wave to the guy who is there to ferry you home, and you stand there for a minute, outside—a civvy, a free man under a blue sky.

Cautious Girls

Milena

Milena Cossutta's father carried her on his shoulders every Sunday. Dorsally moored to her papa, she bobbed above hats and tops of heads, above women's bonnets and boys in baseball caps. Olive-skinned and moon-cheeked, she drifted above the tops of doors as they made their way along Third Avenue or Myrtle Street, Brooklyn, a bug-eyed princess aloft in the sunlight above the flow of pedestrians, as they walked to church or visited family or friends. This they did every Sunday, rain or shine. Her sisters always walked with their mother, a few steps ahead of Milena and her father, always talking, sometimes laughing, sometimes bickering. The rest of the week Milena lived mostly indoors, surrounded by her mother and two older sisters. But once a week, she was free. She would hold her hands in front of her and sway in the air above everything. When they got where they were going—church or a park or someone's house—her father would stop and pivot, pick her up, and hold her in front of him, then toss her into the air. She would laugh and call to her sisters and mother to bear witness, as she became airborne, feet floating in front of her, limbs pulling her into the sky, flying.

In the evenings Milena's father would sit in his armchair with the newspaper and play her the music he loved—Caruso, Sinatra, Roberto Murolo, Carlo Buti. Sometimes, before bed, he would read to her. A peasant from Calabria, Leonardo Cossutta had taught himself to read, and he was one of the few employees at Orlandini & Sons butchers who boasted both literacy and good English, skills that were invaluable on those occasions when a note had to be written to a customer or instructions read. When he returned home each day he washed his hands in soap and rinsed them with lemon and oil, but when she sat in his lap while he read to her, Milena could still smell animal meat and blood mingled with the lemon scent of his hands. When they were out on the streets, Leonardo Cossutta kept his family close and warned of bad men who were capable of doing evil things to little girls. When they were home, they kept the door locked. There were plenty of reasons to stay inside and stay safe. The Genesee River Killer and men like him roamed the streets; muggers prowled. Al Shanker's strike had closed New York City schools, forcing kids onto those unsafe streets for more than a month. There were Vietnam demonstrations, and, somewhere far away, the Vietnam War; piles of trash lined the streets when the garbage workers went on strike; and while Richard Nixon and Mayor Lindsay both promised they would fight crime, everybody agreed that New York was a dangerous place.

Milena celebrated her thirteenth birthday with six girlfriends and ice cream sundaes and Elton John on the juke at Anopoli's, September 1974. It was also the year Milena started going to Manhattan with her older sister Sabrina or riding the Staten Island Ferry to visit their cousins. Their mother allowed them to go out but only when they went together, and as long as they were home by six o'clock. In Manhattan they tried on dresses in boutiques on Madison Avenue and at Macy's and in Little Italy. Once in a while they even bought something. They wore makeup and walked, sauntered, like sophisticated women and Milena sometimes wore a padded bra, with the result that no one guessed how old they were, and the two dark-haired beauties got a lot of attention and many shopkeepers gave them free samples or, at the very least, deep discounts, if they promised to send their friends.

In October, the oldest sister, Maria, married the butcher's son and moved out of the house, leaving Milena and Sabrina each with a bedroom of her own but without an oldest sister as a buffer between them and their parents.

One day not long after her sister's wedding, Milena was on her way back from school when the Greek man who owned the store on Myrtle Street told her he had something for her father, and she followed him into the stockroom at the back of his shop. Once inside, he closed the door, and pinned her against the wall. At first she thought he had stumbled and somehow fallen on top of her. Then he pressed his forearm into her neck, and she knew he had not fallen. She tried to cry out but managed only a muted gagging sound as he mauled her breasts, grabbed here and there, pounding her ribs as he removed her blouse and slobberingly tried to kiss her at the same time. She managed to squirm out of his clutch and ran from the store, her broken-buttoned blouse trailing but her honor intact. Her father was right: there were bad men on the streets of New York City, but she decided not to tell him about this one and what happened that day.

The following Saturday the Greek shopkeeper was sitting on the stool behind the cash register, drinking coffee from the thermos he kept under the glass case of razor blades and batteries, when the bell above the door tinkled. When he stood up he saw Milena standing in the doorway—alone, pretty, smiling.

At first he was on guard, but then put down the cup and followed her when she sauntered toward the back of the store, turning to meet his gaze. She went so far as to bat her eyes and say, in a low voice, "I was scared," as she led him to the stockroom. "I sometimes have naughty thoughts," she whispered as she unbuttoned a button on her blouse and walked inside the stockroom. Her sweaty suitor frowned, but then smiled when she turned to face him and, raising her long arms, shook out her hair. The shopkeeper looked past her when the bell at the front door tinkled weakly again, and together they heard the unmistakable sound of the glass door being shut, followed by movement, shadows across the floor outside the stockroom. And then her cousin Gino appeared, wielding a large knife. "What do I see here?" Gino asked dramatically. The shopkeeper mumbled something and tried to make his way to the door, but Gino blocked his path. "I see you trying to rape this poor young girl."

Again the shopkeeper tried to pass, but Gino pushed him backward and, jabbing his chest, directed him to the chair in the back of the room. Gino pressed his knife against the man's throat and told him to sit down. When he did, Milena tied a rope around his chest and arms, and before he could protest they had bound his arms and legs.

"What do you think her father would say, if we told him?" Gino tied a final knot, tested it.

"I'm sorry. I'll do anything."

"I'm just curious," Milena said. "What makes you think any girl wants anything to do with you?"

"Some of them like it."

"No, none of them. You're a fat Greek ox and you smell like dog vomit, and if you touch another young girl, we will come back and cut off your dick. Understand?"

They'd intended only to rob the man—her idea—but now that he was her captive she found her voice, and she liked it. She liked telling him what was what, and she liked the way he looked—scared.

"I'm sorry. Anything you want."

"Good." The adrenaline had faded and she felt calm, in control, and, suddenly, happy. She noticed the light on the wood floor, a box of shimmering eggplants, colorful boxes of Frosted Flakes and Corn Flakes. "We want your money and your promise."

They left with the cash from the register, the cash in the desk in the stockroom, and his promise. She put her mother's bra back where she'd found it and stashed $250 in her sock drawer.

She didn't gain a reputation, not for that or for anything else. Because she didn't tell, not even her sisters. Only Gino knew what they'd done that day and she'd sworn him to secrecy. Milena knew instinctively the power of secrecy; she knew to lie low. She was pretty, but she wasn't visible. And that was another thing she liked—knowing she could become invisible.

When she was fourteen, three of the senior boys in her school asked her out. She kissed one of them. That year, New York City had no money, Saigon fell, and Maria got pregnant. When Milena went to Manhattan or in the summer took the subway to the Rockaways or Jacob Riis Park, in the company of Sabrina, she knew from the way men looked at them that she was no longer a child.

Hello, Brooklyn

Jimmy

The car is cool and comfortable; an enormous faux leather seat engulfs him. The world rushes past the window—highway, billboards, trees, cars. The prison is behind him and there's no use in looking back now, nothing behind him he wants to know again—cellblocks and razor ribbon, bricks and bars and guard-towers and time, years and years of it, and vengeance deferred. Good-bye, Dannemora. *Well, say good-bye, it's Independence Day.*

The boss sent Jackie Ponzoni to pick him up. The *cugine* looks like a high schooler in his bright sneakers and a tight black T-shirt. They drive parallel to Lake Champlain, with Vermont across the water and thick, green forest in windscreen. They hit traffic near Albany, stop for lunch at a diner on Route Nine. It smells of french fries and bacon grease; Jimmy loves that smell.

He watches Jackie's young, unblemished face, his shiny shampooed hair, as he eats his diner steak, which is thin and brown, but compared to prison food it tastes like Delmonico's. He wonders what they must look like to the bored waitress, one old guy dressed for a funeral, the other in jeans and shiny low tops.

"We coulda flown," Ponzoni says. "Burlington Airport to LaGuardia."

"I know. I wanted to drive. I like the scenery."

"That's cool. I like to drive. I got a lot of respect for you. Everything you did."

"I did my time, that's all."

"You did more than that, I mean, *omertà*."

"Yeah, *omertà*."

Rensselaer County to Sullivan County, and from time to time the bright leaves part and they glimpse the Hudson River. Apart from the river itself, everything is different—the shapes of cars, the black mirrored buildings, billboards advertising brands he's never heard of. They jackknife through Queens. Going home. Whatever that means. Just about all his worldly possessions sit in one box and a suitcase in the trunk. He leans back and listens to the hum of the engine and the *flip-flap* of cars passing.

Brooklyn is not like he remembers—he knew it wouldn't be— and it's not like he imagined it either. Stranger in a strange land. Everything is racing—cars, bicycles, people. Everyone looks busy, as if they're late to get somewhere else. People look younger, more mixed in age, hairstyle, clothing, skin color than he remembers, like a circus or some Technicolor town, only it isn't, it's Forty-Fifth Street under the Gowanus Expressway. Ponzoni drives him all the way to Ashby Street in Sunset Park, rings the doorbell of a frame house with light gray shingles, the door and window frames painted dark blue. A balding man in a faded T-shirt and wire-rim glasses opens the door. Ponzoni introduces Jimmy to Tom DeSapio, then helps carry the luggage, including a new black duffel bag. "A present from the boss," he explains.

Tom DeSapio, Savino's son, shakes Jimmy's hand. "Welcome back." He leads the way around the house, down cement steps to the garden and downstairs apartment. The last time Jimmy saw him Tom was eighteen, maybe nineteen, years old. A college kid. Now he's a balding man, fortysomething, with a paunch under his T-shirt, and a Roman nose just like his dad.

"Here it is. Fully renovated, en suite bathroom." The door swings open with a sucking noise. Jackie carries the bags and boxes inside; Tom hands Jimmy the key, on a square blue keychain, then follows him into the apartment. "The kitchen's got all new appliances."

"Thank you," Jimmy says. "This is great."

"You need anything, something to eat, a sandwich?"

"No, we ate. Thank you."

"Anything else?"

"I'm fine, just going to unpack."

"Sure, of course. We left some things in the fridge, soap in the bathroom, towels. You had two calls. I left the numbers on the pad by the phone. Your brother and your cousin Richie, I think. Anything else you need, just knock. Or call. Our phone number's also on the pad next to the phone."

"Thank you."

Tom is shaking his head. "Welcome. Congratulations. I'll let you get settled in."

"Thank you."

Tom leaves. Ponzoni stands around for a minute, then, seeing that nothing further is required of him, checks his phone and opens the door. Jimmy remembers taking a flight a million years ago and the air hostesses standing at the gangway thanking everyone. That's how he feels now. *Thank you. Thanks for flying.* Alone at last. The basement apartment is clean and he can smell that it's been freshly painted. It's not big and it's slightly dim inside, but to Jimmy it feels palatial. The bathroom smells like ammonia and he sees new towels and a six-pack of puffy toilet paper. He turns on a burner on the stove, watches the gas puff and flare blue and orange, turns it off. He moves his stuff into the bedroom, opens a box, his suitcase, unpacks a couple of shirts and the three photos that sat in each cell with him, watching over him. The duffel bag Ponzoni brought contains a pair of shoes, a pair of sneakers, two T-shirts, a suit, two button-down shirts, the same dark slacks in a few different sizes, and an envelope full of cash. Thank you, Pino Locatelli. He's heard about the new boss of the Ruggiero family. Mostly good things. Everyone says Pino respects the past, his elders, does his best to pay old debts. But the family isn't what it used to be. Some construction money, trucking, union featherbedding. They sold their interest in the casinos and got muscled out of drugs and money laundering. They're still in the garbage removal business and maintain a small protection racket, own check-cashing franchises and some restaurants and long-term storage facilities. He's heard Big Bobby is part owner of two restaurants on Long Island and a popular bar in Islip. As for Pino, he's got some real estate scam going, buys buildings cheap from the government, below market value, resells them six months later. Jimmy's never met Pino. He was just a snot-nosed teenager when Jimmy was coming up.

He opens the door and stands facing the garden, feels the heat, breathes in the smell of trees and grass and humidity—Brooklyn summer. The garden itself measures twenty-five-feet square or so, enclosed on three sides by wood fences of differing heights. The back fence is moldy with long, greenish tears that drip into the flowerless flowerbox. There's a lime tree and several larger trees with big plate-like leaves, rubbery and bottle-green. There's a round wooden table in the middle of the scrubby brown grass, two mottled white plastic chairs kneeling against the table. It's a modest garden, but to a man who was housed in a six-by-nine-foot cinder-block cell with a dented metal toilet in the corner, eyes accustomed to the narrowest window and a view of a brightly lit prison parking lot, it is majestic.

Back inside, he surveys his new home. He has the uneasy feeling that he should be doing something, but tells himself there's nothing, just calm down. The living room and kitchen are one room, facing the garden. There's an electric kettle on the flecked beige Formica counter. When he was a boy they had a stove-top kettle, a massive silver thing, and a bread box and cookie jar, and if their mother caught them taking a cookie from the cookie jar without her permission, she would hit the backs of their hands with a wooden spoon, four hard raps. He remembers the photographs on the kitchen wall. His mother's father, he remembers in particular; he looked like an Italian cowboy—lean and wizened, with a shrewd grin and floppy black hat. He fought against the rich Piedmontese *fascista* armies, then was forced to flee the country for fear of his life. They shot at sight. Jimmy hangs his clothes in the closet. The bedroom is mostly below street level, and the window at the back is a narrow horizontal strip high above the bed, opaque glass covered by a permanent white shade. He prefers the living room with direct light and a view of the garden, and it's there he sits, on a folding wooden chair at the little butcher-block table, alone in his new home, neither tired nor very awake, neither happy nor sad, but free. There's a physical sensation of release, as if he has just tumbled into deepest space, drifting across the universe. His last years in the joint, in honor block, he tended a communal garden—broccoli, kale, lettuce. Maybe he can do that, rent a plot somewhere, or ask Tom if he can plant a small vegetable patch. Like a *fanook*. Who cares. He's too old to worry about that. And let someone say that to his face. No, he will not get in a fight. He will not capitulate, he will not fuck up. He will not go back there. He will not.

Not a lot of money. Bank accounts frozen. The real one and the fake one, in his mother's name. Fucking RICO. The US attorney opened his bank account and took racketeering gains and interest, which was just about everything. Jimmy had stashed some cash in a gym bag at his friend Carlo's house, $10,000 in banknotes, give or take, assuming all of it is still there. He has the envelope from Pino, the money he made in the prison factory, plus the pittance left him when his parents died, and his brother should have another few rolls of bills, if he hasn't spent them. Gravy. Not much gravy. Tomorrow he'll go and collect from Carlo, and he'll buy some things—one of those mini stereo systems and some CDs. Then it will be the day after tomorrow, and he's not quite sure what he will do. Walk around the old neighborhood, maybe visit an old friend or two. There aren't so many of them anymore. Lost, moved away, or dead; even some of the young ones have moved or died. He'll visit his brother and their cousins in Bensonhurst and mattress Richie on Long Island. He knew it would be like this.

He's been away a long, long time. They'll have a small welcome party for him later, Ponzoni said. The world is big and new and the floating man doesn't know many of its inhabitants. He feels like he has just arrived, knows no one, and is seeing the place for the first time.

When he's finished unpacking, he straightens the row of hangers in the closet, collapses the Bankers Box, leaves it tidily angled beside the front door, and sits on the bed. It's vast and comfortable. There's an air conditioner humming. It's nestled high in the side wall, and there's a tiny white remote control on the bedside table. He lies back on the bed in his shoes and socks and stares at the motionless ceiling fan. Brown blades and a frosted glass light. He closes his eyes.

A hot shower, brand new bar of Irish Spring soap, he watches the water bubble and splash and run down the drain. Thirsty brown towel, steam on the mirror. In the joint, you get to shower three times a week (once a week if you're in segregation), in a crowded shower room, with dirty water around your ankles, sharing a single shower head with two inmates.

When he enters the garden again, a little girl is near the back fence, small and thin with dark hair. She's picking up some of the fallen leaves and collecting them in the upturned end of her T-shirt. She turns. He stops, smiles. She looks at him judiciously. Surely they haven't told her that this man was in prison? She waves; he waves back and turns toward his door, where he flips over one of the molded plastic chairs and sits. The little girl watches for several seconds, before returning to her leaves. Jimmy closes his eyes.

When he looks up, the girl is staring straight at him.

"Hello."

"Hello."

"I'm Molly."

"I'm Jimmy."

"I'm six."

"I'm old."

"I know."

She walks toward him, holding the T-shirt-bucketed leaves with both hands. "Can you turn over that chair?" She points with her nose.

He stands up and turns the chair over, pulls it away from the table.

"And bring it over here." Pause. "Please."

He picks up the chair and puts it close to where she is standing. She is so small, wiry legs poking out from her shorts, tiny neck, dark hair. He steps back, away from her. Doesn't want to make her nervous. He's nervous enough. He can't remember the last time he saw a child much less spoke to one.

Savino's granddaughter now climbs on the chair and she loses some of the leaves but she's up now, branch height.

He sits back in his plastic chair and smiles up at her. He wishes he'd brought a newspaper or magazine, and he makes a mental note to buy a few when he goes shopping. He could go today, before Jackie Ponzoni comes to collect him, and he is about to stand up, when she speaks to him again.

"I've been skinning fishes."

"Skinning fishes."

"Yes."

He doesn't see any fish, doesn't smell any. "You can't skin fishes."

"Of course you can. That's how you turn them into birds."

He nods. "Oh."

She selects a leaf, holds it aloft, and lets it drop and it floats to the grass. And then another lands beside it, wobbles, settles, and then a third and there is a small growing mound at the foot of the chair. She drops her skinned fishes one by one and they flutter, green and flapping, to the ground around the mottled brown legs of the garden chair.

Skinning Fishes

Molly

She is the queen of the garden and also a princess and also an inventor, and today she is skinning fishes and after that maybe a tea party. First you must find the fishes that can fly, so she's busy sorting through them, picking only the big waxy ones, when the man appears. This is Grampa's friend; her parents have told her about him. *Hello. Hello.* He sits on the chair near the downstairs apartment, his apartment now, and she goes back to her fishes.

He's thinner, older than she'd imagined. Of course Grampa is dead, but in the photos he's a lot younger than this man and has thick black hair. Mom says they have to be nice to him. *No foolishness.* Molly waves, and the man waves back. His clothes look scratchy. The tenants before were Douglas with big bushy hair, and his girlfriend, Brenda, who used to play with Molly and talk about her dolls and drink tea out of imaginary teacups. Molly liked Brenda and so she liked Douglas. Mom and Dad said they were getting married but she asked Brenda and Brenda said no-well-maybe, and then the apartment wasn't available anymore and they got a month's free rent which sounded like it was a big deal and it was bad timing but what are you going to do. She asked her dad, but he wouldn't talk about it. Grown-up stuff.

It's summer. No school and camp hasn't started. Mom's staying home to watch Molly and Cargo. Maybe today she'll let them go to Eighth Avenue to get ice cream. Cargo likes to watch the softball games at the school on the way back. They stand and watch softball and lick their ice cream cones. Mister Jimmy doesn't look like a man who likes ice cream. Or children. Or imaginary tea parties.

Later she asks him to move the chair so she can make her fishes fly. *You can't skin fishes.* He's not very good at pretend. Not like Brenda.

The man has gone back inside when Cargo comes downstairs. "Mom says stay out of the garden awhile." "But I'm not finished." "Come on." And he yanks her arm, sore. "Go away," she shouts. "Well, come on then." He picks her up and topples her over, and she lands on her side, hard on the ground, the wind knocked out of her, and Cargo sits on top of her for a moment before he lets her up. She runs ahead of him into the house.

Upstairs Mom is in the kitchen, cutting up fruit.

"Cargo knocked me over." She doesn't like to tell, but he does it all the time, and it hurts and it's not nice to do that.

Their mother looks them over, runs a hand through Molly's hair, bends down to look at her.

"Are you all right, chicken?"

"Yes. But he sat on me."

"Cargo. How many times do I have to tell you."

"She wouldn't come."

"Did you ask nicely?"

"Yes."

"No. You didn't."

Mom straightens. "Cargo. Keep it together, okay? If you're good we can get ice cream later." The words settle, and then Mom goes back to the fruit she's butchering.

"Why do we have to stay out of the garden?"

"Just for a little while, Moll. Let Mr. Piccini get settled. He only just got here."

"His mother died," Cargo announces.

"That's right. He was a friend of your Grampa's. Anyway, he's still a bit sad, so let's be nice to him, and be polite."

She knows that everyone dies. Their cat died, and they didn't get another one even though Dad promised. Mom and Dad will die. She cannot think about that for very long. It makes her gulp and have to stand up. What happens? Does everything just go black forever? Do you slowly melt into the soil, like a rock? Or does your soul go and live with other souls in a big house, like when they go to stay with Mom's sister? Does it hurt when you're dead? Can you feel your body rotting? How long before your soul gets to heaven? Do they have TV there? And if it's winter, does your soul get cold floating above Brooklyn on the way to heaven?

Find the Cost of Freedom

Jimmy

Ponzoni returns about six P.M. They drive along Flatbush Avenue, past Laundromats and markets, shiny banks, Golden Krust, Subway, Rite Aid, Best Farm, hardware stores, liquor stores. Some shops have bright awnings, some have neon signs. Cars are brighter than he imagined. Only the tops of the buildings look about the same as he remembers. The pedestrians are mostly young—lots of backpacks, children in strollers, kids on scooters, girls in short skirts. So many people wear headphones, plugged in, tuned out.

Their first stop is Casa Altobelli in Carroll Gardens. Straight out of the past, same sign, same door, new paint job. The social club Jimmy used to frequent is now flanked by a new restaurant and a store that takes Jimmy a minute or two to fathom, until he realizes the bowls and bright tubs are for dogs. A little bell tinkles meekly as the door opens. Inside, Altobelli's is dim. Smells the same—stale cigar smoke and espresso. The unmistakable bear-like outline of Big Bobby Maritato approaches him.

"Holy shit. Look what the cat dragged in." Bobby is upon him, gives him a hug, then holds Jimmy at arm's length, takes a look at him, beaming. "Look at you, you look terrific. You stayed in shape while the rest of us got fat."

"While *you* got fat," someone calls.

"You ain't no string bean."

"Come on, let the man through."

"Whaddya want, his E-Z Pass?"

Everyone laughs. Jimmy's not sure what an E-Z Pass is.

Big Bobby used to drive for Joey Armone. He was a sure bet for captain, maybe even underboss, but Armone got pinched when Jimmy did, another victim of the yellow dog *pentito's* testimony, and Bobby found himself adrift in the family. He made it though, worked hard, proved himself. He was an earner and loyal as the day is long. Now he owns some legitimate businesses, including two restaurants, where, from the looks of it, he spends his days eating.

He squeezes Jimmy, pats his back a few times. "It's good to see you. I've been waiting for this day."

"Me too."

As they walk through, chairs scrape, and everyone stands up. Jimmy recognizes the man in a herringbone jacket and blue shirt from photos. Pino Locatelli, the new boss. Locatelli has short black hair, well groomed, and wears small silver-framed glasses. He lives in Brooklyn Heights, Jimmy has heard, in a brownstone among the bankers and lawyers. So he can't be doing that badly.

"Welcome back."

Same configuration of tables, shelf along the wall, loaded with cups and jugs, SSC Napoli mugs, dog figurines. The crew, such as it is, is all there. Bobby and Ponzoni and Frank Rizzo, Paolo Petrucci and Potito "Mash" Gallucci, Ruggiero family old timers, a few others from the old days, two Gambino guys, all here to pay their respects. Pino Locatelli introduces Jimmy to the guys he doesn't already know, then raises his Sambuca glass. "This is a brave soldier, this is an honorable man. Welcome home." Jimmy smiles and says thank you. Made men and former captains from two different families, Ruggiero and Gambino, stand up and shake his hand. They talk about the Colt, who moved to Palm Springs, where he died back in 2009. They talk about the 125 arrests made on a single day in 2011, a sweep that spanned seven mob families from Rhode Island to Florida. "We dodged a bullet that day," someone says. "None of our guys got nabbed." Rizzo tells Jimmy he's gotta go to Eataly, the new Italian marketplace in Manhattan. They talk about Joseph Armone, the only boss of the family Jimmy ever knew. Racketeering, accessory to murder. Served twelve years. "Shadow of his former self when he got out," Paolo says. "*Mezza morta*, it was sad to see," one of the old timers adds. Jimmy can't remember the old timer's name.

When Armone died, his wife moved to a retirement community on Long Island, Pino explains. Jimmy says he'll go and see her one day, and they all nod approvingly. "And of course Tony Rizzo is still away," Paolo says. "Drugs and racketeering," says the guy whose name Jimmy can't remember. "Didn't see that one coming."

"You probably got a lot of people to see," someone says.

"Not so many as you might think. All that time in the joint, the world kinda shrinks." Shrinks and dies, he thinks.

Bartolomeo Santoro, Armone's *consigliere*, bought himself a place on the beach in North Carolina. He's still there as far as anyone knows. He's lost his mind (Alzheimer's, someone says) but he recognizes some of the old guys. Maybe I'll go and see him too, Jimmy says.

They talk about the old times, who's gone legit, who's in the can, dead, retired to Florida or California or Mexico. Tommy "Fish" Rispoli, of all people, has gone to Mexico. (Fish always hated Mexicans and Puerto Ricans.) Jimmy is glad that they don't ask him about prison. He's happier to hear about other people than talk about himself, still he feels awkward sitting there, like an interloper. Bobby is the one to say, if you need anything, we're all here, am I right? And everyone nods and says sure. Jimmy says thank you and does feel a rush of gratitude and a sense of belonging. Bobby suggests they go to Atlantic City next week.

The old waiter hobbles over with coffees and Sambuca.

"*Cent'anni.*"

They clink cups and glasses.

"*Cent'anni.*"

"This man," Pino says, pointing a knuckle at Jimmy. "This is a man's man. *Salute.*"

Respect, Jimmy thinks. Pino likes that Jimmy is from the old days, you can tell that. They really were family when he was young; now there's not the same trust. Some things like that, they never come back once they're gone. All five families are the same. Less trust, less power, less money. He came up at the end of a golden age.

Someone says, "You're looking good, Jimmy."

"He looks a lot better than you. Maybe you should try a few years in the can."

"Get me away from my wife."

They laugh, clap their hands on their knees, nod at Jimmy.

Ponzoni comes over behind Jimmy, bends to whisper in his ear. "Pino, he wants a word outside."

Jimmy looks over at Pino, who nods and stands up. Someone unlocks the back door and Pino leads the way outside to a small courtyard overhung with oak trees. Brick, rusted metal table, ringed by sturdy wooden chairs. Pino takes a seat, smooths the crease of his pants.

"I wanna say thank you. On behalf of all those people in there and Armone, Savino, everyone. You're a stand-up guy and we got nothing but respect and thanks. All those years, you didn't give the cops nothing, didn't rat on nobody. We've put some money together, found you a place to live, and we're going to keep doing that. You stand for everything we believe in, everything we want to be. We owe you, Jimmy. I know that, everybody in there knows that. Anything you need, you come to me, okay."

"Thanks, Pino. The guys . . . you've been great." He's awkwardly trying to say thank you more effusively or formally, when he realizes Pino hasn't finished, hasn't gotten to the nub of what he wants to say.

"But as far as work, as far as what we are doing on the streets, we can't take risks. You're too hot. Cops are going to be watching you like hawks."

"I want to work."

"I know, Jimmy."

"There's nothing, you know, out of the spotlight?"

He shakes his head, like he's thinking. "There's nothing. I'm sorry. We're not that diversified. Our reach, sorry to say, it's small."

Jimmy wants to say something, but the words won't come. He wants to work. He'd been looking forward to being on the streets, helping out, people coming to him for advice, his opinion sought. But there won't be any of that, just an envelope under the doormat, probably getting thinner and thinner as the months and years go by.

"There's something else," Pino says. "A rumor. I want you to hear it from me. And I want you to know we've got it under control."

"What rumor?"

"Little Mikey. Some people think he's been showing his face in New Jersey, maybe New York too."

"Jesus." He's imagined Mike Rossi alive and well, suntanned and fat, living out his days in Arizona or someplace like that, not here, and not when Jimmy himself just got back.

"Jimmy, there's no proof, just a couple of young wiseguys tossing rumors around, you know how they are."

"Who? Who said they saw him?"

"Someone told someone who told Gallucci. He brought it to me, and we decided to wait to tell you until you got out. We sent a couple of guys to New Jersey, asked around, but none of our guys has seen him, just a coupla Atlantic City buttheads."

Jimmy nods, says nothing, taking it all in, picturing Little Mikey, walking the streets of New Jersey. This was not one of the scenarios he thought about when he talked about forgiveness with the prison priest.

"If we know he's here, then the cops know he's here, and that means heat, which is one thing we do not want," Pino says. "So you stay away. Okay? I swear to you, we see him, we'll let you know, and we'll take care of it."

"Thanks, Pino."

"You know as well as I do we all want him to end up the same way. And not a lot of people know where you're staying, so you

don't gotta worry about that. But I need your promise, Jimmy: you
see him, you let us know. You can call me, any time."

They drive to an Italian restaurant for dinner, past the park, men
in tight shirts and big beards, women with clunky glasses, a home-
less man wheeling a supermarket cart, old brownstones and a new
apartment block dotted with small square balconies. Inside Il Mat-
tone, they are escorted to a private room on the second floor. Soft
carpeting, plates of antipasti in the middle of the table, smooth
jazz drifting down from the ceiling, mingling with the smell of
cooking. A few wives and girlfriends are already there, along with
some young guys who weren't at Altobelli's. He remembers looking for Milena in a crowd of Ruggiero wives and girlfriends. A
lifetime ago. A voice brings him back to the present. "There he
is." The boss's wife kisses Jimmy on the cheek. She's pretty with
blonde hair and a peach-colored jacket. "Welcome home." Bobby
introduces his wife, a young, curvaceous Latina. She gives Jimmy
a hug. "Such a pleasure to finally meet you." They stand around
and clink glasses and make small talk. Some of the younger guys
come over to shake Jimmy's hand. "An honor," they say. "A hero."
They eat, they drink. Midway through the appetizers, Pino points
at the pile of gifts and envelopes on a chair in the corner, and
Jimmy says how grateful he is. "Least we could do." Pino promises
Yankee tickets. "You're not gonna believe the new stadium. Cost
more than a billion."
        Steak, pasta, veal, red wine, white wine, vodka. Jimmy's never
seen so much food and booze. It's the best food he's tasted in
twenty-five years. A lot of eyes are still on him. They ask about
life in the joint and Jimmy confirms that the made men from
all the families, the Italians and Irish, banded together. Some of
them paid Mexicans to be bodyguards. Very loyal, the Mexicans.
He tells the story of some young punk who tried to steal his cigarettes in the can. Jimmy threw him down and kicked him hard
and a couple of the other guys were there in a flash. The guards,
seeing that it was Jimmy and the Italians, didn't intervene for a

few minutes. "You beat him hard once so you don't gotta do it again." Everyone laughs and mutters in agreement. They toast to Jimmy: *A stand-up guy.* They toast the departed and incarcerated: Armone, the Colt, Tony Rizzo, Vincent DeNunzio, Santoro. And the wives: Santoro's wife, Savino's wife, Anna Maria, DeNunzio's wife, Milena. It's the first time Jimmy's heard her name out loud in many, many years. *Salut.* Bobby says, "Okay, let the man eat. Here's to Jimmy. May the best day of your past be the worst day of your future." Jimmy raises his glass. "I'd be lost without you bums." The truth is, he's a bit lost anyway, with or without them. If he needs someone, if he needs a crew to get him out of a scrape or to bust some balls, if he needs to take cold, bloody, violent revenge, who will help him? Not a man among them, not even Bobby. And he couldn't ask Bobby. But they smile and raise their glasses and he smiles back at them.

He stands up. "I ain't gonna make a big speech, but I want to say thank you. Here's to you. Everyone here. You are my family. *Salut.*" And with that, the stand-up guy sits down.

Later, when ties have been loosened, wine spilled, jokes told, and some of the younger guys have left to chase tail, he finds himself at the end of the table with Bobby sipping an espresso and a shot of Sambuca.

"I can't believe it," Bobby says. His cheeks are puffy, like he's holding little balloons in his mouth.

"You and me both. I thought this day would never come."

"Everything all right? Your place with Tom, DeSapio's son?"

"Yeah, fine. It's great."

"Anything you need?"

"Nothing. Thanks, Bobby."

"How's your brother?"

"He's fine. I'll go and see him soon."

It's past midnight when Ponzoni drives him home. They asked if he wanted to go anywhere else. The young guys winked and made gestures he took to mean hookers or drugs. Jimmy just smiled and shook his head. Thank you. Thank you for flying Penitentiary Airways.

Now he asks Ponzoni to stop at a bodega in Park Slope. He's only slightly drunk (wouldn't let himself get juiced at his own homecoming party), so he buys a six-pack of Budweiser and a pack of Marlboros (which costs the same as a carton before his jolt), the *Times* and *Daily News*, orange juice for the morning. It's all he wants. To sit in his garden chair and drink a beer and smoke a too-goddamned expensive cigarette in the moonlight. No guards, no inmates crying and yelling and pounding on cell doors.

He opens a Budweiser and sits at the wooden table drinking from the bottle and looking out at the trees and fuzzy night sky. It's cool enough to sit outside. He's worn orange peels every day, barely remembers what civ clothes feel like—soft against his thighs, these chinos. But it's not all soft-shoe slide. He's got that jittery feeling again, like he should be doing something, planning something. In the can, you get used to being alone, the feeling of time passing around you, without you. The night sky calms him; the peaceful tree. He can just make out the dark leaves, swaying in the breeze. He takes a sip. The beer is cold; the beer is perfection. Distant voices. *Doom-ba doom-ba* music plays from somewhere across the garden. The backs of frame houses are mostly exposed brick, but there's one painted pale yellow. Soft voices from one of the gardens nearby, a man and a woman chatting quietly under the night sky. Another thing that's different about being on the outside: the sounds. Crickets, distant music, the quiet conversation. It's almost unnerving, the quiet, and he has to remind himself this is normal, not the panic of prison's shouted conversations, mess hall fights, and loudspeaker announcements. He didn't come around here much in the old days, a rundown, mostly Latino neighborhood, if he remembers correctly. He can't remember if Savino bought the place as an investment or some Mexican mobster got in over his head and Savino ended up with the guy's house. Jimmy takes another sip of beer, thinks about his friends in prison tonight. He wonders if they're thinking of him, jealous of his freedom, or have they forgotten him already, just another old-timer who got out.

If he's going to freak out, now would be the time. Alone at last, no one around. It's nighttime and he's outdoors, something he can barely remember. But he isn't freaking or frightened, only intensely aware. He is a different person. He's not the same man he was in the can, and he's not the guy he was before, fast-forwarded twenty-five years.

He smokes his cigarette slowly, leans back, gazing at the yellow boxes of light in windows across the yard, at trees and leaves darker than the night sky. He feels a bit drunk and alone, like he may be the only person in the city awake, the only soul on the planet.

Back inside, he locks the envelope of cash in his suitcase without counting it and puts the gifts on the table. *There's nothing. I'm sorry. We're not that diversified.* Not what he was hoping to hear, although not a surprise either. If he knows one thing, he knows you can't count on anything. Like Little Mikey back on the streets of Atlantic City? Would he want a piece of Jimmy? He might. He's a crazy fuck, and he might want to clip Jimmy before Jimmy finds him. Jimmy takes a sip of beer, looks at the stack of wrapped presents but makes no move to open any, looks around his Brooklyn basement. Maybe it's not that big, and maybe it smells a bit of mold, but compared to a prison cell it's a veritable mansion. Freedom is light and quiet and a few square feet to call your own. Cotton-headed, cool, and pleasurably tipsy he takes off his shirt and lies down.

The bed is soft; the air conditioner hums, and cool air tumbles down. There is a strange, quiet ringing in his ears, beneath the hum of the air conditioner, more constant than the traffic sounds. No screams, no cries or groans, no snoring, no banging and clanking of steel doors as he drifts off.

He dreams he is back in the joint, wakes with a jolt in his cool big bed in the middle of the night. He gets out of bed, and stands at the window, looking at the trees and moon-streaked yard. Never mind what Pino said, he's out and no one can take that away. The priest in the can said it would be like this. Another country, another planet. But it's better than being in the joint. Even with Pino turning his back, even with the orphan feeling that comes from all or almost all the people he loved before being gone. He's in Brooklyn, a free man, and tomorrow he can do whatever he likes. He lies back in bed and closes his eyes, listens to the nighttime city rumble around him, and drifts back into a dreamless sleep.

When he wakes again, light splashes around the edges of the curtains. He hears the sound of footsteps and children's voices upstairs. It's Friday, Jimmy's first full day of freedom. He lies in bed and listens to the traffic and birdsong. The bed is so comfortable he wants to cry.

He's up, showered, dressed, and smelling like Irish Spring soap well before eight. He takes a wad of bills, locks the door carefully behind him, and stands in the garden for a few minutes, beneath the deck. Even a skinny lime tree is something to behold on your first blue-skied day of freedom. He makes his way up the steps around the side of the house, his nostrils full of the smell of summer trees. On the street, morning commuters hurry to the subway, checking their mobile phones. Women's heels clip and clop. Kids with bright backpacks, kids on scooters and skateboards. Jimmy walks more slowly. He's got all day. It's strange—no one cares where he is or what he does. He has to fight the urge to return home, because being outside in the world, walking down Seventh Avenue in Brooklyn, feels wrong somehow, like someone else's life. On the avenue, he stops at a deli. It's busy inside and smells of coffee and bacon grease. He buys an egg sandwich and a coffee. He sits on the bench outside the deli, eating his sandwich and sipping his coffee—both goddamned delicious.

Back in the basement apartment, he phones his brother. It feels illicit to pick up a phone and simply dial a number, something he didn't get to do for twenty-five years. Paulie's voice on the other end of the line sounds familiar and yet strange.

"Are you out? You in New York?"

"No, I'm in Madagascar. Of course, I'm in Brooklyn. How you been, Paulie?"

They chat for a while and make a plan to get together.

He goes for a walk in the heat of the day.

To be free is to feel alive.

Takin' It to the Streets

Milena

She propped open her textbook and pretended to read, but she was looking through the grimy, wire-glazed windows, gazing at puffy clouds and the box-top buildings and water towers, the tatty awnings and graffitied brick storefronts. The boy in front of her was picking his nose. The girl beside him had hives on her arms and legs. Milena daydreamed about flying above the buildings and about being somewhere else, it didn't matter where, Manhattan, Paris, Milan. Like many beautiful girls with protective fathers, Milena was careful. Careful not to flirt, careful not to get drunk or attract too much attention or forget herself. She wanted to be a nurse. One of her sister's friends had gone to college, another was a secretary in a law firm in Manhattan. Another became a stripper. Maria, the oldest sister, who had long since married the butcher's son, was raising a family. Sabrina—middle sister, saucy, sexy—had finished high school and gone to Manhattan bars after work with friends where eligible single men drank together. Milena knew she wanted more than that, but she didn't know what exactly she wanted or how to get it. She knew she was clever, and everyone told her she was beautiful. But her Aunt Elisabetta was beautiful and intelligent, and she'd ended up alone, working at a sporting goods store on Nostrand Avenue and clipping coupons at night in front of the television.

From the windows of her high school on Bushwick Avenue, Milena beheld a deli, shoe store, and liquor store, housing projects, an empty lot, tumbleweeds of trash swirling around parked cars. Beyond the brick buildings, beyond the tenements and graffiti, lay a different Manhattan than the one she had seen, a world of prosperity and art, magic and mystery—a world, as of yet, unknown to her.

During the long hot summer of 1977, Sabrina had a job in a clothing store on Knickerbocker Avenue, and on Monday and Wednesday afternoons Milena helped her sister with inventory, folded clothes, and packed returns for five dollars an hour. Son of Sam was shooting women with a .44, targeting single brunettes with long hair in Queens, Brooklyn, and the Bronx. All three sisters had their hair cut, bobs all round. Every time Sabrina and Milena left the house their mother told them to be careful, and they were.

A Wednesday evening, mid-July, the sky a humid, hazy blue. Milena's blouse clung to her back and her hair frizzed out like feathers. They'd gone to see *The Spy Who Loved Me* at the Parthenon on Wyckoff Avenue, and were meandering home, singing "Nobody Does it Better" and pretending to ski like James Bond, taking out bad guys as they carved down the slopes. *Nobody does it half as good as you. Baby, you're the best.* They had skied and slalomed and laughed their way through the song when they stopped for a cold soda, which they drank sitting on the warm stone steps of a row house on Linden Street. It was then that every streetlight suddenly buzzed and flickered. Instinctively Sabrina touched Milena's arm. They were outside and there was still light in the sky, so they thought nothing of it and continued on their way home. Twenty minutes later, they were in Irving Square Park, when they heard a loud cracking sound and then the world went dark, every building, every window, and streetlight black. The only light came from cars and the flickers of matches and lighters. There was a collective hush for a minute or so, and then people started shouting, dogs barked, children yelled, and all around them people started running in different directions. Sirens wailed, car horns honked. Sabrina and Milena ran home in the hot, hazy darkness, sticking close to the road so they could see by the headlights and taillights of cars moving slowly on Halsey Street. They could hear shouting, the sound of glass breaking, and sirens far away, but they didn't stop, didn't turn to look around at the chaos that was engulfing Brooklyn.

Back home they locked the doors and sat in the living room with their parents. Their mother had lit some candles. They looked out at the ghostly city. They'd never seen the skyline so dark, never experienced a night as strange. Sirens wailed and alarms blared, and from their apartment window they could see people running home. After a while the streets went quiet. Their father sat in a chair near the front door, with a baseball bat on his lap. They looked out the window. The block was mostly empty; only the brazen young men stayed out, swaggering, taking it to the streets.

About a month later, in August, David Berkowitz, the Son of Sam, was arrested. Every girl in Brooklyn breathed a sigh of relief. That September, Sabrina found work in a boutique in Manhattan, and most evenings Milena was the only one home with her parents. Milena was allowed to travel to Manhattan once, maybe twice, a month with high school friends and Sabrina and anyone else they could round up. Safety in numbers. They dressed in short skirts and wore mascara and got into any clubs they liked. It was fun; men bought them drinks and they danced and chatted. They liked dancing, liked soul music—Marvin Gaye, Earth, Wind & Fire, Stevie Wonder. Milena brought some of their records home, but her father threw them out. *Our people, our music.* She liked that kind of music too, but she wanted more, she wanted to hear all kinds of music. There was a yearning inside her. She wanted to travel, to see the world. Years later, someone would play her a Springsteen song called "Hungry Heart" and that became the name she would give to her younger self and those yearnings.

Those yearnings, along with everything else she would come to see as her childhood, ended one winter day when her father collapsed on the freezer room floor. By the time the ambulance arrived, he was dead. Heart attack, they said. She never got to tell him what she wanted for Christmas, never got to say good-bye. Suddenly they were poor, without a father or a future. They had a little money in savings and their mother earned a meager wage working for a local seamstress, but without his income they couldn't afford the apartment, the clothes they bought, the colleges she wanted to attend. Her mother wanted to send her daughters to Virginia, to their father's sister, but they wanted no part of suburban southern life, so they helped her move from the apartment where they grew up into a two-bedroom like Aunt Elisabetta's, and their first night there, Milena and Sabrina comforted their grieving mother, told her that they would be fine, and it was all going to work out. She smiled and kissed each of them on the head and held them tight. "I have three beautiful, wonderful daughters. Your father was so proud."

She didn't know it at the time, but that day Milena changed, from feeling she had it all to feeling she had nothing, or nothing she could rely on, from fortunate to fucked. She was sixteen, a sophomore in high school, and cursed her luck. She wouldn't go to college. They'd be lucky to get boring jobs like their aunt and live out their lives with only the TV and each other for company. It was her sister who put an end to her mooning. "Let Mama have her grief. We have to live our lives." Sabrina always seemed to know what to do. Two years older, a woman already, she had a plan, for their mother and for themselves. Perhaps she knew that if she didn't get Milena out of the house she would stay home with their mother, and her beautiful younger sister would grow old without ever having any fun. Whatever the reason, they went out together, mostly in Manhattan. Sabrina knew how to get places on the subway, which stores in Manhattan were having sample sales, how to talk her way into bars and restaurants, and how to flirt with men. Together the sisters went to parties, art gallery openings, fashion week events, Fifth Avenue shops, the movies. "We have to live our lives," Sabrina told Milena. And so they spent what little money they had on clothes and took the subway to Manhattan once a week.

It was in a bar, all the way uptown near Columbia University, that Milena met Chris Benelli, a college boy, handsome, sure of himself and worldly, at least compared to the Cossuttas. It was someone's birthday and the bar was crowded. Preppy guys in khaki pants, blonde girls. Chris didn't quite belong either, wasn't sure how he'd ended up there. He and his buddies were Long Island boys and had driven in from Binghamton for a night in the city. He laughed a lot; he seemed like a guy to take delight in the world, and it was infectious. Smiling, he asked if he could buy her a drink. Everyone was talking to someone else, even Sabrina was already engrossed in conversation. "Can you believe it?" Chris Benelli said, handing Milena a Tom Collins. "Two Italians, one from Brooklyn, one from Long Island, and they meet in Manhattan. *Salut.*" They touched plastic cups. He had a tan, stubble, big warm eyes, and sparkling white teeth. No, his family wasn't from Sicily or Naples. They were from Tuscany. And they laughed at that too. Tuscany was fancy. Tuscany was Florence and rolling hills and wine.

The next weekend he took the train to Brooklyn just to take her to dinner. A week after that they met in Manhattan, took in a band in a club on Bleecker Street, kissed in an alleyway in the Village, and then he rode the subway all the way back to Brooklyn with her and walked her to her door where, after more kissing and giggles, he left her. He said he'd never met anyone like her. After that they met more often, at the public library, at Café Wha? on MacDougal Street, in and around Washington Square. He took her to fancy restaurants. "I could look at you for a week and a day," he said. He told her about Al D'Amato, a town supervisor in Hempstead and vice-chairman of the Nassau County Board of Supervisors. They said he was going to run for president.

"Imagine that, an Italian-American in the White House."

"Is that what you want to do? Politics?"

"Maybe," he said. "But first I have to go to law school, maybe work in Washington."

The world looked so much bigger and more interesting through his eyes. She confided that she wanted to be a nurse or a teacher, but her family didn't have the money for college, because her father had died. He looked crestfallen and said if he could he would help her pay for whatever school she liked. At the end of every evening they kissed but it went no further. "I just want to be with you," he said. He told her he wanted her to meet his parents and sent her a ticket on the Shortline bus. But the day before, he said his mother was sick. They'd have to do it another time. A pity, he said, because he wanted her to see where he lived, see Long Island. It got a bad rap, he explained, but it's really a nice place to live. Instead of dinner with his parents he came to the city and they went to a party in the Village, and she got drunk and they kissed in the kitchen of whoever's apartment it was, and when he touched her breasts, she didn't stop him. "I'd like to see you with a tan," he said, and his forefinger prodded her bra across her breast almost to the nipple. There was only the faintest of tan lines, and he rubbed his hand across it and then let the bra and sweater slide back into place.

"I disappoint you," she said.

"No. Never."

"But I will. That's the problem with high school girls."

"Not if you don't want to."

She didn't know how to answer that, and so she kissed him and let him touch her breasts again, and she liked the way it made her feel, sexy and alive, wanting and not wanting.

He had a friend at NYU and they walked to his dorm room. The friend was in bed with his girlfriend, behind a Moroccan tapestry hung from the ceiling, so they lay on the couch, side by side, talking in whispers, and kissing and touching. "I want you so much," he murmured. She unbuttoned his pants and touched his penis and he groaned and kissed her happily, purring like a cat.

It was hard and warm, his penis, and she stroked it a bit longer like Sabrina had told her, and after a while he came, and she was glad because she wasn't ready to have sex with him or anyone else.

Chris Benelli. Big sweet eyes, mop of hair that he pushed out of his eyes and tucked behind his ears. He had a way of leaning forward when he was earnest, or in planning mode. Europe in the summer was one of his plans. They would see Italy, he told her. Imagine Paris. She'd never convince her mother, but she played it cool. *Paris, sure.* And lit up a mock Gauloise. Would she go with him to Washington when he graduates? If he could get a job on Capitol Hill?

"Oh, Chris," she said. "Depends."

"Depends on what?"

"On everything."

"Maybe you can go to college. Why not? Student loans, my parents would help, and as soon as I can make some money, I'll pay your tuition."

It happened that his roommate's parents had booked a hotel room for a long weekend but had left New York earlier than anticipated, with the result that a hotel room in Midtown was theirs for the night. They laughed and sprawled on the bed, drank the vodka and tonics and ate potato chips from the mini bar. And late that night, when the city below them had dimmed, and she was feeling woozy and warm, she let him undress her and they had sex. It hurt a bit, and she bled and bit her lip, but it was over quickly, and then he kissed her and wrapped his long arms around her, and they fell asleep entwined.

They had sex three times after that. Always in Manhattan. A friend's apartment, a hotel room. He still wanted her to meet his parents, but his mother wasn't well. They hung out with Sabrina and her friends. They had drinks and went to a party together, someone Sabrina had met. Afterward Mili and Chris had sex in his friend's NYU dorm room, behind the colorful tapestry. They had to be out before midnight.

She decided she couldn't have sex again. Not for a while anyway. She told him over dinner in the Village. He'd been planning on returning to his friend's dorm with her, and he looked like a wounded puppy.

"I'm sorry."

"But I love you. I want to marry you."

"I'm not going anywhere."

They kissed on Minetta Lane, and he rode the subway with her back to Brooklyn and walked her all the way home.

She missed her period, and she felt a bit dizzy, a tightening in her breasts and the feeling that she was getting a cold, only her throat didn't hurt and her nose didn't run. She waited until she knew for sure before she phoned Chris. He wasn't there, and she left a message with his roommate. "Just tell him to call me."

Night Fever

Jimmy

Jimmy finished high school, got his diploma, drove to the Jersey shore with friends, slept on the beach, slept in the car, fucked Russian hookers. He lived on White Castle burgers, beer, and cigarettes. It was the summer of 1977 and he was running numbers, taking bets for Silvio the old bookmaker, and shaking down the local drug dealers.

A hot night in July. Dogs barking, cars and buses and children shouting, Mister Softee jingle a couple of blocks away. Jimmy was on his way to The King's Head in Brooklyn, for a cold beer, maybe a burger. His mother would yell at him for not telling her that he wouldn't be coming home for dinner, and he was looking for a pay phone when he paused, stopped by strange sounds, as the streets themselves seemed to buzz and crackle, like the static on a record before the first song starts. Lights flickered, buzzed again, then went dark. Most of the cars on the street slowed or stopped. What was unnerving was the way everything went dark, every light, every window and storefront, and the hush. Only for a minute though, then cars started honking. Sirens and cars and the sound of people running home.

Mothers called their children, lit candles, and locked the doors. Only the men stayed on the hot, dark streets. Jimmy knew he couldn't go home because his father wouldn't let him go out again, so he ran to his friend Eddie's house. By the time he got there he'd seen someone smash a window, metal doors forced open, locks jimmied, glass broken. He grabbed Eddie and, armed with a flashlight, a crowbar, towels and bags, they quietly broke into a jewelry store on Ocean Parkway. Dark inside and out. No one had gotten there yet, and they had their pick of the jewelry. The prize pieces were no doubt in the safe, but there was a lot of gold and silver on display—rings and bracelets, watches and gem-studded necklaces. After that they hit the local liquor store, which was full of looters, more crowded now, past ten o'clock during a blackout, than a normal Saturday evening. They strolled through the upturned aisles of the supermarket. All that food was only going to go bad anyway. They were struggling to carry all the loot home, but that didn't stop Jimmy from helping an old lady he recognized from the neighborhood to get to her apartment building safely. Eddie waited while he walked her upstairs, leaving her with a bottle of wine, bread, water, candles, and a gold bracelet. Back outside carrying flashlights and their bags, Jimmy and Eddie ran home, zigzagging along darkly turbulent Brooklyn streets.

They were on Jackson Boulevard when they slowed from a jog to a walk, accustomed to the dim light now and the clamor of alarms and bells, the distant shouting and wail of faraway sirens. They were walking the riotous streets carrying their bounty. Looking around them as they went, ready to run, but not many people are going to mug two Italian teens, even on a night made for muggers. They turned when they heard the sound of breaking glass and saw a car window being smashed with a cinder block. The world was going crazy; every shop not visibly locked and dark was being looted. There was an ad hoc assembly line removing and bagging things from a supermarket they passed. Sirens wailed, but they were still far away. Meanwhile other looters teetered under boxes of stolen booze, already half drunk. Flashlights and candles flickered in apartment windows.

In their long and mostly criminal travels that night, did they pass two pretty Italian-American girls hurrying home from Irving Square Park? Maybe.

There were 38,000 arrests in less than forty-eight hours. Con Edison took a lot of shit for letting the city go black. The NYPD took shit for not calling in the National Guard. The mayor called for calm as the city patched itself up and went back to work.

They pawned most of the jewelry, then they drove Uncle Frankie's Oldsmobile to Atlantic City where they swam in the sea and watched the girls.

The rest of that summer he and Eddie and their friends went to the Rockaways and Jones Beach and picked up girls and drank and smoked and did blow. For a while Jimmy had a girlfriend, an Italian girl from Staten Island a couple of years older. Not a beauty, but she had a great, curvy body, soft silky boobs and an ass as round as a melon. When she saw him with another girl, she told him it was over, but that didn't matter either. It was a fun summer. He had money, friends, girls, a good stereo system, and big headphones so he could smoke a joint and listen to his music as loud as he wanted when he was home. His dad yelled sometimes, but Fulvio Piccini had all but given up on trying to discipline his younger son.

Jimmy was making some money and enjoying himself, but he wanted more. Not college and not the army like his Boy Scout brother. Uncle Frankie said you can help me out, and so Jimmy started helping his uncle with his late-night runs. Frankie was a trucker who divided his time between legitimate jobs that took him 2,500 miles in a week and nighttime pickups in Newark and other parts of New Jersey. He'd stop by the house to get Jimmy, and they'd eat in a diner nearby, drink lots of coffee. Then they'd drive before dawn to a store or warehouse. They were always lean operations, one, maybe two guys on the other side. You load, you lock, you drive back at dawn, unload them in a warehouse on Kent Avenue. The guy there would give Uncle Frank a fat envelope and a cigar. He would then drive Jimmy home, and Jimmy would sleep until noon.

Jimmy's father wouldn't have approved. Fulvio Piccini believed in hard work and honesty and ideals their mother sometimes mocked, like "giving a man a fair shake." He was a bus driver and proud union member and numbered among his friends Irish and black men who drove buses or worked at the depot on Jamaica Avenue. Jimmy's parents didn't argue often, but when they did it was about politics or the wisdom of befriending people of other races or Uncle Frankie and his dirty money. Fulvio Piccini was the proud American, his wife the nostalgic immigrant. He thought Jimmy Carter's heart was in the right place; she trusted Southerners even less than she trusted the Irish and the Jews. "Land of the free," Fulvio would say, and she would shake her head.

"We're just like the blacks and the Jews," he insisted.

"Nonsense, we're nothing like them."

"We're all immigrants, all making a new life in America. This is the new world, not Italy."

"I know that this is not Italy."

"Sometimes I wonder."

His father tried to get Jimmy a job at the bus depot or the auto parts store. Someone they knew had started out in auto parts and now owned a tire retailer. "I'll think about it, Pops," Jimmy promised, but it all sounded boring, and he knew he could make more money in a day than a tire salesman made in a month.

Once, when he and Uncle Frankie were making a pickup at an electronics store in East Orange at two in the morning, their contact, a night guard, told Uncle Frank he'd heard sirens the night before.

"Fuck you mean by that?"

"I mean what's in it for me."

His uncle peeled off a Franklin from a wad of notes in his pocket and slipped it in the man's front pocket. The guy took it out, examined it, as if it might be faulty.

"That's it? C'mon, Christmas is coming."

Uncle Frankie looked at him, frowned slightly, then punched him in the mouth, coldcocked the sucker. Jimmy stepped forward, but the guy staggered back. He might have been trying to say he was sorry, but Frank punched him again and the guy dropped, saying, "Sorry, I'm sorry," as he fell to the ground.

"Merry Christmas."

As they drove away Jimmy asked if they should take the hundred-dollar bill back.

"No, leave it. He earned it. And Christmas is coming."

On one of those trips, they made a second stop, after unloading on Kent Avenue, at a big house near Brower Park. Everything was opulent, from the heavy dark doors to the thick carpeting the moment they stepped inside. It smelled of cologne or something like it, a good, rich smell. "Who lives here?" Jimmy asked his uncle. He'd never seen such a big house, such classy furnishings. "A rich and powerful man," his uncle whispered. Although Jimmy never met the owner, it was his first brush with the Ruggiero family, a *caporegime*, Giuseppe Simone. A few weeks later his uncle introduced Jimmy to one of Simone's men, told him proudly that his nephew was shaking down the drug dealers in the neighborhood, and held his own when they made their midnight runs to New Jersey warehouses. "He's a smart kid and a hard worker."

Around that time Jimmy started asking people what they knew of the Ruggiero family, *Cosa Nostra,* and Giuseppe "The Shark" Simone. No one in the old neighborhood knew much, or so they said, but Jimmy picked up scraps, names, businesses they protected, businesses they didn't. He also asked a friend of his brother, Paul, to teach him some karate. Jimmy wasn't big, but he was quick and picked up some good martial arts defense and some pinpoint punches and kicks designed to inflict as much damage as possible and felt pretty confident he could hold his own against bigger men.

He was now shaking down the local drug dealers, stealing car stereos and selling them to chop shops, holding up liquor stores.

He was an occasional loan shark and drug dealer, proud owner of a used Volkswagen Scirocco, sapphire blue with Jensen speakers and seats that reclined way back for naps and blow jobs.

They were all home and waiting, that day in early November when his brother rang the front doorbell, and there he was, in blue jeans and a suede jacket with a moustache and smelling of cigarettes, an army duffel at his feet.

"Paulie," his mother sang his name.

"I'm back."

They couldn't ask why, because he'd already told them: he wanted out. "I got my stripes, now I want to be back in the real world. I ain't gonna re-up."

"You got a job or something?" their father asked when they were eating spaghetti alle vongole.

"Not yet."

"You get discharged? You do something wrong?"

"Papa, I didn't do anything wrong. I got an honorable discharge. I get benefits. Okay."

"Fulvio, *basta*." Their mother served seconds, mussed what there was of Paulie's hair. "Paul is home. Tonight we celebrate."

"What about your friend? He out too?" Jimmy asked.

"Who?"

"The one from Oklahoma. Your buddy from boot camp."

"Jasper. Yeah, he's out too."

You're Jerry, the cartoon mouse, clever and cunning. You dance on piano strings, squeeze into the tiniest of holes; you run circles around the big thick cat, the dime-bag dealers, the kids. These are your streets, and you're one step ahead of everyone else. You know you can't get lazy or stupid or let your guard down, and you knew that you won't. Because you are going to make it, because you're wily and smarter than the rest of them.

Because of Uncle Frankie's good name, Giuseppe Simone agreed to meet Jimmy. He dressed in a suit, shook the man's hand, said what an honor, and asked him for a job. Simone thought about it, smiled, said, kid, you got balls, said he liked Jimmy's uncle, and could tell Jimmy was a hard worker and came from a good family. He wrote a name and the address of a social club on a piece of paper. "Tell Al I sent you." The next day Jimmy met Alberto "the Colt" Braglia.

Brooklyn Days

Jimmy

O n Saturday morning, he dresses in the clothes Pino's crew bought for him. Gray suit, black polo shirt. A bit hot for summertime but at least he doesn't look like some idiot who's been out of prison three days—fucktard, the young guys in his cellblock would have said. He glances in the mirror: a clean-shaven, thin man with short hair looks back at him with uncertain eyes. Older than the image of himself he holds in his head, but tough enough and not in bad shape and, most importantly, not freaking out.

Sunset Park is nothing like he remembers it, not that he remembers it well, a neighborhood of dusty storefronts, brick row houses, tire shops, low-slung apartment blocks and public housing. Back in the day, half the block would have been abandoned—not a place you wanted to live. Today the single-family houses have been cleaned up and rebuilt, and the street that greets him is a lot more solid and moneyed than the neighborhood he recalls. The family next door is Asian, as are many of the families on the block. He expected Brooklyn to be black or Hispanic; instead it's Asian, his corner anyway. Where have the Irish gone? The Danes? Where you'd expect to buy a slice of pizza, there's a Vietnamese sandwich joint.

He eats tacos for lunch. Best tacos ever to pass his lips. Takes the subway to Carroll Gardens, walks around the neighborhood he used to know so well. It's all mothers and children and strollers now, and the strollers look like Mars explorers. A bank where the Italian butcher used to be. Drug store, coffee shop, another bank. The row of ATM machines reminds him of fish tanks side by side. Why are there so many banks? He can't make out the name of the clothing store on the corner. The streets are loud, cars and people, the wheeze of a bus. More bicycles than he remembers. A woman in yoga or running clothes gets into a silver Lexus. The sidewalks are more crowded, the brownstones refurbished, other buildings taller, with more glass. There's a brightly lit chain drugstore in the middle of the block. Everything has changed.

Not everything. Not the library. Solid red brick, square and heavy, it looks a bit smaller, surrounded by taller apartment blocks now, but it's the same as he remembers. Through the entrance, past a group of young mothers and nannies with babies on gray carpet. It's story time.

At the information desk, a teenage boy in a baseball cap with a fading picture of a truck asks if he can help.

"Please. Yes. I'm trying to find somebody. Can you help me, you know, Google it."

"Sure thing." The boy guides him to a computer, clicks through a log-on screen, which asks so many questions Jimmy gets jittery, but then the boy says, "Okay, and so who was it you were searching for?" and the screen buzzes.

He types in the name. Her name. The screen fills with words and links. He clicks one at random. Scans the syndicated obituary, the same one he has read so many times.

"Can you search for pictures?"

"Yup, click on images." The boy points, and Jimmy moves the mouse.

"Aha. Thank you."

It seems to take about an hour for him to guide the blinking arrow to the menu bar and click on the images he wants to see. There's her face, older than he remembers. A grid of pictures, a lot of them are the same photo. Some of them are clearly not her.

There's one picture must be Italy. An older Milena in what looks like a town square—small European cars behind her, a fountain. She's holding her hands aloft, as if she's saying, "I don't know," or perhaps she's just released balloons into the air. He looks at the photo for a while, and when he turns around the boy is gone. He clicks on some other photos, then gets up and finds the boy again, asks if it's possible to print a few pages.

"We've only got black-and-white. You need a card. Here, I'll show you."

He leaves with printouts of photos, an obituary he hasn't read from ItaloAmericano.org, and one from the *Daily News*.

Giaccardi's is still the same. *Brutti ma buoni* cookies. The ones she used to love. Ugly but good. He buys one, eats it outside reading the printout. Milena was "well-known among the international travel and tourism community." And: "A volunteer at a children's hospital in Palermo, she was also an activist and philanthropist for Doctors Without Borders and charities for asylum seekers and refugees in Sicily." He didn't know all that. Bobby had said she worked in a restaurant somewhere. He hoped it meant she owned a restaurant, but it probably didn't. A page of photos, black-and-white, grainy and low-resolution and beautiful.

Back in his cool, quiet apartment, he puts Milena's obituary and photos he's carried with him as well as the two grainy ones he printed at the library in the top drawer of the dresser. He goes outside, sits in the plastic chair. After a while he takes off his shoes and socks and walks across the yard to the patch of grass at the back of the garden. It's been twenty-five years since he felt grass and soil under his feet, and he stands there, momentarily rooted to the spot. It's not that the grass feels so special or even surprising underfoot, but it's one of the nameless things he has missed all those years, and it makes his heart feel big and open and empty.

He drinks a beer at dusk, sitting outside, looking out at the hot, still garden. No sign of Molly or her brother. He walks to Luigi's on Forty-Sixth Street for pizza.

He goes to sleep early. Compared to prison, Brooklyn is so quiet at night. The sky dims slowly; the air conditioner hums happily. No one is shouting, no crazy fuck telling the world he is innocent or who he loves. No one else is there. No cellmate, no cell.

On Sunday he makes a list of things he needs to do, things he needs to buy. Stereo, toaster, CDs.

On Monday a reporter comes by the house. He arrives unannounced, rings the buzzer upstairs. Tom phones Jimmy to tell him. "Should I tell him to go?" "No, send him down."

The reporter is young, with a patchy beard and wire-rim glasses, but his business card says *New York Daily News*. Props his iPhone on the table to record their conversation. How many years? What's the first thing he did when he got out? How does it feel? Great, Jimmy says. And he thanks his family and friends who stood by him.

"Did you think maybe this day would never come?"

"Monday? Sure. Mondays come every week."

"I mean getting out. Did you worry you might never be free?"

"Nah. I knew I'd get out. The justice system is stupid but not blind. Still, I'm happy to be here, if that's what you mean."

"What are you going to do now?"

"See family and friends. Walk around New York City, the greatest city in the world. Go to work."

"Do you think you'll have trouble finding a job?"

"Actually I already have a job."

"Well, that's good. So, any regrets?"

"Does a church have Bibles? But regrets are like assholes: everyone's got one and they don't get you anywhere."

"That sounds pretty wise. I guess you learn a lot in prison."

"You sure do. You should try it sometime."

"Any remorse?"

"Sure."

"For who exactly?"

"For who? Myself mostly. And some people I love. Loved."

"What about your victim?"

"My victim? I never killed nobody."

What the fuck did this guy think? That he would deny something for nearly thirty years, then confess to some faggot with an iPhone. In the old days, he'd have knocked the guy's teeth out for asking a question like that, pressed a knee into his pencil neck, and told him what he was going to write in his stupid newspaper. Instead he said thank you and good-bye and sorry no photos and decided then and there: no more reporters. Fuck them. They could write their story without him. I'm not going to be the latest Mafia story for two days, get my picture in the newspaper. I'm no Phil Leonetti or Shellackhead Cantarella. I don't sell my family to the Feds and I'm not going to write some crappy book and spill the beans. *Omertà,* motherfuckers.

The next day he takes the bus to Joralemon Street in downtown Brooklyn for his appointment at the Supervision Unit. He waits among ex-cons, parolees, parents, guardians, girlfriends, and wives and then meets with his realignment officer, a young black woman with very short hair. She fills in a form—address, cell phone number (none), Tom's contact details, Jimmy's employer information. She tells him to get a phone and register the number with the Supervision Unit and come back in a month. She writes the appointment time on a slip of paper.

"You gotta be an upright citizen, Mr. Piccini."

"Upright citizen and stand-up guy."

"This is no joke. You get arrested for jaywalking or loitering, you can get locked up again for a long time. Keep your shit tight, Mr. Piccini."

On Wednesday he wakes up early, makes coffee, does his press-ups and sit-ups, showers, then waits on the street for Lenny Perkins, son of Louis Perkins, a guy he knew in the can. Louis was a

Brooklyn native, smart, tough, with a calm manner and thought-fulness which, combined with the fact that he'd already been in the joint five years when Jimmy arrived, had made him a good guy to know. You kept your distance until you knew a thing or two. Louis was black, and that fact angered some of the Italians, not the fact that he was black but the fact that Jimmy made friends with him. But Jimmy didn't give two shits. He had his loyalties; he wasn't going to go with the other side in a race fight. But Jimmy was something of a celebrity and everyone knew Louis had killed a man, so nobody fucked with either of them.

He waits on the sidewalk. Dry patches of grass, jagged cement, a candy wrapper and beer can in the gutter. Already hot and not yet ten o'clock.

Lenny drives a pickup. A tall man, quiet and considered, like his father, he works for a big building in Midtown, maintenance and crew. Jimmy knows what that means: no crooked stuff, no crime, not with Louis's kid. Lenny drives Jimmy to a Radio Shack where he buys a phone. In the vast new Atlantic Terminal Mall that used to be a wasteland, he buys shoes, socks, and a couple of shirts. Next stop Kmart where he buys a travel bag, needle and thread, socks, T-shirts, and a plastic "ocean set" complete with bucket, spade, fork, cups, seashell-shaped molds for the little girl to use in the garden. Then they go to Best Buy for a boom box and some CDs—Springsteen, the Stones, a Motown compilation. They don't have a very good selection, so he makes a list and pays Lenny in advance to buy them online. He had a boom box in the can, but he gave it away when he left, to a young guy in the cell opposite him. Robbed a bank in Albany, but the unlucky fool got football tackled by a teller. The best-laid plans.

Lenny says he'll get him sorted out on iTunes and get him set up with an Amazon account.

"Okay, good. But in the meantime, you just order me those CDs, please."

"Of course."

"And let me know when you go to see your pops. I wanna send him one of those prison credit cards."

"I'm going next month. Thank you."

The first call he makes on his new phone is to Galluci, but he doesn't have much to add to what Pino said. A high-roller friend of his went to AC. Someone there said a former mobster was in town. Little Mikey Rossi, spotted at Harry's Oyster Bar.

"They say who he was with?"

"This is all hearsay, but he said an old lady and some guy. Maybe his mother, if she's still alive? My guy didn't say nothing, just brought it to me, and I brought it to Pino."

"Thanks, Mash." Galluci's name is Potito, but everyone calls him Mash.

"Of course. Jimmy, I'll keep tabs on my guy, keep the feelers out, you don't have to worry about that."

In the Garden with Jimmy

Molly

She's trying to figure out how ants crawl up and over twigs. And why.

"Hello, Molly."

"Hi, Mister Jimmy. Can I play here?"

"In the garden? Of course. It's your house."

"Mom says we shouldn't. And Cargo jumped on me the other day when I was out here and it hurt and made me cry."

"Your brother."

"Yes, my brother."

"I'm sorry."

"I wish I could be bigger than him. Because then I'd show him what it's like."

Mister Jimmy leans forward in his plastic chair. "Does he do that very often?"

"Sometimes."

"That's not nice for a big brother. If I had a little sister I'd take care of her. Or teach her to take care of herself."

"Like how?"

"Well, if you can't be bigger and stronger, then you have to be cunning."

"What does cunning mean?"

"Sneaky, tricky. But not in a bad way. Cleverer than other people."

"Like how?"

Mister Jimmy bobbles his head back and forth, like there's an idea in there, but it's taking some time for it to come out.

He leans in closer and talks in a quiet voice. "Okay. Tell him if he does it again, you'll cut off his balls while he's sleeping. Whisper it in his ear. Hold your mother's garden shears in your hand when you say it."

She giggles, then frowns and nods. "Thanks, Mister Jimmy."

"Hey, I got something for you."

He goes inside, returns with the bright red bucket full of plastic sea animals—fish, shells, even a lobster.

"Thanks, Mister Jimmy."

Nicky Bariti

Jimmy

He's back inside with the air conditioner on, reading the newspaper when Tom knocks on his door. Is he going to be home for a little while? A water main has broken in Tom's building. He's got to get over there. Could Jimmy possibly watch Molly for a few minutes, half an hour tops. No problem. Tom thanks him effusively.

Jimmy leaves the door open. He can see over his newspaper Molly playing in the garden, building something near the back wall, using an old milk crate, bits of plastic, and blue sheeting like a shower curtain. She's got herself inside her little construction, skinny legs and orange Crocs sticking out.

A little while later, there's a knock on the open door.

"Hi, Molly. Everything okay?"

"Can we get ice cream?"

"Your dad will be back soon."

"The van will be gone by then. Can we go now? Please."

"Sure, why not."

He locks his door, leaves a note on the kitchen counter upstairs, and they lock the door behind them. Molly runs ahead.

"Don't cross the road. Wait for me at the corner."

The ice cream van isn't there, so they go to Eighth Avenue, to the pastry shop. Molly orders a cone, strawberry ice cream and sprinkles. Jimmy orders a cup for himself. They sit at a small table inside under the fan. Outside everyone is moving a bit slowly, drifting in the heat. On the corner, a baby is crying in a stroller, and two boys are shadowboxing.

"Do I know you?"

Jimmy's never seen the man standing beside him. Molly looks, then returns to her ice cream.

"I don't think so, pal." He's close, the man, too close, leaning over their table.

"Hang on, I think I do. Jimmy, right? Jimmy Piccini?"

The question makes him sit up. He glares at the stranger, then glances at Molly, who remains absorbed in her ice cream, licking slow circles around the cone.

"You don't remember me, do you? Nicky Bariti."

He extends a hand. Jimmy shakes it. He remembers a Lorenzo Bariti. Ran stolen credit cards. Vinnie and Tony Rizzo threw him a job now and then. That was all a long time ago. Whatever this douche wants now, Jimmy ain't buying.

"Matter of fact, I don't. You wanna find me, Pino knows where I am."

Dropping Pino's name is a hint like a Mac truck. Or should be. But Nicky Bariti isn't picking up what Jimmy's laying down. "I heard you were back in town. Didn't know you'd gone into the babysitting business."

Jimmy stands up. "You were just leaving."

"Was I?" The guy doesn't move. He's not very big and he doesn't look very tough.

Jimmy presses a finger against his chest, Bariti slaps it away. Jimmy shoves. He's got the guy on the move now, and Molly is watching as they make their way to the back of the café and Jimmy pushes him into the men's bathroom.

"You got no manners," Jimmy says, when they're inside the bathroom.

"You act pretty tough for a babysitter."

Jimmy blocks the exit, standing close to the door, so he is also stopping anyone from entering.

Bariti jabs his palm into Jimmy's chest as if he's going to shove him out of the way.

That's when Jimmy clocks him. Punches him in the face, just to get his attention. When Bariti straightens and raises his hands, Jimmy throws a kidney punch. The guy gets a punch off but it bounces off Jimmy's cheek without inflicting much damage, and Jimmy has all the time in the world to pull back and chop him in the throat, then plant a left hook square on the mouth. Hurts his hand but he's connected. Bariti is gagging now, blood trickling down his chin, and Jimmy knees him in the thigh to keep him from moving too fast, then turns him around and shoves his head into the bathroom tiles above the urinal.

"You heard wrong, pal. I'm not a babysitter. These days I'm teaching manners and doing a bit of dentistry on the side."

He rubs his cheek, runs a hand across his hair, and exits the bathroom.

Molly is still in her chair, almost finished with her ice cream cone.

The First Cut is the Deepest

Jimmy

They threw Mama a birthday party at San Giovanni in Carroll Gardens. Everyone was there, and they laughed and toasted her. Steaming platters of lasagna, veal saltimbocca, and sausages, and Dr. J on the TV above the bar, making gravity-defying slam dunks and his signature layups. At the end of the evening she thanked everybody, spilling tears in her prosecco, and she told Jimmy it was one of the best nights of her life. They said the party was a gift from Paulie and Jimmy both, but it was Jimmy who footed the bill. This was 1980. The year of *Caddyshack* and CNN, Mayor Ed Koch's ambitious housing program in New York, and the botched rescue of American hostages in Iran. Meanwhile in Philadelphia, Angelo Bruno, the "Gentle Don," was blasted in the back of the head in a hit ordered by his own *consigliere*, Tony Bananas. It was also the year Bruce Springsteen released "The River," and Jimmy listened to that cassette every day as he drove the streets of Brooklyn, making collections and running errands, and occasionally hijacking trucks on I-95 and the Brooklyn-Queens Expressway. It was, in his opinion, the Boss's best album.

Jimmy was twenty-two years old, working under Ruggiero captain Alberto "the Colt" Braglia, who told people his nickname referred to his love of horses, but in fact he earned the nickname from his love of the knife or "*coltello*," his weapon of choice. Jimmy had recently moved into an apartment in Douglas Gardens, was banging a waitress called Samantha, and making enough to slip his mother a wad of hundred-dollar bills when he saw his parents, which wasn't very often.

Jimmy was a *soldato*, a soldier, making a name for himself. A made man said do something, he did it. He didn't do stupid shit like most of the other young guys, the boneheads and bullies. He didn't look for trouble, didn't get in fights, didn't yak. He never brandished his weapon or advertised his connection to the family. He never complained, never skimmed. Jimmy listened, learned, worked hard, kept his head down.

The Colt liked Jimmy. And the Colt didn't like many people. He didn't like Jimmy Carter ("fuckin peanut farmer") or Ed Koch ("fuckin Jew Communist"). For his part Jimmy listened to the Colt's tirades and from him learned the structure of the Ruggiero family businesses, who was on his way up, who was on his way down, how to show respect, how to intimidate people, when to keep your mouth shut, and how to approach a boss with a business idea. It was Jimmy's idea that the Colt run more expenses through his legitimate business, like a share in a pizzeria in Little Italy, in which another captain, Salvatore "Sneakers" Battaglia, already owned a share and which had produced a good, legitimate source of income for him. As a result, the Colt would be able to pay for home improvements and write it off. His wife got a new kitchen and furniture and Jimmy a fat envelope.

Fall. The Philadelphia Phillies were playing Kansas City in the World Series. In Brooklyn, the Irish mob started moving in on the Ruggieros' turf, first gambling, then loan-sharking, then protection. They told business owners not to pay the Ruggieros, told businesses to use Irish not Italian builders and contractors. Joseph Armone, the head of the family, said they'd push them out quietly. No bloodshed, no headlines, just squeeze the Irish wannabes out of their neighborhood. It seemed like the right plan up until a Ruggiero captain got clipped in a bar. Maybe he stuck his nose in it, maybe not. But at the end of the night there was a dead captain, one of theirs, on a barroom floor. Taken to the police morgue, like a drunk, like a common vagrant. This couldn't stand. Armone was furious. He'd tried to settle it quietly, was willing to make some concessions if necessary. Now, he said, we need to act, and we need to act swiftly. There were rules, and a sacred rule had been violated, so it was decided the guy who did the deed must go. They debated whether to take out the head of the Irish warriors as well, but in the end, they decided to let him live. Kill the killer: this was justice; this was retribution. This was Armone's way of thinking: it might be a better guarantee of peace if they did not clip the boss. *An eye for an eye—but let the biggest eye see what we done.*

The Colt was close to the captain left dead in the bar; they'd come up together. And Jimmy was just earning his stripes, so they were the team. Uncle Frankie told him, "You got no choice, kid. You do it or you're out." Jimmy even went to see Savino DeSapio, a captain and the family's numbers guy who worked closely with their *consigliere* and whom Jimmy admired, because he favored smarts over muscle. His question wasn't whether he should do it, but how to get the most out of it. Savino nodded. "You wanna sit on my side of the field?" Jimmy said yes. "Okay, so it's done. You gotta make the hit to get a promotion. Then you come and work for me, off the streets, away from the heat."

They staked the place out, Jimmy, Big Bobby Maritato, and the Colt, bought people drinks, talked to the bartenders, regulars. One of the bartenders fingered the guy who'd pulled the trigger, a big, balding man with a mouth full of rotten teeth and a thick gold chain around his neck.

Jimmy tried not to touch the gun in his shoulder holster, drank a couple of vodkas to calm his nerves. Blood would be spilled; anything could happen. Bobby left around eleven. Their mark was still drinking; they'd paid some Mick to get him drunk, and the guy was doing his job well.

In the end, the Colt didn't use his knife. They followed him out, waited for the drinking buddy to peel off, followed him down a back alley. "Now," the Colt said, and the guy turned. They raised their weapons and fired, one shot each. *Boom boom*, head and chest. Blood sprayed the bricks and paving stones. The dying man extended his arms toward Jimmy, looked right at him and reached out as if he were going to hug him. Jimmy watched the man tilt and crumple. He sagged, then fell forward like a log, a corpse. Jimmy felt nothing when he pulled the trigger. This was a war. A soldier had killed one of their own. He was fucked the minute the Ruggiero captain drew his last breath, and now he was dead. They left him there, bleeding black blood in the alley.

They were two blocks away when they heard the sirens.

It was only later that he thought about what he'd done. It wasn't remorse. Cocksucker had it coming. Only a vague nagging feeling, something like doubt. What if they'd clipped the wrong guy? What if there was a witness? How was it that he'd just become a murderer? *Mama, just killed a man. Put a gun against his head. Pulled my trigger, now he's dead.* They were in Casa Altobelli, drinking, but Jimmy didn't feel drunk, only that same doubtful feeling, a kind of guilty shame. The man had a name, Andrew Murphy.

The guys patted Jimmy on the back and said, "way to go" and "whacked that Paddy fuck." Even the Colt told him he'd done good for his first burn. But it didn't feel like he'd done anything good or even necessary. He looked around the room and decided there were three types of guys in the life: the violent guys who loved danger, who thought nothing could touch them and went looking for trouble (Colt, Vinnie, the Rizzos); the cautious few who liked the life and the money but not the danger and violence, not shooting guys in bars or dark alleys (like Savino, Bobby, Jimmy himself); and the old timers, who had done it all and seen it all and now just wanted to sit on a beach or cook or count their money and fuck their *goomahs* (Armone, Santoro, his *consigliere*, a lot of the heads of families and their *consiglieri*).

Just before sunrise they were smoking and laughing in the parking lot of Freccia, a social club in Bensonhurst, Colt drunk and happy. "Go home, Jimmy, you done good." The sun was coming up when one of the young guys drove him home. He'd left the Colt upstairs, playing cards and talking sports with the night owls. Jimmy leaned back in the town car and watched the Gowanus Expressway; cars and trucks and signs and dark warehouses floated past. It had been so easy, to pull the trigger, to turn the guy from alive to dead. Also so permanent. Jimmy couldn't stop thinking about it. Did Andrew Murphy have kids? A wife who called him Andy? A birthday coming up? Parents? For Colt it was all a distant memory, a job he'd done, nothing more, and, other than where to take his next piss, he didn't have a care in the world. Was that what happened to the part of you that saw yourself commit murder—it turned into a Tuesday hangover, it hardened into hardness?

A few days later Big Bobby drove Jimmy to meet Armone. Bobby was a made man, one of the younger ones. "I don't know nothing, but I think you've done it. The Colt likes you, and he don't like nobody. And now you've proved yourself." Armone's house was huge and dark, mahogany paneled, expensive-looking paintings on the living room wall. The boss congratulated Jimmy. "You done good, kid. And Al speaks highly of you. But keep your nose clean, don't get too smart, okay? Don't fuck it up." A week later, he started working for DeSapio in addition to making the rounds with the Colt. No more errand boy.

DeSapio showed him the ropes. They sat in the office he rented above a grocery store on Bedford Street and went through the Ruggiero finances. Different businesses, cash, banks, goods in warehouses. A week after that he sent Jimmy to visit banks from Queens to Long Island. They drew up new plans to stash money, launder money, figured out new places to hide merchandise. DeSapio was setting up complex investment schemes, looking into gold and diamonds, things you could move easily, and he had a crooked banker in Amsterdam ready to set up a bank account for the Netherlands branch of an American olive oil company.

"You gotta worry about the Feds," he explained to his new protégé. "They got a lot of people digging around. Money is stronger than blood. They'll follow it anywhere, so we have to be smarter than they are."

In November Frank "Funzi" Tieri was convicted under the RICO Act. A few days later DeSapio dropped a binder on Jimmy's desk. *Section 901(a) of the Organized Crime Control Act of 1970* and *U.S. Code Chapter 96, Racketeer Influenced and Corrupt Organizations Act.*

"Read it."

"And then, other than fall asleep?"

"And then figure out how we stop doing anything that looks like extortion, money laundering, loan-sharking, obstruction of justice, bribery. All of that shit needs to be tied to smaller fish, not any captains, not the boss."

Jimmy studied the binder. At first his eyes glazed over and he didn't understand the convoluted legal language, but he looked up laws and words he didn't know and eventually got through it. A pattern of racketeering required only two acts, and the criminal activities had to be related and continuous. Victims could seek triple damages and the Feds could seize assets. Jimmy spoke to DeSapio and the Ruggiero lawyer and then made his suggestions to Santoro. Distance themselves from racketeering activities, use code names for anything illegal, put houses in other people's names. Wherever possible orders would come from people on the outside, reliable sources but not captains themselves, and they'd use code to communicate about any illegal activity. That way there would be no trail and no evidence of a continuing criminal enterprise.

Molly and the Mobster

Catherine

When Cath gets back the house is empty. She calls Tom's name, looks in the garden. Where are they? Tom? Molly? Cargo has a play date but where the hell is everyone else? She is on her way to the deck so she can take a look at the garden when she sees the note on the kitchen counter.

> *Gone to get ice cream.*
> *Back soon.*
> *—Jimmy.*

His handwriting is small and neat and looks somehow old-fashioned. She phones Tom.

"You see, she's fine. She's with Jimmy."

"I don't want her with that man."

"I know. But she'll be fine. I had an emergency."

She tries Jimmy's cell phone. No answer. Ice cream could mean any one of a number of places. They usually go to the corner store. But the Italian café and the pastry shop on Claussen Avenue both sell ice cream in the summer, and there's the ice cream van. She hasn't seen it and she doesn't hear the jingle. But, of course, if Jimmy and Molly heard it they may have followed it. She thinks about whether Jimmy would kidnap her daughter. She knows it's an irrational, crazy thought but she can't help it. She imagines him driving Molly away in an old convertible with red seats. She stands up, shakes her head to expel the dark thoughts.

Carrying her keys and phone, she rushes to the corner deli. They're not there. "Did you see a little girl and an older man? Okay, thanks. Just tell them to go home if you do." She walks back to the house. Molly's a clever girl. Tom is right. There's no harm in taking a girl for an ice cream. Or is there? If the previous tenant took Molly or Cargo, they'd be furious. Later they'll explain to Jimmy that if he is alone with her for whatever reason, please do not leave the house. Later she will berate Tom for leaving her alone with him. He's a killer, she can hear herself saying. She tells herself to calm down. Tom was wrong to leave Molly in his care but she'll be fine. If they're not back in half an hour she's going to the police.

She drinks a glass of water. She's about to go out again to try Claussen Avenue or look for the ice cream van when she hears the front door, but it's Tom.

"They're still not home."

"I see that."

"When did you leave?"

"I guess about an hour ago."

"Did you try his phone?"

"Of course I tried his phone. But he doesn't use it much. Cath, they're getting ice cream, it's no big deal."

"How could you leave her with him?"

"I didn't think he'd leave the house. It was an emergency. She's six years old. She'll be fine."

"Listen to yourself. Six years old. Not sixteen, Tom. How do you know he hasn't been planning this?"

"Planning what?"

"Take her, get the family to pay the ransom. You said he's hard up for cash."

"He . . . Cath. Oh, never mind." He turns his back on her, walks out of the kitchen.

"What are you doing? Where are you going?"

He stops, turns. "You stay there, I'll go and look."

"Try the café first, and DiSuvero's."

"Okay."

"Café first. Don't go to the park. She'd know not to go all the way to the park."

"I said okay."

"Jesus, Tom. We've got a mobster downstairs and now he's taken our daughter God knows where."

"Welcome to Brooklyn."

"Don't give me that. The kids, Tom."

"Okay, can we talk about it later? I'll go and look for them. You phone DiSuvero's. Call me if they get back before I do."

"If she's not back in half an hour, we're calling Pino Locatelli."

"No."

"What do you mean, no?"

"Cath, we're not getting the boss of the family involved. Not for this. If they're not back in one hour, we call the cops. But they will be. Don't worry."

Don't Tell

Molly

They go to the ice cream place she likes, the one with colored sprinkles. Mr. Jimmy says she can have whatever she wants and she wants strawberry in a sugar cone, with sprinkles. And for himself he orders a scoop of coffee ice cream (yuck) in a cup. They sit at a table near the front. She licks around the top of the cone so that it won't melt down onto her hand, then a man comes in and says some things to Jimmy and they start shouting, him and Mister Jimmy, and Jimmy stands up. He pushes the man and the man pushes him and they go to the toilet. Jimmy's ice cream is there on the table, and she doesn't eat it or lick it or dip a finger in it, even though she wants to.

When he comes back he says sorry I took so long and is the ice cream okay? And she says yes. She can't remember if his eye looked like that before. Puffy. Ouchy. She says her ice cream is yummy. Jimmy tells her not to tell about the man, and on the way out he gives her five dollars. Our secret. She says, I promise. Because he looks sad, and because Daddy said be extra special nice to Jimmy on account of his mother died and that's probably why he's sad.

When they get home, she can tell her Mama is angry. Maybe because they're late. Jimmy says sorry. Mama smiles her lemon smile. Molly says, thank you, Mister Jimmy.

Mister Jimmy says we got lost. She doesn't remember but maybe they did. She was just walking beside him.

"Don't know my way around. Not Molly's fault. She's a great kid. Terrific. Won't happen again. I really feel like a bum, a real *boombots.*"

She doesn't know that word. Maybe it's Italian. He talks more and her mother stops pretending to smile.

"I'd never let anything happen to her."

Not Everybody Wants to Rule the World

Milena

She didn't need her sister to tell her she'd been played. Sabrina told her anyway. Milena phoned but Chris was never there. His roommate said he was in Spain. Did he have a number for him? "Um, no."

She'd fallen in love with the bum; she'd thought they had a future together, him in politics, two kids, and a nice house. She thought he loved her, and she believed him when he said he'd never met anyone like her because the truth was she'd never met anyone like him.

But Chris wasn't coming back. Forget his face, forget his name, Sabrina told her. Her sister took her for the abortion, paid for it, and brought her home afterward. They told her mother she had the flu, and Milena stayed in bed for a day.

She'd committed a crime against human life. It was a mortal sin, and she was a mortal sinner. She prayed, she cried, but she didn't confess, not that Sunday and not the next. She couldn't bring herself to tell a priest. She kept thinking of a word and that word was: murder. She didn't want to go to hell.

Milena was wretched for a while, then only sad, then confused, then shook her head when she thought about him. Dickhead. Liar. Were all men like this? Her father wasn't, but her dad was dead. She wanted to rip out the part of her heart that Benelli still occupied, or rip out some part of him, yank some organ through broken ribs. *Forget his face, forget his name.* She applied herself at school, and she did well. Maybe she would get to college anyway, become a nurse, do something with her life. She didn't need Chris Benelli or anyone else.

In the winter of her senior year, cousin Gino, who worked for Federal Express, took Melina for a drink, and a friend of his showed up, a darkly handsome happy-go-lucky guy in an expensive leather jacket. He looked very much at ease, comfortable, and in control. When he surveyed the restaurant, his eyes said he didn't give a shit about anyone in the room. His name was Vincent DeNunzio, and Gino looked at him the way you look at a rock star.

Vincent smelled of aftershave and leather, had broad shoulders and muscular arms, a strong Italian nose and strong Italian jaw, and dark brooding eyes that narrowed when he frowned in anger or concentration. When he smoked a cigarette, he left it dangling from his lower lip, like he'd forgotten about it or couldn't be bothered to draw, exhale, and ash like everybody else. He took her to expensive restaurants and nightclubs in Manhattan, a social club in Sheepshead Bay. He bought her flowers, let her drive his Cadillac, stopped by the house with a trunk full of Christmas presents for Milena, her mother, and sister. Her mother thought he was handsome, and when he had a new gas range delivered to the apartment, she and Aunt Elisabetta were sold. Here was a good man, an Italian, who knew the meaning of family, a man with a future. What would her father have said? She didn't know. Sabrina said don't rush into anything.

"You can do anything, marry anyone."

"Like who?"

"Like anyone."

"He's not going to wait around."

"You don't have to get married tomorrow. You're beautiful and smart, Mili. You're something special, don't you see that? You can marry a doctor or lawyer. You can own the world."

The stripper and the college girl told her she could do better. Come and stay with me, they both said. But Milena knew she couldn't do that. She'd be turning her back on her family, on a potential husband whose wealth and social standing seemed secure. And two things her father prized, more than love, more than money, were family and security.

Milena didn't want to own the world; she wanted to live in it. Like Vincent DeNunzio, a made man in the Ruggiero crime family whose life was exciting and fun, brimming and bubbling with friends and parties, dancing, late-night drives down Fifth Avenue and across the Brooklyn Bridge. Vinnie knew how to live, and Milena wanted more than anything to remove her veil of caution.

The poker game heist was all her idea. One warm April evening Vinnie and his friend Enzo took Milena and some of her girl-friends along with a couple of their pals to a private social club in Brooklyn Heights. A bookie had told Vinnie that some of the high rollers would be there. Their plan, Milena's plan, was to dance in and dance out. They would dress the part, flirt, laugh, make their way in quietly and then dash out quickly. Milena knew pretty girls. She also knew a contractor's son, Rino, who could screw L-shaped brackets across a door and doorjamb in less than two minutes. When the haphazard crew had met to run through the operation, Milena knew not to talk much. It was Vinnie's job. But she also knew they had a good plan and couldn't help the flush of excite-ment she felt.

The club was an unmarked brownstone. Drinks and cigars on the ground floor, game rooms and bedrooms on the floors above. Married men gambled there, stayed there, fucked their mistresses there. On the night in question, Milena and her friends rang the doorbell, and only after it was opened, and they had flirted their way inside the wood-paneled, smoke-purpled room, did Vinnie and the men appear. They were dressed in suits and didn't look terribly out of place. Very quietly, doing what he did best, Vinnie persuaded the gray-suited concierge to tell them where Timon and Skelly were playing poker. They headed upstairs, the concierge shaking his head as he scampered away. When they barged into the card room, someone immediately stood up. "You can't come in here." Vinnie pretended to corral the women out of the room. "That's what I told them," Vinnie said. "Come on, girls, wrong room. Sorry, guys." The girls lingered. "There's Mr. Skelly," Milena said, giggling. Of course they stayed, and of course the old farts poured them drinks and let themselves be flirted with, their clothes admired, their suit jackets touched. They sat down to play a hand; Milena asked for a drink.

The women played cards; Vinnie freshened drinks. The other two, Enzo and Rino, the contractor's son, hung back. Before long one of Mili's friends was sitting on the lap of one of the patrician gamblers.

When one of the girls shouted, "Hey, stop that," everyone stopped what they were doing and jumped up, to calm her and separate her from a surprised gray-haired captain of industry. Everyone except Milena and Vinnie who, slowly, pulled piles of cash from the table. Vinnie didn't say anything, just pointed his gun at the wall and made sure everyone saw it. A hush descended over the room and scattered notes drifted to the carpet like falling leaves. Milena noticed the green felt table, the condensation on the glasses, as she stuffed banknotes into two oversized handbags. While they made their exit, Enzo held the door closed while Rino screwed the brackets tight and squeezed Super Glue on the heads of the screws. The flustered gamblers banged and pulled on the door, but the brackets held.

They got away with more than $1,500. They drove to a bar, drank champagne and martinis, got high in the bathroom. After the others peeled off, Vinnie and Milena went to Red Hook and ate arancini and pasta at Ferdinando's, and watched the cars on the Brooklyn-Queens Expressway. It was nearly dawn when they got back to his apartment, and when she took him in her mouth, he purred and stroked her hair. They slept until noon, and she cooked scrambled eggs with onion and tomatoes and garlic like her father used to make. They peeked at their bag full of money. She ran her hands through his hair and kissed him. It hadn't made her feel guilty; it had made her feel strong.

In private Vinnie told Milena they couldn't have done it without her, but in front of the guys he just shrugged and smiled knowingly. Which was fine with her. They were partners, and it didn't matter whose idea it was, or who got the credit, as long as they were successful. Besides, she'd never wanted to steal anyone's limelight. She just wanted to have more fun, plan another heist. Did she feel liberated now that she had done something criminal? Did she have feelings for Vincent not because of who he was or how he made her feel but because they'd done the heist together, because they snorted coke and got stoned, did elicit fun things? Was she confusing love with freedom? Maybe.

The first time they had sex, about a week later, he was drunk, and it was short and brutal and left her sore and shocked, weeping in the bathroom. But the next time he was tender, and it made her feel good, better than Benelli had ever made her feel, that boy, that child. When Vinnie talked about his dead mother, he cried, and she saw vulnerability, a heart in need of love.

They exchanged vows in Saint Cecilia's in Greenpoint. "Will you accept children lovingly from God, and bring them up according to the law of Christ and his Church?" "I will." A traditional Italian wedding followed by a big party. Joseph Armone was there, the Rizzo brothers, along with other captains and made men from the Ruggiero family. She was nineteen years old. The most beautiful bride in the history of the world, Vinnie said. *You're just too good to be true. Can't take my eyes off of you.*

He took her to Las Vegas on their honeymoon. It was the first time she'd flown on a plane. Above the clouds, he told her his plans. He had it on good authority that Korean dry cleaners took their money home in their own cars, usually on a Thursday or

Friday night. Watch for a couple of weeks, figure out the schedule, *bada boom*. He could hit a few of them in a week or two.

"Don't tell Rizzo, more for us."

"No, hon, you can't do that without telling Rizzo."

"Oh, you know all about my business now?"

"I'm just saying, it's good to make friends. You know, show respect. Tell him, ask his advice, split it with him. You gonna be a captain yourself one day."

"And if he says no?"

"Then don't do it. We'll think of something else."

Made Man

Jimmy

$\mathbf{B}$raglia and Savino sponsored him. Jimmy'd made his bones with the Irish cocksucker, although the Colt explained maybe that wouldn't be sufficient, since it was not a solo cleaning job. Different jobs carried different points, different bonuses. The New York Islanders won the Stanley Cup in May. Jimmy started dating a freckled redhead—a waitress with a D-cup and a Chiclet-white smile. In June they went to *Blade Runner* at the Ziegfeld on Fifty-Fourth Street. Jimmy loved it; she thought it was "weird," a word she used a lot. Later that month the Colt told Jimmy about a dirty lawyer who worked for a guy they didn't like, and the Colt said it might happen that they'd ask Jimmy to whack him. It was Savino DeSapio who said Jimmy's work on RICO should make him a captain many times over.

It was Savino who set up the meeting with the Colt, to walk him through the dos and don'ts of racketeering. Mostly don't. "We can't be connected to racketeering in any shape or form," and Jimmy explained how to avoid being a conspiracy in the eyes of the law, what could be shipped, what couldn't be shipped, and the importance of keeping gambling, drugs, murder "two handshakes" away. A week later he told the same story to Armone himself over an espresso at Casa Altobelli, along with a list of rules to follow if they wanted to avoid RICO and Kingpin Statute violations.

The don thanked Jimmy. "You've got a sharp mind," he told him, and called the plan "very forward looking." Privately, DeSapio told Jimmy it was a serious thing he was about to do. *Commitment* was the word he used. "It's a job and a promise and a family, all in one. There's no going back."

"I know," Jimmy said.

The day the Colt came for him, he asked Jimmy if he was ready, then drove him in the back of his car. They stopped on Amboy Street, and the Colt blindfolded him. Jimmy was sweating and his heart was pounding when they led him down clanky stairs to a basement. When they took off the blindfold, the light was bright and the first face he saw was Armone's and he thought, if they were going to kill me they would have done it by now. They asked him if he was devoted, if he'd thought about what it meant to be in the family. He said it was all he ever wanted and he would give his life for the Ruggiero family. He thought about his father, about *Blade Runner*, and answered the questions they asked. Then the Colt smiled and clapped him on the back, and they pricked his finger and he held a picture of a saint while it burned blue and orange, and he repeated the oath and then they hugged him and lined up the shot glasses. He let a long, deep breath escape his lungs and downed a single malt. Jimmy was a made man.

Cadillac Ranch

Milena

Palm trees and sunshine. They drove their rented ruby Caddy convertible down the strip. Vegas was hot and bright, and they had cocaine and every kind of desire. Vinnie drove fast, with the top down, gunned it past shiny casinos, each one taller and more ornate than the last, and the wind drew its hot fingers through Milena's hair. At the Dunes Hotel, he paused to kiss her under the huge sultan statue that presided over the entrance, looked up at the turbaned sentinel, and said, "I love this woman, I do." And she felt very lucky and smoothed his hair and kissed him in the bright Las Vegas light.

They saw Robert Goulet at the Mirage, ate at the Sands where they did not catch a glimpse of Sinatra or anyone else famous. They gambled at the Oasis Casino, did coke in their room, and went out again. By day they swam in the big round swimming pool, and she read her magazines and Vinnie drank and ogled women in bikinis. They drank champagne with lunch. Milena wanted to get tickets for Liberace but the show was sold out, and Vinnie said, "I ain't paying some scalper to see that fag." And that was that. In Vegas, she felt rich; she felt reckless, or maybe it was love. He was handsome and alluring, richer than any man she knew, tough and just gentle enough. A man's man, someone said. He kissed her in the swimming pool and told her he loved her. He promised to bring

her back to Vegas to see Shirley Bassey. He bought her gold ear-
rings and expensive clothes.

Back in New York, she packed up her things and left Bushwick
and moved into an apartment Vinnie found in Carroll Gardens.
A ground-floor apartment with a big living room, huge wood-
veneer Mitsubishi TV, and garden. There were so many rooms.
To fill them, she bought furniture, had carpet laid, wallpapered
the half bathroom. She cooked in the brand-new kitchen, and he
told her she looked beautiful and complimented her cooking and
she decided that she was content and secure and loved, and who
really could ask for more. It was time to put away childish things.

Fortunately there were many adult diversions she enjoyed.
Vinnie took her to expensive restaurants, garden parties, discos,
Broadway musicals. He brought home marijuana and cocaine, and
they did lines in restaurant bathrooms and at parties. She didn't
love it at first, the blow, and then she did. She knew Vinnie occasionally did heroin as well. Once in a while he'd come home with a
young Ruggiero associate he called "Bones," a barrel-chested thug,
and they chased the dragon, then went to the local bar for vodka
and beer.

She liked cooking for Vinnie. They'd smoke a joint and watch
TV. She liked movies; he preferred sports. Sometimes he danced
with her in the living room, and they'd order a pizza and usually
ended up having sex. Sometimes they got dressed up and went
dancing in Manhattan.

They went to clubs with Sabrina and her boyfriend where they
drank champagne and vodka and ate oysters and shrimp cocktails.
After one of those nights, Sabrina asked Milena if she knew what
she was doing, with Vinnie. "Yes, living my life," Milena told her
sister. "He's a good guy. We'll get ourselves on track, and then I
can do whatever I want. He says he'll pay for me to go to nursing school, or college, if that's what I want." What she didn't say
was that she was terrified of ending up like Aunt Elisabetta, and
Vinnie guaranteed her that fate would never befall her. He was

the life of the party, but like a lot of the young Ruggiero bulls, he had a temper. She'd seen him head-butt a bartender, coldcock a stranger, a "jerkoff in a suit," because he looked at Milena too much. He bullied anyone who wasn't his superior in the Ruggiero family, and that included Milena. But most of the time he treated her like a lady. They went dancing at the Underground Club, Celia's, Gazelle, the Jupiter in Chelsea. They danced until dawn and ate gyros on the street outside. He came home with gifts for her—jewelry, flowers, perfume. He was generous, a good dancer, loyal, and attentive. Most of the time.

He moved some cocaine mostly in order to have a free supply. They got it from a guy in Baltimore. Vinnie sent his friend Bones, who made the delivery to a warehouse on the Gowanus Canal. A local dealer Vinnie had been using himself for close to ten years did the rest—cut it, sold it. Vinnie got a free supply and made a tidy profit. But he wanted more. He told Milena of his plan to increase his drug business and add heroin to the offering and sell not to one but to many dealers. She said, be careful.

"Stop telling me to be careful. I'm a made man. I know what I'm doing."

"I know you do, baby."

She knew no such thing.

Police on My Back

Jimmy

He is sitting in the garden, in a plastic chair, halfway through a cold Budweiser, thinking about whether he should walk to Seventh Avenue for a burger or pick up a pizza for dinner when he hears footsteps coming down the cement steps at the side of the house. He can hear by the heavy double footfall that it's not Tom or Catherine or the kids. The first thing he sees is black shoes and then two cops, in uniform, their faces hard and clenched.

"James Piccini."

"Yes."

"Will you come with us to the station?"

"What? Why?"

"We want to ask you a few questions. You assaulted a man at Rocco's Pastry Shop."

"That stupid fuck call the cops?"

"No, he didn't, but the manager filed a report. Mr. Piccini, we know who you are."

"That's good. I know who I am too. Self-knowledge, very important."

"You gonna come with us?"

"I'm coming. Lemme lock the door."

In the back of the cruiser, on the way to the police station, his heart pounds and he feels like kicking himself. *You get arrested for*

jaywalking or loitering, you can get locked up again for a long time.
Could they send him back to prison for punching some mutt in
the face?

The cops are a lot more polite than they were back in the day.
Of course, back in the day, they didn't pull a made man unless he
killed someone in broad daylight with multiple witnesses. Jimmy's
been offered coffee twice by the time he's ushered into an interrogation room with two detectives, both male, one young, one old.
Cup of coffee in hand—decent coffee too—he waives his right to
have a lawyer present. What's going to be is going to be.

The young cop clicks on a digital voice recorder.

"Tell us in your own words what happened," the older one
says.

This is the friendly way. Jimmy can stop talking whenever he
wants. He knows his rights.

"What happened was I took the girl for an ice cream, and I
see this man trying to get her into the bathroom of Rocco's."

Jimmy speaks calmly—he knows how to speak and what not
to say. Even so, his mind keeps coming back to the horrible idea
that he has just lost his freedom, that he's going back to the big
house.

"The man," the younger cop looks down at his folder. "Mr.
Bariti, he was trying to coerce the girl?"

"If that means push into the bathroom, yes."

"Okay. Please proceed."

"I say stop and he doesn't, you know, release the girl, and I
guess we started verbally abusing one another."

"Verbally."

"Yes, and then physically as well. He pushed me."

The two cops lean forward, listening.

"Maybe I overreacted." One thing you learn in the can is that
everyone hates pedophiles. Cops, inmates, wardens, guards, ste-
nographers, everyone. "I don't know, maybe I was wrong." He does
his best to look contrite, or at least concerned.

The older cop nods and Jimmy observes what might be a subtle whatcha-gonna-do gesture.

"But I have this little girl to take care of, she's like a granddaughter to me, and some guy tries to do something with her . . . I, you know, did something. I jumped in. I got to protect her. I mean, a young girl like that."

He says nothing further. They nod. They press stop.

They drive him back to the house in an unmarked car. They speak to Tom, ask him if he was aware of the incident, if his daughter had spoken to him about it.

"Yes. Well, a little." He doesn't look at Jimmy, keeps his eyes on the officers. "Jimmy, he's a stand-up guy, old friend of the family."

"Your daughter say anything about a strange man in the establishment who tried to get her to go with him?"

No one could have seen Jimmy nod, because what he did wasn't a nod. He just lowered his chin a quarter inch and blinked slowly.

"Like I said, I didn't want to press her about the details, but yes, something like that."

"Thank you, Mr. DeSapio."

"Not at all. Thank you."

There's no need to speak to the little girl, they say, under the circumstances. The man in question hasn't pressed charges. Just a misunderstanding. You can see how the manager may have gotten the wrong idea. It's all very cordial. The cops apologize to Jimmy and thank him for his cooperation. He says forget about it, just doing your job.

No Regrets

Tom

"I don't know what happened back there, and I don't want to know. I know you wouldn't have started anything."

"I'd never let anything happen to your little girl. The guy was making cracks about me. So I took him into the bathroom, gave him a slap, came straight back. Two minutes tops. But I'm sorry, shouldn't have left her. I wasn't thinking."

"Let me explain it to Cath."

"Of course."

They're standing outside, sun slanting down. He came outside rather than ask Jimmy in. Better to keep him and Cath apart. He's about to say okay, see you later and head back inside when Jimmy speaks.

"They're great kids. I hope you know your father woulda been proud."

"I'm not so sure."

"I am."

"Can I ask you something, Jimmy?"

"Sure."

"You regret it? I mean seeing how it all ended up for you?"

A softness comes over Jimmy's eyes. "I regret what I've missed out on. People mostly."

"You could have been a very powerful captain. My pops was maybe going to replace Dino as underboss. That would have given you a boost."

"Maybe. Who knows. It's a long time ago. The truth is I got in just in time to watch the thing slide. It's kinda finished now. Bygone era."

"I wanted in, but my father forbade it."

"Smart guy."

"If he was so smart, he woulda talked me out of the solar panel business."

"You've got them buildings," Jimmy says. "That's all right."

"Yeah, and I'm grateful. But it's not as easy as you think."

He explains that one of his properties is stuck with a commercial restriction. Apartments would make a lot more money, but he can't get it zoned residential. Meanwhile residential rents are soaring. "But you don't want to hear about my real estate problems."

Down to the River

Jimmy

He flicks through the *Daily News* every morning and on Tuesday there he is, an old photo. "Brooklyn Mobster Free After Twenty-Five Years." He reads about himself: *wisecracking wiseguy . . . contrite but unrepentant . . . Regrets are like assholes.* No mention of his brush with the police. Still the article makes him sound like a stupid *giamope.* He was stupid to say yes to the interview. Now that he thinks about it, this also means that some people who may not have known he was out, now they know. Like some of the guys he's trying to pay surprise visits, to collect what they owe him. And Mike Rossi.

The next day, Bobby Maritato picks him up in the early afternoon in his slate-gray Cadillac. He shows Bobby the *Daily News* and he reads it and shakes his head.

"Not a bad photo."

"What about the article? I come off like a *scecco*, a total jackass."

"Just a little."

They laugh and he throws the newspaper in the back seat and they roar down the street, away from Brooklyn. They take the Garden State Parkway, chatting, listening to the radio. Bobby's been divorced and remarried. He's got five kids and two grandchildren.

His wife is from Venezuela. "She can cook and she can fuck, and she's a great mom."

They enter Atlantic City from Route 30, passing through the old part of town, Victorian-style buildings, car dealerships, row houses, then a stretch of Queen Anne houses, most of them well restored and newly painted. It's not the Atlantic City he remembers. It's bigger, brighter. There are strip malls on the outskirts of town. Starbucks. Pizza. Subs. It's easy to imagine that the last time he was there the world was in black-and-white. He remembers that day. He's thought about it a thousand times. The last time he was in Atlantic City was the meeting with Little Mikey, *cascittuni* cocksucker. He remembers it well, Mikey sniggering about Jimmy's brother and reminding him that he's a crazy fuck who doesn't make deals with anyone unless he wants to. Well, he made a deal eventually. With the Feds. Jimmy wonders if he saw him again, now, today, would he let him walk by or would he kill him there and then, strangle him with his bare hands or drive a steak knife through his heart? How strong is his forgiveness?

They park at the Tropicana, get some drinks at the bar, play blackjack together for a while. Jimmy is feeling buzzy and happy, the booze making him interested in his surroundings—scantily clad waitresses, an older woman with huge fake tits, the well-groomed dealer, supervisors gliding across the carpets. They stand near the slot machines drinking and chatting, then make their way to the poker tables and play Texas hold 'em at different tables.

Jimmy loses, then wins, then loses. Drinks more vodka and relaxes. He hasn't been able to relax since the police interrogation. He can't let anything like that happen. Gotta keep his shit tight, like the lady said. He finds Bobby and they get a drink at the bar. Bobby's won five hundred bucks.

"How easy was that?"

"As easy as losing five hundred."

"True. *Salut.*"

There's a man in a cowboy hat, a group of Japanese tourists giggling and shrieking. A man in a wheelchair is trying his luck at the one-arm bandit.

His teeth crush succulent bits of crab salad; the juices roll around his tongue. The flickering candles look like little bobbing boats. A martini each. The waitress has big falsies; her name tag says "Loretta." Bobby orders a bottle of wine. Next course: steaks—big, juicy, perfect. It's the kind of meal Jimmy used to dream about. Bobby drinks most of the bottle of wine. He tells Jimmy stories about his kids, his struggles with his legitimate businesses.

"When they got you and Armone, we all got scared. Santoro, he couldn't fill the boss's shoes. We were all jumpy and no one did shit for a while. We all went to work at whatever legit business we owned or didn't own."

They gaze out across two miles of casino lights, skyscrapers lit with light and color stand against the dark sky, the dim gray sea. This is one thing he loves: being able to see for miles. The most any prison window afforded was a hundred yards or so of asphalt, then a brick wall or another building. Some cells had no window at all. In solitary you had a view of your feet.

At the bar, a group of young men is high-fiving and knocking back drinks. "You fucking crushed it," one says.

They're eating desert when Bobby asks about prison.

"It's boring and dangerous and really fucking hard," Jimmy tells him. "It's like you get hollowed out, sitting there, waiting, paying with your time and your mind for what you done."

"You did us proud." Bobby raises his wine glass.

"I endured."

"That's a lot."

"What else you gonna do? A lot of people do it. You know we, America, got more people in prison than any other country. Put them all together and you'd have the fourth biggest city in the country. Bigger than Philly."

"Jesus."

Jimmy nods, takes a sip of wine. "Anyway, I wanted to thank you."

"Me?"

"You came to see me all the time. You were the only one, Bobby."

"Really? All those women in love with you. I'da thought they'd be lining up for conjugal visits."

"You'da thought wrong."

"Not even your brother?"

"Paul. Five visits. Didn't see him the whole time I was in Alabama. I'm going to see him soon. We talked the other day."

"Right. Good." Bobby frowns at his steak. "Listen, I should tell you that I saw him. About a year ago, Paulie came to see me."

"Really? About what?"

"He thinks he saw Mike Rossi."

"What? Why didn't you tell me?"

"I'm telling you now. Pino said not to say anything until you were out. Because of some guy Gallucci knows who says he saw Little Mikey."

"I know. Pino told me about that. So what did Paulie say? Did he talk to Mikey?"

"Nah, he thinks he saw him. Most likely he saw some guy who looks like him. Last time he laid eyes on that bum was a long time ago, remember."

"Where? Atlantic City?"

"No. Some restaurant in Brooklyn."

"Was that around the same time as Gallucci's pal saw Mikey? That would make it more likely that it was actually him."

"Jimmy, I don't know when that guy came to Gallucci, but it was after Paulie came to see me, I know that. Listen, Rossi's deep up the asshole of witness protection. There's a lot of people want that *pentito* fuck dead."

"What restaurant?"

"The joint where Paulie worked. I sent someone there the next few nights. No Mikey. Told Paulie to reach out if he saw him again. Haven't heard from him."

"You're right," Jimmy says. "There's a lot of guys look like that ugly little runt."

"He's stupid, but can't be crazy enough to show his face in an Italian restaurant in Brooklyn. That's like putting a target on his head."

"I wouldn't shed a tear. If someone put him down."

"You and me both. Waiter."

Their waiter appears, and Bobby orders more wine. When it arrives, Jimmy raises his glass.

"You know in the joint you can forget about the world and the world can forget about you. Thanks for not letting that happen. Meant a lot."

"Least I could do." They clink glasses. "You can thank me after you meet the vixen coming by your room later."

They drink and eat tiramisu. When Jimmy fell off his bike, his father scooped him up and held him tight. He'd felt so safe in his father's arms. He never felt that safe again. Why is he thinking about that now? Because it doesn't feel safe outside the can? Because if Little Mikey is running around New Jersey or New York, defying witness protection rules so he can hang out with his old crew or some new casino *goomah*, then he's not going to like the idea of a guy he sent away roaming the same streets, and Mikey may want to get that guy killed, in which case Jimmy is most definitely not safe? Or because Jimmy's contemplating doing some things that are not safe—to Little Mikey for example? Forgiveness be damned, if it's about staying alive, Mikey's going to be the one who gets whacked, not Jimmy. He remembers riding on his father's bus, sitting behind him, watching him drive carefully through traffic. He was always polite, always helpful, their dad. When Jimmy's wandering began, his father implored him to stay in school. He put a hand on Jimmy's head. *You were always the smart one. You can do anything you want.* His papa never expressed regret or recrimination. Still, Jimmy's always felt like he owed him an apology.

The woman who knocks on his door an hour later is Latina, young, with buttery skin and lip-glossed lips. She says her name is Jacinta and takes off her leather jacket, and the first thing he notices is cleavage pressing out of her halter top, straining, like her tits have somewhere else they'd rather be. They have a drink together (vodka for Jimmy, a Coke for Jacinta). They stand at the window, looking at the changing lights of the swimming pool below and Atlantic City traffic. She's got a flat face with a button nose and wide eyes. "You're very handsome man," she says and makes her way toward the bed. She undresses slowly, bending, taking her time with her bra and stockings, bending her legs, then lying naked on her side. She crooks her finger. "Come here." He feels like a teen-ager, undressing, nervous and excited, and in about a minute she's stroking and rubbing him all over and his cock is inside her and all he can think about is not coming. He goes through the names of cellmates and guys who had cells next to his to make himself last a little longer. Right at the end, when he's about to come, he thrusts for all he's worth and she moans and bites her lip. He arches his back and watches her breasts ripple and shake below him.

She runs her nails across his shoulders. "You like?"

"Yes. Very much. Thank you."

"My pleasure."

They lie there for a few minutes. He could get used to this, he thinks. Must get her number from Bobby. He'll come back to AC just for this.

Jacinta says the nice man already paid. He watches her pull on her maroon panties, then her leggings, and suddenly she's dressed and out the door. Jimmy scratches his short hair, smiles, and stretches out—alert but calm, expended.

Driving home he asks Bobby if he knows a service in the city.

"Pipe cleaning service?"

"Yeah."

"Sure. I'll give you some numbers."

"Thanks. Also I need a gun."

"A gun? How come?"

"You know how come. Because there's a rumor going around that Little Mikey's back in town, and if he or one of his old pals wants to take me out, I better have something more than just my dick in my hand when they show up."

"Got it. I'll take care of it."

He's up early Thursday morning. The air is already hot but there's a breeze to go with it. He buys a coffee and walks to Sunset Park. From the crest of the hill he can see Manhattan. He sits on a bench, sipping his coffee, and watches the joggers and kids playing ball. He likes the curve of the grass, the tall oak trees and colorful flowerbeds. In Dannemora the only beauty was the snow that clung to the branches of trees and swirled in the wind. He thought he'd never tire of blue sky and white snow, but he did. Everything a guy sees through bars gets old.

In the afternoon he walks to the Laundromat on Eighth Avenue, buys a bottle of Tide detergent and those little sheets you put in the dryer. When he pulls his clothes out of the dryer, he buries his head in a towel and inhales. Back at the apartment he folds his clean clothes. He likes how it looks, the neat piles of T-shirts in the cupboard, the stack of towels in the bathroom. He sits in the living room with the TV on CNN. Trump is talking about North Korea. Jimmy is aware of sitting comfortably, in this place that is so different and infinitely better than the small, hard, soul-crushing cells he has occupied for most of his adult life—metal chairs and beds, hard institutional furniture, designed to be stronger than you are and to outlast you. You're a different person, not the same guy who sat on that metal bed, looking out of a four-inch window. Of course you have a past, you remember all too well the details of each cell, the size of the window, the shitty view. But you don't feel connected to that past; it belongs to a different man. And you're twenty-five years older than the punk who got arrested, so he's not you either.

On Friday, eight days after Jimmy's release, Big Bobby delivers a gun, a snub-nosed Taurus, untraceable.

Later that day, Jimmy starts putting a crew together. He would have asked Bobby, but the answer was already clear: Pino doesn't want Jimmy working on any Ruggiero business, and because Pino doesn't want him on the street, Bobby can't help him with anything, not anything illegal anyway. Jimmy learned a long time ago: you look after yourself; you count on yourself and nobody else. Anything else is gravy. He can't ask any of the Ruggiero associates, so he speaks to Braglia's nephew, figures any relative of the Colt's must be tough enough. The kid is eager, but the kid is stupid; he's already been arrested for petty theft. Still he'll have to do. Jimmy goes to a titty bar in Williamsburg, meets some construction workers, and buys them drinks. He gets the card of one guy, a Polish mechanic who lives in Newark. Seems like an honest guy and looks like he can handle himself. Could you drive me sometime, if I got an errand to do? The guy says yes, if he's not working. Jimmy's not sure how much he understands, but until he needs him that doesn't matter. What matters is he wants to know there's a crew, however ragtag and unready, a couple of guys he can rely on. Without backup, without a team, he's vulnerable, and he doesn't like to be vulnerable.

One thing he learned serving his time: get through the first year but know how you'll make it through the tenth year too, because you gotta survive the long haul. He's stashed some of the cash at Bobby's office in downtown Brooklyn, some in his new bank account, and keeps a few rolls in the fake pocket he sewed into the duffel bag. Enough for now, but not enough. Of course, as Savino used to say, it's never enough. But he's thinking long term. No pension plan in his line of business. What he puts together now is going to have to last him awhile, at least until he can get a real job or buy into a legit business or, if that doesn't work, by then he should know enough to make a decent score. Fucking money: it can't save your life, but it can kill you. He doesn't want any more skirmishes with the police, but he also doesn't want to be begging for scraps at the Ruggiero table. Nobody said straight time was going to be easy.

He knows what Savino would say. He'd say you just got out of the can, don't take any risks. I'm sorry, he says in his head to the old guy, but I gotta do this. He's collected his cash from Carlo, collected from guys he could still find. Now it's a matter of leaning on a couple of old farts who owe him. He won't get rich, but hopefully he won't get arrested either. He needs the money.

Evening. He sits outside and watches the trees and sky darken and melt together. When he goes to sleep, there are no screams, no cackles or coughs or snores, no one singing or weeping, just the hum of the air conditioner, the rumble of traffic, occasional car doors closing up or down the street. He can't remember ever sleeping so well, or how good it feels to lie in bed.

Because the Night

Milena

The couch and matching armchair were dark green with a fleur-de-lis pattern she thought very European. Vinnie installed a wood bar with mirror-backed shelves, and a side table that housed their new stereo system. The TV, a Sony Trinitron, was spectacular. Vinnie brought home booze—Johnny Walker Black, cognac, champagne, French wine—and videos that had fallen off the back of trucks. They'd do a few lines and order pizza or Chinese food and watch movies until late at night. *Ghostbusters* and *Indiana Jones* were Vinnie's favorites. *Who you gonna call?*

He also brought his work home, in the form of anger, crazy plans, and, mostly, paranoia. She would listen, piece together the background of the stories he told her. Tony Rizzo kept Vincent out of a gang organizing a TV heist. John Perretti had been light last month. Someone killed a drug dealer in the old neighborhood. He was constantly worried about the associates he didn't know well, the young soldiers and mobster wannabes, even the Rizzo brothers themselves were not above suspicion.

"Roberto Cappi's the one you gotta be worried about," Milena would suggest. "Not Perretti."

"What do I do?"

"Stay away from Cappi. He'll implode."

"Stay away?"

"Yes."

She had a better kitchen than her mother had ever owned, clothes her sisters coveted, and Vincent bought her jewels and shoes and gave her cash to go shopping. Sometimes, when she knew Vincent would be out late, she invited her friends over—her sister, high school friends, their cousin Sylvia, their friend Lauren, the one who'd become a stripper. They danced with each other to Kool and the Gang, the Pointer Sisters, and Grover Washington Jr., laughed, cried, ate hot lasagna, and, later in the cold night, smoked cigarettes and drank red wine until their lips were cracked and their tongues stained purple. They asked her if Vincent was in the mob, and she didn't say yes, but she showed them the gun he kept under her camisoles, and they squealed. Vincent didn't like it if he came home and she was drunk and dancing with her girlfriends. Once he kicked them out, yelled at them, as they stumbled out the door. "What's the matter?" Milena asked. "We're just having fun." And he walked over to her, looked her in the eye, and slapped her hard across the mouth. Then he poured himself a scotch, drank it slowly, and went to bed. After that, she made sure to find out when he would be back before inviting the girls over. Most of the time she tidied up after they left. If he asked questions, if he seemed to be getting angry, she'd make a pouty face, kiss him on the cheek, and blow in his ear or give him a blow job if necessary.

She went to a hostess party, organized by Tony's wife, Donatella Rizzo, who was only a little older than Milena. The hostess party was at their apartment in Dyker Heights. All the wives and girlfriends dressed up, talking about hairdressers and restaurants, about their husbands or boyfriends. They traded wedding and vacation stories, compared gifts their men had bought them. All of the men came home late, most seemed to have mistresses, one had been arrested and was serving time for arson. His wife, Jessica, got teary-eyed talking about him. Five years, three if he was lucky. That night she told Vincent one of the husbands was in jail. She was scared; she didn't want Vinnie to go to jail.

"Sweetheart, come on. How many guys you know in jail. That fat *boombots* ain't even a made man. He's a fence. He owns a store, and he got pinched because he burned down the building to collect on the insurance. He was stupid. Do I look stupid? Do I?"

"No, of course not. I just worry, that's all."

"Besides, we own cops and judges. No one can touch us."

Where All Tears are Wiped Away

Jimmy

He pays his respects. Armone's widow, Donatella Rizzo, former captains, aging Sicilian Zips who act like it's the old days. He talks on the phone to Paulie and cousin Richie in Queens. He goes back to Giaccardi's. Old Mafiosi and mobster wannabes are the only ones there, the only fools crazy enough to wear a suit and tie on a summer day, acting like it's 1974 and any minute John Gotti's going to walk in the door. Everyone tells him how brave he was. His respect for the code, his heroism. We need more people like you, they tell him. They pat him on the back. They give him business cards or write down phone numbers. Anything you need, they ask. He tells them no thank you, he's fine. They raise their espresso cups, shake hands. *Cent'anni.* A hundred years. What they don't know is that's exactly what it feels like. It feels like he's been gone a hundred years. Rip Van Piccini.

Bobby fills him in on the family's business interests. "Downsized" is the word he uses. There's less corruption, fewer crooked cops, and a smarter FBI, so shrinkage was inevitable, and margins have gone down.

"Margins."

"Profit margins. Way down."

Jackie Ponzoni drives him to the cemetery, waits respectfully in the car while Jimmy put flowers on the graves. From Calvary he

can see Manhattan smoldering under a hot sky. He lays matching wreaths on his mother's and father's headstones, side by side.
Red and white roses on green leaves. He stands there for a while,
then pulls out his old prayer book. *May they rejoice in Your king-
dom, where all our tears are wiped away. Unite us together again in
one family, to sing Your praise forever and ever. Amen.* He sits down
on a hard piece of scrubby grass between the rows of graves. A
sculpture of an angel looks down on him from a tomb. Instead of
feeling some sort of closure, he finds himself wondering where he
will be buried, and when, and what he will do until then. Can he
scrape together enough money to buy into some legitimate business? Can he find happiness or contentment, maybe even love?
Sitting there, on the hard grass, he doesn't think so.

"It's up to you now," Father Steven told him. "You get to start
again. You're smart, you're able. Whatever happened, that's in the
past. You've got the rest of your life now." When he learned that
Jimmy was going before the parole board again, the priest had
come to his cell for a chat. "It's not heaven out there and this isn't
hell," he said. "Don't expect magic."

"I won't."

The priest smiled. "And don't try to go back to the past."

Jimmy made a crack about liking the past. His friends and
family were there and a slice of pizza was a lot cheaper.

"It's gone. The past is another country. You need to find a new
country now. Well, soon."

He takes Braglia's nephew and Ivan, the Polish mechanic, for a
steak dinner. He tells them he's got a job. Monday afternoon.
They're ready, like puppies waiting for their food. They ask him
what kind of job. "I'll tell you on Monday. But this much I'll tell
you now. Wherever we go and whatever we do, you stick it out.
You run, you leave me inside without cover, you're as good as dead.
Capisce? You gonna get cold feet, get them now."

Saturday he walks around the old neighborhood, has lunch at a
diner counter alongside retirees and teenagers, chats with Tom.

He's a nice guy, a good dad, smart enough but he's nothing like his old man. Jimmy's gone out with Lenny Perkins again and bought himself a lamp and a comfortable chair, hauled out the old striped, squashed armchair that was in the basement apartment. Lenny delivered a box from Amazon with the CDs they ordered—Springsteen, the Stones, and Milena's favorites, Stanley Turrentine, Marvin Gaye, Roberto Murolo. He bought a bottle of single malt, *Time* magazine, the *Wall Street Journal*, *Hustler*, and *Glory Days, Trouble Man*, and *Maria Mari*. He sits outside when the sun is low in the sky, the chair pulled near to his own door, Turrentine blowing his sax quietly.

Bay Ridge to Eighth Street

Jimmy

It comes rushing at you. Cabs and bicycles, people on cell phones, cars, noise and light, and young girls in short skirts. You failed to see your future, to predict or make it safe. You failed to imagine it twenty-five years later, that's for sure. You don't know shit.

Seventeen days after his release, a Sunday, he goes for dinner at Bobby's house in Bay Ridge. There he meets, for the first time, Isabella and their boys. She's cooked marinated beef—or maybe it's pork, he's not going to ask—with rice and beans. It's called *pabellón criollo*, Bobby tells him. Jimmy brought flowers and a bottle of wine, which they are not drinking. What they are drinking is bourbon and bottled beer. Jimmy's alternately laughing and not knowing what to say or how to react. Isabella—plump, pretty—makes sure the boys say hello to their guest and then tells them they can go and play until dinner. She refills drinks, and her easy manner and Bobby's frequent laugh put Jimmy at ease. The boys, seven and nine years old, kick a ball in the small yard, and, after a while, run through the living room to the den to play computer games.

"They play those video games?" Jimmy asks.

"All day," Isabella says.

"They'd play all night if they could," Bobby says. "C'mon."

Bobby gets up first, and Jimmy follows him. They stand in the doorway and watch the boys play. On the TV a boxy man trots up a pixelated hill, passes under pixelated trees, runs around a Lego block building.

After they'd fed the boys and eaten the *pabellón criollo*, Bobby says it's great to see this guy, and Isabella says something about Hugo Chavez, but Jimmy has no idea who she's talking about and just nods and says yes. Bobby agrees. Asks if he's seen Braglia's nephew.

"Yeah," Jimmy says. "Seems like a good kid. We go for a beer once in a while." He thinks about saying more but decides against it.

The next day around six in the evening Ivan, the Polish mechanic, and Braglia's nephew drive him to the house of a businessman he knew back in the day. They leave Ivan in the car.

"You leave us there, or you tell what you've done to anyone at any time, I will hunt you down and kill you."

"No problem," Ivan says. "I stay here."

Brad Chernoff opens the door dressed in shorts and flip flops. He's old now. His legs are thin and pale and wrinkled.

"Jimmy, Jesus. Good to see you. I didn't know you got out."

He pretends he's glad to see Jimmy, shakes Braglia's hand. Offers them drinks. Back in the day Chernoff owned electronics stores, sold stolen goods, made a killing off stolen credit cards and used his bank account to launder money. He owed the Colt and now he owes Jimmy. Jimmy watches his former captain's nephew. He's about as threatening as a hummingbird.

"I'm not happy," Jimmy begins.

"Yeah, of course, of course," Chernoff says. "Jeez, Jimmy, it's good to see you. Holy shit, you been away awhile. Must be good to be out. I gotta tell you, times are tough, things have gotten tight while you were away. I mean, fuck, who's happy?"

"No. I'm not happy with you."

"Listen, you can't just barge in here like this," Chernoff says. "We can chat, but I won't be strong-armed."

"You owe me money."

"If there are any moneys owed, that won't be a problem, but I'll need to check my records and of course you can check yours . . ."

He lets him finish then gives him a piece of paper with a number and his bank details. He follows Chernoff to his study where he takes a wad of cash from a desk drawer, gives it to Jimmy without counting it.

"You'll need more than this."

"Of course, of course."

Half a whiskey later Jimmy walks out with the wad of cash and the promise of a bank transfer. He stops at the front door.

"Come over to the window." He pushes Chernoff's head so he is looking at the car across the road. "You see that man in the car. You don't want to see him again. You know what I'm saying."

The mechanic looks back, stares maliciously, like a dog ready to pounce.

"I know," says the trembling, thin old man.

"Okay. Good. Just to be clear: I don't see that money by Friday, you'll see him again, and you won't like it. You ever wonder who is going to be the last person you see? The very last human being you see? You ever wonder?" He releases the man's head and lets himself and young Braglia out, leaving the door open behind them.

Tuesday in the joint was grits and biscuits. Today it's Frosted Flakes and coffee that tastes like coffee. Breakfast is good but there's a nasty feeling in his gut. Chernoff's gone to the cops. Guy like that would have friends on the force. Even if he doesn't, who are the cops going to believe, the businessman or the ex-con? Jimmy feels something bitter he has not felt in a long time: regret. On the other hand, his demands were modest, an equitable payment of moneys owed, nothing more, nothing less. Did he push too hard, shake down one guy too many? Only time will tell.

Late. Most of the lights across the garden are dark or bedtime dim when there's a knock on the door. A woman stands in the doorway, in a fake fur coat and high heels. Says her name is Leslie.

Puerto Rican or Dominican, large-breasted, lips like ripe fruit, a
goddess. His heart is beating out a rumba. He pours her a drink,
and they talk about the Yankees. For about a minute. "Okay," she
says and takes off her blouse and skirt, slowly, sexily, and lies down,
curved on the bed in nothing but a silk negligee, legs bent and
slightly spread. She hitches up the lace hem, waits for him to
approach before she moves again; she bends forward to kiss him
and touch his face, breasts spilling out of the negligee. He's nervous and happy and hard as a steel pipe. He's worried that he'll
come too fast but he doesn't really care, because she's a professional. She licks her lips and nods. He approaches. She's got the
kind of tits young guys have posted on the walls of their cells. If
they could only see me now, he thinks, as she pulls him inside her.
She coos and coils; he sputters and thrusts.

Afterward the crazy woman runs into the garden. "You can't
do that," he whispers as loud as possible, and she hears him but
she does it anyway, darts across the garden in her cream-colored
negligee, does a spin, and runs back. He pays her, thanks her, asks
if he can see her again. She smiles. "You've got my number."

Wednesday (powdered scrambled eggs in Dannemora), Bobby
picks him up a little after ten. They drive across the Brooklyn
Bridge into Manhattan. Jimmy remembers driving across that
bridge, to a meeting with Savino, to see Milena, or have some fun
with the boys on the West Side. Midtown is taller, shinier, busier
than he remembers. Half the buildings have massive video screens
wrapped around them. More women on the streets, more people
of color too. He asks Bobby to drive through Hell's Kitchen, gives
him an address. When Bobby parks across the street, Jimmy gets
out. He walks up the steps and gets as far as the front door, where
he stops and looks up at the windows.

"You okay?" Bobby appears beside him.

"Yeah, fine. An old friend lived here. Bill Kelly. Stupid, isn't it?
I feel a whole lot of my past when I sit here. It makes me feel, I
don't know, how much I've lost."

Bobby pats him on the shoulder. "C'mon, I wanna show you something downtown."

They drive down Ninth Avenue. He thinks about telling Bobby about Brad Chernoff, but what would Bobby say? And what could he do? They park and walk across Eighth Street. Gone are the bars, the hamburger joint Jimmy used to love, the record store he spent so much time in. Now it's frozen yogurt, coffee shops, exotic restaurants, tattoo parlors, more goddamned banks.

"You see that, Bobby? Electric Lady Studios is still there." He is relieved that there's some reminder of the Greenwich Village he knew from before.

"Whaddaya know."

A Chinese restaurant where Famous Ray's used to be on Sixth Avenue, a shoe store where there used to be an all-night bodega.

There's a health-food store near where Jefferson Market used to be. Well lit, clean, busy. Bobby leads the way and Jimmy follows. Rows and rows of healthy-looking pills, gels, and powders in bottles and boxes—chia, gingko, arnica.

"Salad bar at the back. See how busy this place is. Not yet noon and it's pretty crowded, right?"

Jimmy points to a bottle of horny goat weed. "What the fuck?"

Bobby laughs, shrugs. "The food is pretty good too. And healthy. You eat this shit, your dick will stay hard until you're a hundred."

"Then you can fuck a horny goat. How about we grab a slice, Bobby? Roio's any good? And what the fuck kind of name is that? What's wrong with Ray's?"

"Sure, we don't gotta eat here. I just wanted you to see the place. You know why?"

"Why?"

"Here's your legit business. I just started one, out in Oyster Bay. It's a franchise. They give you just about everything you need, but you can augment, you know, buy additional shit—fruit, vegetables, what have you. And it's cheap. Well, relatively. Coupla hundred thousand for the franchise, plus stock plus rent. After that, you're making profit. But the best news is personnel. You will find someone smart and honest, who doesn't cost a fortune to run the thing for you. What are Americans doing these days?"

"I don't know, what?"

"Eating healthy, chooch. We can go in on it together. Brooklyn, Long Island, whatever. Think about it."

A Ghost in the Garden

Molly

She can't sleep. Or maybe something woke her up. A sound, not the sound of the wind in the trees and not the sound of Cargo going to the toilet or a burglar in the house, something outside. Just then something catches her eye, and she goes to the window. In the garden, there's a ghost, a beautiful woman ghost, dressed in white, with sparkling jewels on her shoulders that flicker in the moonlight. A puff of wind tilts the trees; Molly looks up at the wobbling branches with their flying fish leaves, and when she looks down again the ghost lady is gone. She tiptoes back to bed, and hears quiet sounds downstairs, like laughter or someone singing softly, as moonbeams spill through her half-open curtains.

The Hollywood Scheme

Milena

They knew a guy, Jake Cristal, an old friend of Vinnie's from the neighborhood, who had spent some time working for a Broadway producer and was now making low budget movies in Los Angeles. Mostly horror, slasher and splatter films, sometimes romantic dramas. They flew out to have some fun in the sun—and to see him. They'd gone over what Vinnie would say—he represented some people who may want to invest.

Cristal took the bait. "What movie producer doesn't want investors? Let's do lunch. That's a joke. Come on, we go way back, let's talk." They went to parties in the Hollywood Hills, drove to Malibu, ate lunch at a restaurant overlooking the Pacific Ocean. Cristal took them to a club on Hollywood Boulevard. They did cocaine with tanned, bright-toothed actresses, a Mexican millionaire, a professional surfer. Late in the night Jake told them about his films, almost all of which went straight to video, but if they got a decent distribution deal, and most of them did, then he made money, and his investors made money. Vinnie promised to put him in touch with some investors. Jake promised to give Milena a small part, if they invested.

Her plan was simple. Use different bank accounts to send funds to Cristal's production company. They'd launder money and produce movies at the same time. Rather than take it up the ladder to Rizzo, they decided to go it alone this time. This was California, not Brooklyn, and there were no family interests, and no family eyes could see that far. Besides, they needed a way to wash Vinnie's drug money. (He'd brought in a cousin of his to run a modified version of Milena's drug scheme, buying from and then selling to a few big dealers in Brooklyn and Manhattan.) So Milena and Vinnie became investors in two horror movies, *Ice Cream Man*, shooting the following January, and *Killer Clowns Take Yosemite*, which would be the screenwriter's next feature film. Cristal needed a few more investors, not to mention a script and cast, but promised Milena a small role in *Killer Clowns*. Vinnie and Milena would spend a couple of weeks on the lot, watch the movie being shot, and Milena would be in a scene or two.

Flying home, Vinnie said, "Babe, you're gonna be a movie star." To which Milena replied, "No, I'm not."

On a cool evening in May, they got dressed up and went for drinks and dinner in Manhattan, a new restaurant called The Pearl on East Fifty-Seventh. Tony and Donatella were there, but the host was another captain, Savino DeSapio. Vinnie said he was the numbers man and he and Rizzo had invested in the restaurant. Also present was Alberto Braglia, one of the most feared men in any of the families, Vincent said. There was a story that he once killed a guy for leaning on his car, and maybe it was true and maybe it wasn't, but he was a mean motherfucker either way and you didn't want to get on his bad side. He had a young bimbo with him, drunk, blonde, happy, not his wife, not even his girlfriend and quite possibly a professional, judging from the cut of her clothes and the way she kept putting a hand in his pocket. Also present was another young couple: Savino's young lieutenant, a guy named Jimmy Piccini, and his girlfriend. Thin and quiet, Jimmy had dark, soft eyes that stared intently, like he was about to make a pronouncement, only his lips stayed shut. His girlfriend was named Gina—dark, young, shy. They toasted the restaurant's success, and after another drink talked other things—Ronald Reagan in China and Wayne

Gretzky and Mark Messier and whether the Oilers would beat the Rangers. The girls talked amongst themselves after a while. Alberto's bimbo girlfriend kept ordering more champagne even after she got the hiccups, which she found hilarious. They were talking about *Miami Vice* and *Dallas* and Manhattan hairstylists, and the floozy didn't say much, mostly laughed and hiccupped and commented on the shrimp and champagne. The men, meanwhile, were talking about Italy, and Milena wanted to join their conversation. Savino DeSapio and the young guy, Jimmy, who drank less and listened more than the others, were discussing what it meant that the Communist Party had gained seats in the recent Italian election. It seemed more interesting than whether Don Johnson was handsome or where to get a blowout, but Milena didn't dare say anything.

She talked to Jimmy and Gina when they were leaving. He was very polite, almost shy, and when she said she thought Italy's ruling party would stay the course, Jimmy looked at her, slightly surprised. She was remembering the *New York Times* article that linked the death of a popular Communist Party leader to the party's gaining more seats in the election—and what her father used to say, that the complexity and corruption of Italy made it resistant to change. "Yes, I think so too," Jimmy said. "Craxi isn't going to change anything." Milena said she wanted to go to Italy and that Vincent had promised to take her one day. Then they pulled on their jackets and went out in the warm night to find taxis.

She didn't think much of the shy young man until she met him again at Armone's birthday party, at a club in Brooklyn. A huge party with a cake the size of a bathtub and a live band. Jimmy was there alone, no girlfriends at these events, only wives. She watched him talking with Savino and his wife. There was something about him, a calm intensity. He was not a fighter, she decided, not like her husband, or most of his associates, but a gentler, more refined type, like his mentor, Savino. When she went to the bar to get drinks for Vincent and his crew, she was surprised to find him standing beside her.

"Where in Italy?"

"Excuse me."

"I'm Jimmy. We met the other night."

"Yes, I know."

"Where in Italy do you want to go?"

"Everywhere, but if I had to choose I think Naples and Sorrento and maybe Sardinia."

"Not Sicily."

"Yes, of course, but I think Sardinia sounds more beautiful."

"Most Sicilians don't agree."

She laughed, and he smiled, clearly happy to have made her laugh. She allowed herself to look into his eyes and listen as he described Sorrento and the Amalfi Coast and Vesuvius, a boat on the Mediterranean, restaurants above the marina. No, he hadn't been there, but he too was of Neapolitan descent and wanted to travel around Italy.

Can't Stay Away

Jimmy

Junk changes everything. The Ruggiero family stayed away from drugs because drugs meant cops and addicts and petty crime and real crime and blacks and RICO and Feds and guns and all manner of bad shit. So when they thought about getting into heroin, they argued, debated, listened to outside experts—one of Gotti's guys, a cop on the take. Armone sat on it for a while, talked to his top captains, *consiglieri*, lawyers. In the end, it was decided that they couldn't sit this one out. First, because if they didn't get in now, the other families would later keep them out. Imagine trying now to get into trash-hauling or construction. Second, if they waited it out, they ceded; they looked weak. You never, ever wanted to look weak. Finally, there was a lot of money to be made. A lot of money. And money also changes everything.

They considered potential partners, but because they knew but didn't trust any of the players big enough to be an equal partner, they decided to become "an operator," as DeSapio put it to Jimmy.

"A shipper?" Jimmy asked.

"Transportation and distribution."

"We distribute to the distributors."

"Correct."

"Dangerous business, higher up the food chain, but fewer moves and more profitable."

"Also correct. Which is why we gotta be careful. *Attento*. Stay the fuck away from RICO."

For days they did nothing but read articles and laws and statutes and talk to their lawyer and accountant. DeSapio made all his notes in a small blue notebook that never left his pocket except when he was writing in it. Jimmy did the same. "A bulldog with teeth" was what DeSapio called Rudy Giuliani, US Attorney for the Southern District of New York, who was using RICO to bring down the mob. An Italian, too, one of their own. "Giuliani's waging war," DeSapio said. And RICO meant he could go after crime families, not only individuals—bosses, not only capos and hit men. And the list of what constituted a "pattern of criminal activity" was as long as the Ruggiero family's income statement: loan-sharking, gambling rings, murder, kidnapping, arson, drug dealing, bribery, transportation of stolen goods, mail and wire fraud.

"I'll tell you the trouble with wars," DeSapio said. "They never end, not really."

Jimmy accompanied DeSapio when they presented the plan to "Bart the Shark" Santoro, the Rizzos, and Joey Armone.

"We launder money in the US, send it to legitimate businesses in Europe," DeSapio explained, and then laid out the path for moving money from European businesses to their Sicilian partners so that by the time it got there it was not only clean but untraceable.

Jimmy went through the details—no notes, he did it all from memory. Legitimate businesses they knew or controlled would launder cash—they had pizza parlors and bakeries across three boroughs. Offshore banks and credit unions would turn money and change currencies. A friendly US banker would introduce them to a banker in Amsterdam, who would set up accounts in Geneva. Those accounts would fund payments to legitimate Italian businesses that would, in turn, move funds to their partners in Sicily. A network of banks, intermediaries and shells, no money trail.

Armone leaned forward and whispered with Rizzo and Santoro for a minute, then addressed DeSapio and Jimmy. He complimented their thorough work and said it sounded like the right plan. "We'll go through the details and partners, but this is good." They talked about offshore banks, commissions, and, of course, RICO.

There were secret meetings and more secret meetings. Armone met the Sicilians in Manhattan; Frank Rizzo went to Palermo. As the thing started to take shape, Savino and Jimmy met one of the Sicilians, a captain in the Donato crime family, an old guy in a dark suit. They met in the back of a pizzeria to plan how the money would change hands. They would use bank transfers and suitcases full of cash, to be transported separately from any drugs, sent with couriers on planes. The emissary's English was terrible, and he didn't think much of the pepperoni pizza, but he seemed like an honest man and they got the logistics in place.

Armone had someone handling the drug transfers and several captains, including Tony Rizzo, were organizing distribution, talking to big dealers, guys in other families they could trust. Savino was anxious, going through what-if scenarios. It was a big, messy business, and there was a lot to worry about. One thing he didn't want to worry about was young guys with big mouths. One of those guys was Vincent DeNunzio, and Savino sent Jimmy to talk to him. "Be nice, be friendly. But he's got a big mouth, so you tell him, *stai zitto*." "I'll see what I can do," Jimmy said.

I Want to Know What Love Is

Milena

Milena said yes, when Vinnie invited her along for drinks with his crew, because some of the guys were bringing girlfriends. Yes, again, when they went to dinner with Tony and Donatella Rizzo at The Pearl. She didn't admit, even to herself, her reason for going, who she was looking for, because she didn't know why she was looking for him or what she would do if she found him. There was the added benefit that Vinnie treated her like a queen when they were in public, even if he bossed her around as soon as they got home. When she said no, didn't jump up to cook him dinner when he said he was hungry, or didn't give him a blow job when he tried to guide her head south, his glare was so fierce she sometimes thought he was going to hit her, although the most he ever did these days was yank her hair or curse. Sometimes at night, when he was asleep and the world was quiet, she stood at the open window and smoked a cigarette or a joint and asked herself why she felt so uneasy. What did she want? Another man? It was too late for that. Someone who didn't humiliate her or bore her when they tried to talk about anything other than his work or sports? She wanted to shout at him: *Do you really think this is all I want?*

A *capo* was killed in a shakedown, and although he wasn't in Rizzo's crew and she'd never met him, Vinnie had to attend the funeral, and therefore she did too. She bought a black Donna

Karan dress especially for the occasion. Afterward there was a reception in the private room of a restaurant. And suddenly there he was. Even in a crowded room, he didn't bump into anyone; he seemed to glide through open space. She watched him talk to the grieving widow, bow slightly as he took his leave, very gentlemanly and courteous, very old school.

She excused herself to go to the bathroom, circled the room, and found him talking to Bobby Maritato. "Oh, hello again," she said nonchalantly, and he smiled when he saw her—a real smile— and she felt his eyes on her, roving discreetly. She felt like a high school girl with a crush when she complimented the food, and after pleasantries, said that she kept thinking about what he'd said about Italy. "Maybe I should get a job as a travel agent," he joked, and Big Bobby laughed, and Jimmy said something about wanting to ride a Vespa along the coast of Liguria. She imagined him in sunglasses and a short-sleeved shirt, tanned and smiling. There was the way his dark eyes flickered and sparkled, the crisp knot in his tie, the way he spoke, a low rumble. Here was a man who knew things, she thought, who was going somewhere, a man with goals and dreams, a man with vision and intelligence, a man you could talk to, a man who would become something more than fat or dead, which were the only directions she saw Vincent heading. Three minutes of conversation, five tops, and she had to take her leave, find Vinnie, get another drink, and listen to his stupid jokes and pretend to listen to a conversation about Yogi Berra and the Yankees. She looked for Jimmy the rest of the evening and occasionally caught a glimpse, but she didn't talk to him again that night.

Hello, Jimmy Piccini

Jimmy

"Hello, Jimmy Piccini." It was Milena who greeted him at the door, dressed in Jordache jeans and a blue silk blouse, Milena who mixed the drinks and asked if he wanted something to eat, a sandwich. "Vincent's just finishing up a call," she said. "He'll be right with you." And smiled an inscrutable smile. They clinked glasses.

"Manhattans in Brooklyn," he said. "I like that."

She turned down the volume on the stereo. "Frank Sinatra. I know it's heresy, but not my taste."

Heresy. He liked that too. He asked what was her taste. She tilted her head, and her hair fell like a dark waterfall across her long neck and silk collar, and then she smiled and he felt ripples of warmth, felt them physically like sunshine on his neck.

"Oh, I like all kinds of music. Marvin Gaye, the Rolling Stones, jazz. Horace Silver, Bill Evans."

Jimmy nodded. Ever since Armone's birthday party, he'd wanted to talk to her again, about anything, nothing. "Springsteen?"

"Of course."

"Miles Davis?"

She looked at him before answering. "Mmmm. Love Miles."

"They call him the Prince of Darkness."

He wanted more than anything to listen to music with her, to see her dance, to watch her lips in candlelight. *Dancing in the dark.*

"Won't you sit down?"

"Apologies." Vincent stood in the doorway in a white T-shirt. His hair was messy and he hadn't shaved. "Dealing with some idiots selling swag on my turf. We'll take care of them, but there are problems, always problems."

They shook hands, clapped each other on the back.

"Good to see you," Jimmy said. "Nice pad."

"Thanks. We like it."

Jimmy noticed his puffy cheeks and red eyes.

Milena brought Vinnie a cocktail. The men chatted and when Milena drifted out of the room, Jimmy spoke, in a roundabout way, about how he heard that Santoro yelled at Trapattoni for getting too chatty with one of the couriers they were using.

"Fucking Trapattoni."

"Cocksucker."

Jimmy said it reminded him of a guy the Colt used to use as his *messaggero*, who talked too much. The Colt gave him a beating. "Nearly killed the crazy fuck."

"Our business," Vinnie said. "You can't go yammering about it."

"You gotta ensure discretion."

"You. With the words. But you're right. Another round?"

"Sure, if I'm not overstaying my welcome."

"Never."

Vinnie mixed the drinks this time. Jimmy sipped his Manhattan, relaxed now that he'd delivered his message, subtly, perhaps too subtly. Later he hoped Vinnie would think about Trapattoni and that would be warning enough. *Stai zitto, goombah.* So he made up some bullshit about what he came to see him about: working out secure locations for meetings with the Sicilians, somewhere in Manhattan, somewhere private. Afterward they would show the Italians a good time in the Big Apple. Vinnie suggested a few restaurants and clubs; Jimmy agreed.

Milena did not reappear, and after a while Jimmy looked at his watch, said he was going to visit his parents.

"Let's take the ladies somewhere nice."

"Sounds like a plan."

Strange How the Night Moves

Jimmy

Jimmy's girlfriend at the time was Lee-Ann Harrison, bleached blonde, self-assured in a giddy sort of way, an air hostess with American Airlines, originally from Florida. Not Italian. Not beautiful exactly, with a prominent nose, skin that bore vestigial traces of acne, and too many teeth, but she had emerald-green eyes, a deep hearty laugh that made other people laugh when they heard it, a great rack, and lean, strong legs. She was a good dancer, liked cocaine and oysters, mixed a better martini than most bartenders, and what the tip of her tongue did to his cock was magic. She said she loved Rio and promised to take Jimmy there when he could take a week off. She could get free airline tickets and great deals on hotels.

The Ruggieros' Visa card scam was in full swing. It was simple and it was lucrative. Pay off postal workers, nab mailings sent to cardholders, then do a deal with a shady merchant, like Chernoff Electronics. If a card had a $3,000 limit, they'd split $2,500 with the merchant, and spend the rest having some fun, which, in Vinnie's case, meant nightclubbing. Savino had a different scam, which he and Jimmy ran for a few weeks. They read the obituaries and applied for credit cards for dead people, which they used to get cash advances. They did this twenty times or so and made a bundle, but then Savino put the kibosh on it. If the cops were

125

looking, they'd be able to find him, or whoever he sent, to pick up the physical cards. "You get in, you get out," Savino was always saying.

Lee-Ann wore a shimmery gold top to the Ipanema Club with Vinnie and Milena. They ordered champagne the minute they sat down, and shortly thereafter Lee-Ann slipped away to the bathroom with a small bag of coke Jimmy had given her, and when she came back they clinked glasses and drank the bottle of champagne. Milena said she'd heard so much about Lee-Ann, all good things.

"I like these guys," Lee-Ann giggled. "How come we've never been out with them before?"

"Saving the best for last," Jimmy said.

Each of them slipped off to the bathroom for a line of coke. Then the champagne tasted better, the music sounded crisper. When the waiter, a handsome Latin man who looked to be in his mid-fifties, asked what the "pretty ladies" wanted, Vinnie shot him a dangerous look. After that he was all business, solicitous but terse.

Lee-Ann told them about the places she'd been—San Diego, Rio, London. Her dad was a football fanatic, it turned out, and she and Vinnie had a lot to talk about. She liked Dan Marino but didn't think the Miami Dolphins could go all the way ("Mark Super Duper's a pussy"). Vinnie laughed and clinked his champagne glass vigorously with his fork. They agreed that the Jets had a shot at the playoffs ("O'Brien's one of the all-time greats"). They drank a toast to the Jets, ate and danced and drank some more, did more coke. Lee-Anne danced well, showing off her legs and raising her tanned arms in the air, but Milena looked better, smooth and sexy, rippling her hair, curving her back.

Back at their table they made fun of the old guys at the table next to theirs, working stiffs celebrating a business deal. A flushed man veering around on the dance floor stumbled into a couple, and Jimmy said there should be a law against drunk dancing, and they all laughed and drank some more. They laughed a lot that evening, mostly at Vinnie's off-color jokes ("The old bull says, 'No, son, let's walk down that hill and fuck them all'"). They were drunk and tired, flushed and shiny-faced by the time they called it a night.

At the coat check, Jimmy found himself holding Milena's coat and looking into her eyes. Lee-Ann was in the bathroom and Vinnie was talking to the maître d'—they'd just jacked a truck full of booze and he wanted to unload it.

"Let me help you with that."

"Thank you."

Her walnut eyes stared into his soul.

"Maybe one day we could listen to some of that music you like," he said.

"I'd like that," she said, as he pulled on her coat. And then, "You know what, I'll be with my sister tomorrow. Come by for a drink if you're free." She whispered the address in Murray Hill.

Jimmy smiled and memorized the address.

"Well, that was fun," Vinnie said, coming up behind them. "Good to meet Lee-Ann." He patted Jimmy on the back. "She's a looker, nice too. Knows her football. Milena here doesn't know an end zone from a baseball diamond."

By then Lee-Ann was back. "She knows diamonds are a girl's best friend," she said, winking at Milena.

Thirty years later, Jimmy would still remember that address.

Nespresso Love

Jimmy

He phones the number on the back of his bank card and checks his balance. No money has come in. Waits half an hour, phones again. Still nothing. When you lean on someone, there's only four possibilities. They give you what you want is one. Or they fight back, talk you down, or go to the cops or someone else who can intervene. Chernoff's no idiot, he knows he's dealing with an ex-con, a made man but a made man who had muscle decades ago and is currently on a short leash with the police. The more Jimmy thinks about it the more he regrets his choice. Yeah, he needs money, but he also needs to stay clear of the law. It's a shitty choice. Is that how it's going to be for the rest of his life? He can be free, but only if he's poor. So what's the answer? Stay out of the can. That trumps everything else, because he can't go back there again. It's not worth any amount of money, so why lean on some basically honest citizen, who could go to the cops and make a pretty good case. Who knows, maybe he's got security cameras and caught the whole charade on video. Maybe they're licking their lips waiting to book him. He prays it's not so. He calls the automated bank number again—same damn balance. *Come on, Chernoff, give me a break.* He thinks about going back but that won't do anything. Whatever Chernoff has decided to do, he's already decided. And then there's Little Mikey. How come he has to come back East from wherever he's been hiding? And why now?

He goes for a walk, eats two slices of pizza, drinks a Coke, crushes the can like it's responsible for his bad luck or bad decisions.

He goes to a bar in the afternoon and drinks a cold beer, chases it down with a whiskey, chases that with another beer. After that he feels a bit better, but he's still looking over his shoulder and cursing himself for not thinking more clearly. Tries to talk to the bartender but the guy is all efficiency and doesn't chitchat even though the place is pretty empty.

He has a hangover before his head hits the pillow.

On Friday morning when he phones the bank to check his balance, the money's come through. He feels relief and pride and a small taste of the old high, the thrill of the score. But mostly relief. Whether or not he believed Jimmy's threats, Chernoff made the wire transfer as agreed, and that'll be the last of it.

The next day Jimmy writes a check to Braglia for his uncle's share, and another to Tom for Savino's share of the Chernoff settlement and takes it upstairs. At first Tom refuses. But Jimmy insists—think of it as rent, he says—and eventually Tom relents, accepting the check with thanks.

As a thank you (or maybe he intended to do it anyway), Tom gives him a Nespresso machine, installs it himself, and shows Jimmy how to use it. He even buys two extra boxes of the little cartridges. Now Jimmy has an espresso every morning and one in the afternoon. As he told Tom, he'd forgotten what good coffee tasted like. You forget what you've forgotten. Like the smell of good pasta, or how sunshine feels on your skin, the taste of a martini. In the big house, he got a few birthday and Christmas presents, most years, some years no one remembered. A photograph of Milena on a country road in Massachusetts and those postcards from her sister, that was all he had. *We all miss you, so very much*. He cried when he read that. Pulled his hair and cried, quietly though—can't let anyone hear you cry. Toward the end, he didn't expect anything and he didn't get anything. You need to have a wife if you want a birthday present every year. Armone's wife sent Jimmy something the first few Christmases, probably because her husband was in the joint too. Pino sent fruit baskets or Italian pastries— prison-approved stuff from the website, which was thoughtful considering he'd never met Jimmy.

I'll Play the Music,
Won't You Come Dance with Me

Milena

On a rainy spring night in 1985, Milena put away her customary prudence when she opened the door of her sister's boyfriend's apartment in Manhattan to greet Jimmy Piccini, Ruggiero wiseguy and her husband's associate. He stood in the doorway in a dark raincoat, with flecks of silvery rain in his hair, and he kissed her on both cheeks, in the manner of an old-world gentleman. She watched him walk into the room. He was neither tall nor big, but he had a bearing, a way of carrying himself that exuded a calm confidence. She introduced Sabrina and Bill Kelly, and they shook hands. Bill worked on the stock exchange, was training to become a broker. He'd been told a little about Jimmy and was pretending, albeit not very well, that he knew nothing of his guest's line of business. Bob Seger was playing on the stereo. *Working on our night moves.* Bill was mixing martinis. *In the sweet summertime.* She could hear Jimmy speaking quietly to his host. "No one knows I'm here . . . not tomorrow, not ever." She watched Bill nod, quite seriously—"understood," he said—and shake Jimmy's hand again before putting a martini in it. They clinked glasses and drank and listened to the music and chatted about the weather, and soon conversation turned to Terry Anderson, the journalist taken hostage in Beirut. She knew what Vinnie would have said, something like "serves him right for going to Beirut," and so she was surprised when Jimmy shook his head and said "senseless." Bill Kelly agreed. "You can't just take a reporter hostage."

Another round. Jimmy said you could tell Milena and Sabrina were sisters, and not only because they looked alike. Bill was affable and easy to talk to and very much in love with Sabrina, and Milena trusted them both, so much that she got up and danced when Sabrina put on a Commodores CD and started dancing with Bill, pulling Jimmy to his feet and twirling into his arms. "Come on," Milena sang. "Boogie down white boy. Let's have some fun." And they danced. *The lady's stacked and that's a fact, ain't holding nothing back.* Sabrina sang into her thumb, Milena laughed, and Jimmy danced, surprisingly well. Or maybe nothing about him was surprising at all.

Sabrina put on "Brick House" again and danced across the living room to Bill. Jimmy danced more loosely now, and Milena spun in his arms and let him pull her close and pressed herself against him, then danced away, turning in the corner of the room and smiling at her waiting dance partner. After "Brick House" the next song was "Funky Situation," a slower song, and they all swayed and sipped their drinks and sang along, laughing and shaking their hips. *It's funky, it's funky, it's funky, it's a funky situation.* She remembered her parents dancing, which they didn't do very often, but once in a while, on someone's birthday or when her father was feeling particularly happy (and slightly drunk), they would dance around the dining room table to Glenn Miller or Benny Goodman, her father towering over her mother, and they looked elegant and natural and the girls would join them, dancing with each other and sometimes with their parents too. When they were very little they would stand on their father's shoes and he would dance very slowly.

There was something about Jimmy, his gentleness, the way he remembered things she said at Club Ipanema, remembered things everyone said, his calm way of talking, his interest in music and movies. He spoke in complete sentences and didn't say fuck, fuggedaboudit, or get outta here constantly. He probably hadn't finished high school, but he was smart, educated even. It had taken her awhile to realize what her husband would never be: a gentleman.

With Jimmy, the conversation went up a notch or two. He listened to her. He was attentive, but not once did he look at her boobs. Sabrina sat on the couch with Bill, giggling and whispering, and Jimmy and Milena sat in the armchairs, chatting like old friends.

Did you like growing up in Brooklyn? No one had ever asked her that. Vinnie and his meathead friends didn't give a damn about anybody. Never asked questions. It was a stupid, little thing. Anyone could have asked that of anyone, but Jimmy asked her, and she knew, she just knew, that Jimmy Piccini cared.

She wanted to know more about him. She learned that evening that he'd seen *Das Boot*, a German movie about a submarine in World War Two, he liked clams and Coney Island, and watched CNN.

The next song was called "Patch it Up," and as soon as it came on Sabrina stood and hoisted her sister up. Jimmy and Bill stood together at the window while Sabrina and Milena danced together as they had at home so many times. The men smiled and shook their heads. Milena kept her eyes on Jimmy. She had the feeling that she'd known him a long time. She wanted to dance alone with him, sway slowly to a love song in a flickering candlelit room, walk arm in arm under the moonlight in Tuscany or Sorrento.

"You can see the Empire State Building from Bill's bedroom," Milena said, standing and casting a glance at Jimmy, who stood and followed her down the dark hallway to the bedroom.

Inside, through the narrow window Sabrina had shown her earlier in the evening, they saw lean buildings, dark water towers etched out of gray sky, and there in the Empire State Building's tall spire, white as the moon with red lights on the radio antenna, touching the dark sky.

"Beautiful, isn't it," Milena whispered. Its immensity and grace always gave her the chills

"You're beautiful," Jimmy whispered.

He was beside her now, so close she could smell aftershave. He faced her, then leaned forward and just like that their lips met in a sudden kiss. They stopped and she touched his shoulder, as if to reassure him. She wanted to kiss him again; she wanted to stay right where they were for a very long time. They looked out the window. The Empire State Building was exactly where it was before the kiss, the red lights still winking at the sky.

He drew a finger down her cheekbone, touched her chin. The second kiss was the real thing, long and sexy. She ran her fingers through his hair, kissing and stroking him, a lingering kiss that took her breath away, and the taste of his mouth was not like anything she'd ever tasted before. Chocolate and licorice with a hint of olive.

Later they ordered Chinese food and drank red wine. It was after midnight when Jimmy put her in a taxi, then waited on the wet street for another cab. As she drove away, she turned and saw him under the streetlight, smiling.

Moonraker

Jimmy

As Jimmy Piccini watched Milena's cab drift down the dark mostly empty avenue, and she turned her beautiful head to smile at him, he realized he had never been in love. Or rather, he realized he had never been in love before—and now he was. He decided to walk a bit, and as the taxis on Lexington Avenue floated past, he kept seeing her face. He thought of that James Bond movie where Bond and the sexy scientist end up in a space shuttle and imagined himself and Milena in a NASA shuttle having sex as they orbited the earth, twenty-two thousand miles from home. *Take me round the world one more time.*

They met again a week later at Bill Kelly's apartment. This time neither her sister nor Kelly were there. They had the place to themselves, and she'd brought Italian food from Claudio's in Kensington. Antipasti, prosciutto, mozzarella, breads, cheeses, caponata, and pickled vegetables. He'd bought good wine and cannoli. Enough food for six people, and yet they ate none of it for a while, just drank a glass of wine together, and talked. It was, suddenly, assumed that they would see each other again after this night, and he talked about going to the Museum of Modern Art, joking that no one they knew would ever go there. He didn't want to ruin it by setting a date. She wanted to go to the opera, and he said he would take her.

In the galley kitchen, they unwrapped the cheese and prosciutto, and she licked her fingers, then he touched her hand
gently and licked her fingers, then pulled her close and they kissed.
They ate, they shared a cigarette, they drank more wine. After a
while he stood up. She smiled and sauntered away, and he followed her down the hallway to Bill Kelly's bedroom where they
had sex, slowly, passionately. In the window the red, white, and
blue Empire State Building shone just for them.

Moon River

Milena

It was late; the sky around the Empire State Building was woolly gray. Jimmy made the bed while Milena tidied up the kitchen. She poured what remained of the wine down the sink, and watched the red waves curl around the drain, then she wiped the sink and arranged the flowers, box of chocolates, and whiskey on the bar, their anonymous thank you note. They walked out together, locking the keys in Bill's apartment.

When she saw her sister a few days later, she confessed. She was scared. If Vinnie ever found out, he'd kill them both. But she really liked this guy. He was different.

"We didn't even go anywhere, and still it was the best night I ever had. Oh, Sabrina, what am I going to do?"

"You're going to be very careful," Sabrina said. "You're not going to do anything stupid. That's what you're going to do. There's no way Vincent or anyone else finds out. Okay. And—"

"What?"

"Cool it."

"What do you mean?"

"I mean you don't need to see Jimmy every five minutes."

She looked down. That was just it. That was exactly what she wanted—to see him every five minutes. When she looked up, her sister was shaking her head and pulling a face.

"What?"

"Why couldn't you find someone else, Mili?"

"Because he's special?"

"Because you're an idiot."

Back in Brooklyn, she took a Xanax and lay in bed. Vinnie wasn't home yet; she hoped he would be out late, stay out all night. She wished she were lying next to Jimmy Piccini, and, barring that, wished the Xanax would send her to sleep, which after a while, it did.

Siblings

Jimmy

When Jimmy thinks of his brother, two different versions of Paulie come to mind. The first is the photograph of the marine his parents kept on the mantel—proud and tall in his dress blues, hard cheekbones and jutting chin under the white hat. The other image, one he recalls more vividly, is an unphotographed moment: Paul in civilian clothes, at the front door of the house they both grew up in, slouched and thin—home, vanquished.

When Paulie opens the door of his apartment and sees Jimmy standing there, the brother he hasn't seen outside of a prison visiting room in twenty-five years, his mouth widens and he takes a step backward.

"My God. Jimmy."

They hug and Paulie cups a hand behind Jimmy's head, as if to make sure he's real.

Paulie looks older, thinner. He's dressed in a black T-shirt, jeans, black Converse sneakers, not new but very clean, tied tightly. He must have narrow feet, Jimmy thinks.

"It's good to see you," Paulie says, clapping him on the shoulder. "Jesus Christ, here you are."

"Here I am."

"Come on in. Siddown. Or you wanna go out somewhere?"

"No, this is fine. Hot out there."

They sit in the living room of Paul's small Red Hook apartment. They can see through to the open galley kitchen—spice rack, narrow stove, garbage and recycling bins. It's a clean, neat apartment, not much bigger than Jimmy's basement digs. His brother seems to have few possessions. The biggest thing in the living room is the dark wood sideboard, which he recognizes from their parents' living room. It's chipped here and there but there's still an old-world majesty to its rich wood and shiny bowed legs. So much has gone on without Jimmy and looking at the man with long legs across from him, he doesn't feel so much a brother as a long-lost relative. Fake logs in the bricked-up fireplace, a cord snaking along the wall to the outlet. Jimmy finds himself wondering if the logs actually produce heat or if they simply light up when you switch them on. There are a few photos on the big dark sideboard, along with little plates and vases. Jimmy gets up to take a look. An old black-and-white of their parents, Paul in uniform, Paul with the Oklahoma boy, both of them in fatigues and T-shirts. A man in a suit and fedora, somewhere in the country, just trees and sky around him. Possibly Jasper the Oklahoma guy many years on. Whoever he is, the man in the photograph is not family and not anyone Jimmy knows. There's no photo of Jimmy, not that he expected to find one.

"You want a beer or something?"

"Yeah, sure. Maybe we'll go out later. Any good pizza around here?"

"Sure, not bad."

Paul gets them beers, which they drink from the can. They talk. Paul is working as a doorman, on Montague Street. Nice people, a lot of families. He tells Jimmy how their parents spent their last years. They were both pretty healthy up until their father got the cancer. Then he deteriorated rapidly, and their mother was never quite the same either. Jimmy had gone to the funeral—the one and only time he left prison in twenty-five years. He remembers the misty day, the cold cemetery. He stood beside his mother and she held his hand. Their ma died in her sleep a couple of years later of a heart attack. Jimmy was down in Alabama then and the warden denied his request to attend the funeral. Does Paul have someone special? Doesn't look like he does.

"You look good. Seriously, for a guy who's been in jail all those years."

"Thanks. You exercise in the can, and the food is shit."

Paulie laughs. When they were teenagers they used to tell each other jokes that featured fucking, cocks, loose women, whores, nuns, and laugh raucously. *If I had a pussy, I'd own Manhattan!*

"Well, I'm glad you're out."

"You and me both."

Paulie taps the top of his beer can. "I'm sorry I didn't come to see you more. I knew this day would come. I was hoping it would come sooner. And I knew I'd feel bad. It just took . . ."

"Don't worry about it. I'm out now."

"Do you need anything?"

"Nah, I'm okay. Of course if you still got that stuff of mine."

"Sure, I got it."

Paul disappears for a few minutes, returns with a cardboard box. "Jimmy" is written on the side, below a Staples logo.

There's a small travel bag full of cash, which Jimmy inspects. He snaps out a few hundred-dollar bills and gives them to Paul.

"Nah, you don't gotta do that."

"I know. Take it."

A plastic bag full of jewelry, his old Nikon camera, a stack of envelopes, some photographs, the journal he used to keep track of who had paid and who hadn't, a silver crucifix on a chain that he kept from the jewelry store heist during the blackout of '77. He was a smartass teenager then. Bits of the past, dusty but intact, in a cardboard box. There's a cigar box full of cash and baseball cards, a gold pen and other little things, a Diamond Print envelope stuffed with photos—Brooklyn, trees, Milena smiling, a younger, happier

Jimmy. For some reason they make him uncomfortable and he puts them back, slides the box away from him.

"Thanks for holding on to this stuff."

"That was nothing."

They both stare at the box.

"Hey, Jimmy, I gotta tell you something."

"You're pregnant?" And then: "Bobby told me. You think you saw Mikey Rossi."

"I seen him with my own two eyes, Jimmy. Came into the restaurant, Campagnola, where I was working. I look up and there he is. He didn't see me."

"You sure it was him."

"Sure enough that I said I was sick that night and never came back."

"Bobby sent someone to the restaurant the next few nights. Even Mikey's not dumb enough to go to an Italian restaurant in Brooklyn."

"Well, I was sure enough that I quit probably the best job I ever had."

"How'd he look?"

"The same. Older, fatter, hair dyed a bad copper color."

"Who was he with?"

"Couple of Italian-looking guys, young fat guy and an older guy."

"Tell me about the restaurant."

"Campagnola, everyone knows it. One of the more famous Italian places in Brooklyn. Been there forever. Pricey, but very good."

"So it's possible, if Mikey was in town for a few days, he might have gone there, for a celebration maybe, nothing to do with you."

"Yes."

Jimmy scratches the stubble on his chin and neck. A coincidence? Must be. If he was looking for Paul, he found him and he would have known that he found him. Unless he thought Paulie would lead him to Jimmy. But he didn't. Jimmy stares at the fireplace and the photos above it. Is it possible Mikey has been staking out Paul's apartment? No, he's not that smart or patient. If he has business to do, Mike Rossi does it.

"You see that weasel again, you let me know, okay. You've got my number. Meanwhile I'll have someone look into it."

He looks around. Is this the house of an old queer? Ever since Mikey said that thing, Jimmy had wondered. Doesn't bother him, not anymore. Back then, back when he got discharged, Jimmy would have been—what?

Sickened, angry. Their pops too. There was a military ban on gays back then. In the can he met a bunch of guys who had been in the army. They still called them "blue discharges." Full benefits, but you never put on your uniform or your dress blues again. He read about Leonard Matlovich in *Time* magazine, the decorated vet who admitted he was gay. He got kicked out, but Jimmy can't remember what happened after that. As for their father, he was a pretty easygoing guy, but he didn't like *fanooks*. If he'd known he had one for a son, holy shit, he'd have given Paulie a beating, probably kicked him out of the house. In the joint you have a lot of time to ponder big questions. Does God exist? Am I a bad person? Why did that fucker rat me out? Will she still love me when I get out? Is my brother gay? In the joint you don't get many answers, and you learn to leave the questions alone. They're like oceans or lakes: you know they're there and you know you must stop at the water's edge—if you dive in, you'll drown. What you do know is: it sucks being there; and getting out, whenever you get out, after five months or twenty-five years, is the best thing that ever happened and it's also a letdown. You don't feel a whole lot wiser, that's for sure.

He takes a cab home, lugs the cardboard box into his apartment, and pops open the lid. His green ledger, its pages yellowed with age, contains notes, names (most of them in a code he no longer remembers), incomes, calculations. He picks up the old Nikon camera, looks through the viewfinder, focuses the lens. There is a roll of film in the old camera, and the next day he takes it to Photo Station on Seventh Avenue.

He is not a spiteful person, refuses to be inhabited by hate, but now and then Jimmy lets himself succumb to fear, or maybe it's the old urge for vengeance sneaking out of the box he keeps it in. Now and then leads him to the jam-packed office of Melvyn Zelniker, a "college-educated guy" Bobby uses when they have to find someone. Melvyn knows everyone, likes no one, and can find anyone. "There are a lot of ways to find a person," Melvyn explains. "CCTV cameras in car parks, airports, bus stations, fast-food joints, toll plazas. You give me the name of that restaurant, the guy's friends and family, and we can plant some hidden cameras. I have age progression software, so we'll have a good idea what he looks like today. I'll need your brother to describe him to me, okay?"

The following day, Jimmy collects a shiny yellow envelope of photographs: Milena in Central Park, Milena that weekend in the Berkshires, framed by rust-licked leaves. *Say cheese.* God, she was beautiful. He looks through the other photos—Brooklyn streets circa 1990, his friend Eddie hunkered beside a Chrysler LeBaron, Bay Ridge, Lindbergh Meat Market—then goes back to looking at the ones of Milena, smiling, laughing, Milena looking away, the back of her head, the slope of her neck.

When Cows Fly

Catherine

"**B**ecause I'm telling you. He's okay. You can trust him."

"I'll trust that man with my daughter when cows fly. Come on, Tom, don't be ridiculous."

"Just give him a chance. You gave my old man a chance."

"I was in love with his son."

"So just give Jimmy a chance. We won't leave Molly with him, but we can't kick him out. He's not going to do anything. Besides we don't have much choice."

She sighs, picks plates out of the sink, and puts them in the dishwasher.

"If you ask me he seems like a nice enough guy."

"So did Mussolini."

"Come on, Cath. What do you think he's going to do? He's an old guy."

"So was the Unabomber."

"Nice to see you have an open mind."

She looks at her husband. "You're scared of him."

"Stop it."

What she wants to say is: having him in the house is like leaving a loaded gun lying around. But she's learned to be less metaphorical, more specific with Tom. Otherwise he goes off on a tangent arguing the big idea not the specific plan of action. Although now she doesn't have a plan of action. She can't kick Jimmy out apparently. She can, and has, forbidden her children from going out with him unaccompanied. She has to admit that no harm came to Molly because of Jimmy and, in fact, he appears to take the safety of her children quite seriously. More than that, Molly seems to like him, and Molly doesn't like everyone, not by a long shot. Instructed not to leave the house with anyone, she said, "You mean, Mister Jimmy? But I like him." Cargo is simpler; he likes baseball—throwing a baseball, playing Little League, watching baseball on TV and the adult leagues in Prospect Park, or practicing his swing, often to the detriment of furniture and flora. It follows that his only question, his only real concern, about Mister Jimmy was, "Does he like baseball?"

"I don't know, why don't you ask him. But don't go off with him, not without one of us. Okay?"

"Okay."

"He's not a grown-up," says Molly.

"Who's not a grown-up, chicken?"

"Mister Jimmy."

"And why's that?"

"Because he's not married."

"Not all grown-ups are married."

But she is shaking her head. "No, he got sad and so he didn't become a grown-up and didn't get married."

That Jimmy got sad and, as a consequence, could not or would not marry, that sadness alters time and people in some ineluctable way—these are things that Molly seems to know, self-evident truths. Which makes prison (even though Molly still knows nothing of Mister Jimmy's real past, of that Catherine is certain) a long period of being sad. How does she come up with these theories? She seems so certain. Cath is about to ask more questions of her daughter, but Molly and Cargo scamper off to the living room where they are soon involved in a secret word game that seems to revolve around "hello willy" and "silly willy" and ends in paroxysms of laughter.

Trouble Man

Milena

When Milena DeNunzio stopped being cautious, she stopped being scared. She just let go. She wasn't looking to have an affair with anyone, especially not a made man who worked with her husband, but when she was with Jimmy she felt a great weight lift from her shoulders, a feeling simultaneously of freedom and falling—freedom to love, freedom to choose, and the exhilaration of falling, in love, away from her strictly maintained persona, leaving her disciplined mask as, for the first time in her life, she allowed herself to take chances and lose control. She took a chance every time she met Jimmy, at Bill Kelly's place, at friends' apartments in Manhattan and Staten Island. They shared books and music, ate, made love, and talked. With Jimmy, Milena felt like she could speak openly about anything and everything. "I can't explain it," she told her sister. "It feels like coming home."

At the same time, it was precisely Jimmy's cautious approach to life, or his life within the Ruggiero family, that she recognized and cherished. She asked about his deal with Savino, knowing as she did that the Colt was officially Jimmy's capo.

"Savino offered it to me and I took it," Jimmy said. "Working for him . . . I prefer it, away from the heat."

"You're cautious."

"I guess."

"It's unusual, in your line of work," she said, thinking of Vinnie's recklessness and propensity for violence.

"I wanna stay alive. That so wrong?"

"No. I want you to stay alive. That would be nice."

In April, they met at the Museum of Modern Art. Everyone they knew was heading to Yankee Stadium. They wandered through rooms of paintings. He paused, wide-eyed in front of a painting by Léger and again when she showed him a Matisse.

"You've never been to MoMa."

"I've never been to an art museum before."

"And? What do you think?"

"Great. A lot better than I expected."

"What were you expecting?"

"I don't really know. A lot of big paintings of George Washington and his horse and kings and queens and shit."

"This is modern art, Jimmy."

"Yeah, I can see that."

They stood before an upside-down bicycle wheel attached to a barstool.

"Art," she announced.

"Must be," he said. "It sure ain't a bicycle no more."

They ate lunch in an Italian restaurant nearby. Jimmy looked very smart in a tie and dark suit. They drank expensive red wine and ate pasta and discussed the Ruggiero family and Vinnie. She wanted to say that he was dangerous, to hear herself say it, to make sure Jimmy knew the stakes. He knew.

"Anyone would tell either of us not to do this," he said.

Later, in a Midtown hotel room, Milena turned from the window to look at Jimmy and said, "I love you, Jimmy Piccini."

He looked at her and nodded. "I love you."

Afterward, they walked in Central Park. They watched a horse-drawn cart clip-clop away and took the risk of holding hands. A toddler was taking wobbly steps; joggers zigzagged past. Jimmy had his new camera and he took a few photos of her, under trees, smiling, and then she looked away, allowed herself to be caught off guard, and imagined Jimmy looking through the photos. Another risk. Photographs were dangerous currency: they were proof.

She kept thinking it was going to end, felt sure that Jimmy would phone out of the blue and tell her they couldn't keep seeing each other, or maybe she'd get scared, but neither of them said anything, and weeks became months, and they kept seeing each other, and there she was waiting in a room in the Sanderson Hotel, wearing a summer dress, bare legged and shoeless. They booked a room there every Tuesday under the name Crenshaw. (Vinnie made collections for Tony Rizzo's sports betting enterprise, always on Tuesdays because most gamblers bet on *Monday Night Football*, and he would be gone all day and spend most or all of the night at the social club in Bensonhurst.) She was early. She read a magazine on the big bed, gazed out the window at the offices across the avenue. When she got up she could see the imprint her body had left on the bed. She stayed late, but she never stayed the night. They never woke up together.

When Jimmy arrived, they kissed impatiently, then he pulled things out of plastic bags—a new Sony Discman, expensive headphones, CDs.

They kissed, and he ran his hands across her body, along her clavicle, and down to her breast. After a while he moved her back toward the bed, one lingering step at a time.

He slipped Marvin Gaye's "Trouble Man" into the Discman, held up the jewel case. "Do you know it?"

"I don't think so."

He curled the headphones over her hair and she lay back and listened and smiled. He ran a hand across her blouse, slowly. After a while, he pushed her skirt above her hips and pulled off her panties, kissing around her belly button and thighs and in between, and he didn't stop until she writhed and slithered and held her hands on the headphones, then bit her hand and wrapped her arms around him, pulling his head between her breasts.

"Oh, my fucking god," was all she said.

They lay together on the bed, and then she put the headphones on him, removed his trousers and underpants and bestowed a slow, silky blow job. When she looked up, she saw a wide, dreamy smile on his face. She could hear the music, tinny and small in the headphones.

Something in the Way She Moves

Jimmy

Savino and Jimmy ran the numbers and looked at different ways to structure the deal; they found seven banks and four legitimate businesses in Europe and the US that they could use to transfer and wash money and nine ways to transfer drugs. One of those methods they called "camouflage" and it had been devised by Jimmy and Milena in Central Park on a warm day in April when they saw Con Edison workers digging up the road. The idea was to ship the drugs inside pipes, standard sanitation pipes—used, if possible—and send them as a shipment. Once they reached their destination they would be removed by a garbage company or construction contractor, not with the rest of the ship's cargo. No value, no inspection, a guy just shows up and takes them away. They were going to try the plan with a shipment from Sicily, rerouted in Barcelona to Newark. The only real trick was the bribe in Sicily to get them on the ship, and that the Sicilian partners assured them would be easy.

Savino flew to Sicily to meet with his counterpart in the Donato family. By then he and Jimmy had a blueprint for financial hopscotch and a safe way to move eighty kilos of heroin from Italy to America. Once the money was in a European business or bank, it could be transferred to one of their accounts in Switzerland or Luxembourg. Those accounts were owned by individuals residing in Europe, individuals without any police record or official blemish, which was important because without an American attached and in the absence of any criminal complaint, the long arm of the American law couldn't touch them. Privacy provisions, God bless them.

He saw Milena every week, often at the Sanderson Hotel, but they sometimes spent the evening in Bill Kelly's apartment (Bill was happy to stay at Sabrina's place in Brooklyn), eating and talking and making love, with the Empire State Building as their witness. He felt as tall as the clouds those nights; he felt invincible. It was his highest pleasure, and it was always cut short. Each time they tidied up and were gone before midnight, and each time he watched her cab disappear down Lexington Avenue and wished he was still beside her or better yet lying in bed with her somewhere. Yet after an evening with her, the world suddenly looked bigger, better, flowers brighter, buildings more elegant, cars sleeker, and everywhere he went he thought of things that she might like—albums, movies, art. He prowled the streets of Murray Hill, Bill's neighborhood, looking for restaurants to take her to, and one day bought her a silver necklace, modest enough that she could tell anyone who asked that she bought it for herself on a whim. It had been going on nearly three years now. He dated plenty of women, slept with some of them, but the truth was there was only Milena. He was hooked, addicted, and one thing he knew about addiction: it was bad for your health.

On March 2nd, 1987, a Brink's bullet-resistant armored truck stopped near the onramp to the FDR Drive in Manhattan when a car in front collided with a mother wheeling a stroller. The driver of the truck found himself wedged between the car that hit the mother and stroller and the van behind it. He checked his rearview, honked, waited. When a pedestrian rapped agitatedly on the window, the Brink's guard riding shotgun climbed out of the cab and rushed over to the felled mother and child. The driver remained in the cab and locked the doors once his guard exited the vehicle, per Brink's standard operating procedures. As soon as the guard was out of the driver's line of vision, Vincent DeNunzio pounded him across the back of the head with a lead pipe and dragged him to the back of the van. At the same time Tony Rizzo jumped out of the van and, keeping his back to the Brink's driver, assisted the felled mother, getting her and the stroller to the sidewalk. A few minutes later the Brink's driver unlocked the door when he saw what he thought was the guard climb onto the step on the passenger side of the cab and the guard's shirt pressed against the truck window. Once inside the vehicle, Tony Rizzo drew a gun and told the driver to keep his hands on the steering wheel. *Now you got two options. You get shot and I do the driving, or you drive nice and slow exactly where I tell you.* They drove to a storefront on West Ninety-Second Street, unloaded the cash in broad daylight, then drove the truck up the Henry Hudson Drive to a parking lot where Rizzo pounded the driver's head with his gun and left him bound and gagged in the parked vehicle. The heist netted $150,000 cash, which financed the first heroin buy.

The Sicilian connection was underway.

And Jimmy Piccini was in love.

Frank Rizzo flew the first suitcase of cash to Palermo personally. Back in Brooklyn he told everyone the food was amazing but the Sicilian women all looked like grandmothers. Skinny Bugliani sampled the heroin at a checkpoint in Amsterdam before it was sewn into cushions and put on a cargo plane bound for New York. Drivers, stashers, couriers, and dealers were waiting in Boston, New York, Philly, Baltimore, Atlantic City, and as far south as Miami. With the blessing of the Gambino family and the backing of one of Europe's top drug syndicates, the Ruggieros were about to become one of the biggest heroin suppliers on the East Coast.

Atlantic City

Paul

In September of 1987 Paul Piccini and Jasper Carabine took the bus from Port Authority in New York to Atlantic City. They flashed their old US Armed Forces IDs when they checked in at the Sands Hotel, and even though the IDs were nearly a decade out of date, the manager gave them an upgrade. "We support our troops," he declared. Installed in their enormous room, they toasted each other and raised a middle finger at Uncle Sam. They took a swim in the pool, drank beers poolside, showered, changed, gambled. Paul lost some, Jasper won some. They got drunk at the bar chatting with tourists, then spent Jasper's winnings on a steak dinner.

It was still early when they finished dinner, so they strolled down the boardwalk, along the strip, stopped at the Oasis for another drink and played the slot machines, then walked home through the sultry evening. They were underneath a streetlight on the boardwalk outside the Sands Hotel, laughing and joking, when Paul noticed three greaseballs in baggy suits. One of them sidled over. The shortest of the three, he was stocky, darkly tanned, with slicked-back hair and a mile-wide smirk.

"Can I help you?" he asked.

One thing Paul knew—he didn't want to help them. A Jersey wiseguy looking for trouble.

The two guys with him, one big, one skinny, crossed their arms and looked on. They'd seen this routine before.

"You boys lose your dates?"

Paul knew the type, knew he was Italian from the way he talked, looked, and carried himself. He'd seen enough army brawls to know he was a troublemaker, a little Napoleon shit-stirrer.

"No, just taking a walk."

"Taking a walk, or were you dancing?"

"Hey, listen," Jasper said, but Paul pulled him back.

"We were walking, okay," Paul said. "We're United States Marines."

"And I'm the fucking Pope."

"We just got back from Fort Benning, Georgia. Maybe you've heard of it."

"Maybe I ain't."

"Then maybe you know my brother, Jimmy Piccini? The Ruggiero family in Brooklyn? He works for them."

And that was sufficient; the guy backed off. "Come on, Mo, we got business."

Jasper asked what that was all about when they were riding the elevator back to their room, and Paul explained that it was probably some mobster wannabe, and he'd used a few names from New York to get him off their backs.

"Walk softly and carry a big stick."

"A big dick?" Jasper said, and they laughed, not an entirely sincere laugh.

He didn't say anything more about it, but Paul was rattled. He didn't like to be singled out, and not with Jasper when they were drunk and silly. Maybe he shouldn't have used his brother's name. But it seemed the quickest way to avoid a fight that could have turned nasty in a hurry. Another drink calmed him down. They undressed and stood at the window watching the strip and the dark gray sea. They lingered there, drank another beer, and toasted each other and their futures and promised to meet again soon. Jasper was the first to move to the bed.

Afterward, after a long hot shower, they stood at the window again, passing a cigarette back and forth. Paul said there's no one like you, and Jasper said, well, there's no one like you either, and they watched the traffic lights change from red to green and back again.

The next day they ordered room service. The coffee was weak but it was coffee, and they both had hangovers, which they nursed in the shade until they felt able, then swam in the sea and ate lunch by the pool. They gambled a bit more, started drinking in the early afternoon, took in a show at the Commodore. They felt too self-conscious for drinks at the hotel bar and instead they watched a movie on the big television in their room.

"Come to New York," Paul said, without taking his eyes off the screen.

"You know I can't."

"We could move somewhere together. San Francisco?"

"I wish I could.

"You could."

Jasper squeezed Paul's hand, and then stroked his hair tenderly. They were heading back to their different worlds—Brooklyn and Oklahoma—and they knew that a year, probably more, would pass before they saw each other again. But tonight they had a big bed and a minibar and *Lethal Weapon* on the TV, and no one watching, and it was just the two of them, high above the dark sea and brightly lit boardwalk. It was enough. It wasn't enough.

Cyclones

Jimmy

On a hot Wednesday in July, Jimmy rides the Q train with Tom and the kids to Coney Island to watch the Brooklyn Cyclones play the Staten Island Yankees. It's "Summer Camp Day" and the stands are full of kids in baseball caps. They find their seats and eat hot dogs, and watch the game, and Jimmy and Tom drink cold beers while Molly and Cargo lick melting ice creams. The last time he went to Staten Island, nearly thirty years ago, he and Milena drove out to use her friend's apartment for a tryst. He finds himself wondering what happened to Milena's aunt and decides to look up her sister and Bill Kelly. Now that he's seen his own brother and what's left of the crew from before, there are only a few other people he wants to see. In lockup he would wonder what happened to so-and-so and there was never any way to find out. Now he can. He knows Sabrina married some other guy, but he always liked Kelly. Maybe they could get a beer sometime, if only so he can thank him for the use of his apartment. Jimmy spent some of the best nights of his life there.

The Streets of Atlantic City

Jimmy

You're in love with another man's woman. You try not to dwell on the downside, which is: if he finds out, you're dead. If Vinnie gets his hands on you, a slow and painful death. If one of the captains or an enforcer does it, a bullet in the back of the head. But you try to put that out of your mind. You meet at the Sanderson Hotel in Midtown. You try not to look too far into the future; just being there together is enough. You don't want to lose her.

Meanwhile, in accountants' offices and back rooms of bars and cafés, the plan to expand the Ruggiero family's nascent heroin business was coming together. It was a bold step into the future, and Armone spent days meeting with his *consiglieri* and capos. Armone listened, and the captains spoke, and then Armone and Santoro asked questions. Some of the meetings took half the day and some lasted well into the night.

The Rizzos would take care of getting the money to cover upfront costs and moving the goods. They had shipping companies and air freight deals and, thanks to Dominic "Ziti" Arcuri, they had DEA agents at Newark Port and JFK and a couple of well-positioned Customs and Border Protection officers at Newark on the take. Just in case they needed friends down the line. People said they couldn't be bought. Ziti said everyone had his price. Banks and stooges were standing by, and now the only remaining issue was domestic—how to avoid turf wars. To figure it out, Santoro and Savino met with families up and down the East coast. "Alliances and dispensations," DeSapio called them. The key to it all was a pact with John Gotti and Vincent "The Chin" Gigante: they would split the heroin trade. Dealers might squabble and there may even be turf wars, but they agreed to keep those down the ladder. Gambinos, Lucianos, and Ruggieros would not go to war over drugs. Any problems, it went up the chain of command. Armone himself took it to Gotti, who had just returned from his vacation in Florida. The Teflon Don liked the idea. He took pride in the peace that existed among the families and the prosperity that it had brought. "Nobody needs to get greedy. And we all get rich." Once Gotti was in, Gigante was easy to convince. They sent a group of captains from all three families to speak to "Machine Gun" Johnny Eng and his gang, the Flying Dragons. In a secret meeting, they gave the Flying Dragons the Chinatown drug trade with one condition: the borders were fixed. Johnny Eng agreed, and Italians shook hands with Chinese mobsters. There was one other requirement: the Ruggieros would be the ones to take care of Philly and Atlantic City.

In August of 1990, Vinnie beat up a Russian gang leader trying to muscle in on the Rizzos' turf around Gravesend Park. Left the guy unconscious on the sidewalk, told his boys to stay gone. When the guy died from his injuries, Vinnie flew to Jamaica for a week until things calmed down, and Milena went away as well, ostensibly to stay with Sherri White, a childhood friend who had moved to New Jersey. Milena did see her friend but only for an hour. She spent the rest of the week with Jimmy, on the top floor of the Hilton in Short Hills. They swam in the hotel pool and drank margaritas. The first night they ordered room service, and talked, made love, then watched movies and fell asleep entwined. The second night they took a car all the way to Harlem to see a soul singer at Londels. Back in their New Jersey hotel room, they stood naked at the window, Jimmy's arms wrapped around her, and looked out at the empty shopping mall parking deck, forlorn and yellow. Two nights in a row, they fell asleep together, and two languorous mornings woke up side by side. They were having breakfast, in the glassed-in hotel restaurant, overlooking the swimming pool, when she said, "If I could leave him, I would."

Her words echoed in his head and he spent sleepless nights wondering if there might be a way out, an escape hatch. The next few days he did little else but think about it, occasionally jotting down notes in cryptic shorthand. They'd been sneaking around for years, but they both knew it couldn't go on forever. All it would take was a single slip, something to alert Vinnie's suspicions, then he could have someone follow Milena, and it would all be over. In the life, there were rules, and this was one of them: you don't steal a made man's wife.

Plan A: Wait it out. He'd become a captain, work with Savino, and eventually replace Savino. The numbers man, he'd keep a low profile, get an apartment somewhere nobody would find them, and Milena would meet him there some nights. Maybe she'd leave Vinnie and move to Florida. Maybe Jimmy would already have business dealings in Florida, a different city, of course. They'd be close, but they wouldn't be together all the time, except when they traveled.

Plan B: Disappear. Clean break, another country. Siphon some of the European drug money from Amsterdam or Geneva, not a lot, just enough to get them set up somewhere. Go to Mexico or Canada under fake passports. In Canada, he might have a better chance of making money. He could probably buy his way into a decent job and work his way up, get some experience, then get his business degree and find work, go legit. That, at any rate, was his plan, to become an accountant or stockbroker. He could live with that if he lived with her. He liked the idea of Vancouver, because it was on the water.

Their last night together in New Jersey, Jimmy initiated the conversation. They were eating dinner in the hotel restaurant.

"Let's just say we wanted to spend more than a weekend together."

"Okay, let's just say."

And he laid out the options. She mostly nodded and said, "I know," when he mentioned a difficulty, like obtaining fake passports or washing mob money. Had she considered it all herself? He sure hoped so. He couldn't tell from her expression while he was talking. She looked at him intently and chewed her lower lip.

"I could do that," she said at last. She said they could disappear, live under fake passports, and they talked about Mexico and Italy and Vancouver. They let themselves dream aloud about Mexico, scuba diving and yachts, grilled shrimp, sunsets on the beach. When they parted that afternoon, Jimmy felt a sudden rush of joy, as if they'd just discussed marriage, which in a way they had.

Two things stood in the way of the pact with the Gambinos and Lucianos: Philadelphia and Atlantic City. In Philly the Lampone family had been flexing muscle they didn't have. The Lampones had gotten into drugs a while back, and now they had the *cojones* to tell everyone else to stay away. Which was crazy, because that wasn't how things worked. You didn't announce to the other *borgatas* a venture of that magnitude. You asked, you consulted. Not the Lampones. They announced that they were running a network of dealers and, furthermore, Southern New Jersey and Philly were their territory.

Jimmy took the train with Savino and Santoro to the City of Brotherly Love to meet with Tommy "Double T" Capeci, head of the Lampone family, a silver-haired dandy in his mid-sixties, with gold rings and a jovial manner. The meeting, held in the back room of a South Street restaurant, was respectful enough, but when Santoro said times were changing and it was up to all of them to come up with a plan to run drugs without stepping on each other's toes, Tommy "Double T" Capeci frowned and shook his head.

Santoro barreled ahead, outlining the major points of the plan: cheaper heroin, delivered to Newark, district sharing. "Margins would go up," he said, "plus this way's safer for everyone."

Two of Capeci's big men whispered to each other, eyebrows raised. You could tell they didn't like anything Santoro was saying. Stupid meatheads, Jimmy thought. Why was "safe" a bad word? What was wrong with talking about their business like it was a business?

"We may not like it, but the only way we can make this thing work is if we work together," Santoro said. "We want profits not wars. And let me remind you, we have a powerful enemy in common, the Feds. We want a bounty on the heads of narcs who make convictions from Maine to Miami."

"I got Newark and highways," Double T said, leaning back and shaking two fingers, like he was chasing off a fly.

"Let me walk you through my projections," Savino said.

This, Jimmy knew, was not the right way to talk Capeci into it. These kinds of guys responded to two things: power and bribes. They lacked vision.

He was not surprised that before Savino could continue, Capeci pulled a face, like he'd just swallowed something sour.

"You're a businessman," Savino said.

"I am."

"Well, and with all due respect, this is a good deal for everyone."

"With all due respect, your boss didn't even come down in person. But you can tell him we don't need no deals. Plenty of room for you in New York. You don't gotta get greedy."

Santoro knew not to say anything further. They shook hands and left abruptly. It was only when they were installed in a booth at Pat's Steaks that Santoro banged the table and said, "That stupid fuck," and nothing further was said about the meeting.

Back in New York, Gotti, Lombardi, and Armone and their *consiglieri* held a secret meeting and decided what had to be done. One hit. They clip the head of the family, Tommy "Double T" Capeci. But the only way you could whack a boss was if a lot of other bosses approved the hit. Privately Armone and Gotti discussed who would take care of Philadelphia, and both thought it best to honor the agreement: the Ruggieros would deal with Philadelphia, as agreed. So it was decided.

In Washington, DC, they met the black gang that controlled the lion's share of the drugs sold in the city. When he was introduced to Riley Davis, the presumptive leader, Jimmy mentioned that his name was the same as B. B. King's given name. "How do you know that," Riley asked, and Jimmy explained that his father was a bus driver and one of his buddies was a big blues fan.

"Your dad's buddy, he a black dude?"

"Yes."

"That's cool."

It wasn't true of course. He and Milena had read the liner notes of a B. B. King album, but he knew it would sound good, and sure enough Riley Davis relaxed and got down to business.

"Okay, let's make this thing happen," he said. "How much you gonna drop? And can you guarantee the price?"

They went over details, and when they had a verbal agreement, Riley made a point of saying good-bye to Jimmy and told him to send his best to his pops.

Then there was Atlantic City. Which was what Savino called a "nuisance." The Rossi family worked the casinos. They held after-hours poker games, put the squeeze on anyone hotels needed squeezed—gamblers, drunks, crooked cops, suppliers. They also ran booze and drugs. Because Atlantic City was a lucrative market and because the agreement with Gotti gave the Ruggieros rights to the gambling town, it was important to get the nuisance out of the way.

The Rossis weren't even a family. They were just two brothers and a few guys. Not a lot of muscle, and at the end of the day they knew they couldn't stand up to the Gambino and Ruggiero alliance. The problem was Joey Rossi and, especially, his brother Little Mikey: they were crazy and they were killers. They'd been given free rein in Atlantic City by Nicky Scarfo himself, probably because they did some dirty work for him, which meant they had the blessing of the Genovose family. Rumor had it Little Mikey once killed a guy because he called him short. Anyway the Ruggieros would have to come to an understanding with the Rossi brothers. You didn't take a shit in AC without telling them first. Savino said, "You be the *messaggero*. Go and talk to Little Mikey. We're not going to war with the Rossis and we're not going to look weak to the Gambinos, not over a few junkies in Atlantic City."

Philly was a different matter. A boss was gonna get iced, and that kind of job had to be done right. They could have used their own enforcer, Molinara, who walked with a limp, owned a farm in Connecticut, and was, some said, richer than the head of the family. Behind his back some called him *Melanzane*, referring to his skin color. But Molinara was known to the Gambinos and quite possibly the Capecis knew or would recognize him too, so he was not the right guy for the job. As the saying went, always use an outsider to do an inside job. It was decided that Jimmy Piccini manage the hit. An outside professional managed by an insider who wanted to make captain one day.

Jimmy hated the idea. Didn't say anything when Santoro put it to him, but met with Savino, who told him what he already knew: they weren't asking. So Jimmy went to Philly. To scope it out, make a plan. A good plan. He sure as shit didn't want to be connected to anything like a mob murder. He knew how Savino would handle it: research and plan and plan some more. The good news was: this wasn't a hit designed to send a message, didn't have to be loud or newsworthy. This was a hit designed only to get a man dead and out of the way. Jimmy stayed a week, talked to people Savino and the Rizzos knew and trusted. They introduced him to a skinny guy called Stein. They met in a pizza joint near the Delaware River. Stein had a mottled nose that looked like some kind of cheese, dressed like a funeral director, charged a small fortune for his services, and told Jimmy he'd never failed, not once. Everyone knew he was the guy that whacked a top guy in the Colombo family. Back in New York, Jimmy went through it all with Armone, Santoro, and Savino. Armone said it sounded like a good plan. Savino gave him cash to pay Stein. It was a good plan, and Stein was one of the best in the business. Still Jimmy was nervous. This was a boss, not some stupid mortadella caught skimming, not your average barrel job. The Ruggieros' crooked judges and cops could work miracles, but they couldn't work a murder rap.

On a cool bright day in September he met Milena at the Metropolitan Museum of Art. Despite the beautiful weather and hushed grandeur of the museum, Jimmy couldn't stop his mind from going over Philadelphia and all the moving pieces. He was anxious, waking in the middle of the night, unable to concentrate by day. ("What's with you?" Lee-Ann had asked in the middle of dinner. "Leave it alone, okay." What could he tell her?) What could he tell Milena? So he stood beside her and followed her past marble sphinxes and fox-like animals and hieroglyphs, and after a while Milena's interest and awe became his and he found himself becoming immersed in the art of ancient worlds, imagining kings and pharaohs.

"I thought they just built the pyramids." They were in the tomb of Perneb, looking at a limestone lion.

"What do you think they put inside the pyramids?"

"I dunno. Dead people."

"Yeah, and sculptures and stuff."

"I guess there was a lot of space to fill."

Their favorite pieces were the sculptures they passed on their way out of the museum. One in particular caught their eye—a beautiful kneeling woman called Fragelina, by an Italian artist.

"She's gorgeous," Milena said. "You want to touch her."

"You're more beautiful," Jimmy said, because she was.

Then he went to Atlantic City. He stayed at the Sands, got there early enough to have lunch and a swim. Made a hundred bucks on blackjack before four o'clock and lost two hundred at the roulette tables. He took a quick walk to get some fresh air and take in the sea and sky.

He met Mikey Rossi at the bar. Two goons patted Jimmy down before they took their seats.

He was a small man, Rossi—no surprise there—with a crooked nose that had met its share of fists, a big jaw, and darting eyes. Alert as a bantamweight stepping into the ring.

"I met your brother," was the first thing Little Mikey said.

"You mean Savino? He's not—"

"No, I mean your brother. Paul, right."

"That's right."

"He was here."

"In Atlantic City?"

"No, on fucking Mars. Yeah, he was here. Siddown. What can I get you?"

"Bourbon, rocks."

"Beansy, get this man a drink. What are you, deaf? Go. Yeah, with another guy. Practically kissing. Made me sick." Rossi waved his nubby fingers in front of his face for effect.

"I think you've got it wrong. US Marine brother. I know his girlfriend."

"Yeah, he said he was a marine. I was going to pop those *fanooks*."

Eventually they got down to business. Jimmy said: you don't want to fight us on this. Mikey laughed. Me, I don't like to fight anyone. Good, Jimmy said, not laughing. That would be nuts.

Jimmy scratched his head, rolled the ice cubes around in his glass.

"Okay, I'm listening," Mikey said. "What do you want?"

"The question is: what do you want, Mikey? Here's a couple of ideas. First, you keep Atlantic City, all of it. Sell all the heroin you want. But you buy from us. Exclusively. Same price you can get elsewhere, and we'll be more reliable."

"Or?"

"Or we divide by casinos. You get half, we get half. We get the boardwalk and boats. You get the inland neighborhoods and buy from whoever you want but not us, not any of the New York families."

"Or?"

"Or nothing. Or there's no deal and you take your chances. I don't like your chances, but up to you."

"I always like my chances."

"Not this time. You don't want to tussle with Gotti and Armone. Stay in your box, Mikey." He stood up to leave. "I gotta meet someone for dinner. I'm staying in the hotel, so you leave me a message. Let me know what you wanna do."

They shook hands and Jimmy left. He didn't like Mikey, didn't like the stuff he'd said about his brother, his cocky belligerence or lack of respect. Years later he would wonder if there were signs he'd missed. Did Mikey give any indication that he was a traitor, that he was weighing his options, possibly already talking to the Feds? Any tell that could have alerted Jimmy to actions Mikey would soon take that would be Jimmy's downfall and the downfall of Armone and the Ruggiero family as they knew it? When had he turned? Was he wearing a wire that day? Jimmy would mull those questions over in prison for many years. He never reached any satisfactory answers.

He went for a walk, back to the lobby, checked out the swimming pool. Lots of drinkers, no swimmers. When he returned to the smoke-filled bar, Mikey was holding court with the two fools still at his side, Mo and Cannellini. And they did look like two beans, a bear-sized cannellini and a string bean. Stupid punks in their leather jackets. Jimmy didn't stop at the bar to say good-bye.

Finding Mikey

Jimmy

Melvyn Zelniker has planted three hidden cameras: one in the bushes outside Beans's house, another on the porch of Mo's house, and the third in the lobby of Mike Rossi's mother's apartment building, inside a hollowed-out Glade plug-in air freshener. He's scanned the footage from his cameras and run CCTV footage through a software program that compares faces against the age progression composite. He's checked travel records. There's no Rossi coming in and out of airports, train stations, or bus depots within a hundred miles of Atlantic City. Not that he was expecting a guy in witness protection to use his old name.

"Anything at all?" Jimmy asks.

"Nothing."

Jimmy thanks him and pays what seems like an exorbitant sum.

He meets Bobby in a bar in Kensington. "You think Little Mikey wants to come back East?"

"Who knows, Jimmy."

"If he wanted to kill me, or talk to me, he coulda done either one while I was in the can, a whole lot easier."

"He ain't here for you."

"Yeah. You're probably right. Let sleeping dogs lie."

There's no evidence that Mike Rossi wants anything to do with Jimmy or anyone else in the Ruggiero family. In fact, he probably wants to stay as far away as possible from Jimmy or anyone with any connection to the men he helped put away. But knowing that Mikey knows Jimmy's whereabouts and has been back to Atlantic City and New York rankles Jimmy. And then there is the urge he has to kill the lousy prick. But it's hard to imagine a scenario where he kills Rossi and doesn't get arrested.

Jimmy starts sleeping with a gun under his pillow.

No Way Out

Milena

She worked out a plan. It was simple really, like owning a franchise. Set up a guy as a small dealer, someone local and friendly, who plays by the rules. He buys from some of the big dealers, and when they trust him, he comes to them with an offer. The stooge gets rich; the big guys get a cheap reliable supply, but more importantly Vinnie has a sales channel and the operation flies under the Ruggiero radar. Vinnie knew plenty of people, good trustworthy *cugines*. It was "morning in America," according to the politicians, but a lot of guys couldn't find work. Vinnie said he'd think about it, and maybe because it was her idea, or because he didn't like the idea of some two-bit dealer being able to strong-arm him, or because he was greedy and didn't want to make some two-bit dealer rich—she never found out why—he told her no.

Things got worse. It happened one evening when she said she didn't want to go out with Vinnie and some of the younger guys.

"I don't feel like it."

"What the fuck?" Vincent said. "You don't feel like it?"

"What's the big deal? You go."

That's when he hit her. She heard it before she felt it, a loud snapping sound, then her chin and jaw shot with pain. She was in her bathrobe, and after he slapped her across the face he pulled off her robe and threw her onto the bed, pulling her arms behind her back, and then jamming his elbow across her throat until she gagged. He gouged her breasts with his fingers; they cut into her like knives. She was trying to get out from under him when he pulled back, let out a snort, and walked out of the room. He left her there, curled up on the bed, crying, half naked. She prayed that she'd hear the sound of the door, but the only sounds she heard were the TV and the clink of ice in a highball glass. Half an hour later, dressed, drugged, and detached, she descended the stairs and they got into the car and drove to Manhattan. "Don't make me lose my temper, doll," was all he said, looking out the window as they crossed the Brooklyn Bridge.

A few days later he brought her a necklace. She said thank you, but not effusively. The necklace didn't change anything. She couldn't be bought, and she couldn't help reevaluating the man she'd married. Vinnie was a selfish lover; he had no tact, no art, no soul. He wasn't smart or kind or funny. Sure, he was handsome enough and he was charismatic, the way Mafioso motormouths are charismatic, and when she'd been young and poor and scared, he'd appeared on the scene like a knight in shining armor, rich and reliable. And that was what she needed. Then. Now she needed something entirely different, someone entirely different.

She didn't say anything to Jimmy. The only person she told was Sabrina, and at first her sister laughed because Milena imitated her husband, mimicked his accent and way of talking, his short-stepped walk, the way he raised a soft fist and feinted a jab when he made a joke or finished telling a story. Sabrina laughed and then she gave her little sister a warm hug, but she didn't seem as shocked as Milena that he'd hit her, or that he ignored her. Walking home from dinner, Milena told her sister they could pull off her plan themselves.

"What? Us?"

"Sure. Finance a small-time dealer, buy drugs that he then sells to the bigger dealers. I know the guys to go to. All we need is a bit of seed capital."

"Listen to you," Sabrina said. "Seed capital. And where you gonna get that?"

"I don't know. We probably have enough in savings."

"Oh, now it's we?"

"No, not necessarily. I could ask Jimmy."

"Why?"

"Why what?"

"Why do you want to start a drug ring behind your husband's back?"

"Money in the bank, that's why. My own money. In case anything happens to Vinnie, or I need it. Remember what happened when Papa died?"

"Listen to me, Mili, don't play with fire. You're talking about a guy who hit you because you didn't want to go out one night. What do you think he'll do if he finds out you forgot to tell him you started a drug ring? He'll go apeshit."

"Okay, okay," she agreed. "I won't."

The following weeks Vinnie stayed out most nights, and she went out with her sister and girlfriends more often, and sometimes that was just an excuse to see Jimmy.

Milena talked to Donatella, Tony Rizzo's wife. They'd grown quite close. She trusted Donatella, could confide in her. But more than trusting her discretion, she trusted her wisdom.

"He won't do it again," Donatella said. "And if he does, you leave. Walk out of that house. Come and stay with us, check into a hotel, doesn't matter. That's how they are, our guys. We can't change them, but we can make sure they don't bring it into our house."

"I don't love him."

"What's love got to do with it? Remember Rosalie Sutti? Her husband, Richie, cut off her pinkie in a fit of jealousy. He'd seen it on TV, a Japanese Yakuza tradition. He didn't take her to a hospital, not for a while anyway. Gave her amaro, and she sat drinking, holding the glass in her bloody hand. Later, with the guys, Richie joked that was one less finger he'd have to buy a ring for. The truth was she never did nothing, just talked to some man."

"Jesus. She stayed with him? After he cut off her finger?"

"Where was she gonna go? The guys made fun of him, called him 'Pinkie' to his face. He bought her a fur coat. They're still married."

"Donatella," Milena said, "how's that going to make me feel better?"

Donatella laughed and then Milena laughed and they clinked glasses.

"Listen, Rosalie was unlucky and Richie's a psycho. But we all have to put up with some shit. We just don't let it happen again is my point."

"It's funny," Milena said. "Or not funny. I got married because I wanted to be free. Now all I feel is trapped."

"Sister, you're not trapped. Love the one you're with. Love the life you've got. You can do anything. You can buy a lot of things, drive a nice car, you can go on all kinds of holidays. If you want to go on a yacht, you make him take you on a yacht. A big one. Drugs, clothes, maids in your kitchen, a nanny for your kids, fun, even men, discreetly, very discreetly. Only one thing you can't do: leave. There's no divorce and there's no way out, except in a casket."

Anyway, Anyhow, Anywhere

Jimmy

He made a list in a dollar-store notebook and he's crossed off just about every item. A few people left to visit, a few old scores to settle, some unlikely money to chase down. It's the one thing he didn't predict, the odd feeling of having nothing you have to do, nowhere to be. In the joint, you can't do anything and you dream of doing everything and it drives you crazy. Outside, you can do anything, but you end up just sitting around most of the time, wondering what it was you were in such a hurry to do out in the world. Maybe it's because you've stopped dreaming, and you need to learn how to dream in order to learn how to live again. *You gotta have plans,* Lou Perkins used to say. *Plans keep you alive.* But Lou had kids and Lou was one optimistic son of a bitch, and Jimmy was never one for prison yard philosophizing.

On the outside, everything is too loose—too much time, too much freedom. It's all just a bit overwhelming. *Anyway, anyhow, anywhere I choose.* You can walk, you can sit in the sun, you can drink a cold beer at your own pace and nobody tells you what to do, when to eat, when to piss. He's walked the streets of Brooklyn, seen young lovers kissing, men holding hands, families eating dinner together, a man on a unicycle, Rollerbladers and cute girls on bicycles; he's seen a man walking with a snake around his neck, people playing soccer and Frisbee in the park, girls wearing hardly anything at all, people playing guitar, a woman playing a sitar. He's seen his old apartment block and the building on Bedford Street where Savino had his office. He's had dinner with Paulie a couple of times, talked about old times, talked about Paulie's plans, which include catering and moving to New Jersey. About the only people left to see are Sabrina, Milena's sister, and her old beau Bill Kelly.

An evening at home. He watches a talent show on TV. The first contestant is a young Indian guy, dressed in those cotton pajamas Indian men sometimes wear. He sings a love song, complete with a falsetto. There's a young woman with a chin full of acne, a bleached blonde teenage girl from Delaware. She can really sing, raps in the middle of the song too. After a while he turns off the TV, pours himself a bourbon on the rocks, and plays one of his new CDs. Sits outside with his drink and the music playing quietly behind him. Roberto Murolo's melancholy love songs make him think of his father and of Milena, the woman who loved him who can no longer love him. He wishes he could talk about her, to reminisce, let his memories out. That's why he wants to see Sabrina. Bobby said he can get in touch with her. There is the fading light and the smell of hot ripe leaves and Renato Carosone crooning quietly from the boombox. *Quanno 'o cielo è scuro, primma me dice sí, po' doce doce mme faje murí.* When the sky is dark, first you tell me yes, then softly you let me die.

He hopes Paulie is happy. He wonders if he is. Jimmy wants to be happy too. The time for repentance is past. The thirty-four-year-old Jimmy would have wanted vengeance, but the fifty-eight-year-old Jimmy just wants to enjoy his freedom, to live his life. He doesn't want to be rich or famous or fuck a lot of women or be the most popular guy in the neighborhood. He wants only happiness and maybe a bit of security, but he's not sure where to find happiness or even if he'll recognize it when he does. It's been so long.

And what about Little Mikey? Most likely the little prick just wants to come back to see family or the so-called crew he used to run. Jimmy's been out three weeks and a day, and nothing has happened. He tells himself that Mikey has done all the damage

Mikey is going to do. And yet he worries. Worries that one day he'll look up and some big guy in a black suit will be pointing a gun at his head and that's the last thing he'll ever see. He knows that if someone wanted him dead, they had twenty-five years to get the job done, and it's a whole lot easier to ice someone in the can than back in Brooklyn. But that's the thing about Mikey: he's a crazy fuck, always has been. No reason that would change. Maybe he didn't know Jimmy was getting out. Maybe that throws a wrench in the works for Mikey, just when he's getting used to hanging out with his old crew and visiting his ma. He knows people who know people, and he's got the money to pay a window painter. He wouldn't have to get his hands dirty. Is it possible that Jimmy got out just in time to get shot or shivved in Brooklyn, in broad daylight? That's not something he can tolerate. It's not about revenge; he may need insurance. Kill Mikey before Mikey strikes: eliminate the problem.

Blood and Summer

Molly

Last week they made breadboards, and today they're making flowers from wire and beads to take home to their mommies and daddies. Her summer day camp is not the same camp Cargo goes to. He does swimming and sometimes art-cherry which is bows and arrows, and later in the summer they'll both go with Mom to visit Grandma and Grampa in North Carolina, but that's later.

One day she's running in the playground after lunch with her friend Melissa and she trips and falls, hits her chin and lip and even before she gets up she knows it's bleeding, and she is trying to be brave but she can't help crying. The girls call the counselor and the counselor calls one of the grown-ups and they carry her inside and she lies down and someone gets water and bandages, and the nicest counselor, Georgina, stays with her and holds her hand. They call her mom, but her mom is in the city and her dad is far away somewhere at a meeting, so it's Jimmy who comes to get her. They say Jimmy's her uncle even though he's really not her uncle.

They start walking home, but she feels sore and tired. Everything is still ouchy and it's hot and bright and the sky hurts her eyes. Jimmy asks, "Are you okay?" And she tries to tell him what happened and then she starts crying again. "Do you want me to carry you?" She looks up and nods, and then he picks her up and she's glad he does. At the puppy store, she says, "Can we stop and look?" And he says yes and they go inside and look at the puppies rolling and sleeping in their newspaper rooms. Mom never lets them go in the shop, but here they are, and they let her pet a little brown puppy, soft and warm with a hot wet mouth that wants to kiss her. She wants to take that puppy home but she knows she can't ask Jimmy. Like he knows what she's wishing, Jimmy says, "If your mom and dad say okay, I'll buy you a puppy." "Really?" "And help you walk it and train it too." "Thanks, Mister Jimmy." They stop at the corner deli and Jimmy says, "You can have anything you want," and she picks an ice cream and a candy bar and then she feels bad so she picks a candy bar for Cargo too. Almond Joy, his favorite. They sit on the bench in front of the store, and she eats the ice cream, and it makes her feel better, and she looks up at Jimmy and she can see that she's left a bit of snot and blood on the shoulder of his shirt and she hopes he's not going to be mad at her. It's not really her fault. He smiles. "Feeling a bit better?"

Killer Clowns Take Yosemite

Milena

Ice Cream Man came in on time and on budget, and was picked up by distributors. Vinnie and Milena watched the video, stoned, laughing. "About as scary as *The Karate Kid*," Vinnie scoffed. But they'd made a good return on their investment, and put money into Jake Cristal's next slasher movie, *Killer Clowns Take Yosemite*. In the end, they didn't go to LA for the filming. Vinnie was too busy and Milena wasn't enamored of the role—a tourist who gets killed in a canvas tent. Essentially she'd be playing a corpse. They'd make a nice return and take clean money when the payout came— and that was the primary objective. Cristal promised her a role in his next movie, an action film. She'd play the love interest of the reluctant war hero. At Milena's urging, Vinnie brought the idea to Rizzo and DeSapio, who complimented him for devising a smart way to launder money and make a good investment at the same time. Once again Vinnie got all the credit for Milena's brainchild, but that was okay. It made him trust her. He bought her flowers, took her for dinner at Rao's, and over candlelit clams told her let's make some babies. She smiled and said, yes, but didn't stop taking the pill.

When Vinnie went to Atlantic City for a few days with the Rizzo brothers, she told him she was going to visit her sister, Maria, on Long Island, but instead drove with Jimmy to a bed-and-breakfast in Massachusetts. It was early fall, leaves just starting to take on colors, splashing fire and bronze over the trees. They walked, talked, took in the shops on the quaint main street, made love on the creaky poster bed with the windows open to the sky and mountains. She told him about Jake Cristal and their B-movie investment scheme. He was impressed. He asked if she'd ever seen *Casablanca*. She hadn't, and he promised to rent it so they could watch it together.

The following day they took a picnic hamper and a blanket to the state park and found a secluded spot at the bottom of a grassy hill. They lounged in the warming sun. Occasionally a car drove past on the road above. Birds flapped around the treetops. Jimmy had brought a couple of tabs of Ecstasy and they washed them down with champagne. At first they both thought the drug wasn't working, and that was okay because they had booze and food and the weather was fine, and she lay her head on Jimmy's chest and smelled him and saw the trees and sky around him, a halo of leaves and sky around his hair. The trees and the branches looked alive, glowing with color and very beautiful against the sky, and when she looked over at Jimmy his eyes were soft and sparkling and he grinned down at her and they both started giggling.

"This is cool," he said, and his voice sounded like it was coming from the bottom of a big tin can. *Cooooool.*

"Very." Her own voice sounded strange too, rubbery. *Virrry.*

"Everything looks different."

They wrapped their arms around each other, and lay there, wide-eyed, taking in the bright green grass and the swimming sky. After a while, they stood up, shook their legs out, and shared a sandwich. They left their blanket and hamper and went for a walk. There was a stream at the bottom of the hill. Jimmy extolled the benefits of the drug—a new way of seeing, making the familiar more beautiful, heightened feelings, even more in love. She thought, for some reason, of her father and how he would have liked this man. The trees were majestic, the stream a splendor of light and movement, and Jimmy's arms felt just right around her, and she wanted this moment, this ecstatic beauty, to last forever.

They talked late into the night. Through the windows of their B&B room they could see swaying branches and a sky splashed with stars. They talked about the country, the calm and quiet.

"If we went to Vancouver, every night would be like this."

"I don't think Vancouver looks like Massachusetts," Jimmy said, but he squeezed her hand.

"Well, they've got a lot of parks and forests in British Columbia," she said. "It's really pretty there."

"Can you ski?"

She shook her head.

"We can learn."

After a while they stopped talking; he kissed her and she pulled him close and they lay together entwined, gazing at the star-speckled sky.

Tom DeSapio's Blues

Tom

He'd never understood the buildings his dad had accrued. He couldn't have bought them as an earnest attempt to amass real estate wealth or leave his heir profitable properties around New York. Nor did he come to them by lineage or gambling. His parents died penniless, and Savino didn't gamble. The only plausible explanation was that he took them from losers who owed the mob money and couldn't pay, possibly kicking the owners out on the street. A small garden apartment in Kensington, a row house in Sunset Park, a walk-up in Bushwick, a warehouse in Williamsburg. Savino had amassed a curious real estate portfolio, and Tom had done the best he could with the walk-up, selling it and the garden apartment, and used the proceeds to buy the building in Red Hook. He lived in the Sunset Park row house (surely not what his dad had intended), and rented out the warehouse by the floor, but the money wasn't very good. Nobody needed warehouses anymore, and Tom had been trying since before Molly was born to get the building zoned for residential or mixed-use. He'd applied three times and three times been rejected, while a block or two away similar buildings went residential. He'd found someone who said he could get it done, and they formed a partnership and although the guy got no further than Tom had with the labyrinthine departments of zoning and housing, he managed to spend every penny of the few thousand dollars in the joint account. Tom went to a lawyer, but he went too late. Story of his life: too little, too late, smart in hindsight.

He'd had offers on the warehouse but they'd all been low, and he doesn't want to sell only to see his building blossom into a hipster apartment block in the hands of some asshole real estate *cognoscenti*. If the building were zoned residential, the price would be three, four times what he'd been offered, and then maybe he'd sell. But until that happens, if that ever happens, the building remains a reminder of another glorious invisible world, of which he is preternaturally deprived.

They're drinking espressos in the kitchen, Jimmy savoring each sip like it's the best coffee he's ever tasted. Molly is in the den, watching cartoons and drinking milk, blood on her knees, a bandage on her chin. All bets are off; she could have a meltdown any minute or just fall asleep. He's thanked Jimmy, and Jimmy has said it was nothing. Now they're drinking a coffee together and Tom is confessing the blues.

"There was a squat down the block, a real shithole, and guess what?"

"What?"

"They got the variance."

He wouldn't have told Jimmy all of this had it not been for the thing with Molly. Jimmy helped his little girl, picked her up when she fell at day camp, and carried her home. Maybe that's what his dad had seen in this guy all those years ago, someone you could rely on, someone who would help when there was blood and tears, someone you could trust with your daughter. But try telling Cath that.

Jimmy drains the last drop of coffee. "Maybe it's just luck."

"It's not luck."

"What then?"

"Knowing which lever to pull or palm to grease. Another coffee?"

Woh, Mexico, It Sounds So Sweet with the Sun Sinking Low

Jimmy

Moving ill-gained money was as likely to get you pinched as coming by it in the first place. In order to wash American money and pay for large quantities of drugs, they were buying into legitimate businesses in Europe and making use of offshore bank accounts from Switzerland to Luxembourg. The legitimate companies they used to move money would pay capital gains tax, but they could get a foreign tax credit on European investments. Finally all the pieces were coming together, but for fee agreements and on-the-ground logistics.

At Vinnie's house, an informal council of younger guys talked about those logistics—moving heroin shipments from docks and airport freight centers to warehouses and from there to the network of buyers, middlemen, and trusted dealers. "Ziti" Arcuri had brought a map, and they wrote names over different parts of Manhattan, Brooklyn, Harlem.

"What about Atlantic City?" asked "Skinny" Bugliani, a captain and the oldest person in the room.

"Yeah, we got a little road bump," Vinnie said. "We gotta take care of Little Mikey."

"That little prick," someone said.

"Fuck him," came another voice.

"No," Jimmy insisted. "We don't want a war."

"Fuck him and his mother," Vinnie said, and everyone laughed, even Jimmy.

"Big picture," Jimmy said. "We want contracts. We need Atlantic City."

"AC needs us," Arcuri said.

"Little Mikey's a punk. No respect."

"Jimmy's right," Skinny spoke at last. "Armone doesn't want a war, even a small one. Okay? Good. Now, let's talk about Rocco Russolo's book of business."

Russolo was retiring, moving to Florida, and Skinny was going to divide up his contracts between the younger guys.

Milena was there. It was strange seeing her coming out of the kitchen with a plate of biscotti, seeing her as another man's woman.

"You look nice tonight." He leaned in as he took a cookie, quickly, just enough to smell her.

"Thank you, Jimmy."

He couldn't concentrate after that. He wanted to be with her, alone, not here with these idiots.

Jimmy was the first to leave. He made some excuse about meeting someone in the city.

"Who can be more important?" someone asked.

"Some guy DeSapio wants me to meet. Runs a trucking company."

"Or are you going to meet your *goomah*?"

"Actually, I'm going to meet your *goomah*," Jimmy said, pulling on his leather jacket.

Seeing her, but not being able to touch her or even talk to her, made him weak with yearning, and he staggered home. She was the wife of another made man, and when he thought of Vinnie touching her, having sex with her, he felt physical pain, a knife in his heart and in his groin.

The pain continued another three days, until they were able to spend an afternoon together at the Sanderson Hotel. She sat on the bed to remove her shoes and he buried his head in her hair and kissed her neck. The smell and touch and taste of her was like a drug.

"Was it weird being in my house the other day?"

"Yeah. Of course. I don't like being reminded that you're married, that Vinnie's your husband."

"Okay."

"Okay, what?"

"Just making sure. I didn't like it either. Seeing you and not being able to kiss you."

"You can kiss me now," he said, and she did.

He unbuttoned her blouse. Her neck smelled like some kind of exotic fruit—pear and jasmine. She stood up and they removed the rest of their clothes, and her legs were silky and hot, and they fell onto the bed, her legs wrapped around him, his heart pounding, his body aching for her. She was grace; she was a gift from God, divine.

They had unhurried sex, whispering and moaning, rolling around the soft bed, with the hotel radio bestowing WFUV jazz on their slice of heaven.

Afterward they went downstairs for coffee and cake. She'd said she'd go anywhere with him, that night in Massachusetts, and that made him think differently, plan differently. He imagined a future with her. He couldn't imagine one without her. He'd played out all the scenarios in his head. Could he funnel some money? Yes. A lot of money? Possibly. Or could he get out with Armone's blessing? Not likely. Not if he knew about Milena. No, if they wanted to be together, they'd have to disappear somewhere no one could find them. They could run a hotel on the beach maybe. He pictured them checking in guests, walking on the beach, a dog lapping at their heels, or maybe children.

They talked about when they would meet again, and her mother's health problems. She was having chest pains, and Milena was taking her to a doctor the next day. They looked out across Lexington Avenue—office workers hunched at desks under fluorescent lights. She stroked his shoulder and ran her hand along his arm and whispered, "Mexico."

Zeppole to Nachos

Jimmy

Maybe he was trying to make a deal with the Gambinos, maybe he was trying to go it alone, independent of the five families, or maybe he was simply holding out for more. Whatever his reason, Little Mike Rossi wouldn't make a deal.

"I need you to make a decision," Jimmy told him. Ever cautious, he'd made the call from a pay phone. "We need an agreement here."

"All right, I'm coming," Mike said. "I'll call you. We can meet."

But days passed and there was no phone call.

So Jimmy phoned one more time, but still Mikey waffled. "I gotta talk to my brother."

"The time for talking to your brother is over," Jimmy said. "Now is the time for being decisive and getting rich. Are you an observant man, Mikey?"

"Me?"

"No, the Pope. Yeah, you."

"What the fuck, Jimmy, we talking religion now?"

"No, I mean do you notice things, watch what's happening around you?"

"Yeah, sure. What're you asking me? I miss something?"

"No, but you might. Okay, you watch Philadelphia, watch what's going on down there."

And he hung up.

DeSapio made Jimmy write up all the duties and bribes at each of the ports and docks, using a code. Zeppole meant Sicily, Nachos was Newark, Parma ham was Palermo. Mili had helped him come up with the code names. In another book, using another secret code, Jimmy went through the details of his other plan— the Jimmy and Milena plan. He'd finally cracked it, when Savino explained that money was the way they could get nabbed, so they wanted a flow of funds that was labyrinthine, because complicated was good. Jimmy's plan was simple: a piggyback. One more European business, one that he alone controlled—it could be anywhere, Rome, Amsterdam—linked to an offshore account. And if a payment went missing, or a step in the flow of funds took a bit more time than usual, the Ruggieros wouldn't miss the money, not for a while, because once their thing got going there would be money flowing in both directions. At the end of the month, DeSapio and Santoro would do the books, but that gave them plenty of time. Italian bank to Italian business account to offshore bank to Mexico City. Money in, money out. It was doable, but it was dangerous. Jimmy and Milena risked their lives if they stole from the Ruggieros. But it was possible, with the right plan. The hijacker D. B. Cooper had done it. Jumped out of a plane with two hundred grand, parachuted to freedom, somewhere south of Tacoma.

Leaving Him

Milena

They ordered room service in the Sanderson Hotel, and watched the night cloak Manhattan. She violated their unspoken rule and talked about Vinnie. She said she was scared of him.

"Why?"

"You know Vinnie. He's addicted to violence."

Jimmy considered her words. "You're right," he said. "You should be with someone else. Listen to me, I sound like my father."

"You sound like *my* father."

Long ago Sabrina had told Milena to be careful, to choose wisely. "You're so pretty," she said. "Look at you, you're beautiful." "So are you." "No, Mil, not like you. But beautiful women attract all men, and that's not going to be easy." Sabrina seemed to know so much better how to use her attractiveness to her advantage, how to spend the currency of her own beauty. Sabrina was more ambitious, better equipped with feminine wiles. She seemed able to divine the future, and was certainly better at playing the part of a sophisticated and cool New York City woman, a gal on her way, and she took up with men on their way, like Bill Kelly. She had an easy, reliable manner and, a few years later, she would find an easy, reliable man. Meanwhile Milena fell for Vinnie, because he was cool and tough and handsome and he was the one man she'd ever met that other men looked up to. He'd offered her security, from poverty, from other men. And now she wanted out, but it was not so easy. It might even prove impossible.

Had she found her prince only to be denied? She might never have Jimmy, not properly, not all the way. Maybe it was true that we only love what we do not possess. Or what we are denied. Could life be that cruel?

"Would you come away with me, if it meant we had to run away?" he asked.

"I already told you I would."

Below them a chain of yellow taxis idled at the light.

"If we couldn't come back. We could see our families, and live somewhere nice, like Mexico or Vancouver, but we couldn't come back, not ever."

"Yes."

They said nothing for a while, each lost in the contemplation of an imaginary future. Milena was squirreling away hundred-dollar bills in an envelope she kept underneath her sweaters. She was ready.

"I've always wanted to live on the beach," she said.

Surveillance

Jimmy

Ponzoni sleeps, snoring. Jimmy's eyes rove—apartment block entrance, street ahead, rearview. You have to catch a guy on the way into the building or all you'll see is the back of his head drifting through the glass doors. Pleasantville, New Jersey, about seven miles west of Atlantic City, is quiet tonight, this street anyway. Jimmy massages his neck. No one's gone in or out of the building in the past half hour.

Ponzoni coughs himself awake. "He show?"

"Whaddaya think?"

They look at the road. Ponzoni blinks.

"We can get outta here," Jimmy says. "We've checked the cameras. No reason to think he's coming tonight." He looks at his watch. "Old people don't like staying up past midnight, not even Mike Rossi's mother."

"We're here. Let's give it another hour or so."

"Fine by me."

Ponzoni had insisted that he come along. Jimmy asked only to borrow his driver's license and a credit card so he could rent a car. The kid asked where he was going, and Jimmy told him. "Heck, I'll drive you," he said. Ponzoni spent the evening at the bar at Harrah's where the young punk Galluci knows had heard someone talking about Little Mikey. Ponzoni dressed like a high

roller and came armed with a wad of Franklins to lubricate any
rusty lips. But no one was singing tonight, apart from a couple of
drunks looking for a free round.

The apartment building is brown brick with white siding,
four floors, glass doors, and a brightly lit lobby where Melvyn
Zelniker installed the hidden camera. If Little Mikey visits his
mama, chances are they'll catch it on film. A few hours ago,
Ponzini walked into the lobby and pretended to ring a buzzer,
just so Jimmy can go back to Melvyn and confirm that his camera
is working.

Jimmy switches on the radio, finds a jazz station. The car
smells of stale coffee.

"What's he look like?" Ponzoni asks, not for the first time.

"I told you. Short and ugly. But he struts around like he's
Mike Tyson. I'll know him if I see him. Used to have dark hair,
but that was a long time ago. Now I'm told he has copper hair,
like one of them fancy dogs."

"Labradoodle or some shit."

"Exactly."

"And you're not going to pull a gun and try to shoot the
motherfucker?"

"I'm not even carrying a gun. Besides, we ain't gonna see him.
Not tonight. Jesus, I'm too old for stakeouts."

"They cost a bundle, but they're good if you got allergies."

"What?"

"Labradoodles. They're hypoallergenic."

They watch the glass doors and the halogen-lit lobby. No one
goes in or out. Now and then a car rumbles past without stopping.

"What if you do see him?" Ponzoni asks.

"What do you mean?"

"You said we're not going to see him, but what if we do, or
what if you do, not tonight but tomorrow or next week?"

"I dunno. Maybe if I know his whereabouts, or where he goes,
then I can call in some house painters."

"Jesus, Jimmy. Not a good idea. You can't whack the guy who put you away. You know better. Are you seriously contemplating that?"

"I don't know. Maybe."

"Listen, you come to me first. You catch a whiff of the little fuck, or you have any reason to believe he's out to get you, you come to me, okay?"

"Okay."

He has a drink with Bill Kelly at a bar in Greenwich Village. Men in suits, men with beards like topiaries, women in tight T-shirts. Bill is fatter and has less hair than the man Jimmy remembers but other than that he's aged well. In his khakis and tortoise shell sunglasses he looks like a successful broker—plump, preppy, happy. They're the oldest people in the bar. They drink expensive martinis and talk about the Cossutta sisters, the fun they had in Kelly's apartment all those years ago.

"Good times," Bill says. "Sabrina and I used to talk about whether you and Milena would run off together."

"And?"

"She said no; I said yes."

Jimmy asks if he is still in touch with Sabrina, but he is not.

"Last I heard she was married with children, out in the sub-urbs somewhere."

"I looked her up," Jimmy says. "But there's no listing."

"She got married, took her husband's name. I don't even know where she lives."

Bill explains that he manages retirement accounts and offers to help Jimmy open a brokerage account online. "You know, if you've got some money you want to invest."

On the subway home, he thinks about money and whether he'll ever have enough of it to open a brokerage account. Then he thinks about Tom and what he said about his commercial zoning restriction. Pino may know someone who could help them get that changed. Jimmy could ask. He'll talk to Bobby first, but he figures he can count on one big favor from the head of the family.

A Good Turn

Tom

"I know a guy," was all Jimmy told him.

"You know a guy."

"Who knows a guy."

And what that guy has managed to do is convince someone in the department of buildings to approve the application for a variance. According to the document and cover letter Jimmy gave him, there was a hearing before the Board of Review, and now the building is zoned for Residential Use, Group Two.

"Holy crap. Thank you."

"You're welcome."

"I don't know how to thank you."

"You already have. You've given me a home."

He doesn't want to knock on Jimmy's door, so he sits down to write him a note.

"Don't promise him the world," Cath says.

He looks at her and shakes his head.

"Just saying. This is how they get you."

"And you know this how?"

She shrugs.

"I'm thanking our tenant, my dad's old friend, for doing me a good turn. Okay? This is not how they get you. They've got us. We have to give this man a home. Do you not understand that? It's a Ruggiero family thing. We can't say no."

"Okay."

"Thank you."

"Turnip."

It was Molly's favorite new word for about a week, and it's enough to make him smile. Where does Molly get these ideas? For some reason neither of them could figure out she began to call people and places turnip. *Come on, Turnip, Dad's waiting. Mom's gone to the superturnip.*

The next evening they drink a beer together, sitting in the mildewed plastic chairs outside Jimmy's apartment. He's figured out something he can do for Jimmy, a thank you gesture: better outdoor furniture, wood with cushions he can bring outside when the weather is nice.

They clink beer bottles. Tom asks again if there's anything else he can do, anything Jimmy needs. Jimmy says no, nothing, again. The setting sun splashes amber streaks down the trees and lights up the back fence. A few dandelions float earthward.

"You were like a son to my dad," Tom says. "I was a bit jealous, and then when you went away I felt bad that I'd ever been jealous. I know my dad felt terribly guilty; he felt like it was all his fault."

"I know. It wasn't. I told him."

"He used to tell me Cosa Nostra is one long memory."

Jimmy chuckles. "Yeah, that's exactly what I was worried about."

"What do you mean?"

"Long time ago. There was a woman. I was worried we'd get caught and if we did someone would blow my balls off."

"Like Romeo and Juliet, someone from the wrong family?"

"Something like that."

The Philly Hit

Jimmy

They stayed in a hotel in downtown Philly, Jimmy and his driver, a kid called Bonchi. Didn't need a crew; the fewer people the better. Bonchi drove him to meet Stein and his guys, skinny white punks in leather jackets and baseball caps. House painters. Killers. They didn't speak much, went over details, confirmed the timing of the second payment. Stein knew all the places Double T frequented. They wanted to stay away from his house or places the Lampones conducted business. Someone would shoot back if they shot him there, and they didn't want a gunfight at the Double T corral. That's why they chose a Friday night. Double T would go out for a drink or dinner. If he goes for a drink at a social club, wait until he gets to his next destination. On the street in front of a restaurant was probably the easiest. When the meeting was over, they shook Jimmy's hand and thanked him. It was all very civil. "We'll get it done right. Don't worry." Jimmy had checked them out. Everyone said they were the best at their job, which was shooting people, usually in broad daylight, usually up close and personal.

They ate lunch in the hotel restaurant. Bonchi ate like a horse. Jimmy was too nervous to eat. This was a big hit, nothing like taking out a drunk Irish soldier in a dark alley. Back in his room, Jimmy read the local paper—*Police Shooting Spurs Rioting in Capital . . . Lenny Dykstra Slams Sports Car into Trees.* He thought about Mexico. He'd heard Mexican passports were easy to come by. They had beaches there. He liked Mexican food. Did Milena? He'd never asked. Changing money, bit by bit, would be easy enough. In Mexico, there'd be lots of guys who could clean cash, or take a bag of dollars and turn it into pesos. Plus they could buy gold in Mexico City and sell it slowly wherever they ended up. Setting up an offshore bank account to funnel money wouldn't be too difficult. The rest—Mexican bank account, clean cash, gold—could wait. When? He wanted to talk to Milena. They'd need some time to make a plan, figure out where to meet and how to disappear without attracting attention, right at the time a large amount of money was mysteriously transferred to an offshore account DeSapio and Santoro couldn't touch. When? Next month? July?

The phone shrieked, but it was only Bonchi. "Sit tight, kid." Jimmy paced, turned on the TV. If Stein and his guys didn't burn the boss, or even if they did but the Lampones got their hands on the killers, Jimmy and Bonchi wouldn't make it out of Philly alive. On TV, a college girl jumped up and down when she guessed the cost of camping equipment on *The Price is Right*, and Bob Barker walked across the stage, describing the features of a Whirlpool washer-dryer as if they were scientific marvels.

The call came around seven from Stein. "The windows got painted." Jimmy went to a pay phone, dialed Santoro's private number. "The package was delivered."

His bag was packed. He wiped the room before he left and made sure Bonchi did the same to his.

Outside the restaurant the first thing they noticed was two police cruisers parked on the sidewalk, then the yellow police tape, and a cluster of uniformed cops under the awning. Bonchi slowed but didn't stop, slow enough to see the blood, or what was left of it; the restaurant entrance and sidewalk had been washed and hosed. You could tell from the dark wet stain and the sheen on the tiles how big the pool of blood had been. Water was still running in the gutter, washing away the last trace of a man's life. A few passersby stopped, stared, then walked on.

"Drive."

And Bonchi drove.

Things are a Bit Hot

Milena

Vinnie showed her the papers, and it was on TV and the radio. *Tommy "Double T" Capeci, head of the Lampone crime family, was gunned down in front of an Italian restaurant in South Philadelphia. So far no arrests. The police . . .* Vinnie didn't say much, but she knew it was a Ruggiero hit—and they'd just clipped a boss. That night they went out, but one restaurant and two bars later Vinnie was still agitated—eyes darting, jaw working. When Mili tried to coax some information out of him, he snapped. "I don't know, leave it alone." The next day, Sunday, they spent in front of the TV, nursing hangovers and eating pizza.

Monday. The only real conversation was about breakfast. Vinnie jumped when the phone rang, had terse, mostly mono-syllabic conversations. *Yeah, no. Don't know.* He jiggled his leg the way he did when he was nervous. Tuesday he stayed home most of the day, paced the apartment, switched on the television, switched it off almost immediately. Wednesday he was out all day, didn't say where he was going, not even a good-bye. Milena visited her mother, phoned Jimmy, but he wasn't home. His voice on his answering machine sounded thin and elongated. She waited, left a second message for Jimmy, then watched TV, hoping that he'd phone before Vinnie came back. But the phone didn't ring. Vinnie returned, drunk and sweaty, well past midnight, banged into the kitchen wall, yanked open the refrigerator door, cursed at it.

"You okay?"

"Yeah."

He took cold meat and sliced cheese out of the fridge. Rolled them, dipped them in mustard, and popped them in his mouth, standing in the white light of the open fridge.

"Something happen? What's going on?"

"Don't ask me about my business."

She hated it when he quoted the goddamned *Godfather*. "Okay. I'm going to bed."

Two days later, Vinnie told her that a rumor was going round that there had been arrests. "I might have to take off for a while, keep my head down until this blows over." Who did they arrest? He didn't know. He speculated they were either random arrests to flush out the killer or an attempt by the cops to bag someone high up. Everyone was under orders to keep cool; no one was going to the mattresses over this. Keep running the businesses but keep a low profile, use the phone as little as possible, steer clear of the cops. She called Jimmy when Vincent was out and this time he was home.

"So good to hear your voice," he said. "But I don't think we can meet, not right now. Things are a bit hot."

"I know, I know, lay low. Just . . . I miss you. Next week, okay."

"Call back Thursday. We'll figure something out."

"Okay. Thursday. See you next week."

Out of Sight

Jimmy

Savino was MIA. Rizzo was in Vegas. Armone was on the run. Rumor had it he'd gone to Canada. The Colt said, "Don't worry, just go quiet, drop out of sight for a while." But Jimmy was worried. Skinny Bugliani phoned to tell him the restaurant had caught some fish, meaning there had been arrests. The next day it was in the papers, six arrests in Philly and Atlantic City in connection with the murder of mob boss "Double T" Capeci.

Jimmy's apartment suddenly felt small. They were supposed to have a phone call with their Italian bankers, and he went to Savino's office on Bedford Street, but Savino wasn't there, and the phone didn't ring. He tried Vinnie and Milena's number from a pay phone but there was no answer. Back in Savino's office he listened to the news on the radio, but there was no mention of the Philly hit or mob arrests. The sunlight dropped out of the sky and streetlights came on, and still the phone didn't ring. He tried to reassure himself. The job had been well planned and well orchestrated. If the cops had something on him, he'd be in a jail by now. But he wasn't so sure. He dialed Savino's home number and Bobby's but no one answered.

He left Savino's office around eight o'clock and bought himself a sandwich on the way home. Back at his apartment he ate his sandwich and watched TV. He thought about the bad shit he did when he was young, Mickey Mouse kid stuff. Skipping school, hanging out with rough kids, drinking, smoking, taking the subway someplace far away and holding up a liquor store. He was afraid of only one thing back in those days: his mother. When she caught on that Jimmy had been smoking pot, she punched him in the gut. Hard. Twice. The woman had quite a right hook. She asked if he had a stash at home. "No." Boom. Kidney jab. He surrendered his bag of weed. But she couldn't make him go straight. He hated school, liked hanging out with the bad kids. Paulie's summer job before he enlisted was loading and unloading boxes for UPS for ten dollars an hour. Jimmy and his pals could spend five minutes in a liquor store and come away with four bottles of the Captain and a hundred bucks apiece—on a bad night.

He watched TV, drank a scotch, slept badly, woke up with the morning light. He left early, ate breakfast at his favorite diner, and then left a note for Savino at the office, signed Giuseppe, a nickname Savino had given him a long time ago. *Let me know if you know anything about Mr. Blue, or want to meet.* On the way home, he stopped at a pay phone and tried Vinnie and Bobby again, but either they were gone or they weren't answering their phones. On his way home, he realized he'd started looking over his shoulder.

He couldn't stand being in his apartment, waiting, wondering, doing nothing. He wanted to know what was going on, wanted things to go back to normal, and, more than anything, he wanted to see Milena.

If the cops were looking for him, they'd try his home address, but they didn't know about Savino's secret office. He packed a bag with cash, a change of clothes, and his gun, and took the subway back to Bedford Street.

Trouble

Milena

Thursday morning Vincent was in a bad mood. She heard him on the phone while she was scrambling eggs. When he entered the kitchen, he told her what he heard: Armone fled. He got a tipoff that the cops were coming. Santoro was acting boss. When she asked where Armone had gone and what it meant, Vinnie shrugged her off.

"Just some things going on. Don't worry about it."

"But I am worried."

He poured himself a cup of coffee, picked at his plate of scrambled eggs, washed them down with more coffee. When the phone rang he said don't answer it. A few minutes later he hurried out of the apartment without saying where he was going. She waited a few minutes then called Jimmy but he didn't pick up. She tried Donatella Rizzo, but there was no answer at the Rizzos' either. The world had turned to stone, every molecule suspended in a gray wall of silence. She waited. She hated waiting.

Vinnie came home, still agitated. Again he told her nothing. He lay on the couch with a cold beer and a basketball game on the TV. When she went to check on him a little while later, he was already snoring. She left a note—*Gone to see my Mom, back around 7*—and tiptoed out of the apartment.

The subway rumbled and bumped along to Court Street, and she walked to Jimmy's apartment. She rang the buzzer, but there was no answer. She bought a coffee from a bodega around the corner, sipped it standing on the street. From a pay phone she made two calls, first a message for Jimmy telling him to stay put if he came home, then she spoke to her mother to confirm her alibi in case Vinnie called. "Tell him I'm sleeping."

She walked back to Jimmy's apartment, but there was still no answer, so she left a note in the doorjamb. (She didn't have a key—they never met there.)

> *J—*
> *I'm going to the museum, then the bar at the Pierre.*

There was no need to sign it; he'd recognize the handwriting and know which museum it referred to.

The subway clunked and rattled its way through gray tunnels and graffitied stations. In Manhattan, she stopped at a pay phone and tried Jimmy's number again, but there was still no answer. She walked down Fifth Avenue. The only way to know if he phoned was to go home, but home meant Vinnie—and staying home or going out with Vinnie.

Inside the Museum of Modern Art, she stopped in front of a series of collages made of shreds of torn posters, bus stop ads, patches of newspaper and magazines, like jagged islands. If you looked closely you could discern images hidden in the camouflage layers—a face, a hand, a circus tent, the head of a dog. Step back and the collage looked abstract again, yellow and red splotches on top of blue, almost like smears of paint. Jimmy would like these, she thought. He'd like the way they looked different close up and far away. There was something mobile about the little islands of color; they seemed to be drifting apart, as if they were trying to burst out of their frames. She looked around, lingered at the entrance watching people come and go, but Jimmy was not among them.

She left after twenty minutes and walked up Fifth Avenue to the Pierre Hotel. She was in no great rush. If he was there, he was there. More than likely she'd wait awhile. One of Sabrina's favorite bars, that's one reason she picked it. That and the fact that there was a row of phones at the back of the lobby.

At exactly five o'clock she used one of the hotel pay phones. Still no answer. He hadn't seen the note. He had to come home eventually. He had to know she was trying to get in touch. The bar was almost empty. Three men in suits, talking business or sports. She ordered a gin and tonic, sipped it, watching the bartender, and tried to relax into the upholstered hush.

"Excuse me." The voice was soft and the speaker stood a good foot away. "I was wondering if I might buy you a drink." *Ah was wond'ring*. Southerner. He was not handsome but was dressed in an expensive suit and well groomed, a big flat face like a friendly dog, and a gap between his teeth. He grinned when he spoke. "Don't mean to intrude."

He introduced himself and insisted on buying her a drink and smiled his gap-toothed smile. He's from Texas, in finance. She told him she's an art dealer, waiting for her husband.

"Excuse me one moment." She stood up, crossed the lobby to the pay phones. But Jimmy was still not back. She didn't leave a message. *Maybe he's on his way.* She called home but either Vinnie was not there or he was not picking up.

Back at the bar her Southerner was waiting, grinning and examining the bowls of peanuts and fish-shaped crackers. She made small talk while she waited, finished her drink slowly, then took her leave.

"Perhaps another time." He handed her a business card.

She made two more calls from the lobby. Home and Jimmy. But there was no answer on either end.

She went to a diner, where she ordered an omelet but ate very little of it. There was a pay phone right outside, and she tried Jimmy, then hailed a taxi.

Back in Brooklyn, the cabbie waited on Tilden Avenue while she used a phone.

"Hello."

"Jimmy, I've been trying to reach you."

"I'm sorry. I'm . . . Christ, I'm on the run. Bad stuff happening, as you probably know."

"Yeah, I know."

"I'm worried."

"Me too."

"Vinnie know anything?"

"Not much. Only that Armone is on the run and there have been arrests in Philly. What's going on?"

"I wish I knew. I'm going to my brother's. He's listed. Call me there tomorrow evening?"

"Six."

"Okay."

"I love you."

"I love you."

She knew nothing more when she hung up than she did before she called, and yet his voice was there and love was there, and that was enough for now.

Before They Make Me Run

Jimmy

You could run. There's always a bit of time before the cops get their shit together. And yet you don't. It's not about wanting to get caught or guilt or fate or anything like that. You know enough not to leave clues, you know not to visit the crime scene, how to cover your tracks. But things get confused. You're not quite sure what they know or who they are (the Feds, the cops, DOJ, FBI, the Lampones). You sure as shit don't know what they've got on you. You are also riding the rush of the crime right when all of this is happening. You go from elated to contrite in a matter of hours, think you've gotten away with it, and also regret what you've done.

Years later he would look back on those fateful days and wonder if he could have changed the way things turned out. He didn't know what was happening, and the family was on high alert. He couldn't talk to anyone and didn't know the truth. Like what the cops had on him or who had been arrested or whether the FBI was on his tail. Ask anyone in the joint: ignorance is the biggest mistake you can make. And Jimmy was just a rookie, the guy who hadn't been there before, who didn't have finely tuned instincts about cops and stakeouts, where to run and how to hide. If you don't know the truth, don't know all the facts, you're liable to do stupid shit.

At his brother's apartment he waited for the phone to ring and read the papers. *Suspects in Philly Mob Boss Killing Arrested.*

Arrests

Milena

And then they knew. Armone and Sonny Strazzullo had been arrested although no one knew the charges. Vinnie heard from Tony Rizzo, who heard it from Santoro. Some said they pinched five guys, some said more like a dozen and they weren't done yet. Everyone knew it was trouble with a Federal badge. A lot of guys were on the run. Vinnie was fidgety; he paced around the apartment, glared at the TV as if it meant to do him harm, drank too much coffee.

She asked if he'd heard anything about Frank Rizzo or Jimmy.

"No, doll, I told you."

"What'd Tony say? Should we be worried?"

"Jesus, can you . . . Nobody knows shit, okay."

"Sorry."

It wasn't easy being in the same apartment. She hid her Tampax and then said she needed to go to the store to buy some. Vinnie offered to go, said he could use some fresh air.

"Want to pick us up some dinner too?"

"Sure, doll."

She smoked a cigarette, turned on the radio, turned it off again. There was no news of interest to her, and the agitated newsroom chatter made her nervous.

Time passed slowly. Just before six o'clock she dialed Jimmy's brother's number.

"It's me."

"You've heard? A bunch of arrests."

"I heard. Do you think we're safe?"

"I don't know. Nobody knows what's going on. I can't get in touch with Savino. Can I see you?"

"Maybe tomorrow. I can say I'm going to see my sister. How do I get in touch?"

He gave her a number to call.

"Where are you going?"

"Queens."

Vincent came home smelling of bourbon. He'd bought baked ziti, and they ate quietly. She'd never seen him like this: frightened. He said maybe they should go somewhere until things blew over.

"But they've got nothing, right? Nothing on you?"

"That many arrests, who the fuck knows? Baby, if all of those guys are going down, then of course they've got something on me. Anyone who's got something on Armone's got something on me."

She knew Vinnie was no angel. She knew it, and the police surely knew it.

She took a long hot bath, watched the bubbles melt and slither down her knees. Mob wives stuck with their men. They got arrested, you visited them, and you waited for them. You could do whatever you liked while they're inside, except leave, and you were there when they got out. What did he mean, go somewhere? And for how long? She thought about staying. *You go, I'll be fine here.* But she knew she couldn't, because if you stayed and someone wanted to hurt him, they'd hurt you. Even the Feds. They'd think you might talk, you might know something. Even if the cops or Feds didn't come knocking, the family would be worried. And Ruggiero captains didn't like to worry.

When she emerged from the steamy bathroom, there was an open suitcase on the bed. She pulled the bathrobe tight around her waist.

"We're going?"

"Yes. I'm not sitting around with my dick in my hands waiting for the cops. We gotta skip town. Wait until this thing blows over."

She sat on the bed. He sat beside her and took her hand. *We.* He skips town; she skips town. It was that simple.

"I spoke to the family lawyer. There's a warrant for my arrest. One for you too. So don't feel left out."

At the foot of the bed he'd made haphazard piles—a stack of clean shirts, a pyramid of socks, envelopes and papers, and a shoebox she'd never seen before.

Here was Vincent the schemer, the planner, the guy who talked too much, favored bravura over caution, but managed to keep himself and his loved ones out of trouble.

"What's in the shoebox?"

"Everything they need to put me away. They can search the apartment, but they won't find nothing. Remind me to put that in the suitcase."

The guy with a sense of humor, in good times and bad.

She was thirty years old, and yet she felt like a little girl again, adrift in a world both chaotic and capricious, a world that robbed you of your father unexpectedly, where you're planning a party one day and on the run the next.

Vinnie put a hand on her knee. "Don't worry. We'll be okay."

She said nothing. She was thinking about when she would see Jimmy again, when she would see her sisters, her mother. It occurred to her that they might think she'd been arrested. She found herself wondering when she would take another bath in her own bathtub.

"There's a guy who can get us a car. I've got some cash. No use in sitting around. Come on, get some things packed. We leave tonight."

"Where we going?"

"Florida."

Feel Your Collar

Jimmy

Chances are you are also very tired. The adrenaline has drained. You're spent and you want to sleep; you don't want to run.

He moved to a hotel in Queens, paid cash, laid low.

That's where they got him: in an Italian restaurant in Queens. He was eating alone. They must have been on his tail for a while, days maybe. They'd probably staked out his apartment. Maybe a waiter or beat cop recognized him and tipped them off. Maybe they canvassed hotels. Did they watch him eat? Decide when to do it? He'd finished his plate of pasta when two men in bad suits approached him. A badge appeared on the table next to his glass of wine. Slid toward him.

"You've got the wrong guy."

"Let's talk about that." Big yellow teeth.

"Let's not talk about anything. Not without a lawyer."

"You have a right to have a lawyer present," the other one said. "But until then, anything you say can be used against you in a court of law."

"Okay?" Yellow teeth nodded, leaned on the table. "We're going to stand up, and we gotta cuff you. I'm sorry."

He'd always remember that, the plainclothes cop apologizing. *I'm sorry.* It was the last civil thing anyone said to him for a long, long time.

Handcuffed, uncomfortable, freaking out in the back of the police cruiser, he wondered what they had on him, whether they were rounding up a bunch of them. Was it just his unlucky motherfucking day, or had they managed to connect him to Philly? He wanted to know, but he knew better than to talk to the plainclothes dicks in the front seat. Thoughts kept scattering; he couldn't concentrate; he couldn't breathe.

You're driven from Queens to a police station in Brooklyn, where you surrender your watch, wallet, shoes, lucky bracelet. You get booked. You still can't think clearly. It's like your brain has been jumbled. You tell two different officers your name, address, and phone number. They ask a bunch of questions you know enough not to answer. You want to scream, run away, do something, but there's nothing you can do. You wait. Your cuffs are on too tight. Finally, you make your phone call to the family lawyer. The lawyer says don't say anything. You know that already.

He was fingerprinted and photographed before being led downstairs to a holding cell populated by an assortment of thugs, drug dealers, drunks, and delinquents. They all glared. Jimmy glared back, then looked away. The room was hot, smelly, and crowded. No window, no clock on the wall. A stainless-steel toilet and sink, no toilet paper. He stared at his shoes and felt like he was floating.

They drove him to the Brooklyn Criminal Court building for his arraignment, and that's where he met the Ruggiero family lawyer, a friendly looking guy, listing under the weight of an oversize briefcase. He was big shouldered with copper-wire hair that hovered above his head like an orange cloud, a graying Tom Selleck moustache, and big teeth. They barely had time to shake hands and for Howard Gutkin to say, "Don't say anything unless I ask you a question," before being led into a courtroom. The judge was younger than Jimmy expected, thin, with black hair and yellow skin. He didn't look particularly interested in Jimmy. He was reading the contents of a manila folder, and when he looked up, Gutkin nudged Jimmy and they stood together in front of the judge, close enough that they could see flecks of dandruff on the judge's robe. Jimmy had been indicted by a Kings County grand jury for racketeering, gambling, tax evasion, solicitation to commit a crime of violence, and conspiracy to commit murder. He was to be held until trial, the young judge said. "Based on the evidence presented, Mr. Piccini is considered a flight risk." Gutkin approached the bench, tried to say something, but the judge batted the lawyer's words away, and that was it. Folders were put back in briefcases and Gutkin was pushing Jimmy out of the courtroom, promising he'd work on getting bail.

They led him downstairs, through a labyrinth of halls, then locked him in a cell. He stared at the wall and shook his head. "Fuck, fuck, fuck," he said aloud. He wondered where Milena was and who else they'd nabbed. He thought about his mother and his father. After a while the lights went off, and after that the guy in the next cell started screaming that he wanted to see his lawyer and he'd been framed, and there was some commotion and either he was crazy or they took away his clothes because next minute he was yelling that he wanted his clothes back.

Mostly Jimmy sat and waited, for the lawyer, for time, for a judge—he didn't even know what he was waiting for. His head felt jumbled, thoughts flickered like faulty light bulbs, and he felt like he was floating in space again, even as he sat on the metal chair going nowhere. He wouldn't have guessed he could be so scared and so bored at the same time. That word. *Murder*. He felt small because he was small, a speck in the vast universe of the legal system, a tiny, weightless speck—powerless, fucked.

A woman judge presided over the pretrial hearing. Gutkin said she wasn't bad. Not a mob-buster at any rate. She also hadn't read whatever was in his folder, because the first thing she did after sitting down was read silently. After a while she looked up and spoke to Jimmy's lawyer, mostly confirming names and counsel.

With her big glasses and black hair just starting to gray, Jimmy thought she looked like someone's mom.

She called the lawyers to the bench and they had a little conference that no one else could hear. Then Gutkin and the prosecutor sat back down and the judge read aloud. They discussed evidence and went through a witness list. There would be no bail.

Jimmy wrapped his jacket around himself and tried to sleep. But sleep didn't come. Every few minutes his heart lurched and a bright light flashed inside his closed eyes and he sat up, heart pounding, his head churning with sounds and words, that one word in particular: *murder*. He felt faint and lay back on the narrow bed. He lay there in the half-darkness for the remainder of the night. He must have slept at some point, although when the lights came on in the morning he had no recollection of sleep.

He spoke to Gutkin. The good news was that apart from Philly his file was light. Another night, same cell. By then it was sinking in. Good news? There was no good news. They'd linked him to Philly, and he would be tried for murder. First-degree, second-degree, conspiracy, didn't matter, something ending in murder. That word again, stabbing his brain. It wasn't a good time to be a made man on trial in America. The purge that had started with US Attorney Giuliani's mission "to wipe out the five families," and reached a crescendo with The Mafia Commission Trial, was still going strong. Jimmy tried to think of scenarios where the charges went away—someone confessed, they paid off the judge, it wasn't Jimmy but some other guy—but none of them stuck. He cursed aloud and wondered what would happen next and what his mother would say. He wondered where Milena was and whether Vinnie had been arrested. He'd fall asleep and wake up with a violent burst, terrified and sweating.

Turns out you're not Jerry, you're Tom, the goddamned cat. One minute you're dancing on a rooftop or about to eat a slice of cake or catch that stupid mouse or you're conducting an orchestra in top hat and tails and, *wham*, hit by a flying hammer, arrested by Brooklyn PD.

He spent the next few days in the jail cell, battling his own courage. When they let him use the phone, he reached Colt at his club in Bensonhurst. "It's sunny here," the Colt told him, "but the shadows are all out and we're expecting rain." That meant people were still staying out of sight and the shadow leadership was in command—Santoro, Arcuri, Bugliani. "Boss, Ipanema, the brothers, soap, they're all playing golf somewhere nice." That meant Vinnie, the Rizzos, and Savino were all on the lam.

Gutkin said they were hard at work on Jimmy's defense. If there was a judge they could bribe or threaten, they would do it. Beyond that there was nothing they could do for him.

He spoke to his parents. They were talking to a lawyer. He told them not to, that he had it covered, told them not to worry. He'd never heard his mother so worried, and it made him want to comfort her. "I'm okay, Ma." He was the furthest he'd ever been from okay. He spent a lot of time sitting on a metal chair gazing at the walls and floor and metal bars. He wasn't floating anymore, he was fucked. The fear had abated and mostly he felt a sadness so powerful he didn't recognize what it was at first.

Wicked Game

Milena

Brooklyn to Maryland to Virginia in a rented Buick Regal, cars and billboards drifting past. *Dollar Meal Straight Ahead. Travel with Taste.* She used a pay phone from a service plaza on I-95 outside Richmond, dialed the number Jimmy had given her, but there was no answer. Vinnie did most of the driving. They listened to pop radio, guzzled Doritos and Butterfingers, stayed in a Howard Johnson's the first night, a Best Western in Walterboro, South Carolina, the next.

The Ruggieros were well connected in Miami, with a network of aging mobsters, shylocks, drug dealers, and fences. Vinnie met a guy, returned with a fat envelope. They paid cash for their South Beach hotel, restaurants, everything they needed, making themselves effectively invisible, at least for a while. Vinnie spoke to the Ruggiero lawyer again. "It's hunting season all right," Gutkin told him. Vinnie sent a couple of his guys to get cash from his hiding places in Brooklyn, and they wired money to the Western Union in South Beach.

They ate lunch at the pool at the Raleigh Hotel, overlooking palm trees and beach and sea. It was a beautiful day.

"What are we going to do?" Milena asked.

"Stay here or go somewhere else."

"Where?"

"Away. They connect me to the Russian job, I'm fucked."

Vinnie was the type to get caught. Visible, brash, bad-tempered, possessed of a big mouth, he'd left a trail of witnesses and enemies. She was pretty sure the Feds watching the Brooklyn mob knew exactly who he was, pretty sure he hadn't covered his tracks meticulously. And they wanted her too. Accessory, accomplice—she was part of the California money-laundering scheme; there were payments in her name. Jimmy was different, the careful one, the guy always looking over his shoulder, the one who worried about cops and consequences.

"I've always wanted to go to Italy," she said.

"I'm thinking Canada. Closer to home."

"Too cold. Besides, what's the use of being close to home if you can't *go* home. Let's go to Italy. It'll be like a vacation. When it's safe to come back, we'll come back."

Of course if they went to Italy, she'd be one step closer to Jimmy. They'd get in touch with the Sicilians; Jimmy knew them, and they could get word to him that Vincent and Milena were there. Or she'd tell her sister, and someone would get word to Jimmy. She could send a cryptic postcard that only he would understand. *Greetings from Zeppole.*

Vinnie didn't say yes immediately. He told her he'd think about it, assured her he was not opposed to trying something new.

"Come on, Vinnie, your idea of trying something new is smoking a cigarette while you take a shit."

He never told her what it was that persuaded him, but in the end they booked a flight to Italy and bought stolen passports from a shyster lawyer.

Milena called her sister from a pay phone. "We have to go. I don't know when we'll be back. I'll call you soon. Tell Mama not to worry."

At Miami International Airport they handed over the stolen passports with some trepidation, but the agent stamped their passports and grunted, and soon Mr. and Mrs. José Casares were drinking vodka from plastic cups on their way to Rome.

Johnny 99

Jimmy

You feel lockup, and it feels you, skin on skin, brick on skin, cuffs on wrists. You strip before fat guards who look in your mouth, under your balls, up your asshole. You wear a scratchy orange jumpsuit with your inmate number stenciled in black ink. You sign papers, hand over your watch and wallet. In return you get a pillowcase and sheet. Finally, you get to your cell—uncuffed, alone. It's small and smells of piss and bleach and the other sweaty humans sharing the crowded cellblock.

You touch your fingers, feel your flesh, bang your head with your palms. The bars are real. Everything happens slowly. Time passes slowly, your body moves slowly—your thoughts and feelings are powerful but lethargic, shock and anger slowly rising and crashing like an interminable, frozen wave inside you. It's too much to contemplate. Fifty years is a lifetime. You'll be eighty-three if you serve your whole sentence. You can't imagine spending fifty more days.

Fuckin Little Mikey. Jimmy found it hard to believe that one little scrotum sack's testimony was sufficient for a grand jury, but it was. Cops had been looking in all the wrong places for Double T's killer. But once they knew it was the Ruggerios, they started looking in different places, all the right places, namely the Ruggerios' contacts in Philly. Take away the Lampones themselves and there weren't so many suspects. They found Stein eventually. He knew all the mobbed-up guys and everyone knew he did bad things for people. His car had been spotted; there was money in the bank; bank transfers led them to the button men; eyewitnesses confirmed their meetings. The window cleaners spilled. It was the one thing you didn't think about when you were planning a clean hit. You assumed the cops wouldn't have any idea who did it. It was the one weakness in Jimmy's plan. As soon as the cops had reason to believe that you did something, they started pulling together disparate things, and if they did their job right, you were going down. Because you had a motive, you came to town, and you solicited another to commit murder in the first-degree, and if they have a witness and a confession, it adds up to a Class-A, level-one felony. It adds up to fucked. Once they had Stein and his *strunzi* button men in custody, and they showed them the indictment and talked matter-of-factly about lethal injections and the slim chance of clemency, the killers sang and Jimmy was sunk.

Welcome to Clinton Correctional. Population: 2,865. They told him it was going to get cold in winter. They told him Lucky Luciano had served time there, so had Lucchese hitman Richie Bilello. They gave him an illustrated booklet, *How to Deal with Prison*. Avoid showing emotions, keep fit, try not to cry out loud, don't be someone's punk, don't get raped. There was an illustration of a guy with lipstick and high heels and a chain around his neck, being held by a man with bulging muscles. *Try to remember that the justice system has imprisoned you in an effort to rehabilitate you, enabling you to make better choices upon your release . . . Do not urinate more than necessary.* He was told his parents would receive a copy of *Handbook for the Families and Friends of New York State DOC Inmates*. They asked if he wanted to see the priest (yes) or join the Catholic church group (no). He had the Italians to look after him. He got respect from day one. Jimmy had a pretty good steely-eyed look, and his reputation—mob boss killer—preceded him. The first couple of weeks he mostly cursed his luck and didn't sleep and watched his back, ate very little, made contact with made men, and let his sentence be known. A serious motherfucker— mean, mobbed-up, and a killer—that's all he wanted everyone to know. The book they'd given him was most likely right: the first month would be the hardest.

"Do you want me to hear your confession?" asked the priest, a young guy, Filipino, but a college boy, as Jimmy would later find out.

"No."

Mostly the young priest listened. Jimmy told him he couldn't believe what had happened to him, that it didn't feel real. The priest nodded and said, very quietly, "It is real, at least for now." There was a Bible in his cell, but Father Steven didn't look at it or say anything about it. Before he left, he said something Jimmy would always remember: "The tragedy of life is not what you suffer but what you miss."

He could survive the first month. He was in the fish tank, aka administrative segregation, for new guys only, which meant he didn't meet the general prison population. It was the next ten years he was worried about. And the ten after that. And the ten after that. The booklet probably wasn't written with murder raps in mind. He thought a lot about whether he would rather kill himself now than die an old man in a cell. There was one good reason to wait, same reason not to die in jail: to kill the cocksucker who put him there.

He made himself forget Milena and the pleasures that had been his life. He wasn't that guy anymore. If he was to survive, he'd have to block all of that out, erase his memory. His life started now. They gave him more booklets about exercises you can do in your cell, anger management, meditation. He made a list of ten friends and associates who could visit, in addition to family.

His sixteenth day in lockup, Jimmy had a visitor. Bobby Maritato. Bobby was on his visiting list, along with Savino, Vinnie, Milena, Paulie, his parents, Lee-Ann, Carlo, Uncle Frankie, and his old pal

Eddie. Before he got to see Bobby, Jimmy was patted down and reminded that they could shake hands but have no other physical contact—don't pass anything, no fighting, no yelling.

By the time he entered the visiting room, a bright windowless room filled with blue and white molded plastic chairs and tiny orange tables and patrolled by several guards, Bobby was waiting, looking huge and uncomfortable. He wore a gray suit and white shirt, had dark circles under his eyes, and his skin was pale. They'd both looked better, Jimmy thought, as they shook hands and sat down.

Lights buzzed above them, and the air was thick with disinfectant.

"You look like shit, Bobby."

"Yeah, whaddaya expect. You ain't looking so great either, Jimmy."

"No? Well, they don't cook so good in here. It's good to see you. Jesus. Fuck. So what's going on?"

"They got some other guys too, and some guys are gone. It's a mess. We're doing everything we can to get you outta here."

"Thanks, Bobby. I don't know if I can last in here."

"One day at a time."

"Yeah," Jimmy said. "It ain't gonna be fun."

"Probably not."

Nearby a middle-aged couple was talking to a young man, probably their son. They were listening to him, both with the same incredulous look on their faces, like they were watching a ghost. How could this happen to our boy? Jimmy thought about his own parents. He wanted to see them, to reassure them, but what on earth could he say to make them feel better?

After a month he was moved to the general population cellblock— bigger, louder, more dangerous. Shit happens when you're the new kid on the cellblock. Someone is going to come for you. It's called a "party" and its only purpose is to show you who's boss. It was the Latin Kings, but it could have been any of them. They got him between the cellblocks and the cafeteria. No one around; they must have paid off the guards. One of them had a length of lead pipe, the others used their fists and kicked. He tried to say something, offered them money, threatened, but it was no use. They weren't listening. The lead pipe pounded his ribs and he stumbled and a rain of punches and kicks followed. It took only a few seconds before he felt his head hit concrete and blood and bile burst inside him, followed by his lunch. The blows came in waves, and some of them felt like blades, cutting deep inside him. There wasn't much he could do to protect himself. His eyes were blurry with blood and he went stupid with pain. He noticed one guy's gold tooth, blood spattered on the pipe. After a while they slowed down and he could hear them speaking, mostly in Spanish or if it was English he couldn't understand it. When a kick glanced off his chin, breaking a tooth and snapping his head sideways, he allowed himself to imagine Milena. There she was, under a tree, wearing a white skirt, and she was waving to him when the next blows came. He no longer felt any pain. He tried to protect his face; he rolled when he saw the bottom of a boot raised above him. After a kick that might have split a rib, one guy hunkered down beside him. "Take a look *pendejo*. We did this to you. We can do it again." He spat. They disappeared. The last thing Jimmy remembered before he blacked out was their footsteps and the sound of his own blood sluicing through him.

He spent three days in the infirmary. He was relieved his parents would not see him that way, his face red and raw, right eye swollen just about shut. A prison dentist fixed his tooth.

Off the Map

Milena

Rome was sunny and bustling and foreign. Fountains, cafés, gelaterias, restaurants. Everyone smoked and men checked her out openly. The women wore miniskirts, and everyone talked with their hands. By then Vinnie had worked out a plan: they would travel from Rome to Palermo and hide out in Sicily. They didn't need their passports to travel inside Italy, and in the unlikely event that the Feds were able to track Mr. and Mrs. José Casares, they'd get no further than Rome.

"For how long?"

"Long as it takes."

They stayed in a big hotel near Via Veneto. They visited the Vatican and the Borghese gardens; they ate pasta and drank too much wine and paid with stolen credit cards and cash. Vinnie had gone from scared to elated. He made conversation with other Americans. His happiness was not contagious. It didn't feel quite real to Milena—nor did she see any reason to celebrate. Even as they were eating great food and getting drunk with American tourists, she was growing restless, anxious. They smoked pot with a couple of waiters near the Spanish Steps. Milena reminded Vinnie to reveal nothing.

"Don't say your name, or where you're from. You're Frank, from Florida. You sell insurance."

"What the fuck I know about insurance?"

"Vincenzo, it's insurance. You insure stuff. Otherwise you can't talk to every asshole you meet."

"What, I can't be friendly now?"

"That's right. You wanna be friendly or you wanna stay out of jail? Think, Vinnie."

They read about the arrests in the American papers—Jimmy and Armone and a bunch of guys she'd never heard of. Twelve arrests in New York and Philadelphia. There was a photograph of a Philly gangster called "Lumpy" Fontini, quotes from the district attorneys. No photo of Jimmy; still, her heart froze at the sight of his name. Jimmy was in prison. How was that possible? She wanted to cry, she wanted to see him, touch him, talk to him, but she couldn't even say one word about it, not to Vinnie. She couldn't even utter his name.

"Coulda been me," Vinnie said.

"Coulda been you." *If only.*

It felt more like purgatory than a vacation. She wasn't going home anytime soon, and she wasn't going to meet up with Jimmy in a couple of days. Milena told herself to stop worrying, stop thinking about Jimmy, at least for a while, and enjoy her unanticipated vacation.

They used fake names and real money to buy tickets for the short flight from Rome to Palermo. They were met at the airport by a captain in the Donato family, a man called Facchi, known by the Ruggerios. Short and stout with big teeth and heavy eyes, he said, "Hello, welcome," but taxed his English no further as they headed south on the highway away from Palermo.

They drove for nearly an hour.

"Officially lost," Vinnie said. "Off the map."

They passed lemon trees and olive groves, old train tracks under rocky mountains, small towns, and ancient-looking viaducts. Signs for Marineo and Ficuzza and the Azienda Forest.

"It's beautiful, isn't it," Milena said.

Facchi looked at her in the rearview.

She smiled. "*Bello.*"

Vinnie shot her a sideways glance.

"What?"

After driving for well over an hour they arrived at the house of Elio Cornaro, head of the Donato family and one of Sicily's most powerful men. The house was in the hills between Vicari and Roccapalumba, a renovated eighteenth-century farmhouse built of pale stone, with a swimming pool and four-car garage.

"We stop," Facchi announced and climbed out of the car. He groaned and stretched in the sunlight. "Leave it the valiges."

"Leave what?" Vinnie asked.

But Facchi was already walking toward the door.

"I think he means suitcases," Milena said.

They met Cornaro at a table in the courtyard beside the pool. A servant in black uniform brought wine, bread, *caponata,* and fried *arancini* balls.

"*Salut,*" said the don, arms outstretched. He was bald and powerfully built with bronze skin, a gold necklace, and sunglasses.

"Thank you for meeting," Vinnie said, gazing at the big stone house that surrounded them, and into which they had not been invited.

"You are welcome in my house. Have you seen *il planetario?*"

"Have we seen what?" Vinnie said, frowning.

"Not yet," Milena said, smiling. And to Vinnie: "I think he means the planetarium."

"Like I give a crap about the planetarium."

"Pretend," she hissed.

"La Rocca, the mountains, very beautiful."

"We would love to do some sightseeing," Milena said.

But Cornaro smiled happily. "Facchi, *guidare.*" He looked at Milena. "Facchi take you."

After complimenting the food and the house, Vinnie began to explain that he had connections in America. "We can move cars," he said. "You know, buy cars, sell you cars." He gestured driving, hands on an invisible steering wheel.

"*Si, si*, cars."

"My guys in New York, they can get you any cars you like. Cadillac, Mercedes, old Ferraris, anything. And if you have cars here, we can move them. You know if the car is made before 1967, then that is good, because no emissions, no, um, inspection."

"*Ispezione*," Cornaro offered.

"I mean that's just one example," Vinnie was babbling now. "We got, or we can get, electronics, stereos, cigarettes." He continued for a while, talking about CD players, VCRs, dropping Armone's name.

Cornaro frowned pensively, picking arancini crumbs off his plate with his fingertips.

"Is Brooklyn near to New York?"

"Yeah," Vinnie said. "Yes, Brooklyn is in New York. Manhattan, Brooklyn, Queens, all New York."

"New York City."

"That's right."

"And Buffala?"

"Buffalo. That's far away. Up near Canada. You don't want to go there. Cold."

Facchi bared his teeth and nodded, pressing his big chin into his big neck.

"*Bah-fallo*," Cornaro repeated.

A Sitdown with Mr. Jimmy

Cargo

"Were you a gangster like my Grampa?"

"Who told you that?"

"Kids at school. They say he was in the mob. Like Tony Soprano. And he knew John Gotti."

"They don't know shit."

"You're not supposed to use that word. Were you?"

"No. He wasn't either. Anyway, ancient history. So tell me, what do you want to be, when you grow up?"

"Mob boss."

"C'mon."

"Just kidding. Baseball player or pro skateboarder. Or an architect."

"An architect?"

"I like to draw buildings. Imagine if someone built them how cool would that be."

"Like what?"

He explains the idea of a building that looks like an elephant. With trees on top, and a heliport.

"It looks like an elephant. But it's a building?"

"Yeah. Are you Italian-American like us?"

"What a question. Sure I'm Italian-American. *Come stai, va bene.* See, I can even talk some Italian."

"I learn Spanish in school."

"*Que bueno.*"

"My dad says we're going to Italy next summer. Have you been?"

"Me. Never. We thought about it but never got there."

"We?"

Molly runs over. She's always interrupting. "Can we go for ice cream? *Pleeease?*"

"Sure, we can. Just make sure it's okay with your mom and dad."

A Sitdown with Ponzoni

Jimmy

Jimmy treats Ponzoni to a steak at DeStefano's in Williamsburg. It opened while Jimmy was away, but the restaurant is so old school, so cozy and familiar, with its pressed-tin ceiling and gas lamp style lights, it feels like it's been around fifty years or more. He thanks Ponzoni for accompanying him on the stakeout, for everything he's done. He knows Pino would tell Ponzoni to stay away, if the kid ever asked the boss.

"You don't gotta thank me," Ponzoni says, speaking through a mouthful of red meat. "And anything you need, ask me, please."

"I will. Thank you."

"Listen, old man, you're kind of a hero to me."

"I'm not that old. And you need a better hero."

"You're probably right."

Sensing that now may be the best time to ask another favor, Jimmy lets it slip. "There may be something you could do. If you're serious."

"What'd I just say? Of course I'm serious."

The idea came to him while he was talking to Cargo. What would Savino do? He was wily, trusted a con as much as a show of force. "I'm thinking maybe you could get someone to visit the old lady, bump into her outside her apartment building, that kind of thing. Ask about Mikey, in a friendly way. Reminisce a little, talk about all the guys, Mo, Beans, and mention Jimmy Piccini . . ."

"I don't get it. Why?"

"It'll have to be someone older than you, someone who looks like Pino. Short hair, those silver glasses Pino wears. Mikey's ma ain't gonna know the difference—when this guy says he's Pino Locatelli, she'll believe him. He'll make sure she catches the name, and he'll send his regards to Mikey. Tell him we miss him, he should come and visit."

"And?"

"And Mikey will think that Pino is watching his mother, and if anything happens to me, they'll whack her."

Ponzoni nods, takes a sip of wine. "Smart," he says. "Nobody wants to bring trouble to their mother."

The Sky is Gone

Jimmy

You don't speak. Unless spoken to. Even then sometimes. You watch your back and pray to Mother Mary that your reputation preceded you. One "party," one broken rib, and one broken tooth are enough. You're scared and angry and bewildered. Your heart hammers in your chest. You feel like your head might float off and fly away, like something in a cartoon. Prison is worse than any nightmare because of the thing you know for sure: it's not a dream. Your ribs heal; your face heals. You get through the days, and at night you convulse in anger and self-pity, in your cold hard cell, surrounded by snoring, yelling, smelly criminals. You hate God, then don't believe in God, then you wonder about the universe, humans, fate, death, reincarnation. You settle on unbelievably bad luck. After a few months you stop worrying about all of that. And after that, days go by when you feel only the slow passage of time and all the sadness and rage and regret inside you turning to stone. No sky, no sun, no heaven, no God, no meaning.

Pretty soon just about everyone in the cellblock knew Jimmy was mobbed up and a convicted killer, and he had some Italian muscle behind him, so most guys kept their distance. But prison is full of crazies, and one of them, a tattooed, semi-toothless skinny white guy from Nevada, attacked Jimmy in the middle of a poker game, because he thought Jimmy was cheating or because he was just a crazy violent fuck who did things like that. One minute they were all considering their cards, the next minute the cracker from Nevada was flying across the table, punching and scream- ing. Jimmy took a punch in the face, then got out of range and kicked the guy hard. He'd been playing with an old Italian from another family, "Two Boot" Tardelli, and the old guy's bodyguards were on them a few seconds later. They socked the guy, then held him while Jimmy went Balboa on his kidneys. Which got Jimmy a month in the box, but that was a whole lot better than a repeat of what the Latin Kings had done to him, or all of Dannemora knowing he got his ass kicked by a skinny white punk.

There were guys you stayed away from, big guys, tough guys, men covered in scars, men with teardrop tattoos, who had been fighting and killing all their lives. One of them was Joe Box. More than two hundred pounds, strong, and mostly gentle, but occa- sionally he went "5150"—batshit crazy. Look at him wrong and he might just jump you, and if he jumped you, you wound up in the prison hospital or a body bag. There were mean motherfuck- ers who carried shanks wherever they went, just looking to cut someone's face and watch him bleed. You bribed those guys with cigarettes, reefer, tailor-mades, whatever it took.

There were wiseguys and mob guys in the yard, like Tardelli, like Casati from Staten Island, and from him he heard they'd arrested Frank Rizzo. One day a guy just starting his bid made himself known, an Italian-American kid from Yonkers who'd run an auto theft ring. From the kid he heard that word on the street was the Ruggieros were getting out of drugs completely. Bobby visited. He brought food, arranged for cigarettes, cartons of them. From Bobby he heard that Vinnie and Milena got away, and were hiding out, somewhere in Italy.

Time creeps up on you, gradually, like the slow rising high the time he and Milena took Ecstasy, only in reverse: prison brings you way, way down. The sky is gone. You spend thirty minutes a day outdoors.

They installed a small television in his cell. On its flickering screen he learned that Sammy the Bull ratted out John Gotti. The Teflon Don was convicted of five murders and sentenced to life without parole.

He got a couple of postcards from Sabrina, but none from Milena. *We're all thinking of you. We keep you in our hearts.* He wondered if Milena told her to send them. Possibly. He tried not to think about her. Prison was no place to have a heart. But he couldn't stop himself dreaming of her. If he could change one thing, he'd get his time with Milena—one more day, one more night. He longed for her and knew that longing was wrong, stupid, and tried to banish her from his mind and heart. And still he longed. To kiss her neck and smell her hair and watch her sleep with the moonlight draped over her. And still he missed her, sometimes desperately, the way you might miss air or water or life itself. But time did to desperation what it did to hope, turned it into regret and sadness.

In the joint everybody is nobody, the warden was always saying. And he was right. Jimmy was nobody. Sometimes he didn't even feel human. He felt like a thing, like the stainless-steel shitter bolted to the floor of his cell.

He spent his thirty-fifth birthday in prison. Angry, confused, knowing he'd be there for his next birthday and the one after that. He wasn't a new guy anymore. He may have been a nobody, but everyone knew him. He did his push-ups and sit-ups; he kept to himself.

He didn't want to laugh, or desire anything, or need anything, because there's nothing to laugh about, not really, and desire turns into anger and need makes you weak. He lived curtailed.

"Do you think you might be able to forgive the guy who put you here?" Father Steven asked.

"Yeah, sure. As soon as I kill him."

The priest took off his glasses and rubbed his eyes. "Forgiveness is a journey."

Sitting awkwardly in the visiting room chair, with his knobby knees, big teeth, and long hands, Paulie looked like a rabbit. He told Jimmy their mother had a stroke. She was okay, on meds, slightly demented, and pissed off half the time. "In other words, nothing new," Jimmy said. And Paulie laughed. Jimmy said to tell her he'd be out soon. Paulie frowned, then said okay. He told Jimmy he was thinking about moving to Florida or California, somewhere warm.

His parents' visit was more painful. He told them the same thing: he didn't kill anyone. His mother had lost weight and her mouth was locked in a permanent scowl. His father looked sad, almost in tears, and Jimmy could tell he was in a hurry to leave.

His only regular visitor was Big Bobby. Thanks to Bobby, Jimmy got cash and cigarettes delivered to his cell by one of the guards and prison-approved gifts every month. Thanks to Bobby, Jimmy was rich in the can.

Bobby told him what they'd learned about Little Mikey. The Feds had been onto him for a while, and they had enough on him to put him away for a good long time. In Little Mikey, they saw someone they could crack—and someone who, even though he was a two-bit mobster himself, had dealings with three of the five families. They put the screws on and squeezed. Probably right around the time Jimmy was trying to negotiate with him. Bobby said they were trying to find him, but witness protection was hard to penetrate, and so far they'd gotten nowhere. As for the house painters, they were doing time as well. Separate trials. One of them, the one who pulled the trigger, was doing time in Ohio. Back in Brooklyn, Howard Gutkin was still working on a retrial.

They didn't even need to kill Double T. That was the thing. They could have leaned on him through his underboss or one of his *capos* or his *goomah*. Jesus Christ, they could have got to him a dozen ways. And if they were going to clip him, why did Jimmy have to be the one? Cocksuck luck? Fate? History? Maybe they were all the same damn thing. If they were going to kill someone, why not Little Mikey for chrissakes? Or at least get to him before he got to them. Little Mikey was crazy but even crazy people had their weaknesses, buttons you could push. If things had gone a little bit differently, if the cosmos had tilted slightly, there'd be no murder to hang on Jimmy, no snitch, no hoosegow, no cellblock blues. If. Thinking about it only made him want to cry, or talk to God, or kill someone, but all he could do was sit on his crappy prison bed and stare at a crappy prison wall.

You cannot love in the can. You cannot show weakness or break down or freak out or cry or let anyone intimidate you. You cannot lose your shit. You can be cold or callous or indifferent; you can be all of those things. You can fight and you can hate, but that won't get you anywhere. Memory is one alternative to love.

The Sun in Sicily

Milena

The sun was like a song, and even when they were speaking, the locals sounded like they were singing half the time. Sicily was cobblestone streets and a sparkling sea, old Palermo, the Giardino Inglese in full bloom, the busy port at Arenella, where ferries plied the waters from dawn to dusk. It was the farthest from Brooklyn either of them had ever been. They ate at local restaurants and Milena trotted out the few words and phrases of Italian she remembered from her parents and grandparents, learned some more. It was fun, a game, until you wanted to have a real conversation. "Things will sort themselves out," Vinnie insisted. For her part, Milena thought things didn't sort themselves out, you had to sort them out, but she knew better than to contradict him. They sat in the café near their hotel, watching the town and its inhabitants. They drank a lot, ate a lot. They told the locals Vinnie sold insurance and they were spending a month in Italy. But Milena couldn't shake the feeling of waiting, of not having arrived at all, as if Sicily were a big departure lounge and they were still waiting to get wherever it was they were really going.

Facchi phoned their hotel to tell them they were moving. Only when they were in the car did he inform them that their destination was Enna, a hilltop town roughly in the middle of Sicily.

"Enna è *bellissimo*," he told them. "Big *castello*, and much *conveniente* to Catania and Siracusa."

"Syracuse?" Vincent said.

"Siracusa," Milena corrected him.

"Fucka offa."

About an hour into the drive, Facchi explained in his terrible English that they could not stay in Palermo because the *Direzione Investigativa Antimafia* would soon know who they were, especially if they were seen in the company of Cornaro or any known Cosa Nostra, and they didn't want the cops to "make to look."

"Mister Falcone," he said, holding his nose. "Very bad for us."

"Falcone," Vinnie said. "Yeah, we heard about him. Trying to bring down the Mafia, like Giuliani in America."

"*Si, preciso.* Like Giuliani. You know the Maxi Trial? Many people arrested. Now we must be very careful."

"Many people arrested in New York too," Milena said. She had to hold her breath. If she said anything else, she was not sure what she'd say, or if she'd be able to fight back the tears.

They drove for an hour, listening to Italian pop on the radio and looking out at the knapweed and thistle and dry camel-colored scrub on either side of the *autostrada*. They stopped for lunch, then drove some more. The sun was going down when they reached Enna, an ancient hilltop town surrounded by green valleys. Facchi carried Milena's suitcase into the lobby of a small hotel, leaving Vinnie to battle with the rest of the luggage. Gesturing broadly, Facchi spoke to the concierge, gave Vinnie a crumpled piece of paper with his phone number, and, with a wide, stained-tooth smile, waved good-bye and, thanking the concierge and hotel staff, walked out of the lobby. Only when they had their bags in their room and Milena fished out their guidebook did they realize how far they had traveled.

The concierge gave them a map of the town, and they spent a couple of days walking the cobbled streets of Enna, buying bread

and cheese, eating pasta, and taking in the sights—the duomo and
ancient Federico tower, the green countryside surrounding their
hilltop aerie, old buildings, churches, and little farms down below.

Most nights they walked to the square near their hotel and ate
pizza and drank bad red wine. In the parking lot sat a truck piled
high with eggplant—the owner quietly hawking his vegetables.
Was his name Colossi, or were people just pointing out his size?
It came as a surprise when they heard American accents, and apart
from hellos and how-are-yous in restaurants and cafés, they spoke
exclusively to each other. They stood together at the hotel window,
looking at the apartments opposite, the old *nonna* down the street
who sat in a chair most of the day, the little shop that was the
Sicilian equivalent of a *bodega*. There was a greenish tint on the
road and if you stood to the left of the hotel window you could see
the restaurant sign spilling green light onto the street—Trattoria
Camillo. And just like that her life had turned into something she
could never have predicted.

The owner of their hotel spoke English, and after they'd been
there a few days, a British couple and their toddler checked in. The
other guests were mostly Italians or Germans traveling through
Sicily. One young couple could have been Scandinavian.

Vinnie made a call from a pay phone in a restaurant. Milena
watched from the bar. She didn't have to hear what he was saying
to know he was speaking to Rizzo. He was on the phone for a
while, shaking his head and pulling a sour face a lot of the time.
When he sat down, he ordered a vodka.

"We can't go back. I'm too hot."

From one of the old hotel porters, she heard that there were
sea monsters guarding the Strait of Messina between Sicily
and Calabria. You couldn't see them, but they were there, waiting.
The mob was another monster invisible to most people but even
here, high on a mountain and far from Palermo and the strong-
holds of the Sicilian Cosa Nostra, she could sense the long hand
of the Mafia. But neither mob nor monster wanted anything to

do with the American nobodies who had washed up on their shore.

After a week, Vinnie phoned Facchi. With help from their innkeeper, he asked his question in halting Italian: "*Possiamo visitare Don Cornaro?*"

"Mr. Cornaro, he is very busy now. Maybe soon. Is there something I can help?"

"No, that's okay. Thank you." He banged the phone down, and slumped on the bed, shaking his head.

In Calascibetta, a mountaintop village near Enna, they sipped *macchiatos* at an outdoor café, facing the old church and modern clock tower.

"So what are our options?"

"Options. There aren't many."

For once, he'd succinctly summarized a situation. She wondered if she could go back without him, if Vinnie would allow it, and if she could enter the USA without getting arrested. There was a warrant for her arrest, after all, and if the Ruggiero family didn't want Vinnie in New York, then they didn't want her there either. If she did return, it would mean going somewhere far afield, like San Diego or Orlando, living under an assumed name and always looking over her shoulder—and that was not going home.

"What do you think?" Vincent asked.

"I think we should stay right here awhile, might as well make the most of it."

He didn't say what he wanted, didn't talk about home, or being shunned by the local Mafia. She didn't talk about Jimmy, didn't say his name out loud. They drank wine and smoked Italian cigarettes. She knew she was putting on weight; she could feel a thickening around her midsection and ass. Another woman's body. It was as if all the unspoken secrets, the isolation and anxiety were being absorbed inside her, and she was expanding, growing large with loss. She missed her family, her friends, shops, pizza by the slice, their grumpy superintendent. Mostly, she missed Jimmy; it was like living without sunlight.

They didn't discuss being on the run or going home or things they missed or money. They talked about the menu in front of them, the shops they passed, and, occasionally, their own families—what so and so must be doing, this one's birthday, a baptism. Sometimes in the middle of the night, she thought about Jimmy, about what it would be like if he were there with her, not Vinnie. It was silly and painful, but she couldn't help picturing him beside her, walking along mountain paths and cobblestone streets. *I've been waiting so long to be where I'm going. In the sunshine of your love.*

They used a pay phone in one of the smaller squares, outside a *salumeria*, to call their families. "When are you coming home?" Sabrina asked. "Not for a while, but come to Sicily." They chatted and gossiped and laughed, but on the way home Milena cried.

Afternoons she left Vinnie drinking at the hotel bar and wandered the streets of Enna. She perused the supermarkets and pottery shops, bought blouses and summer skirts, picked her way through the markets, marveling at the fish stalls and piles of vegetables, tasting cheese and olive oil. Mostly she walked with no destination in mind, around the bay, under the soaring *duomo*, along Via San Luca with its modern apartment blocks, past pale stone buildings, restaurants, *gelateria, pasticceria, pizzeria*, ancient churches, and broad *piazze*. Occasionally, and always by accident, she caught the eyes of the old men and women sitting on chairs outside, leaning on windowsills, gazing patiently at the town squares. They didn't make conversation with her.

They agreed they should find somewhere cheaper than a hotel. Vinnie asked Facchi, but he expressed no interest in helping them, and once again after talking to him Vincent crumpled as if he'd been punched. So they asked the hotel manager and the waiter at their favorite restaurant. It was the waiter who found an apartment for them at the bottom of the mountain, in a zone of unremarkable apartment blocks of fading yellows and browns. There was a bakery down the street, a *farmacia* and a supermarket nearby, but the nearest restaurant was a twenty-minute walk, on the way up the mountain. The other direction led to Lake Pergusa. The apartment itself was small: tiny kitchen, living room, bedroom, metal shades on the windows, bars to hang laundry. The appliances and bath were old and chipped, and the place had an odd fishy odor, but they didn't speak of that either. It was cheap and clean enough and gave them more space than a cramped hotel room, and the view through the living room window of old buildings and the crumbling fortress walls of Enna and the sky was pretty enough that their first night they pulled chairs to the window and watched the world in all its flora and foreign splendor and got drunk on cheap red wine. They smoked cigarettes and ended up having sex on the thin mattress. They woke up to the sound of boys kicking a ball.

Vinnie learned how to order his favorite dishes and the names of wines he liked and figured out which hotels carried the *International Herald Tribune*, but there his knowledge of and curiosity about the island, country, and language ended. He mostly viewed Italians with benign mistrust, and suspected that their indecipherable customs and language were things they affected in order to confuse tourists. If a store clerk spoke only Italian, Vinnie shook his head and muttered, "oh, come on," and narrowed his eyes as if to say, "I know you're pretending so knock it off." The magic of Sicily that Milena grasped turned to malice in his eyes. From his perch, in the rickety chair pulled close to the apartment window, where he sat, usually with a glass of wine or vodka and a pilfered newspaper, Vinnie watched Sicily, and was always aggrieved to find people watching back, staring right at him from their balconies and window perches.

Down in the Hole

Jimmy

You don't change lockup; lockup changes you. You become a different animal. You think less; you see more. Eyes in the back of your head. You can smell trouble. Like a dog. Like a dog in a cage with other dogs. You're aware of minutes but not months. You obsess over new choices in the prison vending machine, how much whiskey you can get for a carton of cigarettes. You try not to think about time, or people you love. Loved.

Little Siberia, they call it, seventy miles south of Montreal. He gets books, cards, fruit baskets, backgammon and chess sets, credit cards that can only be used with prison vending machines. Bobby and the Colt get cash and cartons of cigarettes smuggled to him. Gutkin's motion for a new trial has been denied.

You live behind bars and concrete and locks. Bed, desk, toilet, and sink are all bolted down. You lie on your hard, narrow bed in the broken light and you want to cry, but your eyes won't shed tears. You are no one and you are nowhere, and there is nothing to do, nothing to do but wait and watch and not go apeshit.

Bourbon and Regrets

Tom

Cath takes the kids to her sister's house for a few days. Tom stays behind. The new zoning license means he has work to do, the sooner the better. He's meeting with his architect and soon he'll have plans to register with the building commission. He knows Cath's still angry at him. He's just got a zoning variance, which has the potential of making him a lot of money, but all she can think of is how they can get Jimmy out of the house.

Tom and Jimmy drink coffee together one morning and talk about the weather and, eventually, Tom's business. "Look at Red Hook, Astoria, Weehawken, New Jersey," Tom says. "Prices going up, up, up." He shows Jimmy realtor listings, Zillow.com maps with building prices and rents. Jimmy shakes his head at the computer screen, and Tom can't tell if he's impressed or not paying attention. "Amazing, the Internet," Jimmy says. Eventually Tom gets around to explaining that he would like to do it again. He's had his eye on a couple of buildings. "If you're looking to invest of course . . ." He's being presumptuous, but he can't stop himself. He tells Jimmy he knows realtors, architects, good construction companies. He starts to illustrate how a project might work and the possible returns. "Let's say we can buy an industrial building for one and a half mill." He can see that Jimmy isn't really paying attention, so he keeps it short.

"Sounds like a solid plan," Jimmy tells him. "I'd invest if I could."

"Sure, sure." He knows Jimmy's not a rich man, and he feels like a fool for throwing around big numbers. *One and a half mill.* Jackass.

That night they walk to the bar on Kessler Avenue. Dark wood, old barstools, mirrored shelves. The bartender is a young woman in a skimpy top with a tattoo of a bird on her shoulder. It's early and the place is quiet.

"I always wanted to become a made man," Tom confesses when the bartender is out of earshot. "But my father's dying wish was that I stay out, and I honored that wish. Didn't have much choice."

Jimmy strokes his chin, says nothing. Maybe it's a prison thing, listening more than talking.

They sip their beers. There's a couple kissing in a booth in the back, two preppy guys sitting at the window.

"Can I ask? Tell me to shut up if you don't want to talk about it."

"What?"

"Any regrets? I mean, you paid a high price."

"Everyone's got regrets, no?"

"Probably."

"I thought I had all the time in the world. I believed the family was all-powerful, believed the Ruggieros and Gambinos could do anything. When I was a kid and I saw the kind of mansions those guys lived in, saw the kind of money they made, I thought they were gods. For a while, in the can, I believed they'd get me out somehow."

"I'm sure they tried."

"Yeah."

One song ends and another starts, music trickling down from the speakers above the bar, and they're finishing their beers, and the place suddenly feels warm and friendly.

"My pops always said you can't have a family and be in the family," Tom says. "Even though he tried. He said the two didn't really go together."

"Yeah, I guess he was right," Jimmy says. "By the time I realized that, it was too late. Maybe that's changed now. I don't know. But the golden age is gone."

"Did you ever see her again?"

"Who?"

"The woman you told me about. Your star-crossed lover."

Jimmy's eyes light up like he sees something he recognizes, but only for an instant, then his eyes go dim, or maybe it's sadness or regret he's looking at. "No," he says at last.

Here's what you don't do. You don't say, "Do you want to talk about it." Not to a made man who served a twenty-five-year jolt in a maximum-security prison. You don't hug it out. You say, "Jesus, Jimmy," and buy him a cold one.

Sunny and Lonely, with a Chance of Showers

Milena

They had a system. Vinnie made a collect call from a pay phone in the minimarket near their apartment; Rizzo refused the call, then phoned back. There was good news: his brother Frank was out. They couldn't pin anything on him. Armone would serve a year, two at most. Only Jimmy got his ass put away good. They talked about Cornaro's insouciance, and Rizzo said, "What are you gonna do. His turf. Crazy fucking Italians." Vincent reported all of this back to Milena. She wanted to send a message to Donatella, but Vinnie said no. "What the fuck message you going to send her?" He was right. She wanted to see people, not send them word that she was okay or talk to them without saying anything incriminating.

"What about Jimmy?"

"Who knows. He'll do a long stretch. Class A felony. Conspiracy to murder in the first-degree. Nothing anyone can do about it."

The apartment in the foothills of Enna was too small; it had roaches and the walls were so thin that Vinnie and Milena heard every sneeze, every piss pissed, and shit shat by neighbors on either side. The hallways smelled of smoke, and the neighbors and their kids were loud. And the town itself was too small, too tranquil. Maybe if they were with family or friends, in a villa with a swimming pool, it would be fun. But alone together, cooped up in a low-rent apartment, they were going stir crazy.

They met the secretary to the local bishop, who introduced them to a man who owned property, and at his urging they paid a small bribe to a very tall man they met so briefly they didn't know what he did or who he was, only that he knew people who knew people, and, presto, they were able to rent the ground-floor apartment of a low-rise on the outskirts of Taormina, a hilltop town on the east coast of Sicily.

Perched above the Ionian Sea, at the foot of Mount Etna, Taormina was home to a Greek amphitheater, an Arab-Norman cathedral, Byzantine ruins, cobblestone streets, and flowers everywhere— orange blossom, olive and palm trees, oleander, jasmine tumbling from crumbling walls, cascades of fuchsia bougainvillea. The town was much bigger than Enna, their new apartment twice the size of the one they left—sunnier, cleaner, and it boasted a small garden, which was an overgrown mess, but Milena loved it. They were below the *stradone* but it was an easy walk to the old town, close enough that she could set up shop as an English teacher, working from her living room. Taormina was home to more professionals and rich kids than Enna, and that meant more potential students. Truth be told, she needed something to do that didn't involve Vinnie.

They phoned Facchi and told him they'd found a new place to stay. "*Si, si.* Taormina very good," he said. A week later he stopped by unannounced, presented them with a box overflowing with fruit and vegetables, nuts, olive oil, pasta, canned vegetables, *caponata*, wine. Asked whether his boss might want to see Vinnie, Facchi said only, "Mister Cornaro is very busy."

Vinnie punched the wall after he left.

"You can't be surprised, hon," Milena said.

He downed one of the bottles of wine from Facchi's gift box like it was a soft drink, grunted, burped irately.

"Fuck that, I'm offering him amazing deals. Besides, a little respect."

"Vinnie, they're in the middle of a war. You know what that's like. They're not interested in deals right now. For what it's worth, I'm sorry. It would have been good."

"Yeah, and we could use the money. They're fuckin' retarded here. They don't tell you nothing straight up."

"That's the Sicilian way," she said.

"Well, it sucks. It ain't the New York way."

Spring came to Sicily. Vinnie watched soccer on television. Milena read whatever English-language novels she could find and bought paints and paper and tried her hand at painting watercolors. She sat outside on a folding chair near the sea and tried to paint what she saw. But her renderings resembled children's pictures—the sea immobile and too bright, the ancient walls like a gingerbread cottage. But there was a serenity that came with sitting and painting, and the concentrated looking, and over time her pictures began to improve. She liked the big forgiving sky and experimented with the horizon, diluting the brush with water as she moved upward with horizontal strokes. The results were more impressionistic but more striking, and she pinned them up on the walls in the kitchen, replacing one with another when she finished a good one. Other than an occasional "nice," Vinnie didn't register her artistic endeavors.

"Do you want to go home?" he asked over dinner one night. Pasta again.

"Yes. But not without you." *And not if Jimmy is in prison*, she thought. Or rather, her desire to return was not as strong if Jimmy wouldn't be there. "Do you?"

"Sure. But I can't. They'll arrest me at the airport."

One day around that time, she was walking home from the market, when a man of roughly her age approached her. Probably a tourist, certainly no one she'd ever seen before. His face broadened into a smile as he approached.

"Paola."

He was evidently so happy to see her and kept calling to her, even if it was the wrong name, so she smiled back as he made a beeline toward her.

"Paola." His voice was friendly.

She looked at him. Yes, without doubt, he was looking right at her, or rather at someone he took to be Paola. As he approached, his smile flickered and faded.

"*Il mio nome non è Paola*," she said. She didn't know how to say you must have me confused with someone else, so she left it at that.

The man did indeed look confused, hurt almost. He muttered an apology and turned quickly, returning to a woman and little girl, and Milena continued on her way home. Who was Paola? For a moment Milena imagined that she might have been transformed, in that instant, become Paola, whoever she was (long lost friend? old flame?), and Milena would simply disappear and cease to exist. She had, after all, gone a long way toward becoming a new person, someone unrecognizable to the people of her past. Why not go all the way, become Paola? Her old self could just melt away and she could find herself living another woman's life, like something from *The Twilight Zone*.

Summer. They walked along the craggy beach, ate ice cream in the sun, swam in the cold sea. In August they learned about the murder of Antonio Scopelliti, one of the top Mafia prosecutors in Palermo. A few weeks later, a businessman leading the campaign against the "pizzo" extortion rackets was gunned down in broad daylight.

And then it had been a year since they'd left America. Milena had begun to work out the social hierarchy of a small Sicilian town. Tourists were economically vital but socially incidental.

Married women couldn't talk to men, not without going through an intermediary—a father or brother or another married woman. Everyone talked to old people and children. Very few people—innkeepers, restaurant owners—spoke English. Her father and mother spoke a bit of Italian at home sometimes, but Milena's Italian, even after a year, was rudimentary at best, and so she hired Amalia, a young woman from the interior who lived nearby and worked mornings as a housekeeper in a hotel. Twice a week Amalia came to the apartment or they met in a café, and she did her best to teach Milena Italian. It became easier when the mail brought *Let's Learn Italian,* a book Milena had ordered from Palermo. *Come ti chiami. Io mangio, tu mangi.*

One of the English speakers in town was Claudia, owner of a restaurant called Isola Bella. Claudia had been to America; she loved Los Angeles, jazz, George Clooney, Mexican food. A strong woman, on the verge of stout, Claudia was in her early fifties, with a kind face and big dark eyes. She'd lost her husband to a heart attack three years earlier. Milena told her about New York, her old life, and when she explained they had some trouble back home, Claudia didn't pry. They talked about the restaurant and Sicilians. Claudia sat in the back of the restaurant at lunch, keeping an eye on the staff and doing the books, and she invited Milena to sit with her when she had finished the accounts. From Claudia, Milena learned the identities of some of the more celebrated locals—the rich architect who owned buildings on Via Pirandello and down near the beach, the manager of the Hotel Timeo, the head of the bank, the painter, the former professional soccer player, the former model.

Milena watched, observed the social structure. For men, the structure was hierarchical. You didn't talk to a father without first talking to his son, didn't talk to a boss without talking to a subordinate. You were loyal to a few cafés and bars and one church, and you found a way to pay a tribute to the priest and Mafia boss, no matter how little you had. As for women, they were not exactly servile, but they were connected to a husband or father, or in some cases brother. Vinnie didn't figure any of that out, and it was one of the reasons he screwed up his one meeting with the Mafia boss. *Guardare* Vincenzo, Milena's auto-didact father would have said. He didn't watch, didn't try to understand. Every day he knew nothing more than the day before; it was like he'd just arrived.

The language came slowly. Her tongue slithered around the words like a snake around ice, and she couldn't seem to remember the rules and vocabulary from one week to the next. Yet she studied her book every day, practiced words and phrases. She liked the way people treated her when she spoke Italian, even bad Italian.

She was aware of becoming a different woman, a person who spoke a different language outside of the house, a woman who was more polite, but also more independent, than the one she left behind. She remembered dressing up with her sister Sabrina and cousin Stefano, younger brother of Gino, who was about her age. Sometimes Milena dressed in his clothes and wore a baseball hat. They'd say her name was Joseph, and when a ball rolled across the park she ran to get it and other little girls stepped back. That's how it had felt to be a boy and not a girl, and she liked it. Now she was pretending again.

She missed her period, and her breasts felt like they had flames inside them. She hadn't been taking the pill since she ran out a few months after they arrived in Sicily, because she didn't know how to get a prescription in Italy and because they had sex so infrequently she didn't give it much thought. She told Claudia, and they walked to the *farmacia* together to buy a pregnancy kit, and later huddled over it in the restaurant bathroom.

She waited a few days before she told Vincent. He raised his arms in victory, kissed her, hugged her tight, then loosened his arms, as if hugging her too tightly might harm the lima bean embryo deep inside her. She stopped drinking.

She thought about the life she was carrying inside her, the new soul safe and warm inside its amniotic sac, and couldn't help thinking of the life she'd carried inside her all those years ago, the one she'd aborted, snuffed out, the way you snuff out a candle. Now there was another light.

When she started showing, she bought dresses that were too big. She could not find a single shop selling maternity clothing. "*Sono piena*," she said with her dimpled smile. "I'm pregnant." Everyone congratulated her and wished her well. She'd done something good. *Stei sano come un pesce,* some of them said. Be as healthy as a fish.

She bought clothes and toys for the baby—a bassinet, a rocking chair, onesies, swaddling clothes, knitted caps, and booties. One day Vinnie returned home with a big set of bottles, colorful bibs, and tiny blankets decorated with sheep and birds.

"We're going to have a baby," he said, and she took his hand.

They laughed and hugged.

"I hope it's a boy," he said.

"You can't say that."

"I know. I'll love him, or her, anyway, but if possible, I'd like a son."

"Do you want to find out?"

"No, let's have one more surprise."

One thing she knew already: she'd have no sisters here, fussing over the child and dispensing motherly advice, nor her own mother. This was not how she'd imagined having a baby, and it hurt her inside when she thought about it.

Giacomo. Her baby. Her miracle, her beautiful, tiny son with huge black eyes. Their son. Her son. In the hospital bed, still wrapped inside the pain and muck of giving birth, she felt her heart swell and soar. Giacomo. Jack, in America. Or James.

After Giacomo was born she stopped being alone. She'd accepted her loneliness, worn it like a cloak. As to the question of whether to leave Vincent and return to America, she had worried about it for so long that one day she'd simply stopped worrying even though she didn't know from one day to the next what she would do. But none of that mattered now that she had someone to care for, to live for. A little bright-eyed boy who looked at her with love and wonder. She told him everything, and he gazed up at her with his wide dark baby eyes and when he smiled she thought her heart would melt with joy, and so she unburdened it to him. Her oldest sister, Maria, had two children, a boy and a girl, both in school, and when they spoke on the phone, they discussed diapers and baby food, bedtime routines, cures for colic.

Milena changed her wardrobe, going with the local predilection for floral patterns and brighter colors, dresses, not slacks. In Sicily, with Giacomo at her side, she made friends with other mothers, and there was a small group, centered around Claudia and the restaurant—the two regular waiters and a couple who lived nearby. When the restaurant was slow, drinks sometimes led to dinner. Vinnie never joined. Without friends, family, or work, he grew frustrated and quick to anger, drank by day, brooded at night. Even the cute, fat, dark-haired little being sharing their house, eating, crying, making guttural baby sounds and slurping mother's milk, seemed to bring Vincent little pleasure. He drank too much, smoked too much, ranted at strangers in English, blamed Milena for things that were not her fault, and rarely touched her except for occasional and increasingly unsatisfying sex. He'd got it into his mind that it had been her idea to run away to Sicily. "Vinnie, you're fucking nuts. I came home and you were packing the suitcases." "That ain't the way I remember it." They were strangers together, like castaways. She thought of a Frank Sinatra song her papa used to listen to: "You're lonely and I'm lonely." Only there was no change in the weather, no crying on each other's shoulder. They shared an apartment and a bed but no longer shared thoughts, fears, dreams. They cried, drank, changed diapers, talked to English-speaking tourists, did pretty much everything they did, alone—roommates, fellow travelers.

Milena continued to study Italian, still met Amalia at the café nearby, and together they fed and played with baby Giacomo while they talked and studied her book together, with coffee and cannoli. Now, in addition to weathered English paperbacks she borrowed from the lending libraries of local hotels, she read children's books in Italian to Giacomo, and to herself when he was sleeping. She continued to paint with the help of a video of a guy she saw on public television in America, a bearded, bespectacled, and excessively enthusiastic watercolorist. "Look how wet it is. Gorgeous. Now let's paint a few birds." The video taught flat wash and how to balance warm and cool colors and paint wet-on-wet.

They grew accustomed to being parents, to vomit and diapers and crying in the middle of the night, to lack of sleep and waking up tired every day, making formula, making baby food. She did most of the feeding, cleaning, bathing, burping. Vincent never got up in the middle of the night or early morning. She knew she could fight him over it, but he would win because he would refuse and yell at her. She didn't mind. She loved Giacomo, her *bambino bimbo*, loved his tiny hands and puffy cheeks, feasted on his easy smile and baby smell.

They watched the Barcelona Olympics on TV. Cuba won gold in baseball, to Vinnie's disbelief and horror. The dream team won gold in basketball. Meanwhile on the mainland the *mani pulite* campaign took aim at corruption and kickbacks. In America the Colombo family boss "Little Vic" Orena was convicted on RICO charges and sentenced to one hundred years in prison, and Bill Clinton was elected president.

After Cornaro spurned him, the local mafia all but ignored Vinnie. Milena recognized it before he did. Every *borgata* had them, the hangers-on, the empty suits and uninvited, the types of guys Vinnie used to mock. He railed against the Sicilian crew, against fate, the Feds, even the Sicilian pasta was not above Vinnie's scorn. "I liked Italy before we came here." When it was just an idea, those heady, scary days when they'd been on the run after the first few arrests, Sicily seemed like paradise. But paradise was different when you lived there. No one spoke English, and you couldn't get a hot dog or a hamburger or even watch the Yanks on TV. Vinnie complained about their son, about Cornaro, about destiny and chance, and his bad fucking luck. There was, it seemed, no end of injustices and grievances for Vinnie to complain about.

They rented another apartment—farther from the center of town, but it was bigger, cleaner, and more comfortable. Bright and decently furnished, it had a proper bedroom for little Giacomo and a courtyard garden where they sat outside at a metal table when the weather was fine, Giacomo in his high chair, spitting, dribbling, and throwing his food around him. Their neighbors were hard-working locals, most of whom had never left Italy. Hotel workers, porters, bus drivers, taxi drivers, a train conductor's widow. Vinnie complained; Milena didn't. Anything could set him off—the weather, a conversation with someone in town, a conversation with someone in America, not having a conversation with someone in America, Milena's cooking, or asking him to pick up behind himself or clean the bathroom or kitchen. He drank, smoked, and railed against something or other. This was what passed for conversation between them. Milena knew somehow that she must remain silent, that their relationship, their tenuous togetherness depended on her not fighting and not telling him what she thought, not all of it. She was aware of living in the present, day by day, trying to do meaningful things, spend time with Giacomo, with Claudia. She was not happy but she was trying, whereas Vinnie had stopped trying long ago.

One of the first warm days, they walked together to the beach with Giacomo, who had just turned one. Vincent lifted his face to the sun. "Still fucking cold. The heat don't work and the sun don't shine."

Milena felt jubilant in the sunshine. "Come on. It's nice in the sun."

Giacomo held her hands and took tentative steps across the rocky sand.

Vinnie watched for a minute, then shrugged. "Suit yourself," he muttered as he walked back up the beach.

She watched him pick his way through the rocks toward the road. *You're a small man. If I could do it all over again, I'd do it without you. You have no imagination, no soul, no love of art or music or beauty.* So many faults. He was shallow, lazy, his favorite music was Vic Damone and Bon Jovi. He hated classical music, art, had never taken the time to learn anything that could enrich his life. She imagined saying it to his face, as his dark figure grew smaller and smaller, drifting up the cement steps to the street.

Some evenings, she left Giacomo sleeping in his cot and went to the restaurant to sit with Claudia at her table near the kitchen. They spoke a mixture of Italian and English, and Claudia always offered Milena a glass of wine and a plate of pasta or the special of the day. Claudia explained that her husband used to come to the restaurant at the end of the night, and they'd walk home together. She was happy to have the company. "It's hard to make new friends." By the time Milena returned home, Vinnie was generally drunk and mellow or fast asleep. She'd kiss the sleeping one-year-old, inhale his sweet milky breath, and straighten his blankets.

One day Claudia drove the three of them to Catania. They didn't have a car seat, so Milena wrapped her arms around the boy, and saw the roadside through his wispy dark ringlets. Compared to Taormina, Catania was a big, bustling city. They walked along the Via Etna, the vibrant shopping street, and Claudia and Milena shopped, one of them trying on clothes while the other entertained Giacomo. Vinnie waited outside or at a nearby café. They bought a *giocattolo spingere* toy car set for Giacomo, and even Vinnie bought himself a couple of elegant shirts. At *La Pescheria* outdoor market, Claudia shopped for fish, spices, and herbs, and they ate a long lunch at an *osteria* near the marina. The restaurant was owned by a friend of Claudia's and they chatted animatedly, while the waiters amused Giacomo with breadsticks and fed him teaspoons of *casata*, and he toddled on wobbly baby legs between the tables.

But not every day was a sunny day, inside or out. One day Milena paused in front of the mirror and was surprised to see tears pouring down her face. She was still lonely, despite being a mother and falling in love with her own son—her cute, needy, cuddly little human. She was making the best of it, and she knew that was the right approach. Stop looking at what was wrong and look at what was right. But sometimes, not very often, she doubted herself. She told herself to be grateful and focus on the positive and think about how much worse things could have turned out, but the voice in her head sounded like a bad self-help book, and she wasn't sure whether the burden she carried was worth the weight. Here she was, nostalgic, years older. She missed her family; she missed Brooklyn. She pictured a ladder, and with each step she lost a person, a piece of her past, a piece of herself. And she just kept going because it was like getting old, something inexplicable and unstoppable, climbing higher and higher up the ladder, toward the place where everyone else was invisible.

Time Flies Like an Arrow,
Fruit Flies Like a Banana

Jimmy

You don't notice it. The postcards stop coming. There are fewer and fewer visitors. You stop waiting for your brother's visits or a new trial, for new facts to emerge, for the dumbfucks who pulled the trigger to say it wasn't you. As for *strunzo* Mikey Rossi, he's so deep up the sphincter of witness protection, he's pretty well impossible to find. You dream of clipping him, as unlikely as it may be. You picture the doorway of an apartment building, or an empty lot. He turns, sees you. Hello. *Bang-bang.* First shot in the stomach.

This is what you do in prison: you do time. You piss, you shit, you eat, you sleep or you don't sleep, you mark the days, in a place inhabited by crazy men, angry men, boys, punks, bitches, killers, lunatics who killed their mothers, old guys who've lost their marbles and spend the day shouting at walls, jazzed-up guys, the lifers waiting around to die, diehard criminals, the wrongly convicted, the crazies who think they're Jesus, men who think they're the devil, and a few normal guys.

You don't interfere in other people's business, you don't break up a fight, because curiosity gets you shivved. You don't talk to the crazies or the Muslims. You steer clear of the Nazis, the Aryan

Brotherhood, the Spanish gangs, the black gangs, the Islam Brotherhood, the Latin Kings, the bitches, the pimps, the Mexican Mafia, Dead Man Inc. You stick to your own people but you talk to whomever you want, because you're a made man, because you're serving a long stretch and no one, not even the Italians, tells you what to do. In the joint, you learn every day is the same as yesterday, and there is no beauty.

By his fourth year in Clinton Correctional aka "Little Siberia" aka home, Jimmy had witnessed a prison yard murder and countless fights, seen grown men flood their own toilets and cut themselves so they could smear blood and shit on the walls and door; he'd watched cell extractions where guards in riot gear pulled the crazies out, seen guys return to their cells glassy-eyed and twitching after a month or two in Seg.

Some newbie punk, a yoked-out white supremacist from Albany, talking Armageddon and spewing bile all across the yard, had a jones for Jimmy. "Where's the fucking Mafia now, tough guy?" Jimmy tried to mollify him. "I don't know. C'mon let's move along." "You gonna make me, mutt?" "C'mon pal." That's when the guy coldcocked Jimmy in the chest, knocking the wind out of him, and before he could get away, he was on the receiving end of two pretty good punches. Jimmy recoiled—the key was to stay standing—turned, pivoted, moved just enough to put some daylight between them and shout, "knife," and inmates closed in on them to take a look. There was no knife, but the punk paused, looked at the gathering crowd. Big mistake. Jimmy took another step, and now they were far enough apart that he could land one, two, three roundhouse kicks to the solar plexus. *Ichi, ni, san*, Bruce Lee'd the bitch, shoe connecting with flesh and gut. It brought little pleasure, but Jimmy knew if he didn't fuck him up today, he'd be back tomorrow. The guy was picking himself up when the Italians arrived. They herded Jimmy away from the fracas, then pinned the kid and punched and shoved him across the yard, under the indifferent eye of the guards.

In his home upstate, a room bright by day and dim at night, a room that measured six by nine feet, Jimmy learned about space and time. He learned how long a day was, how long it took the sun to move across one bar of a narrow prison window, how long a man could cry at night—not Jimmy, some pussy two cells down. He learned that he might serve twenty-five years and he might serve fifty. He read a lot. For the first time in his life. He read a poem about a guy who eats his own heart. He read the story about Rip Van Winkle, who went for a walk with his dog and returned to a place he'd never seen before. He read about parole hearings and Mafia guys who got off.

Jimmy did push-ups and sit-ups in his cell and used the gym equipment in the yard, took correspondence courses on the prison library computers. He learned about the Milky Way and elliptical galaxies and the expanding universe. He learned that the mayfly only lives three or four hours and that most hummingbirds don't make it to their first birthdays. He learned that Hindus are different from Muslims and read about the Hindu age of vice, when things went from bad to worse. It didn't surprise him to read that he was living in the dark age of Kali. He read about a king called Gilgamesh who tried to find the key to immortality and traveled across the world only to learn that humans cannot be immortal. Gilgamesh didn't want to die but Gilgamesh was mortal, and he died. Jimmy prayed he would not die in Clinton Correctional. He didn't want to leave in a coffin—back-door parole.

His parents visited again. His mother's face had screwed itself into a bitter expression since the stroke, but her mind was still sharp. At times they looked like they were holding back tears. Maybe they wanted to cry over the injustice of it all, maybe over seeing their little Jimmy locked up. He never asked. He didn't want them to worry; he didn't want them to cry over him. He always assured them he was fine, he was strong, he'd get out soon. When? "Soon. I won't serve out my term, my lawyer promised me." A rush of memories always followed their visits. Christmases, Sunday lunches, ice creams at Jacob Riis Park, falling asleep on his father's chest.

He was transferred to a private prison in Alabama. June bugs, kudzu, poison ivy, marsh, sweat, country music, country criminals, and a new kind of heat—heat that was forged in hell.

Sicily Time

Milena

Vincent's sister was their first visitor. They showed her around Taormina, and she said how wonderful it all was and how lucky they were, and they left it at that. She lived in Florida, so she didn't know much about Brooklyn or the Ruggiero family or the life they'd left behind. Nor could Milena ask her about Jimmy or her own family. They ate pasta with sardines and *scaccia* and got drunk on local wine. After three nights in Taormina the siblings drove to Catania, leaving Milena and the one-year-old.

A month or so later Vinnie, Milena, and Giacomo flew to Rome where they met Tony and Donatella Rizzo. It's Giacomo's first time on a plane, and he cried and threw up on her new blouse.

"Never thought I'd be in Italy for more than two weeks," Vinnie told the Rizzos.

They were having lunch, and Tony looked around—piazza, stylish Italian men, attractive Italian women, shoe store, bakery.

"Doesn't look too bad to me."

"Yeah, it's okay," Vinnie conceded.

"Must be hard to have a little one without your mama and sisters nearby," Donatella commented.

"It is. Vinnie's been a big help."

They shopped together and visited the Vatican. Some nights Milena ordered room service and stayed in the hotel room with the boy while Vinnie hit the town with his old *capo* and Donatella. Some nights they all went out, started early and had boozy, raucous evenings, each of them taking turns holding, walking, and playing with Giacomo. Only Donatella seemed to grasp the sacrifice of having a baby with no family and no help. "It can't be easy," she said. "Our men, they don't do much until the kids are a lot older."

They visited the Spanish Steps, ate at Alfredo's, toured the Keats-Shelley house, where Milena read that Keats's grave was inscribed with the phrase: "*Here lies one whose name was writ in water.*" She thought about her life and where she would be buried, and how impermanent it all was, how fleeting—a name written in water sinking and dissolving and floating away.

Sabrina arrived in June. The sisters and baby Giacomo stayed two nights in a nearby hotel, and then rented a car and drove to a big hotel near Messina. They swam in the hotel pool, walked along the rocky beaches, drank cocktails at the port, and watched the sailboats. It was so easy, being there with Sabrina, even sharing the joys and difficulties of traveling with a petulant toddler, so right that it moved Milena to tears because it was so temporary. Neither could guess when they would see each other again. Her sister asked if Milena was coming back, and she said only, "If I do, it will be without Vinnie," and Sabrina said she'd been thinking about going it alone as well, leaving Walter. If she wanted a shot at a second marriage, it was best to start now. Milena sent her back with presents for their mother and Maria. And then the season of visits came to an end.

Vinnie rented a car and they drove to Sciacca, a village on the other side of Sicily, where Vinnie got in a shouting match at a restaurant, swaying drunk and hurling curses in English while they swore at him in Italian.

She thought about her father and what he would make of it all. He probably wouldn't have approved of a Mafia man for a husband, but he would have approved of an instinct for survival and would not have berated her for fleeing to Italy. She couldn't imagine what it must be like to live in a prison, locked in, guarded. She and Vinnie were in a type of prison too, she sometimes thought. No guards, better food, and a more pleasant place, but a prison nonetheless, with their jailer waiting across the Atlantic. The thing about Vinnie's being a made man in the Ruggiero family was the sense of belonging. But now they didn't belong to the family, not really: they weren't there. And they sure as shit didn't belong to Don Cornaro and his team.

She offered to help Claudia at the restaurant when they had a wedding booked and not enough staff. Milena admitted that she couldn't cook very well. "Doesn't matter," Claudia replied in English. "You can peel and fry and carry." And that's what Milena did. After the wedding, they cleaned up and ate with the rest of the staff, and Milena carried home foil containers of pasta with pistachios, artichokes, ham.

One night she brought Vincent to the restaurant. He got drunk on vodka. How could she tell him: you don't order vodka unless you are paying, and you don't order four rounds?

It had taken nearly three years, but she was finally accepted by the locals, not only her fellow restaurant workers but the patrons. Men now spoke to her, with their wives present of course. One of Claudia's regulars, Braucci, a retired civil servant who'd lived most of his life in Milan, made a point of talking to her in broken English. On the street, she sometimes turned and waved when she heard, "*Ciao, Milena.*" She liked the way they said her name, soft and sing-song, *mi-leh-nah*. "*Ciao,*" she answered. "*Come sta?*" She made a bit of money at the restaurant and from her English lessons, so in addition to the funds that Vinnie was able to get out of America and the donations made by Armone and the Rizzos, they now had Milena's paltry income.

Vinnie flew to Brussels to meet Tony Rizzo. He was gone four days and when he returned he didn't say much about the trip, but it was clear that Tony gave him some money, because he was wearing new clothes, gave Milena a silver necklace, and shortly thereafter bought a case of expensive booze.

One night Vincent appeared in the restaurant. She was at a table near the kitchen, chatting with Claudia and old man Braucci.

"Come on," Vincent spat, grabbing her arm painfully.

He was drunk, and she slipped out of his grasp and tried to lighten the mood. "*Ecco*, Vincenzo."

"*Ciao*, Vincenzo," Claudia called.

But he ignored them. Grabbed her arm again, even more tightly this time. "We're going home."

"What's wrong? Giacomo all right?"

"No, he's not all right."

He yanked her upright and pulled her painfully out of the restaurant.

"What is it, is he sick?"

But Vincent didn't say anything, just walked off, and she followed him home.

Little Giacomo was snoring happily.

"What's going on?" Milena asked.

"You tell me. That guy your boyfriend?"

"Boyfriend? Don't make me laugh. Old Braucci is seventy years old. He's just one of the regulars at the restaurant. Is that what this is about?"

"Oh, one of the regulars. You see him a lot?"

"What about Giacomo? Is something wrong or not?"

That's when he hit her. Slapped her with the back of his hand. She was too astonished to move or say anything, and he hit her again. She felt her lip split open, and tasted blood. She turned and crossed the kitchen before he could strike her again, picked up Giacomo from his cot, shushed him when he stirred, and continued out the door.

She walked until the weight of the boy hurt her arms and back, then made her way home. Vinnie, nursing a drink and smoking at the small kitchen table, watched her take the boy into his room, where she settled him in his cot.

"Baby, I'm sorry," he said, when she returned to the kitchen.

He moved his chair back to stand but she put a hand on his shoulder to keep him seated. She pulled a chef's knife out of the kitchen drawer and stood in front of him, holding the knife close and steady before him.

"You see this? You hit me again, and I'm going to hurt you more than you hurt me. *Capisce?*"

Vinnie started to protest but then thought better of it and nodded. He was too proud to say anything, but she knew Vinnie. If he didn't punch her or shout, or at the very least tell her why she was wrong, then he agreed.

She stabbed the knife into a melon on the kitchen counter. The blade went in with a quiet hissing sound.

"And don't you ever leave Giacomo unattended or tell me there's something wrong with him when there isn't."

Back at the restaurant the following day, Claudia drew her out.

"What happened?"

"I fell on the street."

"How is Vincent?"

"Fine."

Claudia shook her head. "Did he hit you?"

"No. I'm fine."

"You've got to tell someone."

She spoke, saying only that he wanted to do her harm, but he won't try it again, because he knew she can repel him.

Claudia nodded. "He has been given the *fattura*, the evil eye."

"I don't know about any evil eye. He's mean and he's stupid, but he's weak."

"A *fattura*. He is afflicted."

Milena said nothing. God knew the Ruggiero family could use a trusted partner in Sicily, but sadly Vincent didn't know how to make that happen, and she knew now that it wouldn't happen.

He was a drunk, adrift, dissipating, a washed-out shell of a man with no ambition and no future, waiting to go back to America to get his life back. Well, he should just go. Go to prison like a man, then go back to the Ruggiero family.

Claudia got up from her barstool and hugged Milena.

"My sister, if there's anything you need, if you ever need to stay with me, you are welcome."

"Thank you. He's not going to hit me again."

"You know that?"

"Yes."

New Deal

Jimmy

Tom lays them out on the narrow kitchen counter, color print-outs of maps with little arrow stickers pointing to properties. Red Hook, Kensington, Sunset Park, Borough Park. There's a spread-sheet of loans and interest, architect's plans, a page of dense-colored charts. "Residential is a sure bet," Tom says, and he talks about "spikes" and "debt ratios" and "sweet spots."

Later, after they've had a drink together, he studies the spread-sheets and maps, with his reading glasses this time. Would it be possible to get another variance? No. It was a one-time deal. A favor from the boss of the family who made it clear Jimmy can't say thank you, may I have another. But if he could, wouldn't that be nice. Real estate investment—he likes the idea of telling people that's what he's doing. But there's no way.

He calls Melvyn Zelniker. The hidden cameras are still in place. Melvyn has run the program, and there are no matches on Mike Rossi. "Okay, I'll run it again. If there's anything close, I'll call you. Yes, don't worry, I won't tell anyone else."

Palermo

Milena

When he was a little more than two years old, Giacomo fell ill. It started with a cough, but it didn't go away, and soon he was thin, pale, and droopy-eyed. He cried all the time but wouldn't eat and couldn't sleep because he woke up wheezing. The local doctors didn't know what to do. They prescribed baby aspirin and hot baths. Amalia and her mother swore by cool fennel tea with lemon. None of it worked. Wide-eyed and baffled, Giacomo sucked phlegmy air into his lungs, grunted with the effort of each breath, coughed for hours on end. When he did eat, he usually vomited immediately after. Nothing made him better; he clung to his mother, burrowed into her and she held him tight, wishing she could make him better, or carry his pain. "I'm cold," he said, his little forehead furrowed, his eyes moist. She wished her sisters and mother were there to help her. They'd know what to do.

They drove to Palermo and took him to the big hospital. They phoned Facchi, and they were seen immediately, by two nurses and a young doctor, who peered down Giacomo's throat, and warmed his stethoscope before listening to Giacomo's chest, then drew blood from the screaming child. The doctor was swift and calm, and as soon as the syringe was withdrawn began comforting Giacomo, cooing to him. They would return when they had test results, soon, the young doctor promised, and he asked if there was anything they needed.

They didn't have to wait long. Giacomo had pneumonia. They said he'd need to stay a few days, maybe a week. They'd give him antibiotics, make sure he got fluids, which if necessary they would give him intravenously. Milena didn't want to leave the boy's bedside, not even to go to a hotel. She and Vinnie talked about it and decided he should return to Taormina. Milena stayed with the boy. She slept in a chair in his hospital room, watching his pale face, attending every twitch of his tiny sausage fingers, holding him when he coughed, her face pressed to his, whispering, "I love you, my baby. I love you and I will take care of you, *il mio angelo*."

The young doctor's name was Roberto Tardelli. A quiet young man, still in his twenties, she guessed. He was tall, thin-limbed, thin-lipped with an angular face, high cheekbones, and a bad shave and a habit of scratching his head vigorously before he spoke. He moved the stethoscope around Giacomo's chest and back and listened intently, looked in his ears and down his throat, pressed his long fingers against the boy's tiny stomach and along his back. He spoke very little to Milena, but he cared about her little boy, she could tell; he watched as Milena fed him antibiotics, a whitish fluid the boy sucked tentatively from the plastic syringe and then spat out, and before he left every evening the young doctor came to check on Giacomo.

In slow but precise English, Dottore Roberto suggested Milena buy honey and fruit juice which they mixed with the medicine and thereafter the boy drank the liquid antibiotic. Pear juice was his favorite. She reached through the rungs of the crib, stroked his tiny arm, and he fell asleep like that. When he woke she picked him up and cuddled him, and eventually they fell asleep together, cheek to cheek. Her boy. Her sleeping, wheezing son. She'd carried him inside her for nine months, fed him from her body, held him every day since his birth, and he was her world or the most important person in it by a mile.

Dottore Roberto warmed his stethoscope before applying it to the boy's chest. When he understood that Milena wasn't leaving the boy's side they moved him to a bigger room and wheeled in a portable bed for Milena. She slept nestling Giacomo, moved him to his cot, went for a walk when the nurses came each morning, washed and changed in the women's bathroom, fed him the honey and antibiotic and pear juice mixture, rocked him to sleep.

After a few days his color returned, his appetite too. He laughed for the first time in a month, toddled up and down the shiny hospital corridor. Dottore Roberto pronounced the antibiotic was doing its job. Giacomo had regained some of the weight he lost, and smiles had replaced the bouts of crying. The next day Dottore Roberto put down his clipboard and told Milena the boy was "*guarito*" or "most better." In the meantime, she could leave his bedside. He suggested they go out for dinner. He could have a nurse stationed in the room beside the boy.

She put Giacomo to sleep and then left him in the care of a stout smiling nurse. The restaurant was a short walk away, on a square off Via Dante Alighieri. She worried; the doctor assured her the boy would be fine and discussed infant pneumonia and lungs and antibiotics. He said it was lucky they brought him in when they did. After dinner, they walked back to the hospital along cobblestone streets. At the entrance to the hospital she thanked him again, and quite suddenly pulled him toward her and kissed him. Because she was so grateful, because he hadn't asked anything of her, not a solitary thing, had only given, and because he was a man who didn't look at her the way other men did, who looked at her only as the mother of a sick child—with sympathy and concern. He blinked his dark eyes, then kissed her back, and they stood under a streetlight kissing for a while, then straightened and walked back inside the hospital. The boy was sleeping, and the nurse said he had barely stirred. They took turns listening to his quick breaths, which came fast and clear now, not wet with mucus and distress. She kissed Giacomo's forehead. *Sleep well, darling boy.* She thanked the nurse and when Milena walked out with the doctor, she thanked him again, touched his shoulder, leaned on him briefly, and took his hand. He looked at her and she tilted her head slightly, answering yes to his unasked question, and he led her to an empty room, which they entered silently. The linoleum tiles were washed with dim streetlight from the small window. They kissed more passionately this time, eventually lying on the creaky hospital bed where he laid a hand on her breast and she unbuttoned her bra and guided his fingers across her body. Because she loved her boy, because she loved the man who made him better, and because she was lonely. After a while she unbuttoned his trousers and gave him a slow, quiet blow job. He purred. *Dio, oh mio.*

She stayed another day, and the doctor, who lived with his mother, booked them a hotel room. She brought little Giacomo along. The doctor didn't seem to mind. He carried the toddler to a nearby restaurant, helped to feed him, and then they returned to the hotel, where he went downstairs while she put Giacomo to sleep. He entered the room quietly, checked on the sleeping child, then unwrapped a chocolate bar, which they ate side by side and then had quiet sex, kissing chocolate kisses. Giacomo snored through it.

Back in Taormina, Giacomo gained weight, toddled around vigorously and was happy and healthy enough to resume his favorite new pastime, singing. His repertoire consisted of "Twinkle Twinkle" and an Italian children's song, courtesy of Amalia. "*Il coccodrillo come fa, non c'è nessuno che lo sa.*" Asked his name in English or Italian, he answered proudly, "*Djako.*"

Milena fell pregnant—a bit of a surprise, but a happy one—and their daughter was born in September 1994. They called her Mariela. Their neighbor, the train conductor's wife, a shrewd old Sicilian woman with whom they had dinner once in a while, told them it meant "bittersweet joy."

When Mariela was six months old, Milena took her to Palermo, leaving Giacomo with Amalia. She said the nurses at the hospital recommended the visit because there was no system of postnatal checkups in Italy. You had to bring your child to a good hospital. They didn't want what happened to Giacomo to happen to Mariela. No, of course not, Vinnie agreed. And off she went. They left the baby with Dottore Roberto's mother and spent the afternoon in a hotel. When they returned, the baby was sleeping, and his mother had cooked a feast. No questions.

A month later Dottore Roberto checked in at the old hotel in Mascali, in the shadow of Mount Etna, and Milena said she was going to visit Claudia's sister for a couple of days. Their neighbor would take care of the children and put them to bed, she told Vincent, and off she went.

Mascali was a large town, partly destroyed in 1928 by an eruption of Mount Etna, and subsequently rebuilt. The hotel was large and lavish, gilded and marbled, but not anywhere they would be noticed. It had a decent restaurant and was located just a block away from the beach. It was winter, and they ate dinner in the heated solarium restaurant, and then walked along the boardwalk to the beach. Milena enjoyed speaking to Roberto again—his intensity, his spark. He was lithe and lean and strong, a boy really, and when they had sex it was just as good as she remembered.

They walked along the foothills of Mount Etna. She showed him photos of the children. He didn't think to ask if the baby might be his, and Milena had decided not to tell him. First, because she was not even sure herself. Second, and more importantly, because she wanted to be in control of that kind of information: it was her secret.

She returned home on a Thursday night, after the children were asleep. Vinnie was drunk, chain-smoking, in front of the quietly yip-yapping television.

"I told you, no smoking in the house."

"I been exhaling out the window."

"Yeah, right. Come on, Vinnie. These are your children."

"Okay, okay."

A few months later, Roberto and Milena met again at the hotel in Mascali. Why don't you have a wife or girlfriend, she asked him?

He shrugged, shook his head as if it was an obscure question. "*No lo so.* Anyway, if I had a wife, I wouldn't be here." They ate dinner, talked, then had slow passionate sex. He stirred something inside her; she felt like a woman again. Afterward they walked on the beach and shared a cigarette. He was a sweet, serious young man, the first in his family to go to university. They talked a lot about his future. He was thinking of joining Doctors Without Borders or going to medical school in America to specialize. *What is Chicago like? How about Atlanta?* His future, of course, did not include her, and she never mentioned that the baby girl at home might be his.

Sabrina visited again. The children loved her, especially Giacomo who couldn't get enough of "Zia Bina." In the spring Milena's mother visited. She cried at the sight of her grandchildren and said, "Come home, Milena. It's not right for you to be so far away." "Soon, Mama. It's not so easy." With those brief, intense bursts, she kept her family alive. Hers was a quiet existence, a small life, smaller than she'd imagined for herself, but it was an even existence, sprinkled with happiness, and populated by two lovely, happy children. There was Amalia, and Claudia, restaurant and neighborhood friends, and a few couples with children the same age. Her only American friend during those years, when her children were young, was Ruth, a rich widow from Virginia, who summered in Sicily. The two of them spent many nights together, but that was only during her summer visits. For his part, Vinnie had one good friend in town, an American originally from Boston. Fred—chubby, balding, easygoing—didn't know or care much about baseball, so they didn't fight about the Yankees and Red Sox. He was a loner who watched American videos and claimed to be a screenwriter, although he'd never had a film produced and was seldom seen writing. Mostly they drank and complained about the Italians.

Vinnie went to Palermo for a few days and although he didn't say why, she knew it was to make a pickup. He was happy and hungover when he returned. He kissed the children. He was sweet and kind and soft with them, and surprisingly patient, tiptoed into their room at night, and sat in the rocking chair beside his sleeping children.

Milena was never entirely comfortable leaving the children with Vinnie, but she did it in order to spend another weekend in Palermo. Told Vinnie she was volunteering at the hospital. Dottore Roberto had booked a room in a luxury hotel, and they had sex beneath a gold-and-crystal chandelier and ate *saviordi* cookies and chocolate meringues in bed. She enjoyed herself but decided it must be the last time. If he contacted her again, she would tell him it was over. But she didn't say anything about that, and he was filled with ardor and dreams of his surgeon future, and there was a lot to talk about, and they laughed together, and the sex was good.

Milena's American friend, Ruth, returned for "the season" as she put it, rolling her eyes ironically. She was a bit of a hippie fruitcake type, but she was smart and funny and wealthy and very relaxed about everything, making it easy to spend time with her. They cooked and did their shopping together and drank red wine when the sun set, if the kids were okay and Milena was not working at the restaurant.

Milena thought about leaving. All the time. But the kids were happy and she wasn't so lonely anymore. Besides, divorce was not easy in Italy. If she left, she would have to abscond with the children.

Her children kept Milena focused on the present, on diapers and food, colds, sleep, formula, vegetables. Vinnie helped a bit. He put Mariela to bed when Milena was still busy with Giacomo. Sometimes, on the rare occasion that Vinnie and the children were all asleep and she not exhausted, she sipped a glass of wine or drank tea and let herself think about the past, or different places she might have been. And sometimes she let herself think about Jimmy.

When winter came to Sicily, Vincent talked about leaving, but Gutkin, the Ruggiero lawyer, said that was not a good idea. Vinnie was wanted in connection with the Russian gangland killing in Gravesend Park. "They got a hard-on for you, Vinnie. You won't make it through the airport, and even if you do, one wrong step and boom." All of this was reported to Milena, who listened and nodded but did not offer an opinion. She could see the worry on his face, but she couldn't really understand the existential crisis the news had provoked. It was not worth going to prison for murder.

They didn't discuss it again, but he became increasingly despondent, sulked, helped less with the children, stayed out late at night, and when he was home trash-talked "faggot soccer," Zips, the Italian language, *scungilli* grandmothers with hair on their chins, anchovies, olives, even risotto and caponata were targets of his far-reaching ire.

Vinnie's mood brightened when Tony Rizzo got in touch about a job. Rizzo planned to ship cocaine directly to Europe, hiding it in Chinese car tires they would export from Brazil. They would bypass US ports, which customs and the DEA were watching like hawks, and go directly to Sicily. "I could go to Cornaro," Vinnie told Milena. "Don't go to Cornaro," she snapped. "He never offered a helping hand, and he's not going to start now." Milena knew a small-time gangster through the restaurant, and he knew the 'Ndrangheta Mafia in Calabria, who reputedly moved a lot of cocaine through Europe. Claudia vouched for Milena, and the meeting was set. She asked the Taormina gangster, Papaceno, whose stock-in-trade was stolen electronics and selling drugs to tourists, if he could help them dispose of a large quantity of cocaine. "If your Americans have a good, cheap supply, I will warehouse the shipment and the 'Ndrangheta will move the goods. To them, the only thing that matters is the price and the quality of the goods."

"Just one thing," Milena told him. "Don't tell Vincent we've spoken about it. He has to think it's all his idea, or he won't go for it."

"I understand," he said, tapping his forehead. "*Facciamo finta.* We pretend."

Vinnie got some swagger back. Tony Rizzo still trusted him and needed him. He was Tony's guy in Sicily. They met Papaceno and together they came up with the plan he and Milena had already more or less worked out. A Chinese manufacturer would sell car tires on the cheap to Rizzo to avoid the antidumping duty they'd pay if they sold them directly to Italy. At Port of Santos in Brazil, cocaine would be stashed inside the tires, and in Newark the tires put on jeeps bound for Sicily. Papaceno's Catania shipping agent would warehouse the jeeps, so they could pull the cocaine out of the tires and hide it on a luxury yacht bound for Calabria.

If the cocaine turned out to be fake, Vinnie could wind up dead. But he only mentioned that possibility once, and they talked about it and decided it was very unlikely. Rizzo would test the merchandise, and besides he already had a relationship with the supplier. The weeks that followed, Vinnie acted like a new man; he was better with the children too. He was back in business. They were back in business.

The waiting was the hardest part. The cargo took two weeks to get from Brazil to Newark to Sicily. Papaceno forbade them from coming to the port or inspecting the merchandise. "We must be very discreet," he told Vinnie. A sample was delivered, and they all tried it together and it was top grade. They drank good wine and Vinnie almost cried when he made a toast. Papaceno's crew sailed the drugs to his 'Ndrangheta contacts in Calabria, while a team of mechanics worked on the jeeps. They paid the *bollo* car tax and sent them to used-car dealers, mostly on the mainland. They expected to turn a small profit from selling the Jeep Wranglers. A few days later Vinnie spoke to Tony Rizzo. Mission accomplished. The cocaine stashed in tires would fetch a street value of two million dollars. It was a big, successful score, and Vinnie's take would be more than enough to buy new furniture, bikes for the kids, clothes for Milena, and a family trip to Paris and Nice. He also got cheap, good coke from a local dealer, thanks to Papaceno.

Milena raised two happy, bilingual, good-looking children. The boy was more athletic, her baby girl the more beautiful. Just as it should be. Giacomo was calm, reticent; Mariela more hot-tempered and strong-willed. She was a Taurus, a bull. The Italians put a lot of stock in astrology, and what they said about her baby girl sounded right. Stubborn and loyal. She was also smart, the smartest one in the family. She had slender hands and a face like Milena's, but longer, more angular, like the doctor's.

For his part Vinnie was not a terrible father. It's possible he was a better father than he would have been if they were still in Brooklyn. He rocked and stroked them and sang them lullabies. Not every night, but enough. When she stopped to listen, she usually heard an old rock song, sung low and slow. *It's a Saturday night special, got a barrel that's blue and cold.*

The Future of the Forgotten

Jimmy

Y ou tell yourself to forget. You don't let in the past, don't let in the pain. You tell yourself you were just unlucky. The other option is you're the dumbest fuck ever to grace these penitentiary halls. Who lands a murder rap without pulling the trigger? You.

Jimmy was thirty-seven years old in October 1995 when OJ was acquitted. A month later, Bruce released "The Ghost of Tom Joad," and that's what Jimmy listened to on his prison commissary portable CD player, when he returned to Dannemora from Alabama in a cell on wheels he shared with nine feral, sweaty men.

Back in the old cellblock, he worked in the factory making plastic utensils for fast-food restaurants. Every day was the same: go to work, come back, lock in. But it was better. Fuck the Siberian winter, Dannemora beat Alabama any day. The Yanks won the World Series, Bill Clinton was reelected, and *The Long Kiss Goodnight* was Jimmy's favorite film. He liked a lady who could kick some ass and looked good too. He once knew one of those. Also he felt a kinship with the private investigator because things hadn't exactly come up roses for him. *I ain't handsome, I ain't rich, and the last time I got blown, candy bars cost a nickel.*

His parents visited again. His father complained about the motel. Pops looked old—hunched and shrunken. His mother told Jimmy he looked good and said she loved him. She felt brittle and bony when they hugged. Bobby Maritato showed up, on his way back from Albany where he was taking care of some business—he didn't say what.

The following year Savino visited. He'd paid a Mexican gang to protect Jimmy while he was down in Alabama, and now paid the Dannemora Italians. "Ain't a day goes by I don't wish we could do it all again, you know, kept you out of here," he said. "Not your fault," Jimmy said.

It was in the prison factory that he met Louis Perkins, a black taxi driver from Brooklyn. They talked about the old neighborhoods, New York pizza, burger joints, bagels. Louis Perkins killed a man, but the man had threatened him and was carrying a gun. The jury didn't think it was self-defense. Jimmy got a pen pal, a woman in Minnesota, who wrote long personal letters that stopped as suddenly as they'd started. His brother remembered his birthday each year with a happy-looking card inscribed with something like, "Looking forward to seeing you." *So come and visit, motherfucker. I ain't going nowhere.*

The priest told him compassion was good and forgiveness was a journey. Maybe. *Their sins and lawless acts I will remember no more.* It took years for him to stop hating. Forgiveness was a million miles away.

Everyone loved *The Sopranos*. Non-Italian guys ribbed the Italian guys. Jimmy just shook his head. "It's fuckin TV," he told them. They asked if he knew John Gotti or Joey Armone. "How would I know them? And no one calls him Joey." Half of them laughed. "Did you know Tony Soprano?" "Sure, I knew him. And Big Pussy too." The other half laughed. The truth was you barely knew anyone anymore, and no one outside of these *mortadella* fucks in this life-ruining cellblock actually gave a shit about you.

A new millennium, same prison cell. You turn forty-two. Winter is cold. You turn forty-three. Winter is cold.

Profit and Loss

Milena

The kids were at school when Claudia walked over to the apartment to tell Milena that a couple of young Yanks were looking for two Americans. Not at her restaurant, but at a bar nearby, and apparently they'd made inquiries at some of the hotels as well.

"Men, I assume."

"Men, yes."

"What did they look like?"

"I didn't see them. I'm just telling you what I heard."

With the help of a blonde wig loaned from the local hairdresser, Milena went in search of the young Americans. She found them eating dinner in the hotel restaurant and surreptitiously snapped a photo. When Vincent looked at it, he said he didn't recognize them, and they didn't look like wiseguys, but that didn't mean they weren't looking for him. Papaceno didn't recognize them either, but he recognized one of their T-shirts, from Ibiza, and remarked that they were tanned, young, prosperous looking. Too young to be Mafioso, too rich to be Feds.

"Probably looking for some friends," he said. "If they ask questions, about jeeps or tires, I'll find out. *Non ti preoccupare.*"

Vinnie frowned.

"He means don't worry," Milena said.

After two days the young Americans left town.

In May Milan beat Juventus to win the Champions League. Mariela turned nine in August, and they took ten girls to her favorite *gelateria*, where they ate ice cream and played Sonic the Hedgehog and Donkey Kong, and danced across the café floor, and the birthday girl enjoyed a steady stream of dance partners. She was happy, and that made Milena happy, and when Mariela danced with her drunken father, Milena watched and remembered birthdays when she was a girl, dancing with her papa, and she felt happiness and sadness in layers, like lasagna, she thought, one on top of the other—a layer of joy, a layer of regret.

In September Milena celebrated her own birthday at Claudia's restaurant. Ruth was in town, and they invited Fred, Vinnie's drinking buddy, the parents of a boy Milena tutored, their neighbors, Papaceno, Facchi, the train conductor's widow, the chef and his wife, Amalia, restaurant workers, old man Braucci and a couple of the regulars, and Rosario Crocetta, who owned hotels and restaurants throughout Sicily and was a friend of Cornaro and the Donato family. With the children at a separate table the restaurant was booming, loud, and very celebratory, festooned with balloons and birthday hats and noisemakers, and everyone laughed and they sang "Happy Birthday," first in Italian and then in English, and Milena raised her glass of prosecco and thanked her friends for giving her such a wonderful party.

The next day Vinnie couldn't get out of bed. He said he must have drunk too much Amaro, but he'd been feeling bad and looking thin and pale for a while, so Milena made an appointment with the local doctor who sent Vincent to see a specialist in Rome, who diagnosed pancreatic cancer, which had gone unnoticed at least a year, maybe more. It was, he said, difficult to diagnose, because the tumor caused very few symptoms and was impossible to see or feel. He had surgery a month later, in Palermo, and when they returned home he put on weight and, for a while, appeared to be recovering.

He did not recover. He suffered through gemcitabine chemo-therapy—which almost killed him—and looked like a prisoner of war, which, she supposed, he was, only the war was raging inside him. He was put on what the doctor called palliative therapy, meaning drugs that made him foggy and meek as a kitten.

"We were a good team," Vinnie said one evening, looking at her through heavy-lidded eyes.

She touched his shoulder. "Maybe. Sometimes. We should never have gotten married."

"Why would you say that?"

"Because it's the truth. We stuck together because we were scared—and then because of the kids."

Vinnie grunted, and she couldn't tell if the slight movement was his attempt to shake his head or a surge of pain.

"Can I get you anything?"

Until the last month, he was in little pain and said with a wry smile, "Having the time of my life, the last time of my life." He received a steady stream of friends and family, including his sister from Tampa. The children paid their last respects, and then the priest. He died at home; Milena was at his bedside. You die how you deserve to die, according to mobster wisdom. Once Vinnie told her he expected to die by an enemy bullet. It turned out his enemy was within.

Vinnie's sister returned for the funeral, and every day brought a UPS van, scooter messenger, or *bici corriere* with envelopes of cash, food, bouquets of flowers from Ruggiero captains and Vinnie's old crew.

After the service, friends and family went to Claudia's restaurant to pay their respects and eat. At the end of the night, after everyone had gone and Milena had sent her kids home, she helped clean up, and when the cook and waiter had gone home, she sat with Claudia at the bar, just the two of them, barefoot, their makeup smeared, getting drunk on vodka.

"In honor of Vinnie," Claudia said, and they clinked glasses.

"In honor of getting drunk after you bury your husband."

"*Salut.*"

They drank another round, compared notes on the funeral—who looked good, who looked old, who came, who didn't.

"He wasn't a bad man," Milena said.

"*Ecco*, that's not something I want on my tombstone. She was not a bad woman. Sorry but he was not a good man. He made mistakes, and he didn't respect you, but I don't want to speak ill of the dead."

"I think you just did."

Claudia grunted, and poured another round.

"I forgave him a long time ago," Milena said.

"Then you are a good woman."

"Maybe, maybe not. I think you have to forgive people for the things they do that are wrong or bad or stupid, because in the end you have to forgive yourself for not being a better mother or a better wife or daughter or whatever you yourself did that was wrong."

A memorial service was held in Brooklyn; Milena did not attend.

About a year later, with the help of their old friend Facchi, who had always liked Milena more than Vincent, she was able to get fake police records and acquire from the coroner's office the body of a destitute young woman found dead in a Palermo *casa popolare*, a poor government housing block. The Mafioso fixer didn't seem surprised by her request, just smiled and told her he was happy to help, and she knew that she would have to pay him and a couple of bribes, but they wouldn't cost much. "*Chi non fa quando può, non fa quando vuole*," Facchi said. "You catch the *opportunità* now, yes." She didn't know exactly what that meant but she got the gist—he would help—and did her best impression of a knowing smile.

As a result of Facchi's intervention, the hospital provided one name to the local coroner and another to the US Consulate in Palermo. In America, Milena DeNunzio was dead, killed in a tragic car accident. Only her family knew the truth. In Sicily, obituaries reported the death of Caterina DeNunzio, and even those both literate and inquisitive did not recognize the name. Besides, everyone could see Milena was alive and well. Sabrina flew to Taormina with her husband and children, so she could report back on the funeral that never took place. *There's no way out, except in a casket.* Or maybe there was. The Ruggiero family would think she was dead, and finally she'd be able to travel back to the United States. She'd get a new passport under her maiden name.

There was a memorial service in Brooklyn, and Milena imagined Ruggiero made men and their wives in fashionable black dresses drinking and paying their respects. The day of her own memorial service she drove to a beach and took a long walk on the craggy, rocky shore. At last she felt free, and she found herself thinking not about her own life but about Vinnie's. She loved him once and thought of him mostly with fondness now. Their children were their successes, and Vinnie had loved them in his way, and of course he was once a rising star in the Ruggiero family, but in many ways his life had ended in failure. He never got it together in Sicily; he waited but it didn't come, whatever he was waiting for, never materialized. It occurred to her that was the hallmark of failure: it happened slowly, like a candle burning itself into oblivion, consuming success and hope and time. Was she herself exempt? What would be the measure of her life?

It was with that unhappy question in mind that she climbed the flowering escarpment, perfumed by sweet pea and spring grass, and looked out at the gray sea. Soon it would be time for dinner, and if she wasn't home her children would worry. Somewhere on Long Island, she was being memorialized by mobsters and their wives who barely knew her, while a few miles away an unfortunate waif was buried beneath a gravestone that bore the name, Caterina DeNunzio, Vincent's mother's name. Milena wondered if Jimmy had heard—her fake death would be real to him. Maybe one day they could get word to him, but not yet.

If You See Her, Say Hello

Jimmy

He tried not to become bitter or mean or crazy. He did his best not to lose his temper, his marbles, or his health. He had friends in the cellblock, knew most of the guards, kept his nose clean, steered clear of smoke and drama. There was a prison library, and he took correspondence courses, got his GSD and applied for Pell grants, so the online courses were cheap. He did his home-work diligently and received two certificates from Ohio University Correctional Education, in accounting and Italian.

Jimmy read about his lover's death in a letter from Bobby. They buried her somewhere in Italy, and he wasn't even there. Never got to say good-bye. Hell, he never got to say hello in fourteen years. He requested permission to attend the memorial service on Long Island, but since he wasn't family, permission was denied. All he could do was mark the day and remember her—how beautiful she was, how unfair it was that she went so young, and how he wanted to see her, just once, just one more time. *She still lives inside of me; we've never been apart.*

You feel yourself shrinking, your body, your soul, even your memo-ries. You keep to yourself, don't speak very much, and then one night you realize the sound of some old bum crying in his cell is you.

Hope is a dangerous thing in the can. Hope makes you stupid; hope gets you hurt. It's like a disease; it can rot your soul and scramble your brains. The only thing worse than clinging to hope is losing it, but spend a couple of decades in the joint and lose the one you love, and you're liable to lose hope.

As for love, kicked and half forgotten, love was like a mangy old dog limping around in the shadows. You aren't even sure it's there, but sometimes you hear a lonesome bark. He'd felt alone and isolated for fourteen years, but now that Milena was gone, it was like living without light.

There was nothing he was fighting for anymore. He'd lost years not allowing his grief to consume him, then more years tending it. He was surprised when he saw himself in the mirror—the thin face, hard cheekbones, and the hollow eyes of a sad man.

A White Fly

Milena

An American widow in Sicily was *una mosca bianca,* a white fly, a rare species. It was strange to be the object of stares and whispers, even if a lot of what was said was compassionate. *Che peccato,* they said. *Poverina.* What a pity. Poor woman. Stranger still was knowing that people in America believed she was dead: everyone she knew there, in fact, apart from immediate family and a few close friends, believed she perished in a car accident. Dead in America, alive in Sicily. She was not grieving, not beside herself over Vincent, but his death and her fake demise brought with them a reminder that her taper was burning, hopes and dreams flickering. There was also a physical aspect to the loss; there was the silence, the emptiness that filled her, the absence of someone who had been there, right by her side for twenty-five years.

They attended Easter Mass in the local church. Giacomo, a long-limbed twelve-year-old, took her hand and led her inside. The priest, in a raspy voice, talked about Jesus and the fire that became light. It occurred to her she had become liberated; she was free from Vinnie and the family and fear. She was also alone. Mariela was ten—imperious, feisty, independent. She was a lot like the girl Milena wanted to be at that age.

Not quite alone. She had the kids and a few good friends, her family back home. And after a respectable amount of time, very discreetly, in order to avoid being the subject of further gossip, she added a new friend, Rosario Crocetta, the hotelier, whom she and Vincent had met through Facchi a long time before. He had a wife, girlfriends; nonetheless he took her to expensive restaurants for lunch, usually Regina Lucia on Piazza Minerva, all the way on the other side of town. She didn't mind if they were seen together. No one would tell his wife. When it was warm enough, he took her sailing. They dropped anchor in an empty lagoon and ate prosciutto and cheese and drank champagne. They made love on the narrow forepeak bed and afterward he made coffee on the single burner.

He was a generous man and a decent lover. After sex Crocetta liked to drink coffee. Milena swam naked in a cove; Crocetta watched. She felt young, desired, and very much alive. They met every week but had sex only half the time. He came to the house sometimes, and the kids knew and tolerated him. He never spent the night. A bit of company but not too much, a gentle romance.

Summer arrived, bringing street vendors and tourists, including the other American widow, her friend Ruth. On a hot night in July a woman fell to her death off the edge of a building in Lumbi, and it was the only thing anyone talked about for a week. Giacomo had a summer job working for the Consorzio per le Autostrade Siciliane, which managed the motorways, but he was given plenty of days off, and on some of those days and weekends, the three of them would pile into Ruth's car and drive to nearby beach towns—Nizza, Giardini Naxos, Alì Terme, and one weekend all the way to Messina. They packed up the car with swimsuits and a picnic, and drove with the windows open, listening to loud music. Giacomo and Mariela would meet kids their age on the beach and disappear for the afternoon. Milena loved the sea in summer, running and diving into the cold blue water, sunlight sparkling on the waves all around her.

Another weekend they drove south, just Ruth and Milena. They stopped for lunch in Santa Tecla, a small fishing village, then continued south along Via Argenta, past old houses, peeling ochre and peach paint, following the craggy shoreline. They parked near the town of Acireale and walked along the pebble-and-gravel beach. There were little houses right on the beach, larger houses on the hill above them. Two girls occupied folding chairs; an elderly couple was walking slowly. Ruth and Milena walked for a while, saying nothing, both looking at the stones and pebbles and sea.

"Don't wait too long before you start the rest of your life," Ruth told her.

"What do you mean?"

"I've buried two husbands. They're not coming back. Think of where you want to be in five years' time. Who you want to be with, how you want to live. And start now."

"Who I want to be with!" Milena exclaimed, but she was already thinking about what Ruth said, about where her children would be in five years' time and whether the day would come when she would want to return to America for good.

There was another version of Milena, online, a Facebook presence with a fake name—Red Azzura—and seventy-one friends. Through her Facebook alias she kept up with her sisters and their children, her Italian friends, and a smattering of old American friends. Lauren, the former stripper, now sold real estate in California; Roberto Tardelli was now based in London and "in a relationship."

In December, she read that Vincent "The Chin" Gigante had died in prison in Springfield, Missouri, and she wondered when Jimmy would get out and prayed that he wouldn't die in a prison bed.

Back in Brooklyn

Milena

Just shy of the two-year anniversary of Vinnie's death, Milena decided it was time. Because of what her friend Ruth said about planning for the next five years, and because her life was a lie. She was lying to everyone, including herself, about where and who she was and whether she was alive or dead. She did not want to come clean with Mariela about who her father was, but it was time to go to America, to be herself again, and make her life whole, if such a thing was still possible. Death, it seemed, had bequeathed courage.

She spoke to a lawyer in Manhattan who confirmed there was no longer a warrant for her arrest, thanks to the statute of limitations.

Rosario Crocetta's lawyer accompanied her to Palermo, and together they visited the US Embassy. He did most of the talking, and it was clear that he'd spoken to someone beforehand, and the complex machinery of Sicilian influence was at work. The passport—officially an update, using her maiden name—would arrive by courier within a week. She stayed overnight in Palermo, bought ceramics, spices, glass figurines for her mother, T-shirts and chocolate for her sisters' kids, a pair of shoes, and a new suitcase for herself.

Amalia moved into the house to stay with the kids, and in April 2006, nearly fifteen years since her departure, Milena booked a ticket to New York.

At the airports in Palermo and Rome everyone spoke to her in Italian. It was only when she landed at JFK that people spoke English. The customs officer punched in some numbers, then gave her a friendly smile and said, "Welcome home."

She cried when she saw her sister's children in their suburban home on Long Island, cried again when they drove down their old street in Brooklyn. But the city of her youth was no longer there. There was a new city in town. And there was the shadow that had followed her, because other than her immediate family, everyone she knew thought she was dead. She'd gone online and read her own obituaries, one in the Palermo paper, one in the *Daily News*. "*Donna umiliata*," the *Giornale di Sicilia* called her. A humbled woman. What did they know about women, humbled or otherwise? *Non capiscono niente di nulla*. They didn't know shit about shit.

In America, Milena felt just slightly Italian and more than a bit of an outsider. She stayed on Long Island with Sabrina and her children. Sabrina had visited Sicily many times, but the children had been only once. They drove through the old neighborhood in Brooklyn but didn't walk the streets for fear of being recognized by someone from the old days. They ate at restaurants in Manhattan, went to the Blue Note to see an aging jazz legend. She took the train to Connecticut to visit Maria and the niece and nephew who were now adults. She didn't call any of Vinnie's friends or anyone associated with the Ruggiero family, nor did she apply for a prison visit to see Jimmy. It was too great a risk to take—for him and for her. Besides, she was not ready for a half-hour meeting in a prison visiting room, not ready to see him in a prison uniform, not ready to tell him that she was not in fact dead. She knew it must have hurt him to hear of her death, but she also knew that wound was now old and probably healed. Let the dead remain dead, and leave him in the past—perfect, young, handsome, waving good-bye as her cab pulled away on a rainy street.

Dinner at Sabrina's with her mother and sisters and their husbands and children. Her mother cried and pinched Milena's cheeks like she used to when she was a little girl and said how much their father would have loved to see them all together, so beautiful and healthy, and Milena back among them.

"My baby." She stroked Milena's hair. "You look good."

Her mother looked old and frail, but when she smiled, Milena could see the woman who put her to bed every night when she was a girl, the mama who cooked dinner, mended clothes, comforted them, loved them.

"Thank you, Mama."

"You do look pretty good for a dead woman," Sabrina said, and they all laughed.

"Too thin," their mother said, shaking her head at Milena, who was not thin.

"Maybe if you died you'd lose some weight too, Maria," Sabrina said.

"Hush," their mother scolded. "Don't say a thing like that."

She stayed in a hotel in Midtown, visited the Museum of Modern Art, lunched with Sabrina on Fifth Avenue. She couldn't stop the flow of memories. The Sanderson Hotel, Central Park, moonlight on Lexington Avenue, *I love you, Jimmy Piccini.* She visited a few of her old girlfriends, the only people in America, apart from her family, who knew she was alive and she trusted not to tell. Sitting with Sherrie White, childhood friend, now mother of three, in her suburban living room in New Jersey, Milena realized this was not her home, and she must return to Italy. Of course Sicily may not be home either, but it was home to her children. It was not the life that she imagined for herself as a little girl, or when she was newly married, not the big, happy family with her sisters coming by for Sunday dinners populated by excited children and smiling grandparents. But it was *her* family, her lovely children, and she was content to stay there with them, in Sicily.

ooooo

She returned to her yellow kitchen, her bedroom, to the cathedral on the square she passed on her walk to the restaurant, to old shuttered windows with peeling turquoise paint, to Fiats and Vespas and cobblestones and a lavender afternoon sky, to the sea wall, and the smell of salt and olive trees.

The kids were at school. Alone in the apartment, she made coffee, tidied the kitchen in preparation for a student who would arrive in half an hour. His father worked in a bank, and the boy was polite and punctual, but his English was terrible; he had no ear for languages. She'd bought fish for dinner, a bottle of wine. Giacomo and Mariela would be back around five. She had so much to tell them, about their grandmother and aunts, and presents to give them—iPods, jeans, jewelry for Mariela, a watch for Giacomo.

Years went by. Giacomo worked as an engineer in Palermo, Mariela, at the finest hotel in Ortigia. There was something theatrical about her daughter—part ballerina, part circus master, with her long, slender limbs and fine features and an elegant nose that did not resemble anyone's in the Cossutta or DeNunzio families.

When she heard from her sister that Tony Rizzo, now *capo bastone* of the Ruggiero family, had been indicted, she planned another trip to America, this time with her children. Before they left, she went to see her old friend Papaceno, and called in a favor. His mobster days were long since over, but he was happy to see her, and happy to help his old accomplice.

Giacomo and Mariela had been to Rome and Milan and Paris; nevertheless, they were wide-eyed in Manhattan, awed by the size and speed of the city, the lights, the skyscrapers, the restaurants, the variety of humans, the fashionable women and smartly dressed men, the din of city and traffic and human life that grew quiet at night but was never silent.

Milena went alone to her appointment with the Brooklyn District Attorney's Action Center on Jay Street, where she told an "assistant specialist" that she had information about a crime. The young woman perked up when Milena mentioned drug smuggling and the Ruggiero family, and a few minutes later she was sitting with the prosecutor handling the Rizzo trial.

Assistant District Attorney Sharon Epstein had the face of a once-pretty law student who had smoked too many cigarettes and cross-examined too many criminals.

"Siddown, siddown," the prosecutor said, and waited for Milena to sit before continuing. "So, tell me about Tony 'the Turtle' Rizzo."

"I can tell you no one calls him Tony the Turtle. I can tell you I know him personally. I know about Port of Santos. I know how he launders money."

"I'm listening."

Milena produced the bill of lading for forty-six American Jeeps with Chinese tires and explained that she'd rather not testify because Rizzo thought she was dead and Milena would like to keep it that way.

"I understand." Sharon Epstein looked over the laptop screen at Milena. "Well done."

She'd thought a lot about what she owed Jimmy, and what she could give him. She felt about him the way she felt about her children—a love that is inextricable from the desire to protect. There was a sharper ache as well, something left undone that compelled her to act now, to buy his freedom if she possibly could. And if she had to testify? She would take the stand. Would the Ruggieros go after her for ratting on Tony Rizzo? Probably. Would they go after her kids? No. They were Vinnie's kids too, after all.

Sharon Epstein typed a few notes while Milena provided more details of Rizzo's cocaine trade—the shipping company, the name of a Sicilian car salesman who bought a dozen jeeps (no mention of Papaceno of course). The prosecutor asked a few questions and wrote down Milena's addresses and phone numbers in New York and Sicily, in case she needed to follow up.

"There's one more thing," Milena said. "I want to talk to you about a crime committed twenty years ago. I have some new information."

The beginning of a smile as the prosecutor looked up from her laptop. "I knew I liked you."

Milena knew that someone snitched, that's how they got Jimmy; she knew that Sammy the Bull's testimony put Gotti away. With Vinnie gone, she was pinning complicity on a dead man. She looked around the cluttered office and began. First she explained that Jimmy didn't plan the hit on "Double T" Capeci; it was Vincent who planned the murder. Jimmy was there only to pay the killers and confirm that the job got done. That's hardly conspiracy to commit murder. How did she know? She was married to Vincent DeNunzio, and he confessed it to her before he died. She had a signed letter that confirmed it. Could that help Jimmy's chance of getting parole or his sentence commuted?

"You can't get the sentence commuted, not for something like this. And I'm afraid there's not enough here for a retrial," Epstein said. "This man, James Piccini, he family or a friend?"

"A friend. And he got a bad deal a long time ago. He deserves a future."

"Okay, let me check it out, and I'll see what I can do. I can't promise anything. But you've been a great help, and if this office can help your friend, we will."

She felt like hugging the ADA but restrained herself. "Thank you."

She'd been back in Sicily almost three months when a registered letter arrived from Sharon Epstein. It was a copy of a letter to the warden of Clinton Correctional. "After reviewing new evidence, I believe Mr. Piccini's role in the murder was a minor one. These considerations do not warrant a retrial but do shed favorable light on his parole application, especially given his good behavior while incarcerated."

There was a handwritten note from Sharon Epstein. Rizzo was found guilty and sentenced to ten years for drug trafficking and racketeering. The letter ended: "As for the other matter, it's entirely the decision of the parole board, but hopefully the enclosed letter will help."

She reread both letters, then put them in the desk drawer that was home to tax documents, the mortgage, passports, and so forth. She felt like a felon for the next few weeks, but there was nothing to do but wait. And worry. If Rizzo found out that she was alive and what she did, he could have her killed—even from a prison cell, the *capo bastone* could order a hit on the other side of the world. But looking over her shoulder was better than looking into her heart and knowing she did nothing to help Jimmy.

Between her meager inheritance from Vinnie, the life insurance payout, and unfrozen funds from his Civil Asset Forfeiture, dating back to when there was a warrant for his arrest for killing the Russian, Milena was, if not rich, a woman of means. She hired an investment advisor and, at the same time, began looking at small properties to buy, in Taormina or on the coast somewhere— a small house she could share with the kids on summer weekends, or visit with Ruth or other friends.

She became aware of the African migrants in October of 2013, when a boat capsized off the island of Lampedusa, killing nearly four hundred. That year the Italian coast guard rescued many hundreds from Libya, Syria, Eritrea, all over North Africa. Those who made it, tens of thousands of them, arrived on small wooden fishing boats. She saw pictures in newspapers, watched TV, Facebook, and YouTube footage of mothers and fathers carrying little children to safety. She made donations to charities that helped refugees and worked with Claudia and the restaurant staff to collect clothes and cook food and drove them to a settlement in the town of Mineo, inland, about one hundred miles south of Catania.

"I'm an immigrant myself," she told Claudia.

"Yes, but not the same."

"Still. We can help a little."

"*Si*, Milena. We can help a little."

Freedom

Jimmy

He's fifty-eight years old, serving out his sentence in honor block where he can cook in his cell and spend more time outdoors; he's had an operation for a stomach ulcer, been stabbed once, given reading glasses, and almost stopped caring about anything, when his parole is granted.

Louis Perkins, beaming, gives him a hug. Jimmy tells him he'll get his parole hearing soon—he probably won't—and they'll see each other in Brooklyn.

"I'd like that just fine," Perkins says, staring into a future they both know to be far, far away.

The day before his release, Father Steven comes to see him one last time.

"I'm not going to give you a Bible. You can buy your own. I'm just going to wish you good luck. Enjoy it out there, Jimmy. I think you will."

"You're okay, Father. For a prison priest. I was expecting some devout old asshole with bad breath."

"There's still time."

"You never told me why you ended up here? Where were you before?"

"Detroit."

"And you didn't like it? I've never been."

"They didn't like me."

"How come?"

"Usual story. Got in with a bad crowd, got caught, Archbishop ran me out of town. No references, no recommendation."

"You miss it?"

"Sure. I used to miss it more. But I like this job better than my old one. Jimmy, you take care of yourself. I don't want to see you back here."

"You won't. And you find yourself in Brooklyn, you look me up. Casa Altobelli, Giaccardi's, just ask around, someone will know how to find me. I'll buy you dinner."

"Okay. See you at Giaccardi's."

Row Jimmy

Jimmy

They're in a steakhouse in the Village. Everything is big: Stetson-sized steaks, home fries like small bananas, massive wine glasses, large men in suits. The rib eyes are ridiculously expensive and impossibly delicious.

"So I spoke to Sabrina," Bobby says through a mouthful of red meat.

"She doing okay? What'd she say?"

"She said she'd like to visit you. She lives out on the Island, but her daughter is in Brooklyn. She'll be there later in the week. That okay?"

"Yeah, that's great."

So many memories. *Boogie down white boy. Let's have some fun.* What if she tells him he ruined her sister's life? Well, he'll find out soon enough. Why do happy memories make him sad, he always wonders.

There are the other memories too—getting arrested, his first days in prison, the unbearable weight of knowing he would spend decades, maybe even the rest of his life, in that shithole or one just like it. He's been thinking about Little Mikey. Jackie Ponzoni did his part, hired a guy to dress like Pino. Ponzoni and a friend accompanied him, so the guy looked like the Ruggiero family boss, in Atlantic City on business with a couple of young captains. With

Zelniker's help, it was easy for them to intercept Mikey's mother as she was walking to visit a friend. The guy did a good imitation of Pino, was solicitous, charming, told her she looked like she could be Mikey's sister. She was a bit rattled, but she knew better than to disregard the words of a New York mob boss. She'd get the message to Mikey, and he'd stay away from Jimmy. The way Jimmy sees it, Mikey just wants things to stay the way they are, and with Pino Locatelli showing up in New Jersey, he knows that nobody—not his mother, not Mo and Beans, not even Mikey himself—is safe. Of course there's no guarantee, but chances are he'll be more careful about coming back East, won't be seen eating oysters at Harry's, won't set foot in Brooklyn or mess with Jimmy.

Jimmy thinks about saying something to Bobby, but he doesn't want to put Ponzoni in a difficult position.

"It'll be good to see Sabrina," he says. "Thanks, Bobby."

"Come on, eat your steak. *Salut.*"

The Things We Do for Love

Jimmy

Sabrina has aged both copiously and gracefully. She's a large, soft-skinned woman, with the warm twinkly eyes he remembers and long velvet hair. They sit in the garden. He makes them coffee with his new machine, and he's bought biscotti, and carries the plate of cookies and coffees outside, to the weathered table. Now that he has a guest, his first real guest, he wonders if the garden and his basement apartment look shabby to her.

They talk about the weather, her kids, how long he's been out.

"I had a drink with Bill Kelly," he says.

"Bill. No shit."

"No shit. He was so sweet on you."

"I thought I was going to marry the guy, but it just kind of ended." She scans the garden. "Young love. So hard to tell what is going to happen."

She shows him pictures of her children, and a photograph of Milena and Vinnie, taken about a year before he died. He looks at the beautiful woman in the photo, gray-streaked hair, the same warm dark eyes.

Sabrina brings the conversation around to the days and weeks in 1991 that led to Jimmy's arrest and Milena's escape to Italy.

"We were so worried," she says. "Milena and Vinnie disappeared, then the news of the arrests . . ." She shakes her head.

"We thought you'd all be back after a few weeks. No one thought Milena would go away. She just disappeared for a while. My mother wanted to phone the police, thought she might be dead. God only knows what Vinnie must have done."

Just then, Molly appears in the garden, with a broom and a plastic ball. When she sees Jimmy and his guest, she stops.

"Hello, Mister Jimmy."

"Hello, Molly."

He's waiting for her to run off and play at the back of the garden, but she stands her ground, looking at Sabrina.

"Molly, this is my friend, Sabrina; Sabrina, this is Molly, my favorite six-year-old."

Molly walks over, shakes Sabrina's hand. "He doesn't know any other six-year-olds."

"Pleased to meet you," Sabrina says.

"Mister Jimmy used to know my Grampa. Did you know him too?"

"Yes, I met your grandfather. He was a lovely man."

Just as suddenly as she appeared, Molly scampers off. Jimmy makes them another coffee, and they're sipping espresso and watching Molly at play when Sabrina says that she misses Milena.

"I miss her too," Jimmy says. "Every day."

"Must have been so hard for you."

"I loved her. You're one of the only people in the world knows that. I love her still. I didn't tell her that enough. And I probably never told you."

"I knew," Sabrina says. "She knew."

Old Flames, New Burns

Milena

When she hears from Sabrina that Jimmy is out of prison Milena is fifty-four years old.

"He's out?" She's been waiting for this day, and yet when her sister tells her the news she finds it hard to comprehend. "How?"

"Parole, good behavior or something."

"No, how did you hear?"

"You know how the old timers are. News spreads fast, especially rumors and bad news."

"What rumors? What bad news?"

"Apparently he beat up some poor fool in a Brooklyn bakery."

"Who told you that?"

"Old man Mancini."

"Do you know him?"

"Who?"

"Old man Mancini."

"A bit. I don't think he's lying, if that's what you mean."

"Jimmy . . ." Milena says, and the word hangs in the whoosh of Skype silence.

"Mili, I like Jimmy, everybody likes him. It's not about that. Just . . . don't expect too much. He's toughened, Mili. He'd have to. He's been away."

"What'd he say?"

Sabrina explains what she heard from Mancini, who is nearly eighty but still connected to the old neighborhood and the family. Someone, he said—and Sabrina surmised that meant a young punk sent either by Pino or another family—went to check out where Jimmy was staying, maybe ask a few questions, and the guy came back with a broken nose and a cracked rib.

"They're sure it was Jimmy who did it?"

"They are."

"And you? Have you seen him?"

"Yes. Thanks to Bobby Maritato."

Had she really imagined Jimmy would get out of prison a better version of his old self and come calling with flowers and a smart suit? Why? Time waits for no one.

"How was he?"

"Jimmy? Fine. Older, of course. Seemed pretty chilled actually. He's living with Savino's son."

"How's he look?"

"Like an older version of Jimmy. Still handsome. And in pretty good shape."

"That's good."

"Doesn't change what Mancini said."

"I know."

"So, what do you want me to tell him?"

"Tell him to come and see me. Tell him I'm alive and where I live. He can phone or write to me, but if he wants to visit that would be better. And remind him not to tell anyone in the family."

"You sure? I thought you said you weren't going back to any of that?"

"Yes, I'm sure."

Sabrina says nothing.

"What?"

"Mili, men, they are emotionally repressed at the best of times. You know that. With prison, with all that he's gone through, what do you expect?"

"Jimmy."

"I'm just saying, I hope you don't think you'll rekindle any romance. That was a million years ago. That was another guy."

"You think he'll be happy to see me?"

"If he doesn't have a heart attack, I think so." Then, "Mili, you know if he tells anyone that you're alive, I mean, anyone in the family, that could be serious for you. For all of us."

"He won't."

"You're sure about that? You haven't spoken to him in thirty years."

"Twenty-five. Yes, I'm sure. Just send him to me. Don't judge him, or me, don't worry about who will say what."

"Okay, okay."

After they hang up, she tries to imagine Jimmy now, free, walking the streets of New York City, but the image won't cohere. Sabrina is right of course—prison doesn't make people better, doesn't improve them. She's a stupid old romantic, she tells herself, and reproaches herself for thinking he would step out of prison the old Jimmy she used to know, untouched by time, unhardened. She of all people should know that people change; life changes them—it's inevitable.

She finds herself thinking about her children. Giacomo, recently married, works for Finmeccanica in Palermo. When she tells people her son works for an aerospace company, they nod approvingly. Mariela works in hotel management in Rome. She has a boyfriend, a lawyer, a good man from a good family. She speaks fluent English, Italian, and French. She's organized, has a head for numbers. Milena always thought Jimmy would have liked her, both of the children, but especially her feisty beautiful daughter, and would have been impressed with Milena for raising such a strong and capable young woman. She is so proud of them, her children—her *tesori*, her treasures. She's never allowed herself to imagine that Jimmy might meet them, never admitted to herself how much it would mean to her.

And then she waits and wonders what he'll be like. A stranger perhaps, someone completely different from the man she knew twenty-five years ago. Are the people we remember even the people they were, or does remembering someone create a new person—our own version, the story of them that we tell ourselves?

Like Walking in the Rain and the Snow
When There's Nowhere to Go and
You Feel Like a Part of You is Dying

Jimmy

Like praying to a God you no longer believe in that a dead woman is alive. Like buying a passport and credit card from some old sap in Bergen Beach, courtesy of Jackie Ponzoni. Like packing your suitcase and heading to the airport, because the woman you loved and lost is not dead and is, in fact, alive and well living in Sicily.

Skipping town is a serious offense in the eyes of the law. The minute he attempts to board a plane Jimmy becomes a parolee at large, and as such he can be arrested, parole revoked, sent back to the slammer. There's probably a holding cell right here at JFK, he thinks, as he sits on a molded airport chair and watches passengers come and go, centipedes of people crawling toward the Alitalia check-in counters, children pulling tiny rolling suitcases emblazoned with Spider-Man, tigers, owls. He pictures Molly pulling one. They said good-bye with his cab idling at the curb. Molly raced back inside and returned with a jelly jar of coins from which she extracted a euro. From her pocket she pulled a slightly wilted flower. Both were to travel with him to Italy, where he was to plant the flower and spend the euro on ice cream. He smiled and said okay, and they high-fived. "We'll miss you," she said. No one had said that to him in a very, very long time.

And now he is at the airport, getting ready to piss on his parole, a wilted flower and a one-euro coin in his pocket. The fifty-eight-year-old Jimmy is scared shitless; he wants to turn around, hail a taxi, go home, and drink a cold beer. The thirty-four-year-old Jimmy wants to get on that plane.

Jet Airliner

Jimmy

The seat next to him is occupied by a skinny guy in his twenties. Italian-American, eager, chatty, he informs Jimmy it's his first trip to Italy. Mine too, Jimmy says. *Salut.* The kid likes that and asks Jimmy his line of business. "I'm in real estate," he says. "I'm in the safety business," his father used to say, "I keep people safe—I'm a bus driver." What would Fulvio think of his sons? A *fanook* and a *jamook*. A faggot and a criminal. What did he do to deserve the evil eye? All he ever did was slave every day to raise good, decent American children. Not your fault, Papa, not your fault.

The kid fastens his seat belt, babbles about Rome and Milan and the places he wants to go. Jimmy nods. After takeoff the kid watches a movie, and Jimmy looks through the scratchy oval window at the dark, mysterious sky above the clouds. He flicks through the in-flight magazine—movies he's never heard of, bands and singers he doesn't know. He remembers the songs his parents used to listen to. Sunday nights his father would drink red wine and read the papers and listen to music from the old country. He can almost hear the plaintive Neapolitan song. *Si doce comme 'o zucchero.* You are as sweet as sugar. *Nun te pozzo scurdà.* I can't forget you.

The clouds below them are like dark, sleeping animals. He likes the feeling up there, in the sky, away from the world, above everything, above the world, above prison and the past, flying to Milena.

There are other memories, not all so good. His father belting Paulie and Jimmy for coming home late, or lying, or breaking one of their mother's glass figurines. Those big hands were like bricks when they landed on your lip or cheek. Still he was a good man and a good father most of the time. Jimmy wasn't exactly a model son.

He drinks a vodka, watches part of a movie, and falls asleep with the headphones on, words rattling through dreams of his father and mother and brother. When he wakes up, it's dim inside the cabin. The young guy beside him is snoring quietly.

He pays cash for a ticket to Sicily. Flying time to Catania is one hour and twenty minutes. Fontanarossa Airport is crowded and hot. A taxi carves through dusty roads along a coastline of craggy rocks, past little shops and restaurants with plastic chairs on the sidewalk, and children playing soccer in the streets. The windows are open and he smells salty sea and olive groves. In the gaps between buildings, the sea curls against the beach and barnacled rocks.

Isola Bella

Milena

She's asked him to meet her at Isola Bella, at the restaurant, not at her house or his hotel. They'll eat lunch, maybe walk around the town a bit. Now that the hour is approaching, she's nervous. She doesn't often examine herself in the mirror, but today she does. What will Jimmy see? An old love? An old woman? The past mocking the present?

Claudia is not there yet, and Milena says hello to the waiter and the chef, then sits at a table near the back. They have a name for it in Italian. *Cavoli riscaldati*, meaning reheated cabbage. As in: the attempt to revive a failed relationship. As in: usually futile. She knew all of that. But she isn't, she tells herself. Trying to revive a failed relationship. Or cabbage.

He's wearing sunglasses when he enters the restaurant and asks something of the waiter, and she feels the same quickening of her pulse that she felt the time she opened the door of Bill Kelly's apartment and saw him standing there with rain in his hair. She sees him see her, and he smiles, calmly, and removes his sunglasses.

He looks younger than she'd imagined, thinner too.

"Milena."

He kisses her on both cheeks. Puts two fingers on her chin, as if he's making sure she's not a ghost.

"Milena," he says again.

"Jimmy."

She's no longer worrying what she looks like; now she's worried that she may start to cry.

Too many broken hearts have fallen in the river
Too many lonely souls have drifted out to sea

Jimmy

And then it's just the two of them, sitting together under buzzing yellow lights in the back of a restaurant. It's late and the restaurant is almost empty; two couples occupy tables at the front, near the open doors. Motorbikes grumble past outside. He tells her she looks wonderful, because she does, and he doesn't want to say that he has missed her or anything like that, because he doesn't trust what he might say.

"I'm in Italy," he says, unable to suppress a grin, taking it all in. He wants to touch her again to make sure she's real. He's afraid he may bawl like an overwhelmed child. He looks at the menu, looks up at her again.

"Yes, you are." She smiles.

There she is. Crow's-feet at the sides of her eyes, her once lustrous hair a bit thinner, a little more brittle, gray-sprinkled. But still beautiful, still Milena. Maybe more beautiful, touched by time, aged but not hardened. She is fifty-four years old but looks ten years younger. She's wearing a simple blue blouse and white jeans, looking at him with those dark, kind, glinting eyes that no photograph ever captured. It's in Italian, the menu, and he struggles to understand a lot of it. For twenty-five years, he tried not to think about her. When he heard she was dead, even then he didn't allow himself to dream that one day, if he ever got to heaven, he might be sitting somewhere like this, with her, just the two of them. He looks at her hands, her strong, still slender, suntanned fingers. He can't think of anything to say, and he's relieved when she breaks the silence.

"What took you so long?"

"*Meglio tardi che mai.*" He pronounces it the best he can but knows he must sound like a man who learned Italian from a videotaped instructor in prison. Each lesson had included maxims, and it's one of the few he remembers, that is, one of the few he looked up in his notebook before leaving Brooklyn. Actually he has the notebook with him, tucked in his suitcase. In English it means "better late than never."

A look of surprise, before she tilts her head and says, "*Bravo.*"

"I learned some Italian. Took a class. I had time on my hands."

The waiter appears, a gangly man, handsome enough, greasy hair. Milena talks to him, then asks, "Pasta okay? And then fish?"

"Of course."

She goes through the menu and orders, and then she tells him about her children, where they live now and what they do. They drink a toast to Sabrina. Of where he's been all these years, she asks nothing.

They're eating their pasta when a woman enters, stops a foot or two inside the restaurant, smiles broadly at Milena—*Ciao Milena! È questo Jimmy?*—and clip-clops over to them. Milena introduces Claudia, the owner of the restaurant.

"Welcome to Italy."

"*Piacere,*" Jimmy says.

After lunch they walk around the town. They stop for an espresso, walk to the Roman ruins, and sit on the balcony of the Timeo Hotel, which has views of Mount Etna and the glinting sea. There, sitting on the balcony beside an elderly German couple smoking cigarettes, he asks her what it's been like living in Italy, and she says it was like becoming another person; after a while you get used to your new skin.

They walk cobbled streets to the port and sit on a bench on a promontory overlooking rocks and crashing sea. Two fishing boats pass on the blue-eyed sea. Sitting on the bench, she explains that she was wanted by the Feds, but she's not anymore, so she's visited America. She tells him how she faked her own death so the Ruggiero family wouldn't look for her.

On the way back to his hotel they stop at a café, and she buys them ice creams in cups and they walk out to the edge of a piazza, sit on smooth stone. She ordered pistachio; he ordered dark chocolate, and it's the most delicious thing he's ever eaten. He thinks about little Molly, ice cream lover.

"Do you miss America? Do you want to move back?" he asks.

"Maybe. I don't know. That's a question I asked myself for so long I stopped asking. My kids are here. I thought I wanted to go back, then I went back and I wasn't so sure, so I guess I just decided to postpone thinking about it. My kids, you know . . . if I leave them, I'd have to come back a lot to see them. What about you?"

"Someone told me I needed to find another country."

"Travel agent?"

"Priest."

She laughs, that easy, open laugh.

They sit side by side, ice creams melting in their small waxy cups, swirls of green and brown shining in the sunlight.

After Lunch

Milena

She walks him back to his hotel, hugs him, holds him tight for a few seconds, long enough to feel the muscles of his chest press against her breasts, smell his hair, and there, just outside the door, she kisses him on both cheeks. She doesn't know what to say, and so she says nothing. As she walks off, she feels a little light-headed, a little scared. She turns to wave good-bye and walks to the parking lot and sits in her car for a while before driving home. Here he is, Jimmy, just around the corner, flesh and blood. She starts the car and drives slowly, still thinking about him, how he looks and acts—older, more measured, tentative even, and slower—but still handsome, and he's still got that glint in his eyes. It's as if she's just seen two people, or a man and a ghost, Jimmy now and Jimmy then. One thing she knows: we are all fragments, every person a collection of fragments, held together by love and memory and aging skin. He asked what's it like living in Italy, and she wanted to give him an honest answer, something more than a tour-guide response about the country and its history and the beauty of Sicily. But she couldn't say anything about that old fear, now diminished, that she's a completely different person here, that a different soul looks out from her eyes.

She's invited him for dinner the following night, and back at home she makes tea, tidies the apartment, even though it's already tidy. She doesn't want to be the teacher, telling him look at this and that, translating, pointing, but at the same time she wants to be herself and wants him to—what?—appreciate what she has learned, what she's become. And what is that? European? Half-Sicilian? A worldly person? Does any of that matter? He's been locked away for 40 percent of his life. She wants to show him all of herself, but at the same time she's afraid of seeing some facet of him that she won't like or won't recognize—an animal or prisoner inside him. *A domani.* We'll see tomorrow, she tells herself.

Ci Vuole Fiori

Jimmy

He spends the day walking Taormina, going in and out of shops, looking at the locals and the tourists. He gets lost in a maze of alleys and narrow streets. One of those alleys smells of jasmine, with blossoms so close his shoulder grazes them as he passes. He eats pizza at an outdoor restaurant. Best pizza he's ever had, with pistachios. He climbs to the top of the Teatro Antico, looks at the ancient columns and broken arches. Third century BC. You can still see the rows of stone seats, and he imagines gladiators fighting, the roar of the crowd. He walks the bustling cobblestone streets, buys two shirts for himself, flowers to take to Milena, then sits at a café shaded by an umbrella, and drinks an espresso and wonders about the evening that lies ahead.

When she opens the door, he sees a small, tidy apartment, dark furniture, wood table, tastefully furnished. He can smell cooking.

"*Fiori,*" he says, handing her the flowers he's brought.

"Thank you. Come in. *Ci vuole fiori.*"

"Flowers . . . something about flowers." He frowns.

"It takes flowers. A children's song I learned from my kids." She half-sings, "*Per fare il monte ci vuol la terra. Per far la terra ci vuole un fiore.* Do you like anchovies?"

He says he does, even though he can't really remember what they taste like.

She gives him a tour of the apartment and they stand in the small garden. Back inside she shows him photos of her children. They eat dinner at the kitchen table. Pasta with fresh anchovies sautéed with garlic and *pepperoncini* and cherry tomatoes and lots of chopped parsley. And red wine, rich and dark. He can't remember tasting better pasta.

"It's delicious."

"Thank you."

They eat slowly, sip their wine, ask and answer questions. How does he find Sicily? How long has she lived in the apartment? He watches her lips. The candle on the table throws spears of light across their plates and hands. They are silent for a while, eating, thinking, and then she asks about Big Bobby and Brooklyn, Savino's son, the place he's staying. They talk easily and eat and drink their wine. She says that she cannot imagine being locked away for all that time. He says don't imagine it.

"I'm here now."

"Yes, you are."

After the pasta they eat salad and cheese and crusty bread. She takes the dishes to the sink. He likes the way she walks, the way she picks up a plate and puts it down, slowly, elegantly, every movement like a dance.

They sit together on the couch, like teenagers. He makes a comment about the pictures on the wall, one that he particularly likes—a watercolor of rippled sea and sky and a strip of land and a small sailboat. She shrugs, lowers her head.

"That's one of mine."

"You painted that, it's beautiful."

She asks if he's still taking photographs. No? Well, we must get you a camera.

It's then he touches her. He puts two fingers on her cheek and she tilts her head back, and he kisses the lips he dreamed of kissing for nearly half his life. He remembers her taste, her smell, the softness of those lips. It's the same and so lovely that he wants to cry, but he doesn't want to ruin the moment. He tries to smile, but tears well in his eyes and seep down his cheeks and he doesn't bat them away as he leans forward and kisses her again.

They kiss for a good, long while, and then she gets up to make coffee.

"*Vieni qui e baciami.*"

He looks at her, standing at the stove.

"Come here and kiss me," she says.

They kiss again. She doesn't pour the coffee. Instead she switches off the burner.

"Come on then."

She leads him to the bedroom. Purple sheets, very clean, no clutter.

They lie together on the bed and undress slowly, and it's like it was all those years ago, and of course it is also different, it is now, and she is beautiful and naked and she is here, in his arms.

Avanti

Milena

The next day they walk. She shows him the Duomo and the fountain of Neptune in the piazza outside and Madonna della Rocca, an old church on the hilltop, overlooking the sea. She's feeling more comfortable now, pointing things out, telling him bits of history, or simply showing him things she loves, like the calm interior of the church. They eat dinner at one of her favorite restaurants just above the old town walls. The following night he takes a taxi to her apartment. He has flowers and wine, and she remembers him in the doorway of the Sanderson Hotel.

"Anyone can make spaghetti alla norma."

"Not anyone. I don't even know what it is."

"Spicy eggplant pasta. That all right?" She feels bad because she didn't ask what he likes. He might have food allergies or hate eggplant.

"Sounds great. I haven't exactly been watching the Cooking Channel. I do have a kitchen now though."

She slices the eggplant, then hands him the knife. He continues the task, cutting half-inch slices. She wants to say I can't believe we're cooking together. She can't believe she is here, in her house, cooking with Jimmy, and only the smell of onions makes it feel real.

"The trick is you burn the onions and chili flakes. The other trick is you buy this spice mix, which is delicious. You still like spicy?"

"I still like spicy."

She pours them each a glass of wine and they clink glasses, and it's funny to her and must seem funny to him too, because they start laughing.

"*Alla nostra*," she says.

"*Alla nostra*."

He's still grinning, and they clink glasses again, then he goes back to slicing the eggplant, and she to chopping onions. She can feel his eyes on her. She can feel her own skin and the air inside her lungs.

"In Italy, you learn how to cook pasta. And eat."

"In the can, you try to forget what real food tastes like."

While the eggplant is cooking, she dips a wooden spoon in the pan, blows, tastes. She's remembering Bill Kelly's apartment, the evening Jimmy came in from the rain, with sparkles of water in his hair, carrying two bottles of wine in a plastic bag. Is he that man? He's aged, and his eyes have narrowed, and his hair has thinned, but he looks like the same man. On the other hand, he beat up a guy in a café not long ago. Maybe he's put a crew together. They say that prison criminalizes people, that confinement turns them aggressive. But Jimmy was never the smash-and-grab type. He always liked things bigger and farther away. He was discreet, a planner.

She dips the spoon again and raises it toward him, and Jimmy leans forward and tastes the sauce.

"*Deliziosa*," he says.

He's like a little boy, polite and quiet, and there's the way he gazes at her, at Taormina, at the world around him, like it's all brand new, which, in a way, she supposes it is. She wants to reassure him. Don't worry. She wants to say, I love you, and she is pretty sure she will.

But not yet.

They have lunch with Claudia, and she introduces Jimmy to Amalia.
They drink espressos in the square below a crumbling *palazzo*. She
takes him to a pottery studio, shows him her favorite cheese shop,
and they taste the different kinds of pecorinos, and he buys little
jars of spices to bring back as presents, for Tom and Catherine and
Bobby's wife. In the afternoon they separate and then he returns
for dinner, with cheese and figs. By now they've relaxed with each
other; they are louder, laugh more, talk more. She asks about life
in prison, and he tells her. She tells him more about her children,
hears herself saying that Giacomo is James, or Jimmy, in Italian,
and reddens, and one minute they are clinking glasses and looking
at each other and then they are both putting down their glasses,
kissing their way to the bedroom. They undress slowly and have
sex slowly, speaking little, kissing hungrily but too shy to look into
each other's eyes, and she feels both in the moment and in some
kind of perfect memory, a replay of a quarter century ago, the kind
of thing that happens in science-fiction movies.

Milena drives a vintage Lancia Fulvia, cobalt blue. Despite the
dent in the chrome bumper and dings on the driver-side door, it's
a sleek, late 1960s Italian sports car, low to the ground, the kind
of car Jimmy would have loved when he was a kid. In her bat-
tered Lancia, she drives them around the island. They spend the
night in an *albergo* in a small town on the coast, eat in its candlelit restaurant, walk along the craggy beach, go to sleep together
in the low-ceilinged hotel room. They don't feel the need to talk
all the time, being there together is enough. It's like the time in
Massachusetts, minus the drugs. The stillness and completeness of
being there together. They touch; they make love. She notices him
looking at her, and sometimes she takes his hand and squeezes it.
    "You," she says.
    "You."

Back in Taormina, he keeps his room at the hotel but stays with
her most nights. Every morning they sit in her little garden

surrounded by jasmine and waxy green leaves, lingering over coffee with fruit and bread and jam, then they walk out along the boardwalk. One day they walk to a big hotel in town and have a late breakfast and read the English language papers.

"You miss it?" he asks.

"What?"

"New York."

"Sure. New York is home. But this, I don't know, feels more real."

The next day they take the cable car down to Mazzaró Beach and watch the boats and swimmers. It is there, looking at the rocky shore and blue sea, that he tells her he must leave soon. There are loose ends to tie up, back in New York.

"You wouldn't be overstaying your welcome."

"Thank you."

"Loose ends?"

"You know, stuff I gotta take care of."

"Nothing dangerous?"

"I hope not."

The thing about Jimmy is: no poker face. She can see worry and indecision, like he's eaten something rotten and he's trying to decide whether to spit it out or not. Like when he told her about Philly, or the heists they were planning to raise money for the drug trade.

"Spit it out."

"Money," he says after a while. "And Mikey."

"As in Mike Rossi?"

"Yes."

"That's a big loose end. What are you going to do?"

"I'm not quite sure. The priest said leave it alone. He's big on love and forgiveness."

"And? You don't listen to your priest?"

"I listened. I'm taking it under advisement."

"When?"

"I don't know. I'll go back in a week or so. As long as you don't throw me out before then."

"I'm not going to throw you out."

"Good."

"Jimmy, will you tell me?"

"Tell you what?"

"Whatever it is you plan to do, tell me before you do it."

"Okay."

"Promise?"

"Promise. I'm not going to do anything crazy, if that's what you mean. I think we've got old Mikey scared enough that he won't try to touch me. His goons might not listen, but I can live with that. What I can't live with is doing something that means I go back to the can, that means I never see you again."

"Good. That's good."

The Yellow House

Jimmy

Milena drives, and the Lancia bumps along cobbled streets, and then out along narrow roads to the coast. He can't help smiling at the way she drives, swerving in and out of traffic, occasionally swearing under her breath in Italian. They stop in a small town and walk past the fish market, bank, *salumeria*, a café, kids playing soccer in the street. He points out the clothes in the windows of a shop, surprisingly old-fashioned, like something out of the seventies.

Driving. The land is a thousand shades of green, and every now and then, through a gap in the trees, they catch a glimpse of the sea. He smiles to himself, thinking about being a fish out of water, a Brooklyn fish in Mediterranean water, a prison fish in the great wide world. And about being with Milena. At the same time, he feels something like fear, scared that he will say the wrong thing, not know something obvious, about anything— travel, how to tip, how to say something in English, never mind Italian. Milena is a sophisticated woman of the world. She has style and lots of friends; she dresses well, still turns men's heads. What does she want with an ex-con from the old neighborhood? He can't help worrying that it will all come to an end, that she is, in some elaborate way, being nice, the way you are on a date with someone you didn't really like, and when it is over she will say

good-bye and they will never see each other again. He tells himself
not to worry about it, just enjoy today, tonight.

He can't believe how old Sicily is, or all the kinds of trees
and flowers—orange trees, lemon trees, peach trees, bougainvillea,
jasmine, yellow flowers, purple flowers, palm trees. There seem to
be every kind of tree and flower imaginable in this place touched
by the hand of God.

She makes a call on her cell phone. He can't understand much,
makes out "*subito*" and "*va bene*."

"Come and meet some friends of mine," she says. "They live
on the beach. It's not far."

They drive along the shoreline, turn at the sign for Acireale,
and follow a rutted road that ends at the beach. Beyond lies the
sea. They park and walk along the rocky shore, clattering on the
gray pebbles. Waves lap quietly.

She points to a little yellow house with green shutters, nestled
between other houses on the stretch of craggy shoreline that ends
abruptly at a cliff, eighty or so feet tall and topped with cypress
trees.

They walk up wooden steps, and Milena knocks on the yellow
door.

A young man opens it, a young woman slides beside him, and
they kiss Milena like old friends. Milena introduces Jimmy and
they shake hands. The man is muscular with an uneven beard over
a broad face. The woman is tiny, dark, pretty.

The house is small and clean, sparsely furnished. Hardwood
floors, beam ceiling, old orange sideboard, view of the sea.

"Can I tell him?" Milena asks in English, and the couple con-
fers in Italian, then the woman speaks to Milena in Italian, before
turning to Jimmy.

"We are pregnant," she says.

"Oh, that's great. Congratulations. How do you say that in
Italian?"

"*Incinta,*" the woman offers.

"Congratulations," Milena says with a smile. "*Tanti auguri.*"

"*Tanti auguri,*" he repeats.

"Thank you," the woman says in English, touching her belly.

They offer them coffee, but Milena says no, they have to get going. They drink a glass of water together sitting on the steps overlooking the rocky beach and green sea.

"Signore Piccini, thank you," the man says, when it's time to go.

"*Si,*" the woman says. "*Grazie mille.*" On tiptoes, she kisses him on both cheeks.

Milena says something in Italian; the man chuckles.

"What?" asks Jimmy.

They're back on the beach, clanking along the pebbles when Jimmy asks why they were thanking him.

"They think it's your house, and you are letting them stay until the baby comes, or as long as they want."

"They do?"

"Something like that."

"*Perché?*"

"*Perché è vero.*"

"It's true that they're pregnant?"

"It's true that it's your house."

"What?"

"I bought it. It's in your name. Here." She reaches in her pocket and takes out a key ring, gives it to him.

"And I suppose these are the keys."

"Yes."

"You can't just buy a house in someone else's name."

"In Sicily you can."

On the Beach

Milena

She's laughing and he's laughing as they make their way back along the rocky beach, but she also feels a wave of anxiety. Maybe it was too much, maybe she should have waited, or explained it better to him. She tries now to explain. She decided to buy a house when the money from her inheritance came through, and she found this one. She's always loved this little cove. It's quiet and beautiful, and the houses are so close to the sea.

"You know I can't accept that," he says. "It's too much."

"You can. Of course you can."

"Why?"

"Well, I didn't want to put it in my name—I'm dead in America, remember. And my kids would only complain that I should have bought something in Palermo or Rome, where they live. It occurred to me that it could be, well, yours, and the tenants would pay you rent, or I would pay you rent."

"Won't this lead back to you?"

"Nobody knows about it, except you, me, and the bank."

"Not even your sister?"

"Nobody."

She'd decided to buy a house when the money from Vinnie's life insurance and frozen assets came through, and, after spending several Saturdays driving around beach towns with different realtors, she'd found one. She also gave some money to Amalia, the woman who had taken care of her kids, made some donations to charities. Refugee charities? Yes, and Doctors Without Borders. She smiles, and explains it's ironic because it was Vincent's money, and he would have hated the idea of giving money to help poor Syrian refugees.

They climb in the car and drive back up the hill to the winding coastal road.

"What are you doing tomorrow?" she asks.

"I don't know. No plans. Maybe visiting another property I own in Sicily?"

She laughs. "I don't think so. You only own one."

"What then?"

"Let's go to Mount Etna. You can't leave Sicily without seeing it."

Ain't No Mountain High Enough

Jimmy

Rifugio Sapienza is the starting point for the ascent. There they wait with hundreds of other tourists for the cable car that jerks and shakes its way to the summit, about ten thousand feet above sea level. From there they will ascend three hundred feet on foot, which is as close as they are allowed to go today. Unfortunately they cannot go all the way to the rim of the crater, because of recent eruptions.

Their guide, a quick and tiny Sicani with reptilian skin, leads the group from the cable car exit toward the uppermost allowable reaches of the volcano. Fleece jackets zipped, they follow him. Cloud shadows slide over the dark volcanic slopes. The air is thin, the ground crunches under foot—*squak, squok, squak*—volcanic rock, dark and hard and brittle, like the surface of another planet. They plod on. Below them lie splashes of greenery, sprinkles of sunbaked grass, purple Bartsia, and yellow clover; above them a patch of snow clings to the scabrous rock. The top of the volcano is striped yellow and red and black.

The guide turns, says something in Italian, his hands and fingers moving as he speaks. Jimmy can't understand a single word he says.

"Small eruption," he says to Jimmy and the rest of the group, most of whom do not speak Italian. *E-roop-shin.* "It is still going, so we cannot climb to the top." He smiles a tobacco-stained smile.

Their shoes crunch and slip on the jagged lava rock and dust. Up they go, walking into the sky and clouds, crunching over volcanic rock. As they near the summit they can see for miles, down the steep slope to the patchy green land below and, beyond, the sea, still as glass. The guide bounds up, but Jimmy and Milena and the others are walking slowly, unsure of their footing.

Soon they can smell the gas and sulfur of Etna's fume-filled crater. Somewhere deep inside lava is bubbling, red hot, burning and shifting.

One of the Americans says: "Who farted?"

"*Scusami*?" The guide frowns back at them.

The guide speaks about magmatic rivers and sulfur and iron. *Sool-fer. Eye-ron*. He talks about the big eruptions of 1971 and 1981. Recently, a big eruption was contained because volcanologists were able to set off minor explosions and drill man-made craters.

Above them the lip of the volcano is hard, rimmed yellow and red from the *sool-fer* and *eye-ron*. Suddenly the guide stops, turns. "Look, you can see it."

The volcano burps slow thunder and a small cloud of gas and smoke rises from the crater as black lava floats in the air like confetti. Everyone points and takes photos. Milena watches, wide-eyed.

They walk around the windy lunar landscape. After a while the guide speaks again. He points to the summit of a mountain visible across the crater of Etna, and Jimmy hears "Bocca Nuova" but can't understand much of what he says.

The guide squats under an outcropping, out of the reach of the wind, and smokes a cigarette.

Milena picks up a crusty volcanic stone. "Here, throw it."

Jimmy feels its rough contours, then lifts his arm and throws it. It arcs into the blue sky then drops and lands noiselessly. They stand together looking up at the crater. Smoke billows skyward.

"I think I may have changed my mind," he says.

"Okay. About what?"

"Those loose ends."

"I'm so glad." She smiles.

"I like being here, with you. Plus there's a chance I might get arrested if I go back to the US."

"I wondered."

"About what?"

"Whether you can leave the country if you're on parole."

"No. Well, it wasn't such a good idea."

"I think it was."

"Me too."

They stand and survey the mountain below—ravines of hardened black magma, cable cars swaying in the wind. Milena doesn't say anything for a while; he has the urge to reach out and stroke her hair, and he does.

In the Sunshine of Your Love

Jimmy

The first seven years in the can, you crave revenge. You want to rip flesh from bone, drive a knife into the traitor's heart, pull the dying organ out of his broken ribs and smash it. The second seven, it's the kiss of death you seek, preferably delivered by you. And after twenty-five years? After you're out? Forgiveness is an act of faith. You have to love yourself and love the motherfucker who put you there and walk away from darkness. Every day is maybe.

You walk into the light, along Via Cappuccini, past old houses, eucalyptus trees, bursts of purple bougainvillea. Sun sparkles on cobblestones. You stop to buy *brutti ma buoni* cookies. Outside the bakery a child is riding a scooter; an old lady is leaning out an open window. You have nowhere in particular to go and no one you would rather be with, and you're free. It might be a dream, and it may last no longer than today, but it's enough, being there together. It's where you want to be. The afternoon sun washes her face in golden light. She walks beside you, and as she speaks your name her hair floats toward you, the color of dark chocolate flecked with gray, ripples, and then settles.

"Jimmy, where do you want to go?"

She's asking about dinner, but it's a question you've imagined her asking, and you've known the answer for three hundred months.

"Anywhere with you."

Acknowledgments

Grazie mille and thanks a million:

Capos bastone: John "Johnny Brisket" Marks and Caroline "Gianduja" Levy.

Consiglieri, readers, racketeers: Lara Santoro, Jessica Haaz, Alexander Hope, Marc Kristal, June and David Schneider.

Capos libro: Everyone at The Permanent Press, Martin Shepard, Judith Shepard, Barbara Anderson, Chris Knopf.

Books: *Mafia Prince* by Phil Leonetti; *Five Families* by Selwyn Raab; *Wiseguy* by Nicholas Pileggi; *Surviving the Mob* by Dennis N. Griffin and Andrew DiDonato. All errors are mine.